ESAU

ESAU

PHILIP KERR

Chatto & Windus
LONDON

First published in 1996

1 3 5 7 9 10 8 6 4 2

Copyright © Philip Kerr 1996
Philip Kerr has asserted his right under the Copyright, Designs and Patents
Act, 1988 to be identified as the author of this work

First published in Great Britain in 1996 by
Chatto & Windus Limited
Random House, 20 Vauxhall Bridge Road,
London SW1V 2SA

Random House Australia (Pty) Limited
20 Alfred Street, Milsons Point, Sydney
New South Wales 2061, Australia

Random House New Zealand Limited
18 Poland Street, Glenfield
Auckland 10, New Zealand

Random House South Africa (Pty) Limited
PO Box 337, Bergvlei, South Africa

Random House UK Limited Reg. No. 954009

Papers used by Random House UK Limited are natural, recyclable products
made from wood grown in sustainable forests. The manufacturing processes
conform to the environmental regulations of the country of origin

A CIP catalogue record for this book is available from the British Library

ISBN: 0 7011 6281 3

Typeset by SX Composing DTP, Rayleigh, Essex
Printed in Great Britain by
Mackays of Chatham PLC, Chatham, Kent

For Charles Foster Kerr

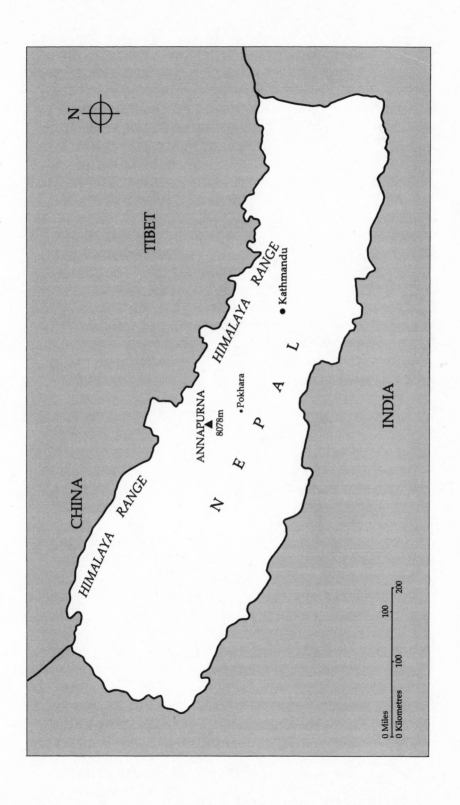

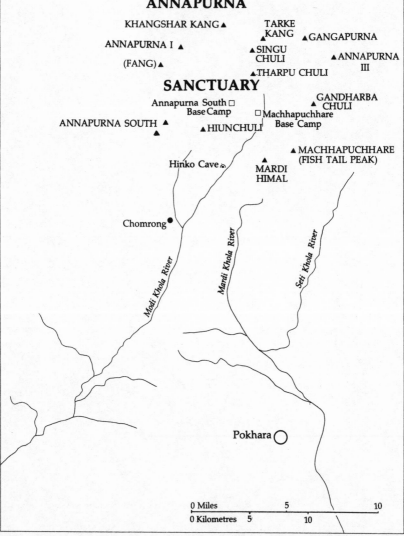

N

ANNAPURNA

KHANGSHAR KANG▲   TARKE
                      ▲KANG   ▲GANGAPURNA
ANNAPURNA I ▲   ▲SINGU
                           CHULI   ▲ANNAPURNA
(FANG)▲   III
                       ▲THARPU CHULI
    SANCTUARY
                                    ▲GANDHARBA
         Annapurna South □   CHULI
           Base Camp   □Machhapuchhare
ANNAPURNA SOUTH ▲   Base Camp
                 ▲   ▲HIUNCHULI
                                  ▲MACHHAPUCHHARE
                                   (FISH TAIL PEAK)
        Hinko Cave   ▲
                           MARDI
                           HIMAL

    Chomrong ●

Pokhara ◯

0 Miles   5   10
0 Kilometres   5   10

'Behold, Esau my brother is a hairy man, and I am a smooth man.'

Genesis 27:11

Part One: The Discovery

'So much glamour still attaches to the theme of missing links, and to man's relationship with the animal world, that it may always be difficult to exorcise from the comparative study of Primates, living and fossil, the kind of myths which the unaided eye is able to conjure out of a well of wishful thinking.'

Solly Zuckerman

One

'Great things are done when men and mountains meet.'
William Blake

The ice ridge, its delicate formations cut deep into the face of Machhapuchhare like dozens of giant bridal veils from a celestial wedding ceremony, soared above his throbbing head in the dazzling, late afternoon sunshine. Beneath his cramponed feet, his toes barely gripping the vertical ice wall, stretched the yawning gap that was the Annapurna South Glacier. Some twelve kilometres behind his back, which ached from the weight of a heavy rucksack, the distinctive peak of Annapurna rose from the ground like a huge octopus. Not that he was looking. Cutting hand- and footholds with an ice axe at six thousand metres, meant there was no time to relax on the rope and enjoy the view. Scenery counted for nothing when there was a summit to be reached. Especially when it was a summit that was officially forbidden.

Western climbers called it Fish Tail Peak, which underlined how the sinuous twisting mountain might elude a man's grasp. At the suggestion of some sentimental Brit gone native, who had himself failed to reach the summit in 1957, the Nepalese Government had declared that Machhapuchhare, three times as big as the Matterhorn, should forever remain pure and inviolate. As a result, it was now impossible to get a permit to climb one of the most beautiful and challenging of all the peaks surrounding the Annapurna Sanctuary.

Most climbers might have let it go there for fear of the consequences. Gaol sentences and fines could be imposed. Future

3

expedition permits could be denied. Sherpas could be withheld. But Jack had come to regard this mountain, Machhapuchhare, as an affront, a mockery of his publicly declared intention to conquer all the major Himalayan peaks. And as soon as he and his partner had successfully completed their officially sanctioned ascent of Annapurna's south-west face, they decided to climb without a permit. A lightning assault that had seemed like a good idea until the bad weather hit.

He pushed himself up on one of the footholds he had cut earlier, reached up with his axe and hacked another handhold out of the ice face.

Bad enough, he thought, that mountaineers were obliged to stop climbing Kangchenjunga just a few metres short of the summit to keep from defiling its holy peak. But that there should be a mountain that you were actually forbidden to climb was unthinkable. One of the reasons you went climbing in the first place was to get away from terrestrial rules and regulations. Jack was quite used to people advising him that this mountain or that wall was unclimbable. Mostly he had proved them wrong. But a mountain you were forbidden to climb, and by a government too – that was something else. As far as their liaison officer in Khatmandu was concerned, they were still on Annapurna; their Sherpas had been bribed to keep silent. Nobody was going to tell him where he could and could not climb.

The very thought of it was enough to make Jack wield the axe with greater ferocity, sending a shower of ice-chips and water-spray into his weather-beaten face, until a crumbling step beneath his boot made him stop to adjust his balance and fumble to insert another ice screw.

Not easy wearing Dachstein woollen mitts.

'How're you doing?' shouted his climbing partner from about fifteen metres below.

Jack said nothing. Muscles aching from his ice-climb, he clung to the wall with one hand as he tried to turn the screw with fingers that were numb with cold. If he didn't get off this wall soon he would risk frostnip. There was no time for a report of his progress. Or lack of it. If they didn't make the top soon they were in serious trouble. Days spent in a hanging tent had cost them valuable fuel. There was only enough for another day or two at the most, and without fuel they could not melt snow for their coffee.

4

At last the screw was tight and he was able to take the weight off his arm. He drew deep breaths of the thin mountain air and tried to steady the alarming pulse in his temple.

Jack could not recall a more demanding piece of ice-climbing. Even the Annapurna had not seemed so hard. Near the top Machhapuchhare looked not so much like a fish tail as a spear point driven up through the earth by some giant subterranean warrior. There was no doubt about it: high-altitude wall-climbing remained the real challenge for any modern Alpinist; and Machhapuchhare's Gothic heights, as sheer as any New York skyscraper, were perhaps the ultimate test of all. What a fool he was. Let him finish the climb before he worried about the authorities discovering what he had done.

The throbbing in his head seemed to diminish.

Except that now he was aware of a strange whistling in his ears. Like tinnitus at first, it grew louder, until the whistling had become a roaring, like the sound of an artillery shell fired from a warship in a distant bay, until the noise filled his ears and he wondered if he was experiencing some dreadful effect of high altitude, a pulmonary oedema or even a cerebral haemorrhage.

For a brief and nauseous moment Jack heard the screws which held him on to the rock face grinding in the ice as the whole mountain shook, and he closed his eyes.

A moment or two passed. The noise ended on the glacier somewhere to the north of him. He remained aloft. The breath he had been unconsciously holding escaped from his chapped lips in an exclamation of gratitude and relief as he opened his eyes again.

'What the hell was it?' shouted Didier, at the bottom of the ice wall.

'I'm glad you heard it too,' said Jack.

'Sounded like it was over the other side of the mountain. What was it?'

'Somewhere nearer the north, I reckon.'

'Maybe an avalanche.'

'Must have been a hell of a big one,' said Jack.

'Up here they're all big ones.'

'Could even have been a meteorite.'

Jack heard Didier laugh.

'Shit,' said Didier. 'As if this wasn't already dangerous enough. The Almighty has to throw rocks down on us as well.'

Jack pushed himself away from the wall and, leaning back on the rope, he looked up at the huge overhang of ice above his head.

'I think it looks okay,' he shouted.

In his mind was a picture of the avalanche debris that he and Didier had seen scattered at the foot of the ridge they were on, an unpleasant reminder of the risks he and his French Canadian partner were taking.

'Well, I guess we'll know all about it soon enough,' he added quietly.

The week before they had arrived in the Annapurna Sanctuary to mount their lightweight, two-man assault on the tenth highest mountain in the world – and then its forbidden sister peak – a German expedition, much larger than their own, had been wiped out by a big avalanche on the south wall of Lhotse, the great black peak that was linked to Everest by the famous south col. Six men had died. According to one of the Sherpas who had witnessed the accident a whole serac, several hundred tons of solid ice, had collapsed on top of them.

To avoid any similar falls of ice, Jack had been following a course to the side of the ridge, but now he was right under the danger area, an enormous boulder of hard ice attached to the rock by nothing more than frost.

If this lot were to go, he told himself, they would really be for it. To take his mind off the danger he began to divert himself by trying to remember the name of the Greek hero, condemned by Zeus to an eternity of pushing a huge stone up a hill. As it constantly rolled down again, his task was everlasting. What was his name?

But even as the question passed through Jack's mind, a long ghostly finger of loose powder snow blew off the crest of the overhang and joined the faintest trace of cloud that rolled across the flawless, bright blue sky. Some of it showered Jack's face, refreshing him like a burst of spray from a bottle of eau-de-cologne. He licked the cool moisture from his cracked lips, lifted his ice-axe and started to cut another handhold on the perilous route he had mentally marked out. It would take him to the corner of the ridge, away from the threat of icy obliteration.

He paused as hundreds of shards of snow and ice came scampering off the crest of the ridge like tiny, suicidal white lemmings, and when at last they stopped he realised that the throbbing in his head had started again.

6

'Sisyphus,' Jack muttered, remembering the Greek's name as he quickly finished the handhold. 'It was Sisyphus, the Crafty.' An eternity of second chances. That's what it looked like. The boulder above Jack's head would only come down once. And that would be it. The terminal descent of man. He tugged a length of rope through the piton runners and moved up the ice arête.

'Sooner I get out from under this bastard the better.'

His ears had started to play tricks on him again. This time it was as if he had gone deaf. Jack stopped where he was and repeated his last sentence, but it was as if the sound had been sucked away from the mountain. He felt the words vibrate in his mouth but heard nothing. There seemed to be some kind of vacuum into which all the sound on the ice ridge was emptying and, like the dead calm before a storm at sea, the sense of menace was overpowering.

He looked down and called out to Didier but once again his shout was snatched away, and the sound merged into thunderous rumble. A second later, the mountain shrugged off several thousand tons of snow and ice, shutting out the blue sky behind the frozen black curtain of an enormous avalanche.

Enveloped in a huge cumulus cloud of stifling snow and drowning vapour, Jack felt himself carried off the rocky mountainous altar.

For what seemed like an eternity he fell.

Trapped inside the belly of the white whale of the avalanche, with nothing to inform his battered senses of the world outside it, he had no impression of speed or acceleration, nor even of danger. Just of overwhelming, elemental power. It was as if he were in the very grip of winter. Kept together by the cold he would melt and disappear as soon as he impacted upon the ground. Jack. Jack Frost.

Almost as suddenly as it had started, the direction of the avalanche seemed to change, and feeling an increasing pressure about his body, Jack instinctively started to swim. He kicked his legs, thrust out his arms and struggled to reach some imaginary surface.

Then everything stopped and all was dark and silent.

His legs were free. But his whole upper body was covered in snow. Struggling backwards, Jack collapsed on to a hard rocky floor. For several minutes he lay there, stunned, and blinded with snow. He found he could move his arms and gently he cleared his nose, mouth, ears and eyes of snow. He looked around and realised that he was in a kind of bergschrund – a big, horizontal crevasse in the rock face. The entrance to the bergschrund was stopped up with snow, but the light shining through seemed to suggest that he was not blocked in too deeply.

The rope was still tight around Jack's waist and led through the snow blockage. Struggling to his knees he gave the rope a hard pull. But even as he crawled through the snow and hauled at the rope he knew that Didier must be dead. That he himself was alive seemed improbable enough.

After several frantic pulls, the the frayed end of the rope appeared. Dragging himself to the mouth of the bergschrund, he managed to peer out. One look at the obliterated slope below seemed to confirm the worst. The avalanche had been a huge one. It had swept the whole lower glacier, from six thousand metres right down to Camp One on top of the Rognon at about five thousand. Like Didier, the Sherpas there would have had little chance of survival.

Somehow the avalanche had dumped him on the very lip of the bergschrund. At a different angle a collision with its hard lower lip would have killed him. Instead the bergschrund had protected him from the lethal icy debris that now rendered the route back, down the north face to the Rognon and Camp One unrecognisable.

Sick to his stomach and yet somehow elated that he had survived unscathed, Jack sat down and began to remove the snow and ice from inside his jacket and trousers, pondering his next move. He estimated it was about four hundred and fifty metres back down to Camp Two at the foot of the rock face. At just above five thousand two hundred, the camp was located where the rock wall overhung the glacier, and there was just a chance that this might have protected the two Sherpas there from the worst of the avalanche, although they were almost certainly buried much deeper than he was.

Even so, he knew that he could not climb down before dark. His radio was gone, and the route down was too difficult to attempt in his condition with the sun already setting. Besides, he had a rucksack of stores still strapped to his back and he was aware that his best chance was to spend the night in the bergschrund and climb down first thing in the morning.

Jack shrugged off the rucksack and stood up painfully to inspect what would be his sleeping quarters for the night, almost impaling himself upon one of the long icicles that hung from the vaulting

ceiling, jabbing the darkness like the teeth of some forgotten prehistoric animal. The icicle, as long as a javelin, broke off and
smashed on the floor.

He opened his rucksack and took out his Maglite.

'Not exactly the Stein Eriksen Lodge,' said Jack, at the same time
as he reminded himself that it might just as easily have been his
grave.

If only they had left it at the south-west face of Annapurna. That
would have been enough for most people. It was their own good luck
that had defeated them, for their lightweight ascent of Annapurna
had been blessed with such fine weather that they had completed it
in half the allotted time. But for his own vaulting ambition Didier
Lauren and the Sherpas on the glacier below might now still be
alive.

He sat down again and flashed the light around him.

The bergschrund was shaped like a funnel lying on its side, about
nine metres wide, and six metres high at the entrance, narrowing
at the rear to a tunnel about one and a half metres square.

With hours to kill he decided he might as well see how far the
tunnel bored into the mountainside. Advancing to the rear of the
cave, he squatted down and shone the powerful halogen beam along
the tunnel.

Jack knew that the Himalayas were home to bear and langur,
even to leopard, but he thought it unlikely they would have made
their home in such an inaccessible place so far above the treeline.

Bunched down on his haunches, he started to make his way along
the tunnel.

About a hundred metres in, the tunnel sloped upwards, reminding him of the long and narrow passageway that led to the Queen's
Burial Chamber in Egypt's Great Pyramid – a journey that was not
for the faint-hearted, the claustrophobic, or the orthopaedically
afflicted. After only a short hesitation, Jack decided to push on,
determined to find out how deep the cave was.

Mostly the mountains were the original Pre-Cambrian continen-
tal crust of the Indian subcontinent's northern margin and con-
sisted of schists and crystalline rocks. But here in the bergschrund
and nearer the summit, the rock was limestone, from a time when
the world's highest range of mountains was the floor of the shallow
Tethys Sea. These early Palaeozoic sediments had lifted almost
twenty kilometres since the onset of the Himalayan mountain

building around fifty-five million years ago. Jack had even heard it said that there were parts of the range that were still rising at the rate of nearly a centimetre a year a year. The Everest that he and Didier had conquered, without oxygen, was almost half a metre higher than the Everest scaled by Sir Edmund Hillary and Sherpa Tenzing back in 1953.

The tunnel slope levelled off, with the roof becoming simultaneously higher so that he was able to stand straight again. Pointing the almost solid beam of the flashlight above his head, Jack found he was in an enormous cavern and, certain only that the ceiling was beyond even the range of his Maglite, he decided that it must be at least thirty metres high.

He shouted out and heard his own voice bounce back off the invisible walls and ceiling, reinforced and prolonged by reflection in a cold, dark resonating chamber that had already left him feeling chilled to the bone. By this sound he might have judged himself to standing not inside a cavern underneath Machhapuchhare Himal but in the soaring vault of a ruined and forgotten Gothic cathedral that was now the hidden hall of a malevolent mountain king. Designed to carry the human voice upwards in praise and prayer, to God in heaven, the vault was filled instead with the silence of the tomb.

How long had this silence prevailed before being desecrated by his presence? Was he the first human to have entered the cavern since the creation of the Himalayas some one and a half million years ago?

At first he thought it was a rock he saw in the artificial beam of his Maglite. It was a moment or two before his untrained eye perceived that staring back at him from the moist earthen floor of the cave, and about the size of a melon, was the bony face of a nearly complete skull.

He dropped on to his knees and immediately began to brush away the dirt and gravel from the find with his gloved fingers. Jack was well aware that the Himalayas contained an abundance of fossils. Only a few kilometres away, on the northern slopes of Dhaulagiri, the seventh highest mountain in the world, he had once found an ammonite – a spiral-shaped mollusc dating from 150–200 million years ago. Muktinath was famous for its Upper Jurassic fossils. To the west, the Churen Himal in Nepal, and the Siwalik Hills of Northern

10

Pakistan, had yielded many significant hominid fossils. But this was the first time that Jack had discovered anything himself.

He lifted the skull clear of the dirt and examined it carefully in the beam of his flashlight. The lower jaw was missing but otherwise it looked to be in remarkably good condition, with a near perfect upper jaw and an unbroken cranium. It was larger than it had looked on the ground, and for a brief moment he thought it might have belonged to a bear until he noted the absence of any large canine teeth. It seemed to be hominid and after a couple of minutes' further scrutiny he felt quite sure of it, but he had no idea if what he was looking at was related to any of the other fossil hominids for which the Himalayas were known, or even if it was a fossil at all.

He thought of the one person who would be able to tell him everything there was to know about the skull. The woman who had once been his lover and who had consistently refused to marry him, but who was rather better known as a Doctor of Palaeoanthropology at the University of California in Berkeley. He knew her simply as Swift. Maybe he would present his find to her as a gift. There could be no doubt that she would appreciate having the skull more than any of the other souvenirs he had promised to bring her back from Nepal, like a rug or a *thangka*.

He could almost hear the unprincipled advice that Didier would have offered him.

'Trust you, Didier,' Jack said sadly. 'Besides, there's still the small problem of getting down from this mountain to consider.'

Jack returned to the bergschrund entrance bearing the skull in his hands. He looked inside his tightly packed rucksack and decided that something would have to be left behind if he was to get the skull down the mountain. But what? Not the sleeping bag. Not the first-aid box. Not the socks, the advance base rations, the Nikon F4 camera.

He started to unpack the rucksack.

A half-full bottle of Macallan malt whisky came to hand. Quite apart from the fact that he and Didier enjoyed drinking it, whisky was a more effective treatment for frostbite than vasodilator drugs such as Ronicol. High-altitude rock-climbing was one of the rare occasions when the medicinal properties of alcohol really could be justified. And this was an emergency.

Jack sat down on the floor of the bergschrund and uncorked the bottle. Then he toasted his friend and prepared to finish the bottle.

11

Two

'Health to the green steel head. . .'

Robert Lowell

India.
The telephone rang.
Pakistan.
The telephone rang again. The man stirred in his bed.

In recent weeks when the phone had rung during the night, it had usually been something to do with the worsening situation between these two ancient enemies.

The man wriggled his way up the bed, switched on the bedside-light, collected the receiver, and then leaned back against the padded headboard. A quick glance at his watch revealed that the time in Washington DC was 4.15 a.m. But his thoughts were sixteen thousand kilometres away. He was thinking that on the Indian subcontinent it would be mid-afternoon on a hot day made warmer by the posturings of the Indian and Pakistani leaders and the dreadful possibility that one of them might decide that a pre-emptive nuclear strike against the other was the best way of winning an as yet undeclared war.

'Perrins,' yawned the man, although he was wide awake. A bad attack of indigestion, the result of a supper cruise down the Potomac aboard the presidential yacht *Sequoia* had seen to that.

He listened carefully to the sombre-sounding voice on the other end of the secured line and then groaned.

'Okay,' he said. 'I'll be there in half an hour.' He replaced the receiver and cursed quietly.

12

His wife was awake and looking at him with a worried expression.
'It's not – ?'

'No, thank God,' he said, swinging his legs out of bed. 'Not yet anyway. But I have to go to the office all the same. Something that "requires my urgent presence".'

She threw back the quilt.

'No need for you to get up,' he said. 'Stay in bed.'

She stood up and slipped on a bath-robe.

'I wish I could, dear,' she said. 'But that dinner. I feel like I'm pregnant again. Pregnant and overdue.' She headed towards the kitchen. 'I'll make some coffee.'

Perrins shuffled into the bathroom and held himself under an ice-cold shower. Cold water and coffee might be the only stimulation his heart would get for the rest of the coming day – just like the day before.

Fifteen minutes later, he was dressed and standing on the porch of the red-brick colonial. Kissing his wife goodbye, he stepped into the back of a black Cadillac sedan that the office had dispatched to collect him.

Neither the driver, nor the armed guard alongside him in the front said anything during the drive north up the Henry G. Shirley Memorial Highway. They were both the speak-when-spoken-to types, servicemen who had driven and protected Perrins for the last year. They knew that a man attending a dawn meeting at the Pentagon might have other things on his mind than the unusually severe cold weather and the way the Redskins had been playing.

Just south of Arlington National Cemetery, the highway deviated to the east and the familiar concrete shape that was the biggest office building in the world hove into view. To Perrins it seemed only appropriate that the US Department of Defense should be headquartered within sight of those Americans who had died in wars.

The Cadillac deposited him in front of one of the Pentagon's many entrances and he made his way into the building. Sometimes he thought that there must be five of everything at the Pentagon: five sides, five storeys, five concentric hallways, and a five-acre courtyard in the centre. For all he knew, there might even have been as many as five thousand of the Pentagon's twenty-five thousand-strong workforce already at their desks by the time he arrived, even though it was five o'clock in the morning. Certainly the place looked busy enough.

The NRO was headquartered in Department 4C956 and although it did not officially exist at all, the Office of Space Systems, as it was sometimes also known, was easy enough to find; 4 indicated the fourth floor, C indicated Ring C: Ring A faced the courtyard, and Ring C was in the middle, 9 was corridor nine; and 56 was the number of the suite of offices.

Perrins went straight to the conference room where he found several men and women, some of them wearing the uniform of their respective service, but all of them grim-faced and awaiting the arrival of the Director of NRO, Bill Reichhardt, who entered the room only a few seconds behind Perrins.

Reichhardt, a tall, thin, grey-haired man in a dark suit, took his place at the head of the table, smiled thinly at Perrins and nodded at a bespectacled man whose round shoulders, shiny bald head, and reverentially clasped hands gave him the look of a devout and supplicatory priest about to ask that the Lord bless their gathering.

'All right, Griff,' Reichhardt said hoarsely, and lifted his collar from his Adam's apple, as if there was something in his throat other than anger at having been roused from his bed. 'Get on with it.'

The priestly man cleared his throat and started to speak.

'I'm sure everyone in this room is now aware of the situation that was reported by the NAADC tracking complex at Cheyenne Mountain earlier this evening,' he said. 'Full details are available in the reports in front of you. Ladies and gentlemen, I have to tell you that the situation has now been confirmed by both Norwegian Mission Control Center at Tromso and the French MCC at Toulouse.'

'Jesus,' said someone. 'Do we know why?'

'So far we've been unable to surface any further intelligence on that.'

'Griff,' one of the naval uniforms asked, 'what's the grade of sensitivity on this material?'

'We're talking SCI.'

SCI was the most secret of all US Government classifications. Affecting matters of truly Olympian secrecy, it stood for 'sensitive compartmental intelligence'.

'So what's the beverage of choice?' said an army man.

Reichhardt looked up from his notepad and raised his eyebrows.

'What do you say, Griff? Any bright ideas?'

'I'd suggest a lower level reconnaissance, sir. We ought to put some U2Rs in the air over that area. Round the clock over flights.'

'Alvin?' Reichhardt was now looking at one of the airforce uniforms.

'Well, sir, I'd be concerned about the conservation of the asset. By which I mean the aircraft. The trouble with the U2R is that it's not a particularly sturdy aircraft. It's designed for one purpose – long flights at low altitudes and low speeds. It was easy enough to shoot down back in the early Sixties, when the Russians nailed Gary Powers.' He shrugged. 'Now more than ever. However. . .'

Perrins had been nodding his agreement.

'My reading,' he said interrupting, 'is that both sides are likely to take a dim view of any perceived American military interference in the region. The Indians see us as Pakistan's natural ally. Trouble is, since this whole thing got going, it's the Chinese who have been backing the Pakistanis, not us. If one of those U2s gets itself shot down it might just jeopardise our ability to honestly broker a peace.'

'Is that what we want to do?' asked Reichhardt. 'Honestly broker a peace?'

'There's no strategic advantage to be gained by letting a war go ahead, Bill.'

Reichhardt nodded slowly and studied the cover of the report in front of him, tapping at it with the point of his mechanical pencil, until the dots began to add up to a whole constellation.

'Alvin? You were about to add a however, I think,' he prompted the airforce man.

'However, when it comes to high-quality photography there's nothing else that can do the job quite as well as the U2. If we were to make sure that we only launched a few missions, when the weather was at its very best, say when the recon' area was less than twenty-five per cent overcast, then I'd be a lot more confident of getting an early result.'

'They'll get a better shot of the ground,' grumbled Perrins. 'But so will the local surface-to-air missile batteries.'

'Can't be helped,' snapped Reichhardt. Glancing over at Perrins, he added, 'I hear what you say, Bryan, but in the short term I really don't see we have any choice but to take the risk.'

'It's your call, Bill,' shrugged Perrins.

'Alvin? I want those U2s launched right away.'

15

'Yes sir.'

'Codename – .' Reichhardt bounced the pencil against his teeth. 'Anyone? I'd rather not have to have a computer-generated codename. They're so damned nonsensical that I can never remember them.'

'How about Icarus?' said Perrins.

'I think not,' laughed Reichhardt. 'I mean, wouldn't that just be tempting fate?'

Perrins smiled back, affecting innocence.

'We don't want our wings to melt. No, we'll call it Bellerophon. That's B-E-L-L-E-R-O-P-H-O-N.' He chuckled again and then added: 'Look it up if you don't know what it means, Bryan. Bellerophon flew to heaven on Pegasus.' He laughed again, with smug satisfaction. 'Benefits of a Harvard education.'

Perrins, who was a Yale man, nodded silently and was about to point out that Zeus had sent a gadfly to sting the horse and Bellerophon was thrown, but checked himself, deciding that it could wait until the next meeting. If the U2s did succeed in uncovering something, then no one would care about the codename anyway. But if the U2s drew a blank, then he could remind Reichhardt of the story behind the name, as if he had only just remembered it. Childish, but enjoyable. In the intelligence game you had your fun where you could. Especially where the Pentagon was concerned.

Three

'God's first blunder: Man didn't find the animals amusing, – he dominated them, and didn't even want to be "an animal".'

Friedrich Nietzsche

Across the Bay Bridge, on Interstate 80 out of San Francisco, the East Bay area comprised Alameda and Contra Costa counties, with Oakland and Berkeley the two most likely destinations for a traveller. Although the two cities were virtually contiguous, something less tangible than a line of foothills separated blue-collar Oakland, a busy port, from its wealthier and more northerly neighbour. Berkeley was a student town, its hills dominated by the University of California. A few more enlightened people regarded Berkeley as the most intellectually important place west of Chicago and the Athens of the Pacific Coast. But for most Americans – certainly those who remembered the peace movements of the late Sixties and early Seventies – Berkeley was still a byword for die-hard radicalism. Drugs, sit-ins and tear gas over People's Park.

The reality was different. Almost three decades after the university had witnessed the largest mass arrest in California's history, Berkeley had a more conservative tilt. There were still plenty of activists and pamphleteers abroad on Sproul Plaza, just outside Sather Gate which marked the entrance to the oldest part of the campus. But in the eyes of Doctor Stella Swift, Berkeley was a small college town with all the vices and virtues of a small college town. And there was little of what was considered radical in Berkeley that would have impressed the really left-wing types she had mixed with as the only child of two of Socialism's leading lights, first in Australia

17

and later on in England. Swift's father Tom, Professor of Philosophy at Melbourne University, Australia and then at Cambridge, was a highly influential writer and thinker, while her mother Judith, a successful artist, was the daughter of Max Bergmann, one of the founders of the so-called Frankfurt School of Libertarian Marxism. Before going up to Oxford to take a degree in human biology, Swift had met everyone who was anyone in international Socialism and, finding herself bored by her parents' world, rejected it, just as one of the young pamphleteers she could now see on Sproul Plaza protesting American foreign policy in the Middle East might have rejected the conservative values of his own parents.

Crossing Sproul Plaza, Swift reflected that being a foreigner and, therefore, someone who was unable to vote, meant that she could more easily ignore politics and concentrate on her research and teaching. It was one of the reasons she had elected to do her Ph.D. in Palaeoanthropology at Berkeley in the first place.

Swift spent most of her working life in the south-eastern corner of the campus, in Kroeber Hall. Entering the building, she made her way up to the first floor, and along to one of the lecture theatres where several dozen freshman students were already awaiting her arrival.

Placing her briefcase on the table, she regarded one of her students, an outsized jock called Todd who was making a show of reading a copy of *Penthouse*, with disdain.

'What's that you're reading, Todd?' said Swift, coming around the table. 'Catching up on a little human biology? Good idea, because from what I hear, it's your weakest subject by far.'

One of Todd's male friends guffawed loudly and elbowed him in the ribs. Taking advantage of this momentary distraction, Swift snatched the magazine out of Todd's banana-sized fingers and turned the pages thoughtfully.

Todd's friend elbowed him again, almost as if he was egging him on to do something.

'Actually,' grinned Todd. 'There was someone in there who reminded me of you, Doctor Swift.'

'Is that so?' Swift said coolly. 'Which page?'

'Page thirty-two.'

'I'll say one thing for you, Todd,' she remarked, turning the pages. 'You're a brave man bringing *Penthouse* on to this campus. I hope someone's read you your Miranda.'

18

'My what?'

'After the US Supreme Court Case that established guidelines for the protection of the arrested individual.'

'He's certainly arrested,' chuckled Todd's elbowing neighbour.

Swift found the page and gave her supposed lookalike her candid attention.

'So?' said Todd. 'What do you think?'

The girl in the photo-spread was tall and green-eyed with a big head of red hair. Her nose was long, but distinguished, and her mouth wide and sensual. She had the same generously proportioned figure although Swift thought her own legs were better. In spite of the pose, Swift perceived an undeniable resemblance.

'So she reminds you of me, does she, Todd?'

'Some.'

Swift tossed the magazine back at him and turning back to the blackboard, found a stick of chalk and started to write in large capital letters. When she had finished she pointed at the word on the board and said, 'That's what you remind me of, Todd.'

Frowning, Todd read the word aloud with some difficulty.

'Ancathocephalus,' he said. 'What the hell's that?'

'I'm glad you asked me, Todd,' smiled Swift. 'Ancathocephalus is a common parasite found in fish. A spiny-headed worm with which you happen to share one unusual physical characteristic.'

'What's that?'

'Its reproductive organs are much bigger than its brain.'

Todd smiled uneasily as the rest of the class started to laugh.

Swift waited for their laughter to deliver their attention. There were times when teaching was quite tribal. When, to maintain your contractual dominance, you had to accept a challenge and defeat your rival in front of the whole social group. She rather enjoyed these occasional trials of strength with young males like Todd. Confident that she had their full attention now, Swift decided to adapt the beginning of her lecture to improvise a segue from her joke about ancathocephalus.

'Despite what Todd might believe,' she said, 'human sex organs do not exist in isolation. Their evolution is inextricably mixed up with the way human females give birth, the size of human brains, and our tool-making skills. And our idiosyncratic reproductive behaviour, even when it's as unusual as the kind of sexual behaviour exhibited by Todd, which reduces less dominant males to the status

19

of mere spectators in the whole reproductive process – is as important as our larger brains in attempting to explain the different evolutionary fate of man and apes.

'Now, I say "attempting to explain" because the origin of modern humans, *Homo sapiens*, people like you and me, is a vexed question among palaeoanthropologists like myself, and the evidence is, quite literally, fragmentary. These fragments might be likened to the pieces of a jigsaw, except that it's not even as if there is only one puzzle. There are many puzzles and lots of jigsaw pieces and they're all muddled up.

'For instance, we don't really have an answer to why our brains should be as big as they are, any more than we know why the human penis should be bigger than a gorilla's. Yes, even your penis, Todd. And if the human penis is larger than a gorilla's, why should human testes be smaller than those of a chimpanzee? Did this come about simply as a corollary of the chimpanzee's greater reproductive activity? Or did man develop his smaller testes in order to facilitate bipedalism?'

Swift sat down on the edge of her table and shrugged.

'There are plenty of theories but the honest answer is that we just don't know. No more do we really know which came first: the bipedal ape, or the brainy ape. What was it about that early environment that demanded that a certain kind of ape should have a significantly expanded brain? Remember, brain size is not necessarily related to intelligence. For example, take the brain weights of two famous poets. Walt Whitman's brain weighed just one and a quarter kilos, while Byron's brain weighed two and one-third kilos, almost twice as much. But does this mean that Byron was twice as good a poet as Whitman? Of course not.

'And yet there would be no point in us having a brain that's about four times as large as that of a chimpanzee if there were not significant benefits to be enjoyed from it. After all, the brain requires a great deal of energy from your body to maintain it. Despite the fact that it constitutes only two per cent of your body bulk, the human brain needs an incredible twenty per cent of your body's available energy. Man's extra brain power evolved for a reason, but quite what the reason was is frankly anyone's guess.

'It's not as if the great apes were a particularly successful group of primates when you compare them with their closest relatives, the Cercopithecoids, or Old World Monkeys. Because in comparison

20

with them, the story of apes is really one of declining diversity. The fossil record suggests that apes were already in decline by the middle Miocene period, some ten to fifteen million years ago, with monkeys more prevalent and many times more diverse.

'If we were able to put aside the knowledge of our simian status and, at the same time, we were able to rent Michael J. Fox's Delorean-shaped time machine and travel back in time some five or six million years, to the middle Pliocene epoch, we would discover that monkeys were the planet's dominant primate. After all, there were so many of them. We might even think that they were the better bet as far as inheriting the earth was concerned, and that their larger, slower, knuckle-walking, brachiating cousins represented a bit of an evolutionary dead-end.

'But then if we could return to our time-travelling Delorean and go forward by another few hundred thousand years – just how far we would have to go is also a matter of considerable disagreement among palaeoanthropologists – we should notice how one particular bipedal ape seemed to be showing considerable evolutionary promise and might be worthy of careful monitoring.

'The question why this one small branch of a numerically unsuccessful species should suddenly develop in such a spectacular way is something that continues to puzzle scientists and, surely, there is no subject of greater interest to us. But the question assumes even greater pertinence the more one comes to appreciate just how much of an ape we really are. Not just Todd. But all of us.

'Some of you will perhaps recall that in 1540, Copernicus published the results of his astronomical observations that overthrew for ever the traditional Ptolemaic view of the Universe, in which the sun and the stars revolved around planet Earth. With good reason, you might think it strange that it was another four hundred years before Palaeoanthropology was similarly able to overthrow the prevailing orthodoxy that saw Man as the inevitable and ultimate product of evolution on earth. We now know that it is wrong to see evolution as a constant progression, like some inexorable assembly line that results in the Ultimate Being – Man himself. Nature is not so clear-cut. And the sooner you are all able to empty your minds of this myth of evolutionary progress that sees the ape as an inferior being left behind by a pushy cousin striving towards its own Nietzschean destiny, the sooner you can call yourselves proper palaeoanthropologists. To this end, I want to spend

21

the rest of our time considering our ape status.

'Back in 1962, Tarzan was being played not by Johnny Weissmuller but by Jock Mahoney. I'm not sure who took the part of Cheeta, his faithful chimpanzee friend, but suffice it to say that there was not a lot to choose between them when it came to acting. Either way one was still able to suspend disbelief and accept the continued validity of the Edgar Rice Burroughs storyline, that Man and Ape were so close that a man might be brought up among apes and indeed, upon growing to manhood, come to dominate them.

'Now around the same time, a scientist called Morris Goodman picked up on something that people had more or less forgotten: the discovery by George Nuttall, a Professor of Biology at the University of Cambridge, that the chemistry of blood proteins might be used to determine the genetic relatedness between higher primates. Using Nuttall's approach on blood-serum proteins, Goodman discovered that the antigens of man and chimp are practically identical. At the time everyone, with the possible exceptions of Tarzan and Cheta, believed that a chimp had more in common with a gorilla than with a man. But Goodman proved that this was simply not the case.

'Since then, using techniques vastly superior to those of Goodman, molecular anthropologists – most notably Vince Sarich and Allan Wilson of this university – have been able to attach numerical values to Goodman's astounding discovery.'

Swift sipped a glass of water and then explained how, using albumin, one of the proteins commonly found in blood, it was possible to measure differences of as little as one amino acid in a hundred and, in effect, how it was possible to establish a precise difference in terms of DNA between one species and another.

'The numbers are quite impressive,' she said. 'And in a way, they're also quite shocking. Whereas the DNA between two species of frog can differ by as much as eight per cent, the DNA difference between a man and a chimp is only one point six per cent. One point six per cent.'

She wrote the number on the blackboard and then paused in order to allow the statistic to sink into her students' minds. She shook her head as if she was still impressed by it herself. She was.

'You know, that is less than the DNA difference between two species of gibbon, between a horse and a zebra, between a dog and a fox and, most importantly of all, between a chimpanzee and a

22

gorilla. In other words we have more in common with a chimp than he does with a gorilla.

'One point six per cent is not much of a difference to account for Aristotle, Shakespeare, Michelangelo, Mozart, Wagner, Picasso and Einstein. But what they achieved is perhaps even more remarkable when you look at it the other way. Maybe you remember Sir Arthur Stanley Eddington's suggestion that if an infinite number of monkeys were strumming on typewriters they might write all the books in the British Museum. But the fact is that every one of those books in the British Museum was written by a man who shares ninety-eight point four per cent of his genetic makeup with a chimpanzee.

'Jared Diamond, who is Professor of Physiology at this university, has argued the case for man as the third chimpanzee. Founding his thesis on a school of taxonomy called cladistics, which says that the classification of living things should be objective and uniform and based on genetic distance or times of divergence, Diamond argues that chimps, gorillas and Man all belong within the same genus. And he says, because our genus name *Homo* came first, that this should take zoological priority. This has the anthropocentric result that we must now think of not one but four species of the genus *Homo* on earth today: the common chimpanzee, the pygmy chimpanzee, Man himself, and slightly more distinct, the gorilla.

'Now that's not a bad idea at all, especially when you consider how the first specimens of ape got their names. It's said that the word "chimpanzee" was taken from a Portuguese-Angolan word meaning "mock man". Orang-utan is Malay for "man of the woods". Also, while the word "gorilla" is Greek, it may in turn also derive from another African word meaning "wild man". Maybe it's only these Latin handles that have made us forget who and what these creatures are. Think about it.

'Four different kinds of Man, when previously we thought there was only one. So much for the question, asked by astronomers and cosmologists everywhere: are we alone? Clearly the answer must be, no we're not alone. We never have been.

'It's possible that some of you will be aware of how, in an effort to protect the dwindling populations of gorillas and chimpanzees from poachers, a number of African countries have taken Professor Diamond's arguments on board, and are changing their laws on homicide so as to include these new species of the genus *Homo*. In these countries killing a gorilla will soon be classed as murder and the perpetrator punished with the full severity of the law. Highly commendable, yes. But it's worth bearing in mind that *Homo sapiens* is not the only species of *Homo* that engages in mass murder of its own kind. Jane Goodall has described how, over a period of years, she observed one group of chimpanzees being systematically exterminated by another. Goodall ascribed the fact that the extermination took so long only to the lack of efficient killing tools of the kind that *Homo sapiens* excels in manufacturing. Dian Fossey's work with gorillas goes a long way to support the suggestion that the average ape – especially infant apes – stands as good a chance of being murdered by another of its kind as the average American.

'As I just said, it's tools that make Man the most efficient killer on the planet. But which came first, brain size, or tools? Now you might think that brain size would be a prerequisite for the manufacture of efficient tools. However the fossil record shows that there is no such clear corollary. It might surprise you to know that forty thousand years ago, Neanderthal Man possessed a brain that was larger than that of a modern human and yet his tools show no great sophistication. Even so, I feel that Neanderthal's larger brain size – about three per cent larger than our own brains – ought to scotch any prejudices that because he had a recessive cranium, Neanderthal was somehow stupid. But quite what all his extra brain power was for, nobody really knows.

'Whatever caused the conventionally held split between Man and Ape – what we like to term the Great Leap Forward – be it brain power or tool-making, the reason must have occurred in only one point six per cent of our genes. Perhaps you'd like to go away and consider what that reason might be. Certainly whatever theories you come up with, they will have no more or less validity than what anyone else has devised so far. As you'll all soon discover for yourselves, I hope, there's little certainty in the world of Palaeoanthropology. Indeed, although we call it one of the Natural Sciences, there's very little that's scientific about it. Empirical method plays very little part in what we do . . .'

Swift glanced at her watch as a sixty-one bell carillon rang out from the Campanile on Sproul Plaza. Three times a day it was the scene of a hand-played, ten-minute concert. This one marked midday and the end of her lecture. Her students were already standing up and putting away their notebooks and pens. 'Okay,' she said,

24

raising her voice above the growing din, 'we'd better leave it there. Just remember what Matt Cartmill of Duke University once said. He said that all sciences are odd in some way, but Palaeoanthropology is one of the oddest.'

'That's for sure,' grumbled Todd. 'Man, I was just getting used to the idea of being an ape.'

'I can't imagine that would take very long,' said one of the female students pointedly. 'I've seen you eating, Todd.'

Todd grinned good-naturedly.

'But four different kinds of men?' he said, shaking his head. 'I can see how that might be good news for one of you. Maybe now you can get yourselves laid. But if you ask me it's kind of worrying. Think about it. All those chimps and gorillas and zoos? I mean, suppose they find out they're not animals at all? Suppose they read the Constitution. Then we'll really be in trouble.'

'Know then thyself, presume not God to scan; The proper study of mankind is man.'

Almost as soon as she had read it as a sixteen-year-old schoolgirl, Alexander Pope's lines became Swift's motto and her whole philosophy of life. It seemed to her that she had always been interested in human origins, and a precociously early interest in sex and the facts of human reproduction was soon replaced by a rather more fundamental quest, to discover her own genetic heritage.

Yet there had occurred one particular moment of revelation when she had realised that she wanted to devote her life to 'the proper study of mankind'. It was perhaps appropriate that the moment should itself have been connected to a scene of symbolic revelation. When, with exquisite caution, the ape had touched the monolith in Kubrick's film *2001: A Space Odyssey*, and was infected with the tool/weapon-making facility, he also touched Swift's youthful imagination. This was the moment when, with a tumultuous fanfare of Nietzschean trumpets, Swift had perceived her way forward in life.

Now, years after the start of her own intellectual odyssey, the riddle of Man's Great Leap Forward – the genetic gift that had made *Homo sapiens* so special – was no less adamantine a mystery than Kubrick's black and brooding monolith. And fundamentally the mystery remained exactly that.

The divergent period between Neanderthals and *Homo sapiens*

25

had occurred only two hundred thousand years before – one-thirtieth of the time taken to separate apes and humans – with less than one half of a percentage difference in their respective genomes; and yet Neanderthals had failed where *Homo sapiens* had succeeded.

Why?

There was not the least clue to chip the hard and ebony granite of this mystery.

The prevailing explanation of the Neanderthal/*Homo sapiens* split – that modern man had developed the evolutionary advantage of language (Palaeoanthropology no longer placed emphasis on man the tool-making killer ape that had so appealed to Stanley Kubrick) – led to an even greater mystery.

What was the peculiar anatomical development that Neander-thals had failed to produce that had resulted in modern man's capacity for meaningful speech?

It was a steep walk home up Euclid Avenue.

Like many of the homes in the Northside area of Berkeley, a quiet leafy neighbourhood popular with professionals and acad-emics, Swift's house was a half-timbered chalet that seemed to have been sculpted from the wooded landscape. The house had been expensive and it was her mother's great bronzes, fetching big prices in the London and Manhattan salerooms, that had paid for.

Back in her airy, plant-filled study, with its book-lined gallery and her baby-grand piano, Swift unplugged the telephone and stretched out on the sofa to smoke a soothing cigarette. She was an infrequent smoker, using tobacco almost medicinally, seeking a tranquillising effect. She took only a couple of deep drags from the Marlboro she held between fingers so heavily ringed with gold they looked like the keys on a saxophone, and then stubbed it out. She was still consid-ering how to spend what remained of the afternoon when she dozed off . . .

Awakening with a start Swift glanced at her watch.

It was five o'clock.

So much for the afternoon.

The entryphone buzzed several times, like an angry wasp, as if someone had been pressing for a while. Who could it be? One of her students? One of her colleagues perhaps? Her neighbour come to complain about her late-night piano-playing?

'Shit.'

Swift swung her long legs off the sofa and crossed the polished ash floor to depress the intercom button.

'Who is it?' she sighed, scowling.

'Jack,' said the voice.

'Jack,' she repeated dumbly. 'Jack who?'

'Jesus, Swift. How many Jacks do you know? Jack Furness, of course.'

'Jack?'

Swift screamed with delight and stabbed the release button to open the front door. Pausing only to check her appearance in the heavy gilt mirror that hung in the hallway, she ran downstairs two steps at a time, and flung open the door.

Jack stood on the doorstep, almost at attention, with a large wooden box under his thickly muscled arm, wearing a navy blue polo shirt, a brown tweed sports coat and a grin as big and shiny as his sportswatch. He was thinner than she remembered, even a little drawn. It was plain from his weather-beaten face that he had endured considerable hardship on his Himalayan expedition. But she knew very little of the tragedy that had befallen him beyond a couple of lines on CNN *Online* and in the *San Francisco Chronicle* the week before about how the two-man expedition to climb all the major peaks of the Himalayas in one year had ended in disaster when Didier Lauren was killed in an avalanche.

Swift flew into Jack's arms and hugged him tightly before drawing back to fix him with an accusing eye.

'Jack,' she scolded. 'What if I had been out? Why didn't you telephone?'

'I did. Your phone is unplugged.'

'I mean why didn't you telephone from Nepal? Or write me an airmail? Or for that matter an e-mail?'

He shrugged. 'For a while I didn't really have much to say to anyone. I guess you heard what happened?'

'It made the *Chronicle*,' she said. 'But it didn't say much more than was on the wire. The report just said that Didier was killed in an avalanche and that you had survived.' She hugged him again and then pulled him into the hallway.

'Not just Didier,' he said. 'There were five Sherpas killed as well.'

'God, how terrible for you.'

'That's what it was. Terrible.'

'I'm glad you're all right, Jack' she said, closing the door.

27

She led him into her living room, pushed him on to a large deep sofa and then fetched him a drink. His favourite. The Macallan.

'When did you get back?'

'Yesterday.'

'Yesterday? And you waited all this time to come and see me?'

'Actually, it was more like last night. Late last night. And I was beat.'

Jack drained his glass and took a long look at her. She was even better-looking than he had remembered. Her legs were tanned and very shapely. These she crossed as she sat down opposite him on a hard little chair.

'There's no one on the scene?' he said. 'I mean tonight.'

'Not tonight, no.'

'Good. Mind if I get myself a refill?'

'Help yourself.'

He stood up, wandered over to the drinks tray where he poured himself a larger malt and then returned to a different position on the sofa, one that seemed to offer a better vantage point from which to enjoy a view of her legs.

'What, no one at all? I can't believe that. C'mon, it's seven or eight months since I saw you last. There must have been someone.'

'I didn't say there hadn't been.'

'Now I'm getting jealous.' He narrowed his eyes. 'Who, for instance?'

Swift shrugged negligently.

'If one is discreet. Very discreet. There are always the students.'

'You're bullshitting me.'

'Maybe,' she said, and uncrossed her legs, allowing him a brief glimpse of her underwear before tugging at the hem of her skirt.

'Anyone can see that you've been celibate while you've been in Nepal,' she said. 'Cut it out will you, Jack? Sharon Stone I am not.'

'Okay, okay,' he grinned. 'Just fooling around.'

'Don't. By the way, what's in the box?'

'A present.'

'For me?'

'Maybe.'

Swift wriggled with excitement.

'What is it? Something I'll like?'

Jack shook his head. He knew her too well to tell her about the fossil in the box. He was looking forward at dinner – the first really good dinner he would have eaten in months – to her undivided attention. He had no intention of eating alone while Swift stayed in her laboratory and played Richard Leakey with the skull he had discovered in the Machhapuchhare bergschrund.

'Oh, I don't doubt it,' he said. 'But dinner first, okay?'

'Well,' he said when they finished the dinner she had made. 'That was almost worth the wait. Best damn dinner I've eaten in months.'

'Is the food so bad in Nepal?' Swift asked.

'Usually it's not so bad,' he said. 'But because we were a lightweight team, and the feasible payloads were critically small, we had to make do with a lot of the same food all the time. Mostly we relied on lightweight assault rations. When we were at base camps the food was better. Buffalo meat. Eggs, dal, goats, and rice. But even then – well, let's just say it's the kind of food where only a brave man farts.'

Swift pulled a face.

'I still can't understand why you do it,' she said. 'Why you go climbing at all. What do you get out of it? Some kind of cheap thrill, I guess.'

'It's hardly cheap,' he objected. 'Considering what can happen. Considering what did happen.'

'Yes, I'm sorry. That was stupid of me.'

'No problem. Disapproval sounds flattering coming from you, Swift. Like maybe you actually care what happens to me.'

'Whatever gave you that idea? Seriously though, Jack. Why do you do it?'

'Why do I leave home and go see all the wonders of the world? I might just as easily ask you why you stay here in this off-the-wall little city.'

'I go places,' she said, bridling. 'Field trips. Fossil hunting. Last year I went to East Africa. But with you, it's not just travel, is it? You go there to risk your life. Jack, you're like a grown man with a new motorcycle. You're forty, for goodness sake.'

'You make forty sound old.'

'Don't you think it's time you settled down?'

'I guess I never found a reason to, yet. Are you making me an offer?'

'No, of course I'm not,' she laughed.

'Then I don't think it's time I settled down at all.'

29

'So, it's all my fault is it?'

'Sure it is.'

'You bastard,' she said and punched him playfully on the shoulder. 'Maybe you like to climb because of the ape in you?' she suggested.

'Maybe. But to answer your question properly, I climb mountains because it's a Passion with a capital P. Suffering, defeat, justice. There's something almost religious about it. Like your own personal Oberammergau.' He laughed out loud. 'Jesus, can you believe the crap I'm coming out with tonight? I've had too much to drink.'

But Swift felt he had let something slip that wasn't just the result of alcohol. Something rare and very personal.

'No, I really want to know.'

Pausing for a moment, Jack took a deep breath and then spoke again.

'The Sherpas believe that the Himalayas are holy. The mountains aren't just named after local heroes or after a supposed similarity with some kind of animal. They mean something religious. For instance, Chomo Lungma, the Tibetan name for Everest, means "Land of the Goddess, Mother of the Earth". And Annapurna means "Goddess of Bountiful Harvests". These people believe that the mountains are sacred and there are some peaks they actually consider to be inviolable – that it would be blasphemous to climb them. Well, this is how it is for me. The fact of the matter is, I almost believe that myself. You see, it's the very blasphemy of it, the confrontation with God, the thrown-down challenge to Him that makes me want to do it. To keep doing it. Even to climb the ones I'm not supposed to climb.

'Maybe, I don't know . . . maybe there's some Freudian explanation for all of that . . .' He laughed again. 'Jesus, stop me, for Pete's sake. I'm just full of shit tonight. I must sound like I'm back at Oxford.'

'You never sounded like that when you were at Oxford,' said Swift. 'You were very practical and American and you made a secret of your intellectual abilities. You were bright without being pretentious. That was what attracted me.'

He and Swift had always shared an understanding about sex: if there was nobody else on the scene, they slept together. Still, it was best to take nothing for granted. If he could only get her into bed before she saw the fossil.

Swift made coffee and carried it into the lounge on a brass-bound Indian tray Jack had brought her after climbing Dunagiri, a seven-thousand-metre high mountain, in northern India. That had been his first Himalayan peak. Didier's too. They had climbed it in preparation for their ascent of Changabang the following year. Jack realised with a sense of shock that it was exactly ten years since that. Maybe she was right. Maybe he was getting too old to go mountaineering.

After a long silence Swift leaned across the sofa and touched his cheek with the back of her heavily-ringed hand.

'What are you thinking?'

Jack told her about the tray.

'I was just wondering who I'm going to partner now that Didier's gone,' he added.

Swift moved closer and Jack put his arms around her waist, squeezed her gently and put his mouth on hers as if he wanted her to breathe life back into him.

Minutes passed. Then Swift drew back and looked closely at him as if reminding herself of what it was she liked about his face.

She hardly hesitated. She stood up, unzipped her skirt and then dropped it to the floor to reveal, with what Jack considered was an impressive lack of panties, the upturned golden divot at the nadir of her belly.

'I thought you said you weren't Sharon Stone,' he said and pressed his face close to her body.

She brushed his hair with her fingers, pleased that he still found her so desirable.

He followed her into the hallway, his eyes fixed on the perfect curves of her bare behind. She mounted the stairs to the bedroom, glancing back teasingly to make sure he was coming after her. It was then she caught sight of the wooden box he had brought with him.

She stopped dead in her tracks.

'Hey,' she said. 'What about my present?'

Turning on the step she sat down and let him push his head between her legs before gathering his hair in her hands and pulling him away.

'After,' he said, bringing a hand up between her legs.

Laughing, she mounted another step to escape his clumsy caresses. 'Oh no. Tribute first. Then reward.'

31

'Can't it wait?' groaned Jack.

'What? So you can change your mind about giving it to me?' She was delighting in her own childishness. 'No way. Besides, you do want my full attention in bed, don't you? I can hardly make love to you properly if my mind is on something else all the time.'

'You don't understand, Swift. That's just the point. That's exactly what I'm worried about. Having your full attention.'

Swift pushed him gently back towards the hallway.

'You've got a lot to learn about female psychology,' she told him, amused by his obvious discomfiture. 'You should have left your present in the car.'

'Damn right,' he said and shook his head ruefully. 'But look here. The thing is. . .this is not the kind of present. . . it's not like some Indian tea-tray. Or a rug.'

'That much I can see for myself.'

'What I mean to say is that it's something scientific and, as such, well perhaps now is not the right time.'

'Now you've really got me intrigued,' she laughed. 'What is it?'

'Shit.' Jack conceded defeat.

He retreated towards the door and collected the wooden box off the floor.

'You've absolutely no idea how much trouble I had getting this through Customs,' he grumbled.

'It's a fossil, isn't it? Oh Jack, you've brought me a fossil.'

She followed him into the kitchen where he laid the box on the table and then found a knife with which to prise off the lid. Lifting it off he collected up a handful of straw to reveal what she immediately recognised the cranium of a hominoidean skull.

Swift shivered with excitement.

'Oh God,' she said breathlessly. 'It's a skull.'

'Go ahead,' he urged. 'Take it out. It won't break. It's really quite sturdy.'

'Wait, wait, wait.'

She ran out of the kitchen for a moment and when she came back she was wearing her skirt again.

Jack tried not to look disappointed and, after a moment, her excitement began to feel infectious and he was keen to see exactly what she would make of his discovery.

Carefully, like a mother picking up her baby for the first time, Swift lifted the skull out of its packing case and stared at it.

32

After a moment or two, she said:

'Jack, it's beautiful.'

'You really think so? There's a piece of lower jawbone in the box. I found that later. And I also brought you a sample of dirt and rock. To help you date it.'

'How did you know about that?' Swift's eyes never left the skull. 'About geochronology?'

Jack shrugged.

'It shouldn't surprise you. Twenty-five years crawling over rocks. I've picked up some geology along the way.'

'Yes, of course,' she said absently.

He folded his arms and leaned against the plain wooden worktop, enjoying her fascination. After a protracted silence he grinned and said:

'You look like Hamlet.'

'You stare at it long enough and it speaks to you,' she murmured. 'Just like poor Yorick.'

'So what's the verdict?'

'The verdict?'

'Is it interesting?'

'You spend most of your fossil-hunting life straining your eyes, looking for odd-shaped fragments. You could go round-shouldered and then blind looking for small pieces of petrified bone. Shattered bits of anatomy. A jigsaw puzzle strewn on the ground. Maybe two or three jigsaw puzzles. A few zygomatics. A piece of jawbone. Half a maxilla if you're really lucky. But this? This is fantastic, Jack. Nearly a whole skull. And virtually undamaged. It's the sort of find that people like me dream about.'

'You really think it might be important?'

'Jack, I've never seen a find that's in as good condition as this is.'

She shook her head as she tried to communicate her excitement and he saw that there were tears in her eyes.

'It's fabulous. Where did you find it?'

He told her about the avalanche, how it had killed Didier Lauren, and how he had fallen into the bergschrund and found the skull on the floor of a cavern deep inside the mountain. He did not tell her that it had been on Machhapuchhare, not Annapurna where he had found it. As far as the Nepalese authorities were concerned the accident had taken place on Annapurna, and the fewer people who knew the truth about what had really happened, the better.

'Just lying on the floor, you say?'

Jack nodded.

'Just like the Neanderthal discovery,' she breathed. 'That was back in 1856. Quarry workers found a skull on the floor of a cave.'

'Is this one Neanderthal too?'

'This? Nothing like. This is much more interesting. Tell me, how far up the mountain was this cave?'

''Bout six thousand metres,' he said evasively. 'I was damn near entombed there myself. Now are you going to tell me what it is, or am I going to have to wait for your paper in *Nature?*'

'Paper?' Swift's tone was scathing. 'I might get a whole book out of this. A whole career, maybe. You know this couldn't have come at a better time. I'm facing a tenure review.'

She turned the skull in her hands as if it had been a crystal ball, but one that was designed not to foretell the future but to illuminate the past.

'To start with it's big, like some kind of giant primate. Do you see these temporal and occipital crests on the front and rear of the cranium? They're quite reminiscent of *Paranthropus robustus* – the South African australopithecines. Only this is strange. The sagittal crest is much higher than one would have expected.'

She paused, raising the skull to the strip light on the ceiling to look at its bony interior.

'As is the cranial cavity. That might suggest a larger brain size. Larger than a gorilla's at any rate. But not as large as a man's.'

She faced the front of the skull, smoothing the thin bowridge over the eyes with her thumb like a sculptor.

'The face is short and not at all ape-like. While the teeth – again these teeth are not particularly ape-like, except for the size.'

Turning the skull upside down she examined the underside of the exposed upper jaw.

'Also the dental arcade is parabolic and not U-shaped. Then there's the enamel on these molars. It looks quite thick. Those two factors alone would persuade me that this is not an ape. Apart from the huge size of the teeth – honestly, Jack, I've never seen a specimen with teeth quite as large as these – I might have placed another tick in the box besides *Paranthropus robustus*. The teeth are certainly similar in shape to those of a *robustus*: the cheek teeth larger and flatter, while the front teeth, especially these canines, are proportionally smaller. But no *robustus* had teeth quite so big.'

She paused, frowning as she laid the skull next to the packing box, and squatting down stared at it along the table top.

'The one set of candidates I can think of is the ramapithecines. One of the best areas for finding ramapithecine fossils is in the Himalayan foothills.'

'The Siwalik Hills,' prompted Jack.

'So far three sizes of ramapithecines have been found,' said Swift. 'My guess would be – and this is just a guess of course, I'm going to have to do a lot of detective work with this guy before I'm sure – that the teeth would be characteristic of the largest of the ramapithecines. Come to that, the largest ever known hominoid, the *Gigantopithecus*.'

She fished in the box, took out the piece of jawbone, and then nodded.

'It's like I said. The size of these jaws suggests a gigantopithecine, while the position of the cranial crests seems to indicate an australopithecine.'

'A hybrid of the two perhaps,' suggested Jack.

Swift was shaking her head.

'But there's something I really don't understand about this skull.'

'What? What's the problem?'

'I don't know.' She paused and then added, 'I guess I'm just a little concerned that this specimen is in extraordinarily good condition for something that must have been around for such a long time.'

'That's a cause for concern?' Jack laughed. 'You are hard to please.'

'It's my job to be sceptical. What were the atmospheric conditions like inside this cave?'

Jack shrugged as he transported his mind back to the bergschrund.

'Well, dry, I guess. The cave – actually it was more of a cavern – well, it was made of limestone and about a hundred metres inside the mountain, at the end of a narrow corridor. Like the entrance to an Egyptian mummy's tomb. Earth floor.'

'Any stalagmites? Stalactites?'

'Not that I could see. But then I'm not sure I really explored the whole cavern. A few icicles out front.'

'Then would you say that it was quite a sheltered spot?'

'Very. I spent a comfortable night there. Thanks in no small part to half a bottle of good scotch.'

'The thing is, you'd expect more petrification.'

'You would, huh?'

'Especially around limestone. Although you say the floor was earthen, right?'

'Right.'

'Even so,' Swift said thoughtfully, 'I'd have expected the skull to have been more stone-like and less like the original bone. Fossilisation is a slow metamorphosis and one we still don't fully understand but even so, this find should show more obvious signs of mineral invasion.'

Swift shook her head and started to gnaw at her lip.

'But for my own preliminary observations – '

'Gigantopithecine with a dash of australopithecine, right?'

'Right. But for that, I might even go so far as to say –'

She scowled.

'No, that's simply impossible.'

'You're tired,' said Jack. 'You're tired and you've had a good dinner and things will look different in the morning. It'll make more sense in daylight. You'll see.'

Jack put his arm around her waist.

'C'mon. Let's go to bed.'

'Maybe you're right,' she said, and yawned loudly. 'I have drunk a bit too much.'

She followed him to the kitchen door. Before she switched out the light she glanced at the skull one more time and laughed at the absurdity of what she had just been thinking.

The absurdity of thinking that possibly the best gigantopithecine fossil ever found didn't look like a fossil at all.

Four

'Every discovery of a fossil relic which appears to throw light on connecting links in man's ancestry always has, and always will, arouse controversy.'

Wilfred Le Gros Clark

Swift hardly slept, although this had less to do with Jack than with the skull. Highly regarded by her colleagues and popular with the students, she knew she was an excellent teacher; but she was thirty-six years old and had published little of moment. Within the Faculty of Palaeoanthropology she faced tenure review and in order to pass – to have her teaching contract renewed – she would have to write a paper of substance. Better yet, a book. Jack's fossil seemed to provide her with something worth writing about.

At six o'clock, she slipped quietly out of bed, dressed quickly and went downstairs with one thought on her mind. Leaving a note for Jack, who was still sleeping, she returned the skull to its box, carried it out to her car, and then drove straight to the university.

Things were quiet on campus. It was too early for the prophets, musicians, craft-sellers, pushers, radicals, artists and assorted academics who were normally to be found along Telegraph Avenue.

As soon as she was in her laboratory she closed the door and locked it. Only then did she remove the skull and the jaw fragment from the box and lay them carefully on a lab table that was specially padded to protect the sometimes fragile fossils that were examined upon it.

She measured the skull carefully with callipers and micrometer, then, laying some rulers on the table as a guide to size, she set up a tripod-mounted Canon EOS 5 with a hundred-millimetre lens, a bounce Speedlite flash, and a ten-metre remote switch cable. When the camera was loaded with Fuji Reala, she started to take her photographs, shooting two rolls of thirty exposures each just to be on the safe side.

Only when she was satisfied that she had a good record of the basic dimensions and appearance of the skull did Swift proceed to the next stage of her working plan, the devising of which had kept her awake for most of the night.

She painted the skull with Bedacryl, a kind of glue that was usually used to harden fragile fossils before removing them from the ground. The skull was as solid an artefact as she had ever handled but Swift preferred to err on the side of extreme caution. Even solid bone would break, if dropped from the height of a table or a workbench.

While the Bedacryl dried she set about heating gypsum to make a plaster of Paris cast. More sophisticated resin and stereolithographic casts could be made later on, but right now Swift wanted a working copy she could handle and carry around the campus in complete safety. Immediately the cast was made, Swift placed the original skull and jawbone in her laboratory safe. Later on she planned to transfer them to the university vault where other valuable specimens were stored.

Swift had also devoted some thought to the securing of her intellectual property in the specimen. If, as she suspected it would, the skull proved to be an important find, it was essential that she maintain complete confidentiality in her work until she was good and ready to publish. But it was also obvious that she could not work in a vacuum and that she would need the help of her colleagues on campus if she was going to classify it properly.

This was her main area of concern.

The palaeoanthropological world was a contentious one in which the discovery of a new fossil often made one person's reputation at the expense of someone else's. Lacking a properly empirical method and populated by people who frequently lacked objectivity, it was a jealous science driven not by experiment but by theory. And there were plenty of theories. Sometimes it seemed to Swift that the public's appetite for popular science meant that there was a new theory about Man and his origins every week. But fossils were at a premium and it was generally accepted that it was upon these

38

that the greatest palaeoanthropological reputations had been built. People remembered Dart, Johanson, Leakey, because they made tangible discoveries. Hardly anyone remembered the theorists like Le Gros Clark, or Clark Howell.

Sometimes the fossils were made to fit the theories instead of the other way round and it was not uncommon for people to buy fossils from the sources of a competitor with the express purpose of demolishing a contradictory theory. Theft was less common but not unknown. And the world of Palaeoanthropology as a whole was still recovering from the revelation in 1955 that the Piltdown skull discovered in 1912 at a gravel pit in southern England had been a blatant forgery.

In 1912, Charles Dawson, an amateur archaeologist, had discovered an ape-like skull in a gravel pit near the village of Piltdown, in Sussex. His discovery appeared to indicate a being of considerable antiquity that also conveniently dovetailed with the prevailing view of a human ancestor equipped with considerable intellectual powers. But in reality Piltdown Man had been a neat combination of human cranium and an orang-utan's jaw.

The one absolute certainty in this uncertain, riven science was that any significant new find would probably occasion another bitter rivalry.

It was perhaps hardly surprising that the first person Swift telephoned to discuss her find was a lawyer.

Harztmark, Fry and Palmer were her mother's lawyers in London, administering a trust set up in Swift's name and paying her a generous annual income through their San Francisco office. Swift had met Gil McLellan, the partner handling her money, only once, but it was always Gil she telephoned on the rare occasions that she needed legal advice.

'Stella,' said McLellan when his secretary had put Swift through. 'Kind of early in the day for a citizen of Bezerkeley. It's not even nine o'clock. I had no idea that anthropology demanded such regular office hours.'

His hollow laughter sounded as if he could just as easily have been coughing.

That was one of the irritating things about lawyers: they always assumed that everyone else was a stranger to early office hours and hard work.

'Listen, Gil,' she said, quickly getting down to business, before he could get around to asking her out to dinner as he usually did. 'I need your help.'

'That's what I'm here for.'

'I want you to draw up a confidentiality contract. You know the kind of thing: the signatory agrees not to discuss or write about something, nor to claim any intellectual property in it, without my written agreement; and if anyone is proved to have used the same confidential information directly or indirectly obtained from me, without my consent, express or implied, he or she will be guilty of an infringement of my rights that is actionable in a court of law.'

Gil chuckled.

'Are you sure you need my help? Sounds like you've got it pretty well covered there. You know, maybe you should have read law instead of anthropology, Stella.'

'Can you do it?'

'Sure. But let me ask you a couple of questions. First of all, what exactly is it we're talking about here?'

'A fossil. An important fossil.' She paused for a moment. 'We'd better call it a skull so that there's no confusion.'

'My second question relates to the quality of confidence,' said Gil. 'Information cannot be confidential if it is public knowledge, okay?'

'Nobody knows about this fossil except me and the person who discovered it. This is not public knowledge.'

'Okay, no problem. I'll draw something up and fax you a draft in half an hour. That'll keep you going until I can get you something on headed notepaper. That always scares the shit out of people.'

'Gil, you're a star.'

'Give me your fax number so I won't have to look it up. Call me back if there's a problem. Call me back anyway. Instead of charging you for this, I'll let you take me to lunch.'

As soon as Swift received by motorcycle courier the final copy of the legal document that Gil McLellan had drafted, she went to see Byron Cody.

The Earth Sciences building was home to the University's Faculty of Zoology, among others, and retained some scintilla of the Hellenic ideal with its mock colonnades. But with its fortress shape, square keep-style towers and central courtyard, the building reminded her more of a central bank, or some federal government institution.

40

She found Berkeley's world-famous primatologist in a different office from the one he normally occupied. It was a room of pleasing solidity that ran almost half the length of the building and housed a collection of immaculate, leather-bound books that appeared to be rarely read.

'My own office is being redecorated,' Cody explained, after he had kissed her on both cheeks. 'I believe this belongs to some botanist who's up the Amazon right now.'

She sat down and declined the offer of coffee from the machine along the hall.

'The reviews of your new book have been good,' she said. 'I'm looking forward to reading it.'

'I never believe my good reviews,' he told her. 'It's only the bad ones I take any notice of. I find I can discount any amount of praise, even when it's wholly accurate. Criticism is like air travel: when things are going well, you pay it little attention, but when you crash you just have to take it seriously.'

Swift smiled. Cody was one of her favourite people.

'You're lucky you caught me. I'm supposed to go and do a signing at Moe's,' he said. 'Although I can't see why my signature should make a difference to anything except a cheque. Really it's not for another hour. I thought I'd do some book shopping first. But I'd much rather sit and talk with you, Swift.'

'Actually, there's something of mine I'd like you to read and sign,' she said.

'Grant proposal, is it? It'll be a pleasure,' he said, tossing McLellan's letter on top of a precarious-looking pile of other papers.

'I was hoping you might glance over it right now,' she said. 'It's not a grant application. It's more of a legal document.'

'Now I'm really intrigued.'

Byron Cody read her document with a mixture of hurt and amusement. When he had read it once, Cody, a slow, careful man with a suitably Darwin-sized beard, read the confidentiality contract again and then sighed loudly.

'What's this all about, Swift?' he asked, removing his half-moon reading glasses and cleaning them nervously with the end of his blue woollen tie.

'As I said,' she explained. 'It's a standard confidentiality agreement. It just makes what I want to tell you a privileged communication. Like a client and her lawyer, that's all.'

'And you're the client?'

Swift nodded.

'I'll say one thing for you, Swift. You're nothing if not thorough. This is the first time someone ever asked me to do this. For most people, intelligence is merely a blessing. But with you it's a moral duty.'

'Then let me come straight to the point. I've found something that might turn out to be really significant. If it is, I want to keep the lid on it for as long as possible. The last thing I want is for someone at IHO to put out a paper before I do.'

'Is that a possibility?'

Swift shrugged.

'Don Johanson based his new species, *Australopithecus afarensis*, on rubbishing some of Mary Leakey's Kenyan fossils before she'd had a chance to talk about them herself.'

'But he did discover Lucy.'

Lucy was the name Johanson had originally given to those *afarensis* fossils he had discovered himself, in Tanzania.

'Yes, but he still had to demote her fossils in order to promote his own.'

'Point taken.' Cody took out his pen, but still hesitated to sign the document.

'Look, Byron, fossils are data. And the naming of a fossil is everything in this business.'

'Business? Now we're getting to it. I thought you people were supposed to be scientists.'

'Science is just business wearing a white coat,' argued Swift. 'Trustworthy methods for the discovery of new truths include covering your ass. If Galileo had been a little slower to take up a definite position on the Copernican theory – '

'Or if he'd had the advice of a good attorney,' grinned Cody. 'Okay, okay. I'm convinced. Hurt, but convinced.' He dashed off his signature and launched the document back across the desk top. 'Now what's the big deal?'

'I want your opinion, as the country's leading primatologist – '

'I can resist any amount of flattery except the truth.'

' – of a hominoid skull that has recently come into my possession.'

'Curiouser and curiouser.'

Swift opened the wooden packing box, removed the cast of the skull and waited for Cody to clear a space before placing it on the

42

desk. Then she took a laptop computer out of her shoulder bag and switched it on, ready to note down his first impressions.

Cody replaced the half moons on the end of his nose, then picked up the skull, turning it expertly in both hands like a melon he was testing for ripeness.

'Nice cast,' he murmured. 'Make it yourself?'

'This morning.'

'Where's the original?'

'Safe enough.'

'Oops.' Cody uttered a malicious little laugh. 'Information only on a need-to-know basis, huh? Not so much James Bond as James Bone. A big fellow, wasn't he? Look at the size of this cranium.'

Swift started to type.

'And these enormous jaws. Only my wife has bigger jaws than these. But that's just exercise rather than anything hereditary. Talking and eating mainly. Wow, I've never seen teeth as big as this on a fossil. They're much larger than a gorilla's. And I should know. I still have the bite radius to prove it.'

'How much larger, Byron?'

'Maybe twice as large? Yeah. Why not? And look at these cranial crests. They're very unusual. The occipital crest – now that's smaller than a gorilla's. However, the size of these teeth would seem to require extremely powerful masticatory muscles, in which case most of them would surely have to be attached to the top of the head, to the sagittal crest. And that would of course increase the height of the head. Quite a bit, come to think of it. Maybe one-and-a-half times the height of a gorilla's head, at the very least? This is really something quite extraordinary, isn't it? You know from the size and position of this occipital crest one might almost assume that the owner of this skull kept its head rather more upright than a gorilla. That might even suggest bipedalism. An ape-like creature that walked on two legs instead of a conventional knuckle-walker. I'm beginning to see the need for your legal acquaintance. Jesus, Swift? Where did you get this?'

'At the moment, I can't tell you that, Byron. All I can say is that this is not an Old World fossil.'

'You surprise me, ma'am. I was just about to suggest it might be australopithecine. Except of course no South African fossil primate was ever so large as this dude. Not even *Paranthropus crassidens*.'

43

Swift looked up from the screen of her laptop as Cody stopped speaking.

'How about a Miocene ape?' she suggested. 'One of the ramapithecines, perhaps.'

'Yes, that's possible,' he mused. '*Gigantopithecus*, maybe. The biggest primate ever known. Of course I've never seen an actual complete fossil. No one has. There are just those three teeth that von Koenigswald found in a Hong Kong drugstore. The so-called Dragon's teeth. This could be *Gigantopithecus*. Goddamit, wouldn't that be something?'

'That was my first thought,' she admitted. 'But I wanted someone better qualified to come through the same line of reasoning.'

She started to underline some of the observations that Cody had made on her laptop's screen.

'The height of the head,' she said. 'You thought, one point five as high as a gorilla's.'

'At least. Maybe fifteen centimetres above the ear. You know I can imagine a scalp that might look something like a Viking's helmet. Rather pointy-headed, same as a big silverback gorilla's, only more so. Much more. And if this is consistent with what we already know about body-size dimorphism in primates and fossil primates, I should say what we have here was almost certainly a male of the species.'

Swift typed 'Male' and then said:

'Body-size dimorphism in primates is nearly always a corollary of males competing for access to a pool of females, right?'

'Right. And also of polygamy.' He weighed the cast in his hands and smiled broadly. 'Yup. This lucky bastard probably had a whole harem of willing females.'

'So that's what turns you on, Byron. And here's me thinking you were a happily monogamous man.'

'Me, monogamous? Whatever gave you that idea? I should best describe my own sexuality as Neo-Confucian. Which is to say that I prefer the kind of heterosexual relationship where there exists a benevolent superior, namely myself, and an obedient subordinate to do my every bidding.'

'Sounds like one of your gorillas,' she remarked laughing.

Cody grinned back at her through his patriarchal growth of facial hair. 'The ape will out, I guess,' he said. 'But socially, you know? I think we have much more in common with baboons. The latest

44

research shows that high-ranking females have their pick of the best males, although only at the price of an increased risk of miscarriage. There's evidence of a similar effect among human females too. Successful career women often find it quite difficult to conceive.'

Wondering if she would ever have a child herself, Swift forced a smile.

'But,' she objected, 'do we get to choose the best males?'

'I don't know about the best,' said Cody. 'But it has been my experience that a good-looking, intelligent, high-achieving woman like yourself can more or less get whatever the hell she wants.'

'Nonsense,' said Swift.

Cody shrugged and then smiled.

'Signed your damn stupid paper, didn't I?'

Sometimes it bothered Swift that she belonged to a university that had effectively built every nuclear weapon in the US arsenal.

A quarter of a century before Vincent Sarich and Allan Wilson had helped to establish Berkeley at the forefront of Palaeo-anthropology, the University Physics Department at Le Conte Hall had already guaranteed Berkeley's place in history when a team of scientists, including the distinguished Berkeley physicist, Ernest Lawrence, met to discuss plans for a new type of bomb.

Lawrence had won the Nobel Prize for Physics in 1939 for inventing the Cyclotron – a device for accelerating nuclear particles inside a circular magnetic field, a sort of nuclear pump. He had built his machine on a hill above the Berkeley campus, a site now occupied by the Lawrence Hall of Science. Experiments in the Cyclotron had resulted in the discovery of Plutonium in 1941, since when Berkeley scientists had developed other bombs and discovered thirteen other synthetic elements including Berkelium and Californium, the antiproton, the anti-neutron, and Carbon-14.

Developed by the Berkeley chemist Williard F. Libby in 1946, Carbon-14 is created in the earth's upper atmosphere by the bombardment of cosmic particles from outer space which pass into the bodies of animals and plants through the food chain. Since it begins to decay as soon as it is formed, Radio-Carbon as it is sometimes also known, has proved to be a useful technique for dating the remains of once-living things. It marked the beginning of accurate geochronometry, a specialised field that now includes many even more sophisticated techniques and for which a department at Berkeley was also to be found in the Earth Sciences building.

Professor Stewart Ray Sacher was Berkeley's outstanding geochronologist. The author of the standard textbook, *Stratigraphic Geology and Relative Age Measurement*, Sacher was also a highly respected palaeontologist and had published several best-selling popular science books to do with the Palaeozoic era, most notably *Future World: Walcott's Quarry and the Cambrian Explosion*, his Pulitzer Prize-winning analysis of a famous Cambrian biota and its significance in the history of life on earth.

A bulky man, with a shock of untidy brown hair and a soup-strainer of a moustache, Sacher was working in his vast laboratory surrounded by various configurations of spectrometer and assisted by an attractive-looking female postgraduate student when Swift caught up with him.

As always, Sacher had a piece of choral music playing on his lab's powerful sound system and from time to time he would stop and conduct a phrase or movement he particularly enjoyed. He was in the middle of just such a moment when he caught sight of her in the doorway and, quite unabashed, he said in his strong Brooklyn accent,

'True hope is swift, and flies with swallow wings.'

He grinned as if pleased with the dexterity of his capacity for quotation and then hugged her warmly. 'How are you doin', sweetheart?'

Swift kissed him on both cheeks and, noticing his trousers and vest, remarked on his continuing fondness for wearing leather.

'I'm a biker, what do you expect?'

'Sometimes I think it's rather more fetishistic than that,' she said, teasing him.

'I would like to present an alternative explanation of what these so-called fetishisms mean,' he declared. 'If all our efforts, intellectual and sexual, represent a striving for godhead, then God has surely given all of us our sexual quirks and kinks to frustrate our efforts in this respect. But for panties and shoes and stinking primeval ooze we would all of us be gods ourselves. What can I do for you, honey?'

'I'd like to talk to you about a dating problem.'

'I wouldn't have thought a good-lookin' gal like you would have much of a problem.' He grinned and shook his head. 'I wish I had a dollar for every time I've made that lousy joke. Take a seat, Swift, and I'll be with you in two shakes of a lead isotope.'

He pointed towards a leather swivel that was positioned in front of a roll-top desk, and next to a trolley supporting several storeys of hi-fi equipment.

Swift sat down and glanced over Sacher's cluttered desk top, searching for the CD case. She recognised the music playing as Haydn's *Creation*, only the recording was rather better than the one she herself owned – the full-price choice as opposed to the budget. Unable to find it, she leaned back in the chair and, trying to ignore the baseball paraphernalia that covered the wall above and around the desk – Sacher was a dedicated fan of the Oakland Athletics – she let the music wash over her.

There was, she thought, an extra pleasure to be found in classical music when and where you were not expecting to hear it. At the same time she wondered what a composer who had once remarked that whenever he thought of God it made him feel cheerful, would have made of someone like Stewart Ray Sacher. Or, for that matter, herself. Whenever Swift thought of God she tried to imagine a biological predisposition in Man to be religious that was like Chomksy's theory of an innate capacity in human beings to learn language. Her own experience of God had been that He was merely a name to be invoked when you needed something urgently, like an all-night supermarket.

'You like this?'

Swift opened her emerald green eyes.

'Haydn? Yes. Of course.'

'What's your favourite bit?'

She thought for a moment and then said, 'The Representation of Chaos'.

'Ooh, that's dark. Says a lot about you, honey. Me, I like the bit when the worm finally shows up on the scene, but only after the tigers and the sheep have already put in an appearance. *In langen Zügen kriecht am Boden das Gewürm.* How's about that for an evolutionary ladder?'

He laughed a heavy smoker's laugh. Cigarettes were the principal reason his voice seemed to have no more range of modulation than the cawing of a bad-tempered crow – a dry, catarrhal rasp made him sound all the more like Al Pacino. His sentences were not so much spoken as expectorated.

47

'You know somehow,' he said, 'I don't think Franz Joseph Haydn would have accepted the idea that we're all descended from a few simple land invertebrates.'

'I was thinking the same thing.'

'So what brings you to my time machine? Got something interesting for me to date?'

Swift opened her shoulder bag and handed him another copy of the confidentiality contract.

'I'm sorry about this, Ray,' she said. 'Really I am. But I think you'll understand the need for caution when you see what I've got. You can't be too careful these days.'

'This must mean you've found something important,' he said interrupting her, and without another word he signed the paper and returned it.

'Well? Come on. Don't keep me in suspense, honey. Where is it? Where's the material?'

Swift glanced around the laboratory for Sacher's lab assistant.

'Helen?' Sacher called to her. 'D'you wanna take those books back to the Bancroft?'

'Sure,' she said, and having collected a pile of library books off the floor, went out of the door, smiling a wry smile at her boss. 'No problem.'

'Ooh, did ya see that smile?' said Sacher when Helen had gone. 'I bet she thinks that you and I have a thing goin'. You know, this is going to be very good for my reputation.' He laughed and took out a packet of Winston Select. 'Thank God she's gone. Now I can have a cigarette.'

'You shouldn't smoke so much,' said Swift.

'Et tu Brute.'

'I worry about you.'

'Hey, these must be safe. They advertise in *Omni*.'

Swift put her hand in her bag. First she took out a small plastic bag containing Furness's rock and soil samples. Then she unwrapped a length of lint and laid the piece of lower jawbone on the desk.

'It sure doesn't look very old,' Sacher grumbled, picking up the bone in his sepia-coloured fingers.

'It does and it doesn't. You're right. It's hardly fossilised at all, and yet it ought to be. According to the existing phylogenetic classification, this piece of jawbone ought to be over a million years old. Even if one discounts the possibility of intrusive burial, this

48

mandible ought to look more obviously rock-like.'

'Why discount it?' said Sacher. 'How did you come by this specimen?'

'It came from a reliable source.'

'How reliable? Has this person ever provided you with fossils before?'

'Never. But he's not the kind who would work some elaborate hoax, like Charles Dawson and his Piltdown Man. Or could work one, for that matter. Dawson went to the trouble of treating the pieces of skull and jawbone to give them a suitable patina of age. If someone really wanted to put one over on me, they would surely have done the same.' She paused, waiting for him to agree with her. 'Wouldn't you think so?'

'I guess so,' he admitted. 'But always let the fossil speak for itself. For the purposes of isotopic dating, what we're really concerned with is this piece of jawbone. The rock sample is probably more or less irrelevant.'

'That's right.'

'It could be that there are some unusual atmospheric conditions that have prevented any petrification.'

Swift described how Furness had found the specimen in a limestone cave high in the Himalayas.

'In which case,' said Sacher, 'it's quite possible that for many thousands of years your find was encased in ice.'

'You mean like a glacier corpse?'

'Exactly. We now know that a body is not always crushed by the shearing force of a glacier. Do you remember that glacier corpse they picked out of the ice in the Austrian Alps a few years ago? I believe it was in 1991.'

'Yes. The Iceman. I remember.'

'Turned out he was a Neolithic hunter who had died over five thousand years ago. His body tissues, his skin tattoos, even his Reeboks were all perfectly preserved.'

Sacher turned away from Swift to blow out a cloud of smoke.

'Now as I recall, the Iceman was found at a height of around three thousand metres. Your specimen was found at what kind of height?'

'Six thousand metres.'

'Okay, that's twice as high. So here's a very early hypothesis. And that's all it is. Like I say, we'll let the fossil speak for itself. But suppose the Iceman could have remained preserved for another five

49

thousand years. Suppose also that at twice the height your specimen could have stayed preserved two or three times as long. Maybe thirty thousand years. Suppose he could have stayed in the ice all that time. Only when the ice melted and the body was finally released did it start to decay, but very slowly. It seems to me that it's quite possible that your specimen could be at least fifty thousand years old.'

'That still leaves us about nine hundred and fifty thousand years short,' she objected.

Sacher shrugged.

'You know my methods, Watson. Data first. Attain the knowledge required and the precision necessary with the least number of analyses. Then we'll re-examine the theories in the light of what the fossil tells us. That's the proper scientific method.'

He extinguished his cigarette in an iron pyrite rock sample that served as his ashtray.

'And what particular method will you choose?' she asked.

'Ordinarily I might suggest a cosmogenic method. With the accelerator mass spectrometer we can get a precise age on as little as one milligramme of carbon. However, the tooth enamel on this piece of mandible is so good that I think I'll try ESR.'

'Electron Spin Resonance,' Swift nodded. 'That's where you measure the energy of the electrons trapped in the dental enamel.'

'Yeah. You obtain a date for the material from the ratio between that and the trapping rate.'

Sacher thought for a moment and then turned off the CD player as he began to wrestle with the choice of dating techniques available to him.

'On the other hand, in this lab we now have Uranium series, or Thorium series. I used Thorium to date some new Neanderthal specimens they found in Israel last year. Did you know that there were Neanderthals living in Israel as recently as fifty thousand years ago?'

'And if this does turn out to be older than that?'

'Anything over one thousand years and we're stuck with using the rock. But from what you've told me I think that it's going to be of limited use. I've never really subscribed to using pieces of rock to date pieces of bone unless they're actually discovered within a geological stratum.'

'Whatever you think is best, Ray.'

'Of course, this is going to take a while.'

'How long?'

'I'll call you when I have something.'

'As soon as, okay?'

Sacher lit another cigarette.

'God knows how long we've already had to wait. A little longer shouldn't make a hell of a difference.'

Swift raised an eyebrow.

'Ray, that's the third time you've mentioned God. What does God have to do with it?'

He shrugged and looked vaguely sheepish.

'I used to think, nothing at all.'

'Ray.' For a moment Swift was too surprised to do anything but open and close her mouth. 'You're an atheist.'

Sacher ran a pudgy hand through his thick hair. There was more grey than she remembered. He wiggled his eyebrows suggestively.

'You're not going soft on this, are you?' she frowned.

'You know, it's said that amputees commonly experience a phenomenon called phantasmagoria, in which they encounter the feeling that an arm or a leg, even a female breast, is still present following its severing. The presence of this phantom limb, especially the hand or the foot at its periphery, may be most strongly felt for several years after an amputation. It may even itch.

'Swift? It's like this. I guess that after a long period of atheism, I'm beginning to find that I have much the same feeling about God. And I've more or less come to the conclusion that this is the best evidence of His existence that I'm ever likely to find. Religious experience may indeed represent the only way of verifying this itch, although I rather doubt that there exists any one religion that could accommodate my kind of heterodoxy. You know what I'm saying?'

Swift stood up, kissed him on the cheek once again and then headed towards the laboratory door.

'Hey, Swift?' he said, laughing uncomfortably. 'Have you got a problem with that?'

She turned on her heel.

'Only this, Ray. Atheism is like standing up to the Mafia. There's safety in numbers.'

He made a gun with his forefinger and pointed it at her.

'Wiseguy,' he laughed.

'Call me when you've got something.'

'I'll call you anyway.'

Five

'O the mind, the mind has mountains; cliffs of fall
Frightful, sheer, no-man-fathomed.'

Gerard Manley Hopkins

From his home outside Danville, Jack Furness tried calling Swift a
few times at her home, and then at her laboratory on campus, but all
he ever heard was the sound of her voicemail service. Over the
course of two or three days he left several messages and, when still
she did not return his calls, Jack put her out of his mind and set about
preparing for meetings he had arranged with the National Geographic Society, and the White Fang Sports Equipment Company,
who had jointly sponsored his expedition to the Himalayas.

He was not much bothered by her neglect. He knew Swift too well
to take it personally. In a way, he was even glad that she had not
called. Not seeing her meant that he was able to devote all of his
energies to writing up reports, preparing the expedition accounts,
and best of all, developing and printing the many rolls of film he had
taken during his six months in Nepal.

Her silence pleased him in another way, too. It seemed to suggest
that she herself was busy and that the fossil might indeed turn out
to have been an important find.

And if it did turn out to be important? What then?

As time passed he began to think that perhaps he had acted a
little impulsively in giving the fossil away. It wasn't that he wanted
the thing back. Far from it. Rather that he began to worry about the
legalities of what he had done. Having no wish to become embroiled
in any legal arguments with his sponsors as to whether the fossil

had been his to give away in the first place, he called his lawyer and was reassured to learn that while the Nepalese Government might take a dim view of the removal of the artefact without proper permissions, there was nothing in Jack's sponsorship contract that interfered with his ownership rights in any scientific or archaeological discoveries made during the expedition.

Jack told his lawyer that he had paid American dollars for the only export paperwork there was to be had in Nepal. But at the same time he decided it would be better simply not to mention the fossil to the people at the National Geographic Society, at least until Swift had a better idea of what the fossil was.

Whenever that would be.

Arriving at Washington's National Airport with only one bag, Jack could see no reason not to take the Metro into town instead of a taxi, and thirty minutes after boarding a blue line train to Metro Center, where he changed on to a red line bound for Dupont Circle, he was checking into the Jefferson Hotel on 16th Street, just around the corner from the Society's headquarters.

Located on a busy intersection, the Jefferson was a small but elegant hotel and a favourite with politicians and senior public servants. The interior was reminiscent of an early nineteenth-century house and many of the rooms were furnished with antiques. Jack had often stayed there and would have chosen the Jefferson even if National Geographic had not agreed to pick up the bill.

It was too late to go anywhere except the mini-bar. So he sat in front of the TV drinking not one but several whisky miniatures, draining each tiny bottle's contents as if it had held nothing more potent than antiseptic mouthwash. There was something so ersatz about spirit miniatures, like something you might find in an outsized doll's house, that he found it hard to take them seriously as containers of real alcohol, almost as if he expected the effect of the spirits to be somehow in proportion to the size of the bottles. It wasn't and he awoke the following morning with a very adult-sized hangover.

Jack met the Sponsorship Director of White Fang, Chuck Farrell, over a breakfast for which he had no appetite.

'Good to see you, Jack,' said Farrell when their breakfast meeting was at last over. 'Next time you're coming to town, give me a call. I've got some new sticky climbing boots I want you to try. They're

53

made of a really remarkable new rubber compound that we think is really going to change the face of big wall climbing in this country. We call it the Brundle Shoe.' He chuckled. 'Think about it. Look, take care of yourself, okay? You're not looking so good right now.'

Jack didn't doubt it and when Farrell had gone he decided that with a couple of hours to kill before his meeting with the National Geographic Society, what he needed most was some fresh air. So he went back up to his room, collected his overcoat and went out to brave a typically cold Washington winter morning.

His footsteps took him south, past the White House and then east along the Mall. Gradually he began to feel better. But he also began to feel cold. In search of warmth he ducked into the Smithsonian, where it was the very last day of an exhibition entitled *Science in America*. Designed to show the impact of science on the United States, a substantial part of the exhibition was devoted to the Manhattan Project and the development of the first nuclear bomb. This was the most interesting part of the exhibition. Jack had never before seen some of the photographs they had of post-detonation Hiroshima. He wondered how keen the governments of India and Pakistan would be to blow each other up if they could see those pictures.

The news was not good. Several Arab countries appeared to be preparing forces for deployment to Pakistan as an act of Muslim solidarity, while the Indian Prime Minister had called an emergency meeting with his military leaders. In an ongoing effort to defuse the crisis, the US Secretary of State was flying to Islamabad and then New Delhi for the fourth time in as many weeks.

Jack hoped the Secretary had a better understanding of the reasons underlying the crisis than he had. Like most Americans he had little idea of why the Indians and Pakistanis should be at each other's throats again.

Leaving the Smithsonian, Jack took a cab back to his hotel and then walked round the corner to the tall, international modernist building that housed the National Geographic Society.

Back in 1888, when the Society and its famous yellow-bordered magazine were founded, it had been intended that proceeds from the periodical should help to support the Society's expeditions. But by the late twentieth century and with almost eleven million readers, most of the Society's activities were supported by its annual membership dues.

Among scientific organisations, the National Geographic Society was one of the richest and most benevolent. Yet while the creed of the magazine may have been 'Only what is of a kindly nature is printed about any country or people,' Jack knew better than to assume that the same kindliness would automatically extend towards himself in the shape of generous sponsorship. He was well aware that there was stiff competition for the Society's patronage and that he could not afford to minimise the disaster on Machhapuchhare.Even if he was still sticking to the line that it had taken place on Annapurna.

During his meeting with the representatives of the Society and the magazine, however, he spoke with a degree of candour and self-criticism that surprised even himself. He knew that what had happened had been an accident. Equally he was certain that there had been no negligence beyond the obvious risk that was inherent in any lightweight, Alpine-style ascent of the Himalayan big walls – particularly those, like his own, that scorned the use of oxygen. But in his heart of hearts Jack still held himself responsible for what happened, for no other reason than that the attempt to climb all the major peaks in this hazardous way had been his idea.

When Jack had completed his account of the expedition, the Director of Sponsorship, Brad Schaffer, nodded solemnly and said:

'I want to thank you, Jack, for a very full and frank explanation of what happened. I'm sure I speak for us all when I say that we appreciate your coming here so soon after this tragedy and giving us the complete picture. I'm sure that it will greatly accelerate the payment of compensation to the family of Didier Lauren. Is that not so, Miss Harman?'

Miss Harman, an attractive, soberly suited brunette from the insurance company, looked up from Jack's accident report and cleared her throat.

'Yes,' she said vaguely, as if still troubled by something. 'I expect you're right.' Glancing back at the report she added, 'However I do have just a couple of questions relating to what happened.'

'Oh?' Jack tried to sound unperturbed in the face of her cool scrutiny.

'Relating to funeral expenses and compensations already paid out to your Sherpas and their families, Mister Furness.'

'Is that right?'

In order to keep his illegal ascent of Machhapuchhare a secret,

55

Jack had been obliged to handle the costs of five Sherpa funerals.

'Yes.'

Jack rolled the track ball of his laptop computer and found the items in the accounts to which she was referring.

'Fire away,' he said.

'You paid ten thousand dollars in compensation to the families of your Sherpas at two thousand dollars each. And you also paid for the cost of five funerals at five hundred dollars each. Is that right?'

'Yes.'

'However, you just told us that you only recovered three bodies.'

'That's correct. Didier and two of the Sherpas are still up there somewhere.'

Miss Harman's sharp little face took on an exasperated demeanour.

'I don't understand,' she said. 'How can you have funerals without bodies? And why is a funeral so expensive in comparison with what you paid out in compensation. Five hundred dollars represents twenty-five per cent of the compensation.'

Jack glanced over at Brad Schaffer, looking for support. But Schaffer shifted awkwardly in his seat and said nothing. Smiling nervously Jack took out a chunk of Exer-Flex silicone exercise putty and, looking back at Miss Harman, started to work it with his fingers.

'All ceremonies in Nepal cost a lot of money,' he said. 'Comparatively. Particularly the death ceremony. Sometimes they save up for years to pay for it. Even if there's no body, and even if they can't afford it, this is still a traditional obligation and one that Western climbing expeditions always take upon themselves. If we didn't, Miss Harman, then Sherpas would be hardly likely to risk their lives along with the rest of us.'

'I see,' she said coldly. 'But surely in the circumstances a contribution towards these death ceremonies would have been more appropriate. Say fifty per cent.'

'I don't think you quite understand,' he started to say.

'No, I don't think I do, Mister Furness. You said yourself, these people save up for years to pay for their death ceremonies. But, well, what about the Sherpas who died? What I'm merely trying to determine is what happened to their funeral expense savings.'

It was a good question. Even so, Jack felt himself squirm with distaste. For a moment he imagined that the Exer-Flex was her windpipe and gave it an extra hard squeeze for good measure.

'Or were your Sherpas just not the prudent kind?'

'If this Society was concerned with prudence, Miss Harman,' said Jack, 'then I doubt it would ever have got started.'

'Amen,' said Schaffer.

But Jack was just starting. He threw the chunk of Exer-Flex on to the mahogany table, hoping that it would make a mark on the highly polished surface.

'Death's a considerable expense in the Himalayas, Miss Harman,' he said. 'People get killed in the most awkward of areas. Why don't you look at these accounts from the up-side? We didn't find Didier Lauren's body so we saved your company the cost of chartering a helicopter to fly his body down to Khatmandu, the cost of a special casket to meet the requirements of international air freight, not to mention the flight home to Canada.'

'Jack,' said Schaffer. 'I think you made your point. No one's disagreeing with your accounts. Miss Harman's just trying to determine precisely what they mean. Is that so, Miss Harman?'

Miss Harman smiled thinly. 'Yes.'

She was about to add something when Schaffer cut her off.

'But we'll leave it there, I think,' he said firmly, and collecting the Exer-Flex, stared quizzically at it for a moment.

'What is this shit, anyway?' he said, leaning towards Jack.

'It develops wrist and finger flexibility, strengthens forearms, improves grip.' Jack shrugged. 'All kinds of stuff.'

'Does that mean you're planning to go back and finish what you started? To climb all the big Himalayan peaks, without oxygen? Didn't you say you wanted to do the Trango Tower next?'

'Sure,' he said, without much enthusiasm, still angry with the way the meeting had gone, with himself most of all. 'I always finish what I start.'

But even as he spoke Jack knew that before he could go back to the Himalayas he had to prove to himself that he still had the nerve for the big walls. Never having fallen before – certainly there were few climbers who had fallen so far and still survived – he had yet to discover if the avalanche had taken more than just a friend and climbing partner from him. Jack had to find out if he could still put gravity to the back of his mind and climb with all of his former *élan* and disregard for danger.

Yosemite Valley was Jack Furness's spiritual home. It was here, high up the western slope of California's Sierra Nevada, in a granite abyss eleven kilometres long, one and a half kilometres wide and three-quarters of a kilometre deep, that Jack had perfected his climbing technique. With its unrelentingly sheer walls, the valley was the centre of American rock-climbing and the kind of place where reputations got made or became permanently stalled. In the twenty-five years he'd been coming to the valley, six of Jack's friends had been killed there.

Six friends and one elder brother.

In theory rappelling, or what the Europeans called abseiling, was one of the safest and most exhilarating parts of climbing. The buzz of bouncing down a sheer face in long graceful curves through space, of descending with the acceleration of a free fall, and then stopping smoothly on the karabiner under full control.

His brother, Gary, had been rappelling down the six-hundred-metre-high Washington Monument when his anchor sling, frayed by numerous rope pull-downs, broke just a metre or so short of Lunch Ledge, a nondescript platform about three hundred metres up. It was nineteen years since Gary had been killed. But hardly a week passed when Jack did not think of him. When he was climbing he thought of him more often.

These days Washington Monument was considered a warm-up climb for the big vertical walls of the Yosemite, and among them there was none bigger, none more vertiginous and none more daunting than the famous El Capitan.

Leaving Danville in the late afternoon, the drive had taken him around six hours and he checked into the Ahwanhee Hotel at just before ten o'clock. The Yosemite Lodge would have been slightly nearer El Capitan, but the Ahwahnee was better, if more expensive. There he ate a big, high-protein dinner, went straight to bed, and was up again the following morning at just after five.

December with its cold weather and short days was not the best time to climb El Cap. Except that the valley was almost empty of tourists and Jack, who had made several other winter ascents in Yosemite, was more or less certain that he would have the rock to himself. Besides, the day had dawned as bright and sunny as the weather forecasters had promised and, up on the wall, too hot could be as bad as too cold. In summer the temperatures could make the rock as hot as a frying pan. This looked like an excellent day for climbing.

Before going to El Cap Jack found a hard boulder and got himself properly limbered. There were dozens of well-established routes up El Cap, but you never knew when you were going to have to do some wide stem or something even more bizarre. It paid to be stretched and ready for anything.

Every year the warm-ups got harder. In his twenties he had been so supple he had seemed almost double-jointed. These days, he was putting a lot more trust in his upper body strength than in his overall agility. Maybe Swift had been right. Maybe forty was too old for this kind of thing.

Walking back to the wall, he strapped his fingers with adhesive tape, to help improve their rigid tendon support. Free climbing was hardest on the fingers' ends, a manicurist's nightmare. There were climbs Jack had done that left his cuticles so badly broken that the blood was oozing from his tips.

Standing at the foot of El Cap's clean brown and white granite face, it was easy to underestimate its height. Looking up at the ninety-degree wall, you might be fooled into thinking that the one solitary pine growing on the cliff face was no bigger than a Christmas tree and the rock itself no more than one hundred and fifty to one hundred and eighty metres. But the tree, a Ponderosa Pine, was twenty-four metres high while the top of El Cap was a heart-stopping nine hundred metres at right angles to the valley floor.

Unclimbed before the mid-1950s, El Capitan, and the Salathé Wall route – rated 5.13 on the Yosemite decimal system of climbing difficulty – that Jack had chosen, looked less of a sporting challenge than a circus feat. Yet there were an increasing number of mountaineers, Jack among them, who had free-climbed the Salathé Wall. Using spring-loaded camming devices known as 'friends' for jamming into cracks, climbing shoes of sticky rubber, and only natural holds for upward progress, but scorning the use of stirrups and karabiners, Jack had made a free solo ascent of the wall as late as 1994.

In the cold bright dawn, he covered his bare hands with chalk, and then checked the friends, wire nuts and curvers, and chalk bag that were hanging off the bandolier on his sit harness. The only karabiners he was carrying were the ones he would use to hook on when he needed to take a rest.

Reaching high above his head, he found a handhold and drew

himself a metre up on to the wall with one arm. Like an ape. In an hour or two, the winter sun would have warmed the rock, making it easier for the Boreal rock boots he was wearing – Jack didn't much care for the White Fang stickies he was paid to wear by his sponsor – to get a grip. It would be the early part of the climb, on cold and sometimes icy rock, that would be more difficult and dangerous. Nine hundred and eleven metres to go.

After his trip to Washington he had been eager for this moment. Quickly he tried to find his rhythm.

The fall on Machhapuchhare had no real bearing on his climbing ability. He had not made a mistake. Surely he was the same crag rat who had climbed El Cap in record-breaking time. But as he progressed up the first pitch he sensed that this particular ascent would be more than just a climb, more than an exercise in self-discovery. He would have to reach deeper into himself than ever before. Where once he had climbed for fun, now he was climbing with an extra piece of luggage. It hung on him like a heavy haul bag. The fall. The death of Didier. His own thoughts and emotions, the smallest hesitation, the least hint of fear, all of them would fascinate him, scare him, intimidate him as never before. And all leading up to the great question set by his own personal Torquemada: was he climbing El Cap with the abandon, the total self-confidence that had marked each one of his four earlier ascents?

For two hours he climbed as efficiently as he had ever done, moving quickly up the steep rock in the early morning sunshine and relishing the silence and his sense of insignificance on the hard grey face. Sometimes he was hanging by only three fingers, or lifting a leg to the height of his own shoulder to find a foothold. This wasn't fun. This was a lot of work. Already his fingertips were feeling as if he'd used them to sand a wooden floor.

He'd seen himself climb on video many times and from a distance he was surprised how much like a scorpion or a lizard he had looked scrambling up a wall. Something not human anyway. Swift might have liked to believe that he went climbing because of the ape in him, but he would have liked to have seen the chimpanzee that had the patience to do a speed solo on a wall like the Salathé. It felt like a marathon. Hundreds of moves over hundreds of metres. Like running a marathon in a day. Except that it was rather more hazardous.

There was very little to recommend the Salathé Wall beyond its sheer difficulty. He'd been just twenty years old when he'd first succeeded in climbing it, with the dumb luck of youth. Certainly it was not a particularly aesthetic climb. It wasn't much of a view behind him. Or below him. Just thin air. Pulling at him with the nagging force of gravity. Like Galileo's famous experiment. The law of uniform acceleration for falling bodies. And in front of him just rock, and more rock, monotonously, implacably, forever in his face.

Wind teased his hair. He never wore a helmet. If any object falling from something this high managed to hit you, you tended to stay hit, helmet or no helmet. Once, jumaring up the rope on another El Cap route known as the Dawn Wall, Jack had dislodged a flake of rock that narrowly missed hitting him. The flake had been as big as a set of radiator pipes. Another time the rope on a haul bag had broken and the bag, heavy with pitons, karabiners, nuts and hammers, had come whistling past his ear. Another reason why he preferred a free climb. Weirdest of all, while Jack had been climbing the exterior of the Transamerica building in San Francisco for a TV commercial, one of the cameramen had accidentally smashed a window and a two-metre sword of glass had come within a few centimetres of his head. No helmet would have protected him from that.

The rock was getting warmer.

Maybe he just got bored with looking at it, but one hundred and fifty metres up on the wall, Jack did something that he had never done before on a free solo ascent.

Something you never did.

He looked down.

Suddenly his whole mind was in travail. Memory flung up in him the exact recollection of how it had felt to fall off Machhapuchhare's north face. This time there was not even a rope to break. And certainly no snowdrift-filled bergschrund to cushion his fall.

Jack's heart leaped in his chest and for a moment all he could think of was himself in bed with Swift, her own mind on something else, the fossil, as he pumped in and out of her body like a mad thing.

Then memory played its ace trump card.

He remembered that it was not nineteen years since his brother had been killed. It was twenty. Twenty years. He tried to put it out of his mind but already he felt his guts collapsing inside him, as if he was about to experience a diarrhoeic cramp.

61

Killed in this valley. Almost twenty years, to the month. It was just a coincidence, but courage slips on such small coincidences and, winded, lies helpless on the ground. By the time Jack had helped it on to its feet again and supported it long enough to get its breath back, he had already started to doubt that he could make it all the way to the top.

Gloved in white chalk, his own hand – the fingers raw and red with blood – appeared from underneath him, jammed a quad-camming friend into a crack, and then hooked him on to the sit harness.

'Take a rest. You'll be okay in a couple of minutes.'

Held firmly to the one spot like the Ponderosa tree growing on the cliff face high above his head, Jack shook his head, paralysed with fear.

'What the hell am I doing here?' he said, pressing his face into the wall. 'I can't do this. Goddamit, this is crazy.'

He sat there in the harness, checking the view, waiting for his legs and stomach to steady a little before he could try to go on. He closed his eyes and tried to persuade himself that he had freaked out before. The king of the big walls was not forced to abdicate so easily. The idea of a ranger rescue never entered his head. Not that he really had any choice in the matter. It was unlikely that any rangers would be looking out for climbers at this time of year.

He could climb up. Or he could climb down. Or he could jump. End of story.

'Come on, you chickenshit asshole,' he yelled. 'You've got to move.'

Minutes passed but still he stayed put and Jack began to think that for the first time in his life he had come up against a very different kind of wall. Perhaps the highest barrier of them all. Himself.

Six

'All beauty comes from beautiful blood and a beautiful brain.'
Walt Whitman

The University of California Medical Center occupied a kilometre-square site on the thickly wooded slopes of Mount Sutro, midway between the red roofs of San Francisco's Haight-Ashbury district and the Golden Gate Park. It was a pleasant neighbourhood and Swift seldom visited the Medical Center without also browsing in a few of the Haight's famously radical bookstores. But on this occasion she went straight to the hospital's radiology department where she had arranged to meet an old friend.

Joanna Giardino was a diminutive Italian-American beauty with abundant dark hair and the kind of come-hither look that made men fall for her like stupid pets. Swift knew her from a time when, as members of the university women's ski team, they had briefly been rivals for the affections of one particular guy on the men's team, a handsome hunk who was later killed in a motorcycle accident. Somehow the two women had subsequently become firm friends and from time to time they would meet at the Edinburgh Castle, an English pub on Geary Street (Swift's choice), or Capp's Corner, an Italian restaurant (Joanna's choice) in North Beach.

As well as being Swift's good friend, Joanna was also one of UCSF's most promising research neurologists with several papers to her name, including one that she had co-authored with Swift on the palaeoneurological border between hominid and hominoid.

The two women embraced warmly under the eye of a good-looking Indian man wearing a white coat and a necktie featuring a selection of DC comic-book characters.

'This is Manareet,' Joanna said, introducing the Indian.

The Indian gave a slight bow.

'He's our senior neuro-radiologist. If there's an intercranial abnormality, Manareet will find it. Manareet, this is Swift. It's not that she doesn't have a Christian name, just that she's rather touchy about the one she's got.'

'Pleased to meet you, I'm sure,' said Manareet, taking Swift's outstretched hand.

His pronunciation was so clear and his manners so impeccable that Swift thought that he must have been educated in England. She had known a few Indians like him at Oxford, most of them fabulously rich Old Etonians with cut-glass accents and better breeding than the British Royal Family.

'I think Swift is a very nice name,' said Manareet. 'Like a bird, or a thought, or a small planet.'

Uncomfortable with any kind of compliment, Swift bit her lower lip as she tried to check the inane smile that threatened to linger on her face.

'Ignore him,' advised Joanna. 'He's too smooth by half.'

'Are you English?' he asked Swift.

'Australian,' she confessed. 'But I was educated in England.'

'Me too. I was at Winchester and after that, at Stanford,' he explained.

Manareet glanced at his watch and then nodded at the box Swift was carrying.

'Is that our patient you have there?'

Swift set the box containing the original skull down on Joanna's desk and lightly tapped the lid.

'In here,' said Swift.

'After your letter, I can hardly wait,' said Joanna.

Joanna had already signed the confidentiality contract, but Swift had decided not to ask Manareet to do so. It wasn't as if he was working in any related field. Besides, he was giving her his time and the CAT scan for nothing.

'Okay, the machine's ready to roll. If you'll come this way?'

Manareet led the way down a corridor and into a large room where the huge, black CAT scanner was located.

'Five or six years ago,' he was saying, 'this machine, the Picher 1200, was state-of-the-art. But these days we hardly ever use it.

Nearly every patient we see now undergoes a different diagnostic process. Nuclear magnetic resonance imaging.'

Despite its reduced status, the CAT scanner looked impressive enough to Swift. Sleek, black, and with a business end that was shaped like a two-metre-high lifebelt, the Picher 1200 reminded her of an expensive hi-fi. The kind you might have to lie down inside to really appreciate.

Manareet removed the skull from the box, commented on its size, and then laid it on the padded leather headrest of a bed that extended inside the lifebelt where the X-ray emitter and detectors were housed. In Computerised Axial Tomography, or CT scanning, a laser beam rotates around the patient's head, and is itself surrounded by several hundred X-ray photon detectors to measure the strength of the penetrating photons from a whole host of different angles. The X-ray datum is then analysed, integrated and reconstructed by a computer to produce the intercranial images on a television monitor. Once they had a picture of the inside of the skull, they could construct an image of the brain that had once filled it.

Manareet made a few adjustments to the controls and then another engineer turned on the laser before retiring behind the protective lead screen with Swift and the two neuro-specialists.

Seconds later a thin laser beam like a strip of red candy began to fire intermittently at the skull.

'All right,' said a businesslike Joanna. 'Let's get the computer to generate a digital image of the brain that used to be inside that skull.'

'No problem.'

Manareet sat down at the computer keyboard and began to type out a series of transactions.

'Do you want 3D or VR?'

'Virtual Reality,' said Joanna. 'Let's get the real Spielberg look for this one. And 3D for the hard copy.'

'Are you planning to have this skull morphed, at some stage?'

'Yes.'

Morphing involved the university's biomedical visualisation lab metamorphosing faces and sometimes even whole bodies to fit skulls and human skeletons, using algorithmic warp and dissolve software that was originally designed by Hollywood for movies like *Terminator 2*. Swift hoped they could graft an image of a living creature on to her specimen.

'Then I might as well give you stereolithographic data as well,' he said. 'Save them doing it.'

'Thanks a lot,' said Swift. 'If it's no trouble, I'd appreciate it.'

'It's no trouble at all.'

In stereolithography a computer-guided laser would harden layers of plastic resin in the shape of the skull's cross sections. A hard replica could later be used by the university's biomedical visualisation laboratory's computer analysts to reconstruct a face on the skull. Computers had almost entirely replaced plaster of Paris and Bedacryl as the tools of choice for rebuilding and copying fossils.

'This will take a little while,' said Manareet, and leaning back on his chair, collected a can of Pepsi off the desk.

The computer screen went black for a moment and Manareet sat forward on his chair.

A minute or two later the computer had recreated the precise intercranial contours and dimensions of the skull and they were viewing a high-resolution colour VR copy that the Picher 1200 had scanned on to the fifty-centimetre Trinitron screen.

'All right,' he said. 'Let's do a little caving, shall we?'

He pushed the mouse forward on its pad, entering the skull through an eye-socket, searching the interior of the cranium as if he had been a real-estate agent showing someone round the image of an empty house.

'Looking good,' nodded Joanna. 'But let's see the brain that would fit this, shall we?'

'No easier said than done,' declared Manareet, and hitting the return on the keyboard, replaced the VR image of the skull with one of a brain.

To Swift the image looked real enough for her to have lifted the brain out of the computer monitor and placed it in a tank of formaldehyde, like Frankenstein preparing to bring a cadaver to life.

'That's great,' she said. 'You can see nearly every lobe.'

'There's no nearly about it,' said Manareet, turning the mouse one way to turn the image around, and clicking once to magnify a specific part, and once again to magnify it even further. 'You can see every lobe.'

As if to prove it, he positioned the cursor over the occipital area and clicked the mouse several times until there was a clear view of a visual cortex.

'How's that?' he said proudly.

'Excellent,' said Joanna.

Manareet clicked the mouse again and several seconds later handed Swift a CD containing all the images and digital information the CAT scan had recorded on the computer.

'A gift.'

'Thanks, Manareet.' She fanned herself with the CD case.

'No problem.'

'Let's take the CD to my office,' said Joanna. 'We can run it through the neurological contour analysis programme.'

Swift collected the skull off the scanner bed and returned it safely to the carrying box. On her way out of the scanning room, she smiled sweetly at Manareet.

'Nice meeting you.'

'The pleasure was all mine,' he said. 'You must let me cook you a meal sometime.'

'Oh yes, you must,' said Joanna. 'Manareet makes the best barium meal in this hospital. Only he calls it a curry. I swear, the one I ate was so hot you could have photographed a perfect outline of my stomach.'

Swift laughed and kept on smiling at Manareet.

'Ignore her,' she said. 'I'd love a curry.'

Joanna inserted the CD in the drawer of her computer, made a choice from the list of browse options on screen and then waited for the selected VR data to load.

'Is he cute, or is he cute?' she said.

'He's nice.'

'It can't be easy for him right now,' added Joanna. 'Given what's happening in the Punjab. Manareet's a Sikh. He's got family there. But if he's worried about them he doesn't let on.'

Swift nodded gravely.

'Does he think there's going to be a war?' she asked.

'He doesn't refer to it at all. And neither do I. I mean what I said about the curry, though,' Joanna said, more brightly. 'Like it was molten magma.'

'I had a lot of curries when I was at university in England,' Swift admitted. 'And some of them were pretty hot.'

'Maybe that's why the English are so tight-assed. You picked it up when you had your empire in India. The stiff upper lip. It was just too many hot curries.'

Swift let the assumption that she was English go. Life was too short for her to be forever insisting that she was an Australian. Especially as it was so long since she had been back there.

Joanna's screen flickered and the VR image of the pink brain on a bright blue background reappeared, floating inside the monitor like a strange undersea creature.

At first glance the brain did not seem to be very different from that of a human being. It was divided vertically from front to back into left and right hemispheres, and both of these were separated into four lobes, each of them responsible for different sets of functions, and Swift thought the virtually real brain looked prototypically hominid.

'Okay,' said Joanna. 'Let's see if we can get a size estimate.' She tapped a couple of keys and then read out the result. 'One thousand millilitres. At the extreme lower limit for humans.'

'But more than twice as large as a gorilla's.'

'I guess if you tie that in with the dentition you'll be able to work out a few life history variables, won't you?'

'I already spoke to a dental anthropologist,' said Swift. 'A specialist on fossil hominid teeth.'

'Did she sign your confidentiality thing too?'

'Of course. She thought these third molars were just erupting when the creature died.'

'I still don't know why you're being so paranoid about this.'

'Not paranoid. Just careful, that's all. Now if you were to assume a growth trajectory about half-way between a man and a gorilla, that would mean the owner of the skull was about fifteen years old when he died. That means a first molar at around four or four and a half years old, and a probable life span of about fifty years.'

Swift tapped the VR image on screen with a fingernail, one of the few she had not bitten away with excitement since receiving the skull from Jack.

'This brain, Joanna. Any left hemispheric dominance there, do you think?'

'Some,' allowed the other woman. 'But not as pronounced as in humans.' Holding the button down on her mouse she rotated the brain to view it from the other side.

'Let's see now. The occipital lobe is larger than a human's,' she added. 'Whereas the temporal and parietal lobes are smaller.'

'That's also typically ape-like,' said Swift.

Joanna clicked the mouse and enhanced the frontal lobes on the VR brain.

'This is quite interesting. These large olfactory bulbs would seem to suggest that the specimen enjoyed a highly developed sense of smell.'

'Well that's something we haven't found before.'

Joanna viewed the underside of the brain.

'Now this could be something. The position of the foramen magnum would be unusual in an ape,' she murmured, becoming more absorbed in the analysis. The foramen magnum was the point at which the spinal cord passed from the brain case into the torso.

'Yes, you're right,' said Swift. 'It's much further forward than a gorilla's.'

'That would mean the head was carried much higher up on the shoulders.'

'And indicate an upright-walking creature rather than a knuckle-walking ape.'

'Exactly. I'm beginning to see why you were so excited about this skull, Swift.'

Joanna turned the image of the brain to view the left side in close-up.

'Oh, wait just a moment.'

Her keen eyes had spotted something. She clicked the mouse, magnifying an almost featureless area of the brain, and then pushed the mouse forward across the pad so that the close-up surface image swooped towards the viewer.

Joanna pointed to a small lump, just above a fold in the brain architecture that Swift recognised as the Sylvian fissure.

'That looks to me like a small but distinct Broca's area,' stated Joanna.

Human linguistic ability was usually assumed by neurologists to have something to do with Broca's area, although it was impossible to say for sure whether or not the faculty of speech was located in or under this insignificant-looking lump.

Swift looked closely at the screen as Joanna tried to gain maximum magnification of this possible language centre in the unknown hominid's brain organisation.

'There's something there all right,' she agreed, cautiously.

69

Joanna altered the angle of magnification so that the lobe appeared very distinctly in profile.

'Yup. There it is,' she said.

'Of course it doesn't mean the hominid could speak,' said Swift. 'But maybe the creature had some extended vocal abilities. A sophisticated mimic, perhaps.'

'C'mon, Swift,' said Joanna. 'Why the sudden caution? Nobody ever found Broca's area in a fossilised brain organisation before. Am I right?'

Swift nodded.

'But we're only dealing with surface features here. There's no telling for sure where basic linguistic abilities might be hidden in hominid brain organisation.'

Joanna turned in her chair and pulled a weary face.

'In neurology nothing's for sure. Even with humans. The more I know, the less I know. Come on, Swift. Admit it. Maybe we really found something here. Evidence of language as an early development in human evolution. Wouldn't that be something?'

Swift was smiling now. But at the same time she remained acutely aware that she could expound no theories regarding the specimen's place in evolutionary history until Stewart Ray Sacher had come back to her with the results of his geochronological tests. She hardly dared to think what the evidence of her own eyes was beginning to suggest. And before she constructed the theory that was already beckoning to her like some silent phantom she would have to be as certain of her facts as the most sceptical of sceptics would permit.

Whenever Swift tried to deflect her mind from some preoccupation, she sat down at her baby-grand piano and, with considerable difficulty, strove to play her self-taught way through one of the pieces from Bach's *Well Tempered Clavier*. The first prelude, in C-Major, with its arpeggiated chords was her favourite and she played it well until a fugue took up the theme, as if stating it in another more confident voice. She wondered if she might reach a stage in her own work when uncertainty gave way to such resolution. The minute she thought of the analogy the fugue collapsed beneath her fingers like snowflakes to the human touch.

Getting up from the piano she found a packet of Marlboro Lites and lit one carefully, holding the cigarette loosely between her bit-

70

ten lips as if it had been an empty balloon. She flicked the spent match at a bin under the piano, failing to notice it land several feet short on the polished wooden floor.

Swift went outside to smoke. For once the sky above Berkeley was dark enough for her to be reminded of her own insignificance. The stars, seemingly fixed, were actually light in motion, travelling from a point in time when ancient Man had first walked upon the earth. Probably even earlier. She shivered, uncomfortable with this reminder of her own apparent irrelevance in the general scheme of things. All those generations, ancestors, precursors – previous, long-forgotten, hardly recognisable. Looking up at the terrible grandeur of that great basilica roof she almost wished that the Catholic Church had been more successful in stamping out astronomy's Great Revolution and that they had burned Copernicus, Galileo and Kepler alongside Tycho Brahe.

The telephone rang. She ground out the cigarette and went inside to answer it. As soon as she heard the urgency and excitement in Stewart Ray Sacher's gravelly voice she felt her heart leap forward in her chest. Even before he told her the results of his geochronological tests she knew that life would never be the same again.

Warren Fitzgerald, Director of the Laboratory for Human Evolutionary Studies and Dean of the Faculty of Palaeoanthropology at Berkeley, rubbed his poorly shaven chin ruminatively. A smile flickered on and off his well-chiselled face which, with the old man's white hair and wire-framed glasses, looked to Swift almost beatifically wise. One of the world's pre-eminent authorities on human evolution, Fitzgerald was best known to a wider audience as the host of the award-winning PBS science series, *Changes*. A Boston man, Fitzgerald spoke with such an over-abundance of vowels that he always reminded Swift of John F. Kennedy.

'Well, if you and Sacher are even half right, Stella, I do believe that this might alter our understanding of the whole timeline of hominid evolution. At the very least it seems to restore the importance of *Ramapithecus* in the search for human origins. But I can certainly appreciate your caution, considering the proximity of our friends over at IHO.

'Re-establishing the phyletic position of *Ramapithecus* is going to play havoc with the biochemists and their work in molecular

71

phylogeny. They'll spare no effort to discredit your data the minute you break cover. For years they had to withstand accusations that their biochemistry was wrong because it didn't agree with the fossils. Now you're saying that the fossils were right all along.'

'I don't think that's exactly what I'm saying,' said Swift. 'At least not yet, anyway.' She pushed her mane of red hair away from her face and looked thoughtful.

'Look, all that the biochemical approach says is that the immunological dates for a divergence between Man and the African great apes provide a separation date of four to six million years ago. Because hominids of the genus *Ramapithecus* date back to the late Miocene about fourteen million years ago, and because *Sivapithecus* – closely related to *Rama* – seems to be more closely related to the orang-utan than to the African apes, it has been generally assumed that *Ramapithecus* is therefore disqualified from being a hominid.

'But here we have a fossil that seems to have characteristics of both *Rama*'s ape and of *Paranthropus robustus*. A skull that appears to be a half-way stage between *Ramapithecus* and *Australopithecus*. Moreover a skull that gives every indication of being considerably more recent in its apparent origins than any previously discovered ramapithecine.'

Swift stood up excitedly and stalked around Fitzgerald's book-lined office as her theory began to be articulated.

'All right,' she continued. 'We've always believed that *Ramapithecus* was around as late as fourteen million years ago. All this skull suggests is that the genus could have survived until much more recently than we had ever suspected before. Until only fifty thousand years ago.'

'This is what I'm not at all comfortable with, Stella,' grumbled Fitzgerald. 'This idea of Sacher's. The glacier corpse. His fifty thousand years is pure assumption. Why not assume a hundred? Or a hundred and fifty? But even then it's a very long way short of fourteen million. Do you really think that some kind of ramapithecine could have survived for the best part of fourteen million years?'

Swift shrugged.

'The dinosaurs survived for sixty-five million years. And that's as nothing beside the coelacanth. The coelacanth was abundant in the world's oceans as long as three hundred and fifty million years ago. We thought they had died out some sixty million years ago. And then a fisherman caught a living specimen as recently as 1938. Now why shouldn't a ramapithecine have survived for a mere fourteen million years?'

'Just how many assays did Sacher make, Stella?'

'Several. And all with different results. He's saying that there may be a number of reasons why there's more natural radiation in the dental material than we expected. He's tried carbon dating but that hasn't been any more accurate.'

'I see. And the rock sample you provided?'

'According to Sacher the rock sample shows that the specimen's environment must have originally been deficient in Carbon-14.'

Fitzgerald sighed and shook his head.

'All that money we waste on all that goddamn machinery of his and he says that there's something wrong with the lousy samples. For the life of me, Stella, I've never seen why we should accept that the amount of radiocarbon produced in the atmosphere has always been constant. Did you know that Sacher once analysed the amount of radiocarbon in a living snail and came out with the result that the creature had been dead for three thousand years?'

'I'd heard that story,' she admitted.

'Anyway, you'd like a temporary release from your teaching obligations to do some field work on this, right?'

'That's right. At this moment I'm preparing a grant proposal for the National Science Foundation and the National Geographic Society with the aim of going back to the Himalayas to study the site where the skull was found.'

'I suppose you know I'm on the peer review committee for the National Science Foundation?'

In the world of academic scientific research, applications for grants were put up to the scrutiny of relevant experts in order that the merits of an application could be judged.

'I know.'

'Money's generally a bit tight right now. So if I were you I'd try the people at National Geographic first. But if your grant proposal makes it, it could make your name, Stella.'

She nodded.

'The thought had crossed my mind.'

'I bet it has,' he grinned. 'Yessir, it could make you as famous as Mary Leakey. This science could sure do with another woman making her reputation. Not to mention the kudos it could bring to Berkeley.'

73

Fitzgerald thumped his desk enthusiastically.

'Might be the most important piece of anthropology done here since Vince Sarich's time. Lord, I really hope so, Stella. I never did like those chemists much. I'm a fossil man, myself. Always have been, always will be. All the biochemistry in the world won't change the fact that it's bones, Stella. It's bones that count.'

Swift came away from Fitzgerald's office feeling that things were beginning to shape up quite nicely.

It was bones that counted. Too damn right. In the field of Palaeoanthropology there were many more scientists than there would ever be fossils. But fossils were everything. Of course the trick was in getting hold of them. Until then all you had were theories and nearly all of them based on other people's finds.

Not that theories couldn't be rewarding too.

In search of some theories of her own she had spent the previous winter working with Byron Cody, helping him elaborate some of his ideas for his now bestselling book about gorillas. It was an experience she still remembered with pleasure.

There had been one particular moment that Swift believed she would always treasure, when she had been sitting in a cage with a young mountain gorilla. She had found herself looking deep into the animal's eyes and instead of looking away, as normally happened, the gorilla had held her stare, leaving her with the most profound, albeit ineffable sensation. She had felt both question and assent, and the nearest comparison she could ever make was that it had been like meeting the unflinching gaze of a small child. Even now she could hardly recall ever feeling a greater sense of empathy for any other living creature.

A gorilla was also capable, like a child, of shedding tears. And Swift had come to the conclusion that Man was not about emotion so much as language. It was certainly true that there were plenty of animals that could communicate at a rudimentary, symbolic level. Like Chomsky however, Swift believed that what made Man uniquely human was his limitless capacity for self-expression and, as a corollary, his limitless capacity for imagining and thought.

She was fond of asking her students the following question: if you had a dog that could talk – a dog that was every bit as articulate and funny as Robin Williams – would you continue to treat it like a dog, or would you treat it like a human?

Sometimes, to underline the importance of human speech or signing in defining what it really meant to be human, she also reminded her class of cases involving feral or wolf children – wild boys who had never learned to speak and who could only communicate within a finite number of symbols. And then she would ask the class whether it would treat a wolf boy more like a human or more like a dog?

Consciousness, she argued, must surely have evolved as a direct corollary of language; and language was merely the most portable means available to ancient Man of transferring a culture from one place to another as the climate changed and the hominid population exploded out of the African heartland during the late Pleistocene period, from 70,000 BC to 8000 BC.

It had been Swift's greatest ambition to find a fossil that would provide some indication of early linguistic ability and, hence, of an emerging human consciousness.

The Dawn of Man.

Except that now she wondered if perhaps she was in possession of something better than just a bone. Bones were always a matter of contention. She had a feeling that this might just turn out to be something of the past that was not gone, something lost that was not irrecoverable.

Seven

'Science must begin with myths, and with the criticism of myths.'

Sir Karl Popper

The Campanile clock had struck six o'clock when Swift climbed into her Chevy Camaro. Feeling that she was probably wasting her time and that the reason his phone was off the hook was because Jack was with some girl he had picked up while climbing in the valley, she drove inland, heading east along the interstate towards Mount Diablo State Park and Danville, and hoping that she could see Jack and then be back in Berkeley before lunch time.

The smoothness of the highway contrasted with the intolerance of Northern Californian drivers for, although it was early morning and there were only a few trucks on the road, their drivers seemed to regard a woman at the wheel of a bright red, two-seventy-five horsepower coupé as some kind of challenge to their masculinity. On several occasions she found herself involved in a bitter war of middle digits.

It was at times like this that Swift thought men were little better than apes, capable of fighting about the least important thing. She wondered how it was that the human species was not as rare as that great reproductive dud, the Giant Panda.

Danville was a small town surrounded by rolling ranch land and campsites and a short ride on the Contra Costa County bus from Mount Diablo. Sixty years before, the town's most famous resident had been the playwright Eugene O'Neill. But O'Neill was largely forgotten by the locals and now Danville's most famous resident was America's number one mountaineer, Jack Shackleton Furness.

Like O'Neill, Jack lived several miles outside of town, in a small ranch situated on the lower slopes of Mount Diablo. Twice, Swift drove past the anonymous-looking road that led to Jack's house before seeing where it diverged obliquely from the main highway and dropped down a steep slope into a short ravine wherein a small creek meandered its way back to the East Bay and, beyond, the ocean.

Mounting the other slope on the far side of the creek, the track suddenly levelled out and Swift caught sight of Jack's house and the black Grand Cherokee parked on a gentle slope facing the Devil's Mountain to the west.

Swift got out of the car and looked around. There was not a soul in sight, not even the signposted 'Mean Dog'.

She walked up the front steps, knocked at the door and waited a minute or so. Then she tried the handle. The door was not locked.

'Jack?' she called, leaning inside. 'Are you there? It's me, Swift.'

Advancing towards the bedrooms at the rear, her glance took in the empty bottle of Macallan on the floor and the overflowing ash-tray and half-eaten dinner that lay next to it. She heard the sound of something hitting the floor in the next room and then a man coughing with resolve.

'Jack? Is this a good time? Am I interrupting something here?'

He arrived in the bedroom doorway, puffing a cigarette and naked but for the Rolex GMT Master he still advertised in pages of *National Geographic*, and a pair of battered docksiders on his feet.

Perhaps it was because he hadn't shaved in several days but somehow he was even hairier than she remembered. And he had also put on some weight.

'God, you look awful.'

Jack snorted loudly, scratched his balls absently, chewed over the bad taste in his mouth and then glanced at his watch.

'Swift. What the hell are you doing here so early?' he yawned. 'Comes to that, what are you doing here at all?'

'The phone. You left it off the hook.'

'Is that so?'

'I've been trying to reach you for days.'

'You're not so easy to get hold of yourself,' he sniffed. 'Tried calling you a couple of times after you disappeared that morning. Left voicemail and other shit all over the place.'

He went over to the empty bottle and retrieved it from the floor. 'I was worried about you.'

'Like hell you were,' he said inspecting the empty. He grinned and shook his head. 'I know you, remember? You want something. That's why you've driven all the way out here. I can tell. Why else would you look so sexy?' He nodded at her clothes as if this was obvious. 'Honey, you be stylin'.'

Underneath her long wool coat Swift was wearing a pink miniskirt, a plain white shirt, and a red and gold coloured toile de jouy waistcoat featuring scenes from the frieze in some Pompeiian villa of mysteries.

'Jack, that's not true.'

'I mean, that waistcoat. If I could see straight I'd bet there'd be a guy with a hard-on somewhere thereabouts. And you're wearing a mini-skirt.' He licked his lips feverishly. 'You only ever wear a mini-skirt when you want something.'

'Something's happened, hasn't it?'

'Something usually does.'

'Something not very nice.'

'Call it delayed grief then,' he shrugged. 'Didier was a pretty good friend of mine.'

Swift considered this for a moment and then nodded.

'Why don't you let me make you some breakfast?'

Jack's eyes narrowed. 'I haven't figured out what it is yet, but I will.'

'I'm just offering to cook your breakfast, that's all.'

He tugged at the end of his penis, almost unconsciously. She thought he looked like a little boy trying to comfort himself.

'I am kind of hungry,' he admitted.

'While I'm doing that, you can take a shower,' she said. 'And then put some clothes on. And when you've eaten, we'll talk.'

'Don't suppose you brought something to drink,' he said vaguely. 'You know. Hair of the dog?'

She shook her head.

He shrugged. 'Breakfast would be nice,' he allowed. 'But on one condition. That you don't read my beads. If I want to go and get myself cocktailed, that's my business, okay? Doesn't mean I'm a drunk. This is my crib and I'll do it my own way, okay?'

'Okay.'

'Just as long as we understand each other, right?'

'Right.'

''Cos I'm not in the mood.' His penis had thickened and he started to grin at her. 'I don't suppose you'd care to doggylock before breakfast?'

'I think you should have that shower,' she said. 'And you'd better make it a cold one.'

Jack finished his ham and eggs, drained his coffee cup noisily and eyed the laptop poking out of her shoulder bag with continuing suspicion. But showered and shaved, and wearing a clean shirt and jeans, he already looked like a different man. Now he sounded like one too.

'I feel a lot better for that. Thank you for a delicious breakfast. And I appreciate your coming over here. I've kind of let myself go these past few days.'

'How much did you have?'

'Whisky? Just the one bottle.' He gave a sheepish sort of shrug. 'Never did have much stamina as a drinker.'

She nodded, awaiting the right moment to broach the subject that now concerned her. She sat back in her chair and lit one of his cigarettes. For a moment she pretended to be distracted by the sound of a couple of jays squabbling in a tree outside the kitchen window. Then she said:

'So how were the people at National Geographic?'

'Oh you know.' He shrugged. 'Bureaucratic. Chiselling about a few thousand bucks I paid out in compensation to the families of the Sherpas who were killed. Can you believe that?' He shook his head and sighed sadly. 'Lousy bean-counters.'

'You didn't fall out with them, I hope?'

'No, I didn't fall out with them.'

She had spoken too quickly.

'Why?' he added, frowning. 'What's it to you?'

'Jack. Don't be so defensive. They're your principal sponsors, aren't they?' She shifted uncomfortably on her seat. 'I just don't think that you should alienate them for no good reason. It's the bean-counters who run everything these days. You might as well get used to the idea.'

'If you say so.'

Swift folded her arms and went over to the window, feeling it was still too soon for her to come to the main object of her mission.

79

'I love it here,' she said quietly.

'If you say so.'

'And now what are you going to do?'

'I'm going to have another cup of coffee.'

'I meant, what are your plans, Jack?'

'Rest up a while. Then I dunno. I guess go back and finish the peaks. Solo, I suppose. Trango Tower looks tough enough.'

'You don't sound very sure.'

'What do you want me to say?' His eyes narrowed again. 'That's what this is all about, isn't it? Whatever it is you're up to.'

'Jack. What are you talking about?'

'The real reason you came.'

Swift stamped her foot angrily. 'Can't I just do something for you without you thinking I've got some ulterior motive? Jack? Why do you have to be so bloody suspicious?'

'Because I know you. Mother Teresa you are not. It has something to do with that damned fossil, doesn't it?'

Swift said nothing, pretending to sulk. This was not going the way she had expected.

'Well doesn't it?'

'All right, yes it does,' she snapped.

Jack grinned. 'That's my girl.'

He leaned forward on his chair, took her by the hand and pulled her back to the kitchen table.

'Now why don't you sit yourself down and I'll try not to look up that abbreviated skirt you're almost wearing while you tell me exactly what it is that you want?'

She sat down, facing him, knees pressed tight together, and smiled. Then quickly she opened and closed her legs as if teasing him and laughed.

'I think it's a new type specimen,' she said excitedly.

'That's good, huh?'

'It's wonderful.'

She collected her Toshiba from her bag, laid it on the table, flipped the screen up, and switched it on. The laptop whirred like a tiny vacuum cleaner, and began to emit a quiet scraping noise as it started up a CD.

'A type specimen is a kind of flagship for a new species, a fossil against which any similar fossil material will have to be compared. It's what every palaeoanthropologist dreams of, Jack. Eventually, I

80

hope, there will be a formal citation that will include the species name or number, and the associated author – me. But everyone will know the fossil by its popular name. I mean no one ever talks of skull 1470, everyone talks of Lucy.'

Jack nodded. 'I've heard of Lucy.'

'I'm going to name this one after you, Jack. With your permission.'

'Jack? Doesn't sound right somehow.'

'No. That's not what I meant. Do you remember what some people called you at Oxford, because you're so hairy?'

'Sure. They called me Esau.' He nodded. 'Esau. I kind of like that. Sounds much more appropriate for an ape-man.' He shrugged. 'That wasn't so difficult, now was it? Hell, you ought to have known I'd say yes. Why should I object? I'm honoured.'

Swift shook her head. 'There's more.'

'Oh?'

'I want you to help me work on a grant proposal for the National Geographic Society. To put together an outline for a plan to survey the Annapurna Sanctuary and explore some of the caves in search of paratypes and referred material. In short, I want you to be the official leader of an expedition to look for fossils that might be related to Esau.'

'Me? I'm no anthropologist.'

'True. But you do know the Himalayas and the Sanctuary better than any other American.' She paused. 'Besides, that shit's only for the grant proposal. In reality I want us to take an expedition to go and look for something rather better than a few bones.'

'Like what for instance?'

'According to Stewart Ray Sacher – he's in charge of geochronometry at Berkeley – the skull doesn't carbon date. In other words, it's less than a thousand years old. He says that the reason for this is that the corpse must first have been in a glacier for at least fifty thousand years, and that only when the glacier melted did Carbon-14 decay begin. Warren Fitzgerald thinks it must have been a lot longer. Maybe a hundred or a hundred and fifty thousand years.

'But the question I've been asking myself is why assume it's older when you can just as easily assume that it's younger. Let the fossil speak for itself, that's what Sacher says. Except that he won't. But what I reckon is this: why not consider the possibility that it is less

81

than a thousand years old? I say: why not consider the possibility that the skull may indeed be exactly what it seems to be? Something that may not be a fossil at all.'

Jack frowned. 'Wait a minute. I'm confused. Let the fossil speak for itself, you said. But now you're saying that this may not be a fossil at all?' He shrugged. 'Well, which is it?'

'Okay, now the prefix Palaeo comes from a Greek word meaning ancient. I think that's the part that may be irrelevant here.' She shrugged. 'I guess that's all I'm saying really. We dump the ancient part.'

'Of course, you mean more than you say. And you know it. So how about you stop bullshitting me and come to the point?'

'Okay. Here's my idea, Jack. What if this skull is recent? So recent that we could go to the Himalayas and find not some bones but an actual living fossil?'

'You mean like a Dodo?'

'Not exactly. The Dodo is extinct. I mean we should go and find something we never knew existed in the first place. A new species.'

'A new species.' Jack frowned as he considered the idea. 'At that kind of height? You have to be kidding. The only new species you might find up there is a mutant strain of cold virus.'

Swift waited for a moment before playing her next card. There was something almost comic, something absurd about all the old names that were the stuff of myth, legend and cheap B-movies. And she thought that in Esau she had another way of saying it.

'Jack, I want us to go to the Himalayas and find one of Esau's living relatives. Not a fossil-hunting expedition at all. But a zoological one. I want us to go back there with the purpose of capturing a new kind of animal.'

Jack frowned as he thought about what she had said. About what he thought she was saying. And then realised what she was driving at.

He leaned back in his chair, ran both hands through his hair, and let out a loud guffaw.

'Oh, wait a minute. Esau nuthin'.' He smiled bitterly, wagging an accusative finger at her. 'You're very clever, I'll give you that, Swift. You're clever. All that bullshit about a living fossil. You must think I'm stupid, Swift. I know what you're talking about and it's – frankly, it's ridiculous.'

'You didn't always think so,' she said pointedly.

He stood up and turned away.

'Let me tell you, it's as ridiculous as the Loch Ness monster,' he insisted.

'That's not what you said ten years ago, when you saw it yourself, on Mount Everest,' she said, accessing the pages from Jack's book she had scanned on to the compact disc in her Toshiba. 'Want me to remind you of what you wrote in your book, *Mountain Mantras*?'

'Not particularly.'

He stood by the window and lit a cigarette. For a couple of minutes neither of them spoke. Then, quietly at first, Swift began to read.

'"By May 20th we had established camp on the North Col at seven thousand metres, with all the creature comforts. This was just as well because the very next day a terrific hurricane set in, driving the thermometer down well below zero. Enquiring of Karma Paul why the weather seemed to get worse the nearer summer came, he told me that it was all to do with certain religious festivals that were taking place at Thyangboche Monastery. The mountain demons were, he explained, attempting to stop the ceremonies by screaming very loudly and that as soon as these religious services were ended the storms would be too."'

'I know what I wrote,' he murmured.

'"We spent three successive nights in the shelter of the North Col while the westerly gale did its worst. But on the fourth day, the weather cleared and I made a small expedition to the Lhakpa La where I obtained a fine view of the northern face of Everest as well as a more disconcerting one of the approaching monsoon that made me nervous about completing the ascent in time, and I resolved to make my attempt without oxygen the very next day. As I was about to make my return to Camp 3, a small bird – I think it must have been Wollaston's Lammergeyer, for no other bird seems to fly as high – flew across my path as if it had been startled by something approaching from the opposite direction and it was then that I saw what looked like a giant ape, standing no more than fifty metres away. At about the same time the creature saw me and for a moment it stopped in its very clear tracks and we just stood there looking dumbly at each other. It is impossible to say more beyond the simple fact that the creature was tall and covered in thick hair, for the sun was at its back and in my eyes, and as soon as I reached for my spotting scope, the creature moved away at a remarkable speed, wading through the deep snow in a manner that would have exhausted me within seconds. By the time I had the creature in the Nikon scope it was no more than a speck upon the horizon. . . ." '

'I know what I wrote,' he repeated loudly. 'I don't need to be reminded of it. Maybe it's you who needs reminding of what happened when the book was published. Some of the reviewers suggested I'd made up the sighting in order to sensationalise what they considered was an otherwise dull book. Cryptozoology, they called it. Then some asshole in *Scientific American* wrote a story about how, like many other climbers before me, I'd suffered a delusion born of high-altitude sickness.' He shook his head grimly. 'Jesus, I even reached the twin status of becoming a joke on the Carson Show and the subject of a sketch on *Saturday Night Live*.'

'And what about you? Is that all you think it was? Just high-altitude sickness?'

'Yes,' he said, without much conviction.

'And what about all those other climbers who've seen it too?'

'What about them?'

She turned her attention back to the Toshiba and started to scroll down through a long list she had compiled on CD of other sightings.

'Five years ago, Hidetaka Atoda reportedly saw a large unidentified creature on the slopes of Machhapuchhare, within the Annapurna Sanctuary. He even took a picture. Machhapuchhare is a holy mountain. No permits are issued to climb it.'

'Tell me about it,' Jack laughed scornfully.

'Apparently he was unable to track the creature for fear of losing his licence to climb in the area.'

'Instead of which he lost his life,' said Jack. 'The Toad was a good friend of mine. He was killed climbing the south-west face of Annapurna only three weeks later. Just like Didier. Avalanche got him and his camera.' Jack grinned at her aggressively. 'So that famous photograph was never seen. And here's another thing. As a mountaineer the Toad was notoriously in a hurry. Never knew him to get himself fully acclimatised. Always rushing ahead. Probably what got him killed.'

'Okay,' Swift said patiently. 'Well, what about Chris Bonington?'

'What about Chris Bonington?'

'He saw it too, on an expedition to climb Annapurna back in 1970. According to his account, he wasn't much higher than the entrance to the Sanctuary itself, near the Hinko Cave, at about three thousand six hundred metres. That's quite close to Machhapuch-hare, isn't it?'

'Maybe,' allowed Jack.

'What's more, he was fully acclimatised.'

'He's a good climber,' Jack allowed. 'The best.'

'In his book, *Annapurna South Face*, he describes seeing an ape or ape-like creature running quickly across the snow towards the shelter of some cliffs. It was, he says, a reasonably powerful animal that left obvious tracks but which his Sherpas later pretended not to see. Bonington was convinced that he had seen the yeti.'

She smiled, almost apologetically.

'There now, I've said it, haven't I? Yeti.'

'Congratulations. You win a furry toy.'

'In 1982, Greg Topham saw the creature while climbing Anna-purna III.'

'Topham.' Jack snorted with derision. 'That hippy dopehead ass-hole.'

'He reported seeing a bear-like animal moving south along the ridge, towards Machhapuchhare.'

'Probably what it was. A bear. Look, what's this thing with Machhapuchhare, anyway?'

'Just that it's three sightings in and around the one mountain. And, what's more, a mountain which is forbidden to climbers and tourists.'

'There's nothing magical about Machhapuchhare, if that's what you're implying,' Jack said uncomfortably.

'I didn't say there was. And you're right, there have been yeti sightings all over the Himalayas.' She glanced back at the Toshiba. 'That's not what I meant.'

'Before Bonington, in 1955, Tony Streather, on an expedition to climb Kangchenjunga, reported hearing a loud whistling noise. The same sound that had been heard two years earlier by Wilfred Noyce on Sir John Hunt's expedition to climb Everest. His Sherpas said the whistle was the sound of a yeti.' Swift looked up from the screen of her Toshiba. 'Do you remember how last winter I helped out Byron Cody with his book on gorillas?'

Jack shrugged.

'You know, what interests me about what this man Noyce says is that a gorilla's alarm call is a shrill and prolonged scream that sounds and indeed looks spectrographically like a piercing whistle.'

85

'It's a small world.' He shook his head. 'Could have been anything. An eagle. A lemur . . . Have you finished?'

'Jack, I've hardly started. In 1951, Sir Eric Shipton photographed and took casts of a series of footprints that he and others observed in the snow of the Menlung Glacier, near Everest, at about five thousand five hundred metres. Shipton and Sherpa Tenzing, who later reached the summit of Everest with Sir Edmund Hillary, followed the tracks until they lost them. Tenzing himself had seen a yeti back in 1949. He described it as being well above man-height, covered in reddish hair, but bare-faced.'

'Is that bare-faced as in bare-faced lie?' laughed Jack. 'And footprints.' He snorted. 'Footprints can be caused by all sorts of atmospheric phenomena. I read about it somewhere. A warm current of air intruding in the colder atmosphere causing tiny patches of moisture that turn to water and, when they fall, become blobs in the snow that look to all appearances like footprints.'

'In a regular formation? A metre or so apart?' It was Swift's turn to look amused. 'That explanation's more fantastic than the one I'm proposing. But even if you could dismiss Shipton and Tenzing, which I don't think you do, can you also dismiss Sir John Hunt, who found not one but two sets of strange tracks near the Zemu Glacier in 1937? He said that the tracks were definitely not those of a bear and he had no explanation for them. Subsequently he stated his belief in the existence of some indigenous higher anthropoid unknown to science.'

Jack looked up at the ceiling as if he wished she would finish.

'All right then,' she said. 'There are still dozens of other sightings of the animal. Montgomery McGovern in 1924, Colonel Howard-Bury in 1924, Henry Elwes in 1921, Major L. A. Waddell in 1899, W. Rockhill in 1884, and Lieutenant George White in 1838. Jack, the legend goes back as far as 1820, in J. B. Frazer's *Journal of a Tour through Part of the Snowy Range of the Himalayan Mountains*. You can hardly dismiss them all as mad, or liars, or hippies, or mistaken. This creature and its footprints have been reported in areas as distinct from one another as Nepal, Tibet, Sikkim, Garwhal, the Karakoram, the Upper Sahween area and Bhutan.'

Jack grunted stubbornly and pressed his forehead against the cool windowpane. Outside the sun was burning its way through cool clouds and a buzzard was slowly drifting in the blue beyond like some passenger jet full of human souls.

'You've seen it, Jack,' she persisted. 'You know you have. What's the point of pretending you haven't?'

'I don't know what I saw,' he said irritably. 'Like I said, it was probably the effects of the altitude. Lack of oxygen causes all sorts of physical problems. Pulmonary oedema, insomnia, loss of appetite, weight loss, and fluid retention. Take fluid retention, for instance. It causes the brain to swell and, pressing against the inside of your skull, it can cause you to hallucinate. If that wasn't enough you're also susceptible to conjunctivitis caused by excessive ultra-violet light. Your eyes feel gritty, then painful, until it's impossible to open them properly.'

Swift nodded. 'Of course,' she said patiently. 'It's understandable that anyone would want better evidence than the sight of some very sore eyes.' She paused. 'So I faxed the Natural History Museum in London, and they Fedexed me some photographs of a plaster-cast made by a Russian zoologist, Vladimir Tschernezky, using Shipton's photographs.'

She rolled the Toshiba's trackball with her thumb and pulled down an image of the cast that she had scanned on to the CD.

'The foot is about one and a half times as large as a male gorilla's,' she said. 'But about the same overall length. And check the size of that big toe.'

Jack continued looking out of the window.

'It's exceptionally thick. I'm no mountaineer but I'd say it was the kind of foot that was ideal for grasping rocks on a steep incline.'

Jack glanced casually at the screen. He pursed his lips critically and said: 'Yeah. It could be.'

'Moreover the heel size would seem to indicate a creature that was altogether larger and heavier than a gorilla.'

Noticing that she now had his attention she accessed a drawing of some comparative footprints.

'That's the gorilla's footprint on the left there,' she explained. 'The one in the middle was found by Shipton as low as five thousand five hundred metres. Some of them even led over a crevasse – a leap of some four and a half to six metres. And there were no claw marks. You can see the difference.'

'What's the one on the right?' he asked.

'This was a print reconstructed using Neanderthal type skeletal remains that were discovered in the Crimea,' she explained. 'As you can see, the breadth of all three feet – almost half as wide as they

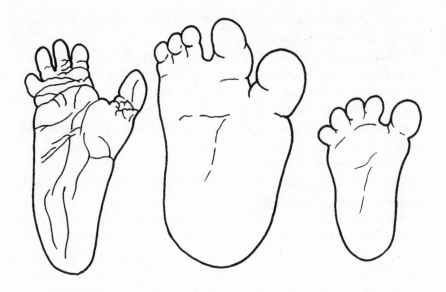

are long – is quite consistent. But only Shipton's prints show such a deviated hallux. Big toe. And such an unusually long second toe as well.

'I had the people in the biomedical visualisation lab digitise an image of the skull you found, in conjunction with the footprints that Shipton found. Using cranial landmarks and tissue depths from the anatomical data of gorillas they were able to effect a full fossil reconstruction of the kind of anthropoid that we're interested in.'

'That *you're* interested in,' he said without looking away from the screen.

Swift smiled to herself and pulled down a short animated CD sequence that illustrated the reconstruction of the creature from the feet up. Hairiness, impossible to deduce from the fossil and the footprint, was not enhanced. But watching it, Jack felt his heart skip a beat, for the computer animation finished to reveal a 3D colour illustration of a bipedal anthropoid he half recognised.

'Jesus Christ,' he whispered. 'How'd you do that?'

'The computer,' she said coolly.

Jack turned away for a moment as if he needed somehow to gather himself.

She paused, waiting for him to look back and when he did she thumbed the trackball up to the creature's head for a close-up.

'I think the interesting thing about this sequence,' she said, 'is how the predicted skull shape exactly tallies with the skull you found in the Annapurna Sanctuary.'

She dragged down a small icon from the corner of her screen and dropped it on top of the creature's head. As she did so, the icon exploded, becoming one of the colour photographs Swift had taken of the skull in her own laboratory.

Nodding with appreciation, Jack allowed that it was a good match.

'I'm glad you of all people think so.'

'You know it might be nice at that,' he murmured. 'To go back and prove some of those bastards wrong.'

'Wouldn't it just?'

'Besides, seems like I left more than just a good friend back in the Sanctuary.'

'Oh? What was that?'

Jack shook his head. 'Amazing,' he said quietly.

'Anatomically speaking,' she said, 'Esau occupies an approximately intermediate position between a gorilla, and the fossil form *Paranthropus crassidens*, also known as *Australopithecus afarensis*.'

Jack was still shaking his head with wonder at what she had shown him.

'That's the creature I saw on Everest. Swift, that's a yeti.'

Swift nodded. 'At last,' she said. 'I'm glad you agree.'

'You really think we could do it?' he asked. 'You know, the Himalaya is a big place. It won't be easy.'

'Not the Himalayas, Jack. The Sanctuary. And more especially Machhapuchhare. You may have found the skull on Annapurna but all the most recent sightings of the yeti have been on Machhapuchhare.'

Jack winced.

'There's something I haven't told you,' he admitted. 'The skull wasn't found on Annapurna.'

He explained how he and Didier had been climbing Machhapuchhare illegally when the accident occurred.

'You know you could be right,' he concluded thoughtfully. 'Maybe there is another reason no one's allowed to climb Machhapuchhare. Maybe the locals know something we don't. Maybe that's why no one's ever found the yeti. Maybe no one's been allowed to find it.'

'In which case it'll be like I said,' agreed Swift. 'Officially, for the purposes of the grant proposal and the Nepali Government, we'll be in the Sanctuary on a fossil-hunting expedition. But the reality will be that we're in and around Machhapuchhare and searching for the Abominable Snowman.'

Jack shook his head.

'To hell with that,' he said. 'Abominable Snowman, bullshit. That stuff's for the comics. This, this is science. We're going there to find Esau.'

Eight

'Nothing is more expensive than a start.'

Friedrich Nietzsche

The Pentagon's guided tour was free and given every half-hour on weekdays between 9.30a.m. and 3.30p.m., except on public holidays. Even non-US citizens were permitted to take it, provided they brought their passports. In the so-called Commander-in-Chief's corridor you could see a model of a Stealth SR-71, an aircraft that technically at least was still a secret. It was this willingness on the part of the military to open its headquarters to the public and to brag about its toys that made Bryan Perrins dislike the Pentagon and its DoD personnel. Either you had secrets or you didn't. Whenever he had a meeting there he always half-expected the door to open and the uniformed tour guide to back in – he always walked backwards in order to keep an eye on his flock of visitors – followed by a group of Okies, their wide-eyed faces still full of hot-dogs bought from the stand in the middle of the Pentagon's courtyard.

In his late forties, Perrins looked more like some up-market clothes designer than the Deputy Director of Intelligence. He wore a sharp suit and a dark, designer-stubble beard and sat well back from the boardroom table almost as if he was attending the meeting of the Committee on Overhead Reconnaissance in the role of observer.

There were a lot of uniformed experts, all of them saying the same thing. Operation Bellerophon, organising U2 overflights in the Indian subcontinent, had drawn a blank. One of the experts, an USAF general, was still droning on with his excuses.

91

'Because of the need to husband our resources, and to ensure that the highest quality photography was obtained from each over-flight, it was the practice not to launch a mission unless weather over the area was predicted to be less than twenty-five per cent. Unfortunately the weather has been stacked against us. Several flights yielded no usable photography at all. Nevertheless we still managed to acquire a moderately complete mosaic of the region, but with zero result.

'Attached to your reports, gentlemen, is a summary of weather forecasts in the area. As you can see we are now firmly in the grip of winter and despite the obvious urgency of the situation I would not recommend resumption of U2 overflights until at least the end of February.'

When at last the airforce general sat down, Reichhardt sighed, took off his lightly tinted glasses, patted his bald head almost as if he had just had his hair cut, and thanked him.

'I had hoped that this meeting would surface some intelligence that might be of use,' he said quietly. 'I must confess that I'm a little disappointed by this lack of progress. However I guess we all knew that whatever we did or did not find the ultimate responsibility for dealing with this Bellerophon situation would devolve to the CIA.'

Perrins smiled and drew himself closer to the table.

'Bellerophon,' he said, shaking his head. 'I looked it up, just as you suggested, Bill, and since this whole responsibility is about to devolve to intelligence anyway, I think maybe we ought to change that codename. Did you know that a letter of Bellerophon means a document that is either dangerous or prejudicial to the bearer? On account of how Bellerophon was thrown off Pegasus when it got stung by a horsefly. We'll let you know whatever name the computer generates.'

Perrins smiled thinly, enjoying Reichhardt's chagrin. The NRO director looked as if he had found something unpleasant on the soles of both of his shoes.

'Naturally we're already exploring a number of lines of action involving field personnel,' continued Perrins. 'Given the background noise in the area, it's always been our view that any action taken would of necessity be covert. You can rest assured that whatever new action programme is decided, we will execute it aggressively and I'm confident that we'll find what we're looking for.'

Aware that the game belonged to Perrins now, Reichhardt

nodded. His own department had failed. There was nothing more to be done except to eat the shit that Perrins was offering to him. But even so he had learned to be pessimistic where the optimism of the CIA was concerned. Perhaps he might still manage to keep a foot in the CIA's door.

'Let's hope so,' he said. 'Let's see now. Our next scheduled COMOR get together is tomorrow. Perhaps you might lay out some of those lines of action then.'

'Bill, why don't I call you?' said Perrins. 'When we're ready to read you the menu.'

'Yes,' said Reichhardt, squirming with irritation. He could see that Perrins was enjoying himself. 'Why don't you do that?'

'Fat chance,' Perrins said to himself, as soon as he was sitting in his car on the way back to Langley.

The headquarters of the CIA were a very different proposition from the Pentagon. An uncomplicated, modern, white, seven-storey building in a pastoral setting of woods and lawns, the nearest Langley got to tourists was the occasional pleasure boat sailing north up the Potomac, the odd demonstration on the CIA exit off the George Washington Parkway, and maybe the Bubble.

The Bubble was a dome-shaped auditorium that apparently stood alone but was in fact connected to headquarters by an underground tunnel. It was where people without security clearances were allowed to come into contact with agency personnel. It was in the Bubble that Perrins's boss had been sworn in as DCI by a Justice of the Supreme Court. And back in the Seventies, it was in the Bubble that TV had been brought into the Agency for the first time with *60 Minutes* and *Good Morning America*.

There were very few journalists allowed through that secret corridor and into the heart of the CIA's headquarters. Perrins was about to take a meeting with one of the few who was.

Having worked as a foreign correspondent for a number of newspapers and television networks prior to his joining *National Geographic*, Brindley had always enjoyed a close relationship with the CIA. At first the relationship had been informal and restricted to the odd conversation on a subject of mutual interest. But over the years the relationship had developed to the point where Brindley agreed to seek specific information or other personnel needed by the Agency.

As a journalist, Brindley had always been something of an action man, the kind of reporter who got into remote and inaccessible parts of the world, often at no small risk to himself. He was the type who joined expeditions to climb unclimbed mountains or penetrate impenetrable jungles and when he first joined the staff of *National Geographic*, it had been as the magazine's senior editor in charge of expeditions.

A fit-looking man in his late forties, but still suffering from the constant glaucoma that had forced an end to his once incessant globetrotting, Brindley saw his former Yale classmate first in the Bubble and then in the latter's seventh-floor office, on the executive row of the CIA. With its view of the river, the old team photographs of the Orioles on the walls, and piles of computer printouts on the carpeted floor, Perrins's office was only slightly less shabby than the rest of the building.

The two men exchanged pleasantries while Brindley opened an English leather briefcase and took out a copy of the familiar yellow-bordered magazine. On the cover was a blurred photograph of a gondola.

'Are you interested in Venice?' Brindley asked and then tossed his latest issue across the desk.

'Not professionally,' smiled Perrins.

'Me, I don't care for it at all. There's something claustrophobic about the place, something corrupt and infective.'

'What was it Henry James said about it? Originality of attitude is utterly impossible.' Perceiving that Brindley had felt the point he smiled sadistically. 'But keep trying. Maybe you'll think of something.'

'Bastard. Beats me what people want to read about. National parks mostly.'

'Well, Dunham, I'll say one thing for you: you usually know what I want to read about. That's why you're here, isn't it?'

Brindley nodded at the magazine lying on the blotter in front of Perrins.

'"Behind the Scenes". About six or seven pages in from the front cover. That's a new feature. The editor's idea. Amusing, sometimes amazing stories from staff members and freelances about their experiences in the field. Piece of shit if you ask me.'

Perrins turned the pages.

'Rock Jock's Himalayan Tragedy,' Brindley prompted.

The DDI glanced at a photograph of two mountain climbers and then started to read aloud from the short piece of copy printed underneath.

'"America's leading 'rock-jock', Jack Furness, abandoned his attempt to climb all fourteen of the highest Himalayan peaks and returned home to California early, following the tragic death of his climbing partner, the Canadian Alpinist, Didier Lauren. Lauren and Furness had forged an internationally famous climbing partnership with an unparalleled record of lightweight first ascents that has been the inspiration for a whole new generation of Alpine style climbing in America. Furness and Lauren, two NGS research grant recipients, were climbing the south-west face of Annapurna, when disaster struck."'

Perrins sighed and looked up.

'Does this have a point, Dunham?'

'Don't stop,' Brindley insisted.

Perrins looked back at the magazine and read the rest of the story in silence. When he finished he nodded slowly.

'Could be,' he allowed.

'He's staying right here in Washington. At the Jefferson.'

'The Jefferson, huh?' Perrins sounded impressed. 'I'd have thought an outdoors type like him would be more comfortable at a Howard Johnson.'

Brindley shook his head firmly. 'Furness is a celebrity.'

'That's why I've never heard of him.'

'People write books about him. Movie people use him. Stallone had him do all the stunts in one. He's made a lot of money. He was a Rhodes scholar at Oxford University.'

'That doesn't mean shit, Dunham. Clinton was a Rhodes scholar.'

'I'm just trying to turn you on to the fact that this is no hard-hat-for-a-brain kid who stinks of camp-fire smoke.'

'Okay, okay, he's Gore Vidal. What's he doing in Washington?'

'Presenting a grant proposal. He and an anthropologist, a woman called Stella Swift, want to return to the Annapurna Sanctuary to look for fossils.'

'Jesus, don't they read the newspapers? There might be a war in the Punjab.'

'That's three or four hundred kilometres away.'

'Near enough if it goes nuclear down there.'

'Which ought to make them all the more valuable to you, Bryan.

95

Right now there are not many people asking for money to go to a potential theatre of conflict.'

'Point taken. A scientific expedition to the area would be good cover for us.'

'Copies of the grant proposal are given to the Research and Exploration Committee. That's about sixteen people. Each of them writes a critique of the grant, summarising his or her evaluations in a rating, ranging from excellent to poor. After all the reviews come in, the ratings are averaged and a grant is or is not awarded accordingly. On paper there's nothing wrong with the proposal. Which reminds me.'

Brindley picked up his briefcase and took out a thermal-bound document that was as thick as a movie screenplay. He tossed it on to the desk on top of the magazine and leaned back in his chair.

'I brought you a copy. I'm not on the committee myself. And here's the problem. From what I hear, they didn't get funded.'

'Why's that?'

'It's just that money's a little short right now. In this particular field. Belt tightening, I'm afraid.'

Perrins's intelligent eyes noted the expensive leather belt that was holding up the pants of the journalist's Brooks Brothers suit and smiled thinly. To the right of the belt's brass buckle the leather showed a dark band that seemed to indicate a belt that had been let out a notch or two to accommodate Brindley's ample stomach.

'I can see that,' Perrins said drily, and picked up his pen. 'So who's on the committee? Maybe we can influence the decision the other way.'

'Brad Schaffer. He's a friend. You've met him before. I think if we levelled with him he might help.'

'Do you mean level with him? Or bring him to a certain level, clearance-wise?'

'Bring him up.'

'Maybe. What about the rest of the committee?'

'You'll find a list of their names in the magazine. It's an International Who's Who. Basically the trustees find the money. Often from their own pockets.'

Perrins turned the pages of his copy of *National Geographic* until he found one that was completely filled with the names of those who had anything to do with the magazine or the Society. Many of the names that appeared on the Board of Trustees and the companies they represented were familiar to him. One name in particular caught his eye.

'Joel Beinart, Chairman and CEO of the Semath Corporation.'

'The electronic conglomerate. Yeah, I've met him.'

'So have I,' said Perrins. 'He used to be Secretary of Commerce. We did quite a bit of work together. Commerce would often pick a country or a field of business endeavour and then ask us to deliver briefings to the appropriate business people. Beinart's always been sympathetic to the aims of this agency. Maybe he could front something up for us. Organise what the Russians call "a joint venture". With an injection of government money via Semath, Schaffer might persuade your Research and Exploration Committee to change their minds.'

'All the years I've known you, it still surprises me when I hear my own ideas coming back to me as if they were yours.'

'Shut up,' smiled Perrins. 'What does this kind of trip cost anyway?'

'It's in the grant proposal,' said Brindley. 'But if memory serves, I think they were looking for something in the region of seven hundred and fifty thousand dollars. Less the cost of any private sponsorship deals.'

'They won't have time to get any sponsors,' said Perrins. 'Three quarters of a mill, huh? You know how much that is out of the 1996 Defense Budget?'

Brindley shrugged.

'I'll tell you.' Grinning like a schoolboy, Perrins was already tapping out numbers on the keyboard of his PC. 'About two minutes' worth.'

'I figured it must be something piffling.'

'What about this Furness character?' Perrins asked. 'Do you think we might recruit him?'

'Possible, I suppose. He did a TV commercial for junk bonds once so he can't be too highly principled.'

'What about her?'

'That I couldn't say. She's Australian or English or something.'

Perrins leaned across the desk and depressed a switch on his intercom.

'Connie. Would you get me the files on – ?' He glanced down at the grant proposal and read the two names on the cover. 'On a Jack Furness. F-U-R-N-E-S-S. And on a Doctor Stella Swift, as in the bird, of the University of California in Berkeley. Oh, and ask Chaz Mustilli if he'd like to come and see me in my office. Thanks, Connie.'

Releasing the switch, he turned the pages of the grant proposal and perused the mission statement.

'Human fossils huh?'

'Palaeoanthropology,' nodded Brindley. 'Haven't you heard? It's the new religion.'

'People have got to believe in something,' shrugged Perrins. 'But speaking for myself I can't imagine a God who would prefer going to church to seeing a movie.'

'Let's stay in tonight,' said Swift. 'Let's have dinner in the hotel.'

She was watching the television news.

'But we had dinner here last night,' objected Jack. 'Wouldn't you prefer to go somewhere different?'

'I'm not in the mood for different. I'm in the mood for staying in and feeling sorry for myself.'

'Okay, if that's what you want.'

'Shit. Wouldn't you just believe it?'

'What?'

Swift pointed at the television.

'The news,' she said dully. 'The Secretary of State has managed to persuade the Indians and Pakistanis to agree to a three-month cooling-off period.'

'What's wrong with that?' demanded Jack.

'Nothing,' shrugged Swift. 'It's just that three months would have been a very convenient window for us to have got safely in and out of Nepal.'

'Most expeditions, it takes at least three months to put them together,' said Jack.

'This isn't most expeditions. At least not any more.'

She kissed him on the cheek.

'I'm going to take a bath, Jack.'

'Can't I stay and watch?'

Swift laughed a silent, embarrassed laugh. There were times when he came on like a high-school kid. But since starting to sleep with him again, she had begun to realise how much she had missed him in the first place.

'Why don't I join you in the bar?'

'I could use a drink at that,' he admitted. 'I hate committees.' He shook his head angrily. 'I still can't believe they turned us down.'

'You're just saying that. You warned me it might be tough.' Swift shrugged bravely. 'Anyway, it's *me* they turned down. Me and my idea. They didn't turn *you* down. They said you can go back and finish climbing the rest of the peaks, if you want.'

'That's not what I want. Not any more.'

'Well then, there's still the National Science Foundation. Warren Fitzgerald's on the peer review committee. He's Dean of Palaeo-anthropology at Berkeley.'

'It's not what you know, it's who you know, huh?'

'Actually it's who you sleep with.'

'You're kidding.'

She laughed. 'Just a bit. Unfortunately I think the National Science people are just as tight for cash right now. So Fitzgerald told me anyway.'

'We'll find the money somehow. We have to. Maybe a newspaper or a television network. There must be many people who would want to get involved with something like this. Maybe if we levelled with them, and told them what the expedition was really all about. . . ?'

'No way,' Swift said firmly. 'The last thing we want is a lot of media interest before we get started. We have to stick to the original plan and keep the idea of a living Esau under wraps. Okay?'

'Yeah. You're right.'

Swift nodded and then headed towards the bathroom. 'I'll see you downstairs.'

The Jefferson's lounge looked like the drawing-room of an eighteenth-century house. Above a green and white marble fire-place, where a large log was burning noisily, was a portrait of Thomas Jefferson and his racing dog, a white whippet sniffing at its master's declamatory hand.

Jack sat down in a large armchair, ordered a whisky from the waiter and settled back to enjoy the fire. The windows rattled against the howling wind and for a moment he thought he could have been back in the Himalayas. On such a cold night he was glad after all to be staying indoors. The widely praised Virginian cooking of the hotel chef was exactly what he fancied. When his drink arrived, he nursed it for a while, drank it and then ordered another, wishing he'd brought something to read. Swift had a habit of staying in the bath too long. Most women did.

'Mister Furness?'

'Hmm?'

Jack looked up from his study of the firelight. The man standing over him was tall and dressed in a conservative-looking blazer that seemed slightly too big for him, although he appeared in excellent shape.

'I hope you'll pardon the interruption, sir,' said the man, and pointed to the other armchair. 'May I?'

Jack nodded and then read the proffered business card.

'"Jon Boyd, Senior Director, Alpine and Arctic Research Institute." What can I do for you, Mister Boyd?'

The waiter returned with Jack's drink. Boyd handed him his credit card, ordered a Daiquiri, and told the waiter to put both drinks on his tab. Then he stretched his hands towards the fire. Jack caught sight of an impressive-looking tattoo. With his buzz haircut, square jaw and short moustache Boyd reminded Jack of the gay clones you could still see in San Francisco's Castro district. Apart from the blazer. That looked like off-duty military.

'The trouble with wood is that there's not much heat in it,' he grumbled, then abruptly changed gears. 'Frankly I was hoping that you might be able to help me.'

'Oh? And how might I do that?'

'I'm a geologist,' explained Boyd. 'But for a while now climatology's been my thing. Do you know anything about climatology, Mister Furness?'

'In my line of work it can save your life if you know something about weather,' said Jack. 'It's a constantly recurring theme in the conversation of most mountaineers, I'm afraid. You learn to blend a little theoretical knowledge with a lot of real-life situation. But mostly it's a question of listening to weather reports on the radio. I'm an expert on listening to those.'

'Is the term "katabatic" wind familiar to you?'

'It's a wind that develops when air cooled on high ground becomes dense enough to flow downhill, right?'

'Exactly so.'

'I know enough about them to avoid camping in valley bottoms and hollows if I want a comfortable night,' said Jack.

'On the Antarctic plateau these winds can reach tremendous

speeds,' said Boyd. 'As a result they often remove recently fallen snow. Which is where I come in. Snow and ice. You see my special field of inquiry is the climatic factors that affect the preservation of snow.'

The waiter returned bearing their drinks and there was a moment's pause as each man contemplated his glass.

'Snow?' Jack tried to sound interested, but he was beginning to regret his tolerance of this stranger. He was beginning to feel a little imposed upon. 'Why would anyone want to preserve snow?'

'Snow *and* ice. In particular the effect of global warming on the great ice sheets.'

Jack groaned inwardly. An ecology freak. Just his luck. Where the hell was Swift?

'Most of our work has been done on the Antarctic peninsula and islands. We hope to understand the outcome of the threatened runaway greenhouse effect. Frankly, there's a lot of conflicting information. The Greenland ice sheet is thickening. And there have been increases in the amount of snow at the poles. Yet the climate continues to indicate that the melting of ice is accelerating.'

Jack glanced at his watch.

'Somewhere between five and ten thousand years ago the sea rose rapidly, in response to the disappearance of global ice sheets. Then it slowed considerably. Currently we estimate that the sea level is rising by as much as two millimetres per annum.'

'Well this is fascinating, Mister Boyd,' said Jack, stifling a yawn. 'But I don't see what it has to do with me.'

'It has everything to do with all of us,' said Boyd.

'What I mean to say is – '

Boyd held up his hand and added quickly: 'It's likely that the melting of mountain glaciers may account for some of this.'

Jack's ears pricked up. Mountains. Now the man was making sense.

'The question is, how much? How much of the increase in sea level relates to melting mountain glaciers, and how much to floating ice sheets. And that's why I want to go to the highest mountain range in the world. To undertake some urgent research on the Himalayan glaciers.'

'At last,' said Jack. 'We connect.'

'Washington's a small place, Mister Furness. When I heard you had applied for a grant to fund an expedition to the Himalayas, I had hoped that I might persuade you to take me along as a paying guest. Share some expenses, y'know? Not to climb. No sir, I have no head for heights. No, it's so that I might conduct my own geological experiments. Specifically, drilling holes in the ice, taking core samples from the glacier, that kind of thing. Frankly the political situation in the Indian subcontinent means that there are not many people like yourself going to that part of the world.'

Jack tried to cut in with his own news, but Boyd was not to be interrupted.

'There's certainly no one who knows the Himalayas as well as you, Mister Furness. No one knows how to put an outfit like this together. That's why – '

'I'm sorry to disappoint you, Mister Boyd, but I'm afraid our grant proposal got turned down.' He shrugged. 'We just heard.'

'No.' Boyd sounded genuinely outraged. 'I don't believe it. Why would they turn *you* down? You're the country's leading mountaineer.'

'It's kind of you to say so. But this time it's not exactly a climbing expedition I'm putting together. We're going to look for some fossils. Either way, it doesn't really seem to matter right now.'

'What can I say? I guess I'll be going on my own then. I'm really sorry. I felt sure – '

'Forget it. And good luck with your work.'

The two men stood and shook hands as Swift appeared in the Jefferson lounge. She looked excited about something. Jack glanced irritably at his watch.

'You'll never guess what's happened,' she said, ignoring Boyd.

'I figured something must have, the time you've been.' He started to introduce Boyd, but Swift was too high on her news to listen.

'The phone rang just as I was leaving the room. It was Brad Schaffer. From the Research and Exploration Committee? He was calling from the National Geographic offices.'

'They're still there? At this time of night?'

'In view of the three-month cooling-off period agreed by the Indians and Pakistanis, some of them wanted to reconsider their earlier decision. And guess what? It looks like they've decided to give us a grant after all.'

'That's great.'

He grinned awkwardly and then glanced at Boyd.

'Swift, this is Jon Boyd. Mister Boyd, this is Doctor Stella Swift. Only don't ever call her Stella.'

102

Boyd handed her another business card.

'Mister Boyd is a geologist and climatologist. He had hoped to be a paying guest on our expedition.'

While Jack was speaking Swift read Boyd's card, turned it over in her fingers as if threatening to make it disappear, and then tossed it on to the table like so much wastepaper. Easily attracting the eye of the waiter she ordered a bottle of champagne.

'I'm in a mood to celebrate,' she said simply and sat down.

Jack nodded. 'What changed their minds? Did they say?'

'They found some more money. One of the committee members, Joel Beinart, was more impressed with our grant proposal than he'd felt able to say at the meeting. And when this cooling-off period was negotiated, he felt that it must be some kind of sign. Anyway, he's found the money himself, from his own company. The Semath Corporation. Oh, yes; there's one tiny condition. Something to do with the tax year? It's a condition of the grant that the money has to be used sooner rather than later so his company can treat the grant money as part of this year's deductible charities and donations.'

'How much sooner?' said Jack.

'End of the month.'

'The end of the month?' Jack guffawed. 'That's less than two weeks, Swift. It takes time to put an expedition like this together. A lot of time. Two weeks? It simply can't be done.'

'Oh, come on, Jack. Where there's a will?'

Jack looked around the room with bewilderment and caught sight of Thomas Jefferson's portrait.

'Like the man said,' he sighed. 'Delay is preferable to error. What's the goddamn hurry anyway?'

Swift shrugged.

'The bean-counters have their financial year to consider. They're even prepared to give us more money than we asked for. A million dollars, Jack. Not to mention a lot of new equipment they want us to test. Besides, there's the diplomatic window to think of now. It would be a lot easier persuading other scientists to come with us if we could take full advantage of what's been negotiated between India and Pakistan.'

The waiter arrived back with champagne. Swift toasted the good news.

'Speaking for myself,' Boyd said cautiously. 'If, that is, you decided that you were able to take me along. And I'd be paying my

103

way. Not to mention bringing along a lot of new equipment that we've already tested in the Antarctic. Well, sooner would also suit me better too. You see there's an Intergovernmental Summit on Climate Control in London, in twelve weeks' time. Now I don't know how you people feel about fossil fuels, but my company opposes any moves on the part of the international community to force through more reductions in emissions of greenhouse gases. At least until people like me have had a chance to predict how much CO_2 the atmosphere can absorb before it triggers catastrophic climate change.'

'And you can do that in the Himalayas?' asked Swift.

Boyd described his interest in taking core samples from mountain glaciers.

'It's vital that we have as clear a set of data as possible, otherwise we may end up committing ourselves to unnecessary targets that will almost certainly have an effect on American economic development.'

'What if your data doesn't support your institute's point of view?' asked Jack. 'Then what?'

'To be honest with you, that's not for me to say. I'm just a scientist, Jack. Governments will have to call a halt to CO_2 emissions sometime. It's bound to be unpopular when it does happen. Very unpopular. No politician wants to take an unpopular decision until the last possible moment.'

'I guess so,' said Jack. 'But two weeks? Have either of you any idea what the weather out there is like right now?'

He drained his champagne glass at the thought of it.

'Quite apart from the effects of high altitude, we'll have to cope with very high winds, temperatures so low they're almost off the scale and less than seven hours of light per day. These are hardly ideal conditions for any scientific expedition.'

Boyd shrugged.

'I apologise if this sounds like mine's bigger than yours, but Antarctica wasn't exactly a Sunday school picnic. And like I say, my institute will be sending some of the latest equipment. Some of the gear we used at the pole was developed by NASA. I mean state-of-the-art.'

Swift nodded. 'It all sounds fine to me, Mister Boyd. Jack? What do you say?'

Jack examined his now empty glass and then nodded grimly.

'Whatever equipment you take, it's never enough. Things go wrong. The unforeseen happens. It's that kind of place. State-of-the-art equipment from NASA, huh? You can bet your last dollar we'll be needing it. Because in winter, the Himalaya is as cold and hostile an environment as – as the surface of Pluto.'

Jack drummed his fingers on the table.

After Boyd had finally left the hotel he and Swift had settled in with a good dinner. He might have enjoyed it more if he hadn't been a little preoccupied with trying to fathom the reason for the Committee's sudden turnaround. It was nagging at him like a persistent toothache.

'You're being very perverse about this,' she told him. 'We've got the money. We've even got a breathing space.'

He grunted with puzzlement.

'I mean, the cooling-off period. What more do you want? The car comes gift-wrapped in pink ribbon and still you want to inspect the tyres.'

'Someone has to if we're all going to ride safely.'

'I don't see why.'

'Companies don't just find a million dollars lying around like that. Like so much backyard lumber.'

'But it's just as I told you. They liked the grant proposal.'

'My guess is that you'd take the grant whatever. Jimmy Hoffa could show up and give you a suitcase full of money and you wouldn't ask any questions. Am I right?'

Swift let herself be amused by him.

'Maybe.'

'So, who's being perverse now? I mean isn't there any part of you that wants to know more about this? That wants to be just a tad cautious?'

'Okay then, tell me. What should I suspect? That someone has figured out the real purpose of the expedition is to find a yeti? If anything I think that would make people less inclined to hand over a million bucks, don't you? What is there that should make us suspicious? Please, Jack, I would like to know.'

'It feels wrong that's all. I can't explain why.'

'Well, you're certainly not trying very hard. I'm a scientist. I need a little more to go on than what's happening in your guts, Jack.'

She stood up.

'I'm going back to the room,' she said. 'Are you coming?'

'No, I thought I would get some air. Clear my head.'

'Good idea,' she said. 'Too much wine makes you paranoid.'

They parted stiffly in the lobby. As Jack headed towards the front door the concierge called to him.

'Mister Furness. There's a parcel here for you, sir.'

'A parcel? For me? I'm not expecting any parcel.'

'Your name is on the label, sir.'

'Thanks, Harvey.'

Puzzled, Jack came over to the desk to inspect the parcel, immediately recognising its White Fang address label. It was from his sponsor. Inside was a note from Chuck Farrell and several pairs of new compound sticky rock boots, all in Jack's size. The concierge, watched as Jack picked one pair of shoes out of the box. With their Velcro fastenings, bright colours and Navajo Indian designs, they looked more like moccasins than climbing shoes.

Reading the name on the shoe box, the concierge said: 'The Brundle shoe. What's a Brundle shoe?'

'Do you go to the movies, Harvey?'

'Some.'

'Ever see a movie called *The Fly*? After Doctor Martin Brundle. The Jeff Goldblum character.'

'Right,' said Harvey. 'But I still don't get it.'

'They're climbing shoes.'

'Climbing shoes. Well, they look comfortable.'

'Not on me,' said Jack. 'Not any more. You keep 'em. Christmas present.'

'Thanks, Mister Furness. But where can you climb round here?'

'You could try the Washington Monument.'

He went out on to 16th Street, braced himself against the cold and walked south, heading past the ornate mansion that housed the Russian Embassy, chuckling quietly. The Washington Monument. Now that really would be a climb. A one-hundred-and-forty-metre obelisk of New England granite. The wonder was he hadn't tried it before. There had been a time when just thinking about it would have made him want to go and do it.

On the corner of M Street he turned right, his footsteps carrying him automatically in the direction of the National Geographic building. He could see a couple of lights still burning on the penultimate floor, where the executive decisions were made. Even the ones you couldn't account for. Why had they changed their minds, and so quickly? Was it really anything to do with the cooling-off period negotiated by the Secretary of State?

It didn't make any sense. It just wasn't the way they did things. Was there some other reason? But what could that be? Swift was right. He had to give her more than just his gut feeling. He had a good mind to go up there and see if he couldn't find some answers. Jack tried the front door, but it was locked. What was the point, anyway? Even if there had been someone about, they would probably just have given him the same story that they had already given to Swift about the Semath Corporation bean-counters and their financial year.

He walked on, staring up at the top of the building and the lights still burning there and, rounding the next corner, saw that someone had carelessly left a corner window open on the top floor. The light was off but he could clearly see a net curtain billowing out into the night air like the sail of a ship that had slipped its rope.

Perhaps he had only to climb up and through the open window to find out why the decision had been changed. Look around someone's office. Someone like Brad Schaffer, on the Research and Exploration Committee. Turn on his computer. Locate a file. It sounded simple enough when he considered the idea. Just climb up there and nose around. It wasn't as if it was a particularly tall building. There was a height limit on all buildings in Washington – roughly the elevation of the Capitol dome and the Washington Monument, so that you could always see the sky and the Capitol downtown. About thirteen storeys. The Transamerica Pyramid he'd climbed for the junk bond commercial had been several times higher. In comparison this one looked positively squat.

Jack walked quickly back to the hotel, his heart racing in anticipation. Perhaps it was as well that he'd had so much to drink. Dutch courage: in lieu of any other kind it would have to suffice. If he was ever going to climb the big walls again, this might just be a quick way to recover his nerve. Either that or it would be an easy way of killing himself.

The concierge was sitting behind the desk reading a copy of the *Post*.

'Give me a pair of those shoes, will ya?' said Jack.

'Sure thing, Mister Furness.'

Jack threw off his coat. He was wearing a cashmere rollneck

sweater and a pair of jeans. He sat down behind the desk and pulled off his loafers and socks.

'Kinda late to be going climbing, isn't it, Mister Furness?'

'It's never too late to go climbing, Harv.'

He laced the Brundle shoes up tightly on his bare feet and stood up, flexing his insteps. Chuck's new shoes felt good. He laid one foot flat on the marble floor and pushed hard. The sole hardly moved.

'Not bad,' he murmured. 'Not bad at all, Chuck.' He looked around the inside of the reception desk. 'You got any band-aids there?'

The concierge produced a first-aid box and let Jack help himself.

'How about chalk powder?'

'Chalk powder?' He looked thoughtful. 'No sir. Can't say we have. But there's some resin in the health club. Guys use it on the rings. Would that do?'

Jack nodded.

'I'll go fetch it.'

Jack started to tape up his fingers, trying to make each finger's tendon as rigid as possible without cutting off any circulation. He had rejected the idea of wearing gloves. It was cold enough, only he was worried about not getting sufficient grip on the fabric of the building. He just hoped he could get up quickly enough before his fingers started to get numb.

The concierge arrived back with a small bag of resin and handed it over.

Jack turned and jogged gently towards the hotel front door.

'You ain't gonna try the Monument, are you, sir?'

'Not tonight,' said Jack and ran out into the night air.

Somewhere inside his head a still small voice of sense and reason tried to tell him that what he was planning to do was crazy. Even if he did make it up to the open window, what exactly was he hoping to find? And where would he look for it? But by now Jack's late-night expedition had become more than just a bit of innocent cat burglary. The climb was now carrying the extra load of another chance at the rest of his mountaineering career.

As calmly as he was able, he walked past the front door of the National Geographic offices. The last thing anyone would be expecting was someone entering the building through an open window on the top floor. Jack kept on walking. Climbing the Transamerica, he had chosen a route up the corner of the building. It was

108

just good luck that the open window was on the corner of the National Geographic.

Jack looked around and seeing M Street deserted he jumped up and caught the first window ledge with one hand. It was about eight centimetres deep. The hardest bit was always pulling yourself up on to the pitch with one arm. Grunting so loudly he thought that someone would hear him, he got another handhold and then swung a foot up, scrambling at the ledge, sliding his face up against the cold pane of the window until he was standing about three metres above the ground. Breathing heavily from this first exertion, he inched his way to the corner.

The building was the standard glass box, clean lines and brutal simplicity, with a steel frame that left a suitable handhold all the way up on both sides of the corner. It was the rock-climbing equivalent of an even-width crack. A 5.9 layback, like the Crack of Doom on Yosemite's Leaning Tower. Or Lightning Dream at Tahoe. Better. There was at least two centimetres of crack between the frame and the glass. And it was a crack unscarred by the jamcracks, pitons, nuts and cams that had ruined many good routes in Yosemite all the way to the top. Just a matter of sliding two sets of fingers under each side of the frame, and with arms at full stretch, concentrating the weight there, pushing up with your toes.

The grip of the new compound rubber was astonishingly sure and Jack made good progress up the corner of the building. The Brundle shoes really did let him climb like a fly. It was as well, he thought, that his vision was not similarly enhanced. Seeing less left little room for his imagination to go to work.

Nearer the top it grew windier. Now he had a good view of Capitol Hill and the Washington Monument: two airplane warning-lights blinking on either side of the obelisk made it look like some kind of fiery-eyed dinosaur. He was going to make it. The window was now just a metre or so above his head.

Jack lifted his foot, reaching for the next toehold, slid his fingers up the crack and touched something alive that was suddenly leaping in his face. His heart seemed to take off into the night sky, flapping madly, like the wings of the pigeon he had disturbed. He moved instinctively backwards to avoid its emergency flight path, just a little too far and missed the toehold he had been going for, as well as the one he had been resting on. For a long, vertiginous moment, he hung there by only his fingertips, his feet thrashing around like those of a hanged man, desperately trying to find another toehold. Seconds passed and his toes seemed foreign to him as they refused to do his mind's bidding. Finally, they connected with the building again and he clung there, like a koala, perspiring freely although it was cold enough for snow.

He took a deep breath, steadied himself, felt the alcohol in his blood and climbed on, reaching the corner window in a matter of a few seconds, and stepping into the empty office with the sense of having conquered more than just an averagely tall glass monolith. He felt a new raw lifeforce. Perhaps he really had overcome his fear.

He could see why the window had been left open. The room was being decorated and smelled strongly of paint. He opened the door and peered into the dimly lit corridor. No one about. He crept along the corridor and down the stairs to the floor below where the offices of the Research and Exploration Committee were situated. The lights were still on, but it looked as if everyone had gone home.

Brad Schaffer's office was easy to find. It even had his nameplate on the door. It was not locked and Jack opened it and went inside, closing the door behind him and turning the T-lock just in case anyone from security came along. Jack glanced at Brad's desktop PC and wondered if he was being a fool to think that he might be able to work out how to use the operating system. He switched it on anyway and while the machine was warming up, noisily initialising and testing its own memory and reading its own operating files, Jack turned his attention to the polished wooden filing cabinets ranged along one wall. He searched among the drawer fronts and their title panels and almost immediately located the one labelled 'GRANT PROPOSALS'. A few seconds later he was sitting in Schaffer's own desk chair and reading the notes that had been attached to the research proposal Swift had carefully prepared with duplicitous understatement of the real aims of their expedition. Alongside the grant proposal were the reports of the members of the peer review committee, generally favourable, and a note from the accounts committee to the effect that money was too tight for the awarding of any new grants before the end of the next calendar year. The next page in the file was a letter formally confirming that the grant proposal had been accepted.

Jack groaned quietly and turned his attention to Schaffer's computer screen. It was a standard Microsoft Windows setup, the same as the one he had on his PC back home in Danville. But trying to access Schaffer's files from the File Manager he discovered that they were all protected by a code word. He stared hard at the Program Manager and its many coloured icons resembling objects in a doll's house, hoping that one of them might provoke an idea about what to do next. One of them did. The Compuserve icon. Jack wondered if Schaffer had bothered to protect his e-mail files. If Brad was anything like himself, the messages just piled up until he could be bothered to delete them.

He clicked on the Compuserve icon and checked the In Tray for recent messages. Straight away he realised that one of these was exactly what he had been looking for. The message was from someone called Bryan Perrins, and there was even an e-mail number for any reply. Jack made a note of it for later investigation.

'Dear Brad, thanks again for your co-operation in this matter. Dunham has told me how helpful you have been. Under the circumstances, the least I can do is put you completely in the picture. Since this situation developed, the Nepalese have been trying to hang on to their neutrality. So this represents our best chance of dealing with our little problem. This really is a very low-risk assignment. About the only real compensation of any fail situation is that if our man doesn't succeed then the chances are very slim that anyone else can pull this off. The man we're sending has already established an excellent threshold of accomplishment in this kind of situation. Given the nature of the expedition it will be Dr Swift who chooses who goes along. I'm pretty sure that when she speaks to him, she'll want to have our man on her team. He is well qualified in his particular scientific field and a natural choice for an expedition of this kind. Despite recent political developments however, there is in our perception still a need for urgency. Thus the insistence on their going to the area ASAP. Finally let me reassure you that beyond the obvious hazards of where they're headed, they've got nothing to fear from our man and I doubt they'll even be aware of what he's up to.'

Reading the message, Jack smiled grimly.

'I wouldn't be too sure of that,' he whispered, and headed back upstairs, towards his exit window.

*

Back at the hotel, the concierge was nowhere to be seen. Jack reclaimed his jacket, shoes, and socks, and went straight up to the room where Swift greeted his appearance with horror.

'What the hell happened to you? You look like you've been crawling along the street.'

Jack looked at himself. It was true. He was filthy.

'I had a bit of an accident,' he said vaguely. 'I slipped on the sidewalk.' He went into the bathroom and hauled off his rollneck. 'It's getting icy out there.'

'Too much to drink more like,' she said coming up behind and hugging him warmly.

'I'm sorry we quarrelled. But don't you see? This expedition means everything to me. It's the chance of a lifetime. The chance to give my professional life some meaning. You can see that can't you?'

'Yeah. I can see that it's important to you.'

'But you're the boss, Jack. The expedition leader. You know the logistics of going somewhere like this.'

Swift squeezed him affectionately and tried to convey an impression of having to struggle to say what she was about to say. She had been preparing her little speech while he was gone and hoped it would convey the right combination of acquiescence and seductiveness.

'If you think there's some reason we should delay,' she said, kissing his bare shoulder. 'Some reason we should tell Mister Beinart, and Semath, and the National Geographic people that we'll find the grant money from somewhere else, then that's fine with me. Okay?'

'No,' he said. 'There's no reason at all.' Perhaps it wasn't necessary that she knew what he knew. Besides, he only half understood it himself. He would just have to be on the lookout but for what, he wasn't sure.

Part Two: The Expedition

'What does the mountain care?
Ah, but a man's reach should exceed his grasp,
Or what's a heaven for?'

Robert Browning

Nine

'The great end of life is not knowledge but action.'

T.H. Huxley

It was an alien, separate world, like something cast adrift in outer space, some asteroid or comet, hostile, unfastened from the rest of earth, a frozen place of snow and rock. In this lost, abstracted place, time and space had different meanings, and sometimes no meaning at all. Ten minutes or ten kilometres – these measurements signified nothing. The Himalayas made the clock run more slowly than in the rest of the world and all that mattered was how far could be walked or climbed from one sunrise to its setting. Mountains made everything relative.

On every side Swift felt their arcane and unsettling presence, like ancient holy men, their bodies shrouded from pointed head to massive toe in long white robes of snow, as if their faces might be too old, too wrinkled and too terrible to behold.

Like the rest of the expeditionary team on the six-day trek up from Chomrong, she seldom spoke and, amidst a mountainous silence that felt unnatural, she began to rediscover the quiet privacy of her own mind. It was like entering a walled garden, long neglected and overgrown.

Small wonder, she thought, that the Himalayas were regarded as a holy place for in such icy, frigid silence, where the only noise was the sound of your own footstep as, quietly growling, it sank into the tight-packed snow, it was easy to mistake the still, small voice of consciousness as the actual spoken word of some immanent being.

Walking slowly up the ever steepening trail that led to the

115

Annapurna Sanctuary, Swift reflected on how much louder that unspoken voice must have sounded to ancient man. Was this how it had been? From where else but mountains did the gods speak to men? The Himalayas, being much higher than the highest mountains of vision that were to be found anywhere else in the religious and mythical world, were endowed with a silence that much more profound, with voices that much clearer, and with a sense of epiphany that much more sacred. For a scientist in the late 20th century, this sense of the eternal and the numinous was both exhilarating and a little frightening.

The Annapurna Sanctuary, a glacier basin as protected and holy as the name suggested, was a natural amphitheatre created by ten of the world's highest mountain peaks. It was Jack's fourth time to the sanctuary, but he never passed by the north-west face of Machhapuchhare, the seven-thousand-metre-high mountain and symbol of Shiva that marked the entrance to the sanctuary, without feeling like a kind of grave robber intent on desecrating the pyramid of some antique king and stealing something precious.

Annapurna Base Camp, or ABC as it was more easily known, lay at the head of a valley filled with deep snow. This had been the site of the successful 1970 expedition to climb one of the Himalayas' great walls, although now as he looked up at the solid mass of rock and reflected upon his own failure to climb it, Jack thought it almost inconceivable that anyone choosing that route should actually have made it to the top.

Perhaps that was why he had failed after all? Any kind of doubt could be fatal on a mountain like Annapurna.

It was like standing in front of an enormous tidal wave of rock and snow that threatened to come crashing down upon his head at any second. But as far away from the foot of the mountain as it was, ABC was reasonably safe from all but the most cataclysmic collapse of snow and ice.

Here, at four thousand one hundred metres, the air was noticeably thinner. At anything above three thousand metres the oxygen concentration inside human lungs starts to drop. To ensure that everyone on the expedition would become properly acclimatised, Jack had insisted that they should all endure the walk up from Chomrong.

The last four hundred metres from MBC – Machhapuchhare Base Camp – had been the hardest walking of all and some of the

116

expeditionary team were already feeling the effects. They arrived fifty minutes behind Jack and the sirdar – the Sherpa leader – breathless and light-headed, and wondering irritably what had happened to the stone huts that were supposed to be there and which the guidebooks had described as simple lodges for tourists during the trekking season. The miscellaneous team of scientists and climbers did not think of themselves as tourists but after walking for six days in all weathers, even the most basic tourist comfort had begun to sound attractive. The mystery of the disappearing lodges was soon solved when Jack, who had never been in any doubt where these were to be found, ordered the porters to start digging in the snow.

He had chosen to pitch camp at ABC instead of MBC, which was nearer to the forbidden mountain of Machhapuchhare where Swift wanted to concentrate their search, for several reasons: for one, the lodges at ABC were of a better standard; he hoped to get the team acclimatised to a slightly higher altitude; but most important of all, he wanted to keep the real search area of Machhapuchhare a secret from the authorities for as long as possible. The first inkling they had that the expedition was intent on violating the terms of their permit and their liaison officer back in Khat would be forced to recall the Sherpas.

Boyd located some of the heavier supplies, including the main tent, that had been dropped near the site by an army helicopter from Pokhara. While Boyd set about erecting the tent, Jack climbed down a vertical snow shaft, several metres deep, breaking through the bamboo thatched roof of one of the buried dwellings – the Hotel Paradise Garden Lodge – and dropping into its perfectly dry interior. Another shaft was sunk in the snow, another roof was broached and soon two horizontal tunnels connecting the front doors of both lodges were excavated and connected. Within a few hours of their arrival, Jack and the Nepalese Sherpas had located all four lodges and connected them through an icy warren of under-snow tunnels. Aluminium ladders were placed in two of the vertical shafts, to become an entrance and an exit, and a system of halogen lights was rigged so that underneath the thick duvet of snow, the lodges, which were simply furnished with bunk beds, tables, and chairs, could accommodate the eight members of the team as well as at least a dozen Sherpas and porters.

The main tent, supplied by Boyd's company and developed for

117

use in the Antarctic, was to serve as the expedition's laboratory, communications centre, and main living area. Jack, who thought himself an expert in storm-proof tentage, found himself impressed by the structure for it was not so much a tent as an inflatable building, of a type similar to those used by the US army during the Desert Storm operation in the Gulf.

The round, twenty-metre-diameter, igloo-shaped structure that Boyd referred to as 'the clamshell' was made of Kevlar – a material most frequently used in the manufacture of bullet-proof vests – with a frame of 'airbeam' tubes, that were about as thick as a beer-can and inflated to about three hundred times the pressure of a standard inflatable dinghy. These tubes provided a series of rigid beams almost as strong as an aluminium beam of equivalent thickness. But as well as being strong, the clamshell, which was about three metres high at its centre, was also warm. Whereas inflatable buildings in the Gulf had been kept circulated with cool air, for the Himalayas, the air inside the clamshell was heated, creating an environment that was sufficiently temperate for members of the team to dispense with outer-layer clothing altogether, whatever the weather outside. There was even an airlock door to prevent spindrift snow getting inside the clamshell. The whole structure was secured to the snow and ice of the glacier basin by 'smart' titanium tent pegs containing shape-memory wires that were designed to expand and then stiffen when subjected to pressure. Boyd said that in Antarctica the clamshell had withstood winds of up to two hundred and forty kilometres per hour.

The same helicopter that dropped in the clamshell also brought in the Semath Johnson-Mathey fuel cell. About the same size as a small car's engine, the fuel cell was essentially a battery that could not run down, generating about five kilowatts and providing the expedition with all the energy it would need to run heat, light and the various items of electrical equipment too delicate to drop from an aircraft, which the porters had carried up from Chomrong. These included four ruggedised Toshiba Portégé laptops, a desktop PC Gel Documentation system, a Toshiba microwave oven to cook the MREs (meals, ready to eat), a portable pressurisation chamber for extreme cases of altitude sickness, and a small digital weather station.

Communications in the field were to be achieved using handheld GPS units, while regular contact between ABC and the expedition

118

office in Pokhara relied on powerful Satcom transceivers: with a broadcast power of eighteen watts, the transceivers were sufficiently powerful to serve the US-Robotics 14,400 PCMCIA fax-modem cards that were inside each laptop computer, providing the expedition with electronic mail links to offices that were several time zones away.

'This is the best equipped outfit I ever teamed with,' Jack told Boyd.

'You ain't seen nothing yet,' chuckled Boyd. 'Just wait until you get to try one of the SCE suits. SCE. That's Self Contained Environment. My institute had them developed by the International Latex Corporation in Delaware especially for exploration work in the Antarctic. They're kind of similar to the EMU suits they made for the astronauts on the shuttle programme.'

'You mean like a space suit?' Jack laughed. 'C'mon, man, you're shitting me.'

'No way. It's like you said when we met, Jack. There's only one place gets colder than up here and that's outer space. Absolute goddamn zero. An SCE suit? Well, I'll tell you, it's kind of like being in a Rolls-Royce. Once you've been in one you won't want to go in anything else. Believe me, Jack, when you have to leave the clamshell in really shitty weather you'll wonder how you ever managed without one.'

Under Jack's watchful eye, the team began to assemble underneath the clamshell, installing computers, checking communications, sorting gear, testing equipment and planning reconnaissance. Meanwhile the porters put away many of the stores in one of the newly excavated lodges.

The sirdar was Hurké Gurung, a wiry, handsome-looking man in his late forties, and an old-style Sherpa, according to Jack. Although he could neither read nor write, his face was full of the quiet confidence and experience he had gained from climbing with some of the world's greatest mountaineers. He had been twice to the summit of Everest – once with Jack – and, as part of an ill-fated Japanese expedition to climb Changabang or K2 as it was better known in the West, on which ten people had died, he was one of the few men alive who had made it to the top of the world's second-highest mountain by its 'impossible' west face. As well as being a proficient climber, Hurké Gurung was also a trained soldier. Before

119

becoming a Sherpa, he had served with the Gurkha Rifles, reaching the rank of Naik, sergeant, and was a skilled tracker. But Gurung had one extra special qualification that made him indispensable to the expedition. Like Jack Furness, he too had seen a yeti.

The assistant sirdar, Ang Tsering, lacked the older man's experience but, having attended the Sir Edmund Hillary School, he could read and write, and had even visited America. Like Gurung he spoke a Sherpa dialect of Tibetan, Tibetan proper and Nepali. His English was better than the sirdar's although he spoke it with such archaic formality that he sometimes sounded like a character from a novel by Henry James. He also spoke some German which Jutta Henze, the expedition doctor, was determined to help him better. Tall, slenderly built, with a sea-urchin haircut, almost lidless eyes, a broad nose, and an uncertain smile, Tsering was a cautious-looking man. In the smart new winter clothes he had been given for the expedition, and with a Yak cigarette rarely absent from his mouth, he reminded Swift most of some cocksure French ski-instructor. Jack told her that this was not so very wide of the mark since Tsering had no experience of mountaineering or scientific expeditions, only of guiding tourist treks, and that the Western women who went walking in the Himalayas often had affairs with their guides.

Jack thought that Jutta Henze was just the type to pick and choose the men with whom she had affairs. Powerfully built with strawberry blonde hair and a shower of russet freckles, she was a terracotta warrior of a woman, a neo-classical ideal of what a heroine on the grand scale ought to look like. The eighteen-month widow of Gunther Henze, the famous German mountaineer killed on the Matterhorn, Jutta was an experienced climber in her own right, with a steely aspect in her blue-jade eyes that seemed to speak of both tragedy overcome and devotion to her sport and the freedom it provided. Swift thought the big German looked ruthless, as if, like Liberty leading the People, Jutta might not care if her way ahead lay across the bodies of the dead and the dying. Swift also thought her an unlikely-looking doctor, but Jack told her that as she came to know Jutta better she would understand that it was this same determination that made her such an excellent choice as the expedition's medical officer. Every member of the team was a strong personality, inclined to make light of any ailment and it took an even stronger personality to give the kind of doctor's orders that

120

were obeyed at all times and without question. Byron Cody, the team primatologist, and Lincoln Warner, a molecular anthropologist, were a case in point. Upon their arrival in Khatmandu, both men had contracted a severe form of dysentery and Jutta had ordered them confined to the CIWEC Clinic in Baluwatar until they were recovered, which meant they were a day behind the main party in leaving Chomrong for the Annapurna Sanctuary.

Dougal MacDougall was the expedition cameraman. A working-class Scotsman from Edinburgh, MacDougall had left school at sixteen to become a joiner until, deciding improbably to make a career in films, he had managed against all the odds to get a place at the London Film School. Despite never having climbed before, his first assignment for the BBC had been to join an expedition to climb the Carstenz Pyramid in New Guinea, since when MacDougall had established himself as a first-class climbing cameraman and all-round photographer of international repute.

Swift thought the Scotsman was more interested in money than in anything so creditable as a professional name. To her, he appeared a stereotypical Scot: crudely tattooed, chain-smoking, hard-drinking, foul-mouthed, argumentative, and generally deficient in manners, patience, and anything that might pass for pleasant conversation. Jack greatly admired him however, having climbed both Everest and the Kangchenjunga North Ridge with the diminutive, brick-faced Scot, and he told Swift that he hoped she and the rest of the team might never find themselves in the kind of tight spot where MacDougall could be relied upon to perform at his very best.

Miles Jameson owed his place on the team to Byron Cody, although as Director of the Chitwan National Park in southern Nepal's lowland Tarai region and as a qualified doctor of veterinary medicine, he would have always been a natural choice. Jameson had been Senior DVM at the Los Angeles Zoo when he first met Cody in connection with Cody's bestselling book about gorillas. Before that the thirty-eight-year-old white Zimbabwean had worked with Richard Leakey in the Kenyan Wildlife Service. Like Leakey, Jameson also came from a distinguished East African family. His father Max was the Director of Parks and Wildlife in Zimbabwe, while his sister Sally had made a name for herself protecting the elephants at

Zimbabwe's Whange National Park. Big cats were Jameson's special area of expertise and, more especially, LA's collection of koalas and white tigers. Tigers were also Chitwan's most important attraction for the park's fifteen thousand visitors a year and it was said that Prince Gyanendra of Nepal had been so impressed with what Jameson had achieved in LA that immediately he met the young Zimbabwean, he invited him to take over the administration of Chitwan, not to mention the command of a force of fourteen hundred soldiers that existed to protect the Park's tigers and rhinos against poachers. Chitwan had seen very few visitors since the beginning of hostilities between India and Pakistan and when he heard about the real purpose of the expedition, Jameson had pressed to join it. Tall, fair-skinned, with dark hair and blue eyes, Jameson had the impeccable manners of a diplomat which made it all the more surprising to everyone that he and MacDougall should get on so famously. They laughed at each other's jokes, discussed trout fishing with endless enthusiasm and bunked together in the Hotel Paradise Garden Lodge where their loud laughter and incessant smoking could disturb nobody but themselves.

Byron Cody preceded the last person to arrive at ABC, who was also the most academically distinguished, by almost sixty minutes. Lincoln Warner was Professor of Molecular Anthropology at the University of Georgetown in Washington and adjunct research scientist at the Smithsonian Museum of Anthropology. He looked exhausted, having carried his own pack all the way from Chomrong, unlike Cody.

'What the hell did you want to do that for?' said Jack. 'You should have got a porter to carry your gear, Professor. That's what they're for.'

'That's what I told him,' shrugged Cody.

The tall black man shook his head and dumped his rucksack on the snow outside the clamshell.

'No way,' he said. 'A porter is just a slave by another name.'

'Slaves don't get paid ten dollars a day,' remarked Cody.

Lincoln Warner glared at the older man and it was obvious that the two had already argued about porterage.

'I think that a man ought to carry his own load in life,' said Warner. 'Know what I'm saying?'

'Oh, and I suppose that computer of yours just walked up here all

122

by itself,' said Jack. 'Everyone else is using an extra lightweight laptop. But you have a desktop PC.'

'I can't do my job without that UVP. If there was a laptop powerful enough for my requirements, I'd have brought it. There isn't. But the point I'm making is that I don't see why I shouldn't carry some kind of load – anything at all – when all these other men are carrying something.'

'Well, Professor, I guess that's your choice,' said Jack. 'But the point *I'm* making is that you did a man out of a job. People round here need the money badly and carrying heavy loads on their backs, which they're very used to doing, and which they do damned well, is about the only way that they can earn it. So there's no need to feel guilty about letting them. Lots of Westerners coming here make that mistake. Fact is, the Nepalese don't understand a man who can afford to pay and yet carries a load himself. They don't think you're a good guy or a good democrat or whatever. They just think you're being mean. Isn't that so, Hurké?'

The sirdar nodded solemnly.

'It is just so, Jack sahib. Carrying loads mean plenty big money for porters. Special with not much tourists right now. For man with family this maybe biggest money all year round, sahib. Ten bucks a day make sixty from Chomrong.'

'I don't remember me saying that I had a problem with mental arithmetic,' growled Warner. 'Look, you made your point. And I'm too tired to argue. Too tired and too cold.' He grinned at Jack.

Jack clapped him on the shoulder.

'I thought you were from Chicago,' he said. 'It gets pretty cold in the windy city, doesn't it, Professor?'

'Lincoln, just call me Lincoln. Or Link. Professor makes me sound about as old as I feel right now. Actually I was born up the coast from Chicago. Place called Kenosha. Kenosha, Wisconsin. There were three good things that came out of Kenosha, Wisconsin. The first was the road south to Chicago. The second was Orson Welles. And the third was me, Lincoln Orson Warner. Like most folks in Kenosha, my momma, well she always had a thing for that old fatman.'

The forty-year-old scientist was not dissimilar to the larger-than-life Welles. Tall, slightly overweight, and with a thin moustache, Warner looked like Welles when he played Othello. Physically he made an impact, like someone who could hardly be contained. And, in common with cinema's *wünderkind*, there had been nothing in

123

Warner's background that had suggested the precocious scientific talent that, before he was thirty, made the molecular anthropologist was one of the outstanding minds of his generation. Warner had published a number of important books on the genetic implications of the human fossil record and on the biological nature of the human race. Currently he was embarked on constructing a theory to account for why some people were black and some were white. But it was his work with the DNA sequences of Australian Aborigines and orang-utans that had persuaded Swift that Lincoln Warner would be an invaluable person to have along, in the event they were lucky enough to capture a living specimen: Warner had argued that the mitochondrial DNA suggested aboriginals and orang-utans had split at a different time than African Man and African apes. From this he posited that human-like creatures had evolved separately in several different parts of the world, and had merged only subsequently. It was as radical a theory as had been constructed in the world of Palaeoanthropology during the whole of the previous decade.

The arrival of Cody and Warner took the team up to ten, not including the sirdar and his assistant who oversaw the cookboys, mail runners to carry film, and the ten or fifteen porters who came and went between ABC, Chomrong and Pokhara.

In Pokhara itself – a small village that was the gateway to Nepal's more popular trails – the expedition and its supplies were administered by Lieutenant Surjabahandur Tuhte who, like Hurké Gurung, was formerly of the Gurkha Rifles. Over a hundred and fifty kilometres away, in Khatmandu, Helen O'Connor, a Reuters news reporter, ran the expedition office from her elegant home overlooking Durbar Square. Fluent in Nepali and Hindustani, Helen maintained good contacts with the Government and, as Jack had discovered on several previous occasions, her knowledge of local bureaucracy and, more especially, Nepalese Customs and Excise, was second to none. It was Helen's good offices they would have to rely on if the Nepalese authorities got wind of the real purpose of the expedition and its forbidden location.

Connected. The digital revolution had made a tremendous difference not just to the computer nerds, but also to the intelligence community. Bryan Perrins could keep in direct touch with any agent in the field through one insouciant touch of a mouse button at the beginning of his day. Only a few years before there had existed whole departments of people manning radio receivers, reading signals traffic, analysing transmissions, and processing intelligence. Today most of those departments had been radically downsized and Perrins could open his own e-mail tray and read copies of whichever agent's reports seemed of greatest relevance. Right now he was most interested in receiving the e-mail addressed to HUSTLER that was coming straight from Nepal. He could even send e-mail straight back via a simple RSVP function that saved him from having to use the agent's codename, which in this case was CASTORP, or his electronic mail number. It was as hands-on a relationship with an agent as anyone had enjoyed since the French Minister of War had slept with Mata Hari.

Normally Perrins disapproved of field personnel including jokes in their reports, but when he read the first piece of e-mail filed from the Annapurna Sanctuary he could hardly resist enjoying CASTORP's crack that he had 'no news yeti of what he was there for'.

'Goddamn bunch of looney tunes,' laughed Perrins.

He hesitated for a moment, wondering if it was at all proper for him to respond with an equal amount of levity. After all, CASTORP might be risking his life. But it was still early days. The guy had only just got there. Why not? A little light relief might be just the encouragement he needed. So Perrins typed an e-mail back:

> **YOUR REPORT SHOWS AN ABOMINABLE LACK OF GOOD TASTE. IN FUTURE PLEASE REFER TO SNOW-PERSON. HUSTLER.**

It would be the last time that CASTORP would cause Bryan Perrins to feel amused.

Jack had no doubt that it was the CIA who had determined to use his expedition as cover for one of their operations. As to what they were up to, his best guess was that it had something to do with the Indo-Pakistan crisis. Despite the cooling-off period, it was still a crisis. There were few well-informed people who did not think that at the end of the three-month period the two sides would be at each

125

other's throats again. But precisely what the CIA were up to he could only imagine since the Annapurna Sanctuary was much closer to Nepal's border with Tibet than to India. A country controlled by Communist China, Tibet was his next best guess in accounting for the interest of the CIA. Tibet had been invaded and occupied by the Chinese in 1950, since when it had been almost impossible to gain a permit to climb a Himalayan mountain from the Tibetan side. No reasons were ever given by the authorities, but ever since he had been in the Himalayas, Jack had heard persistent rumours that the Chinese were using Tibet to build secret factories for the production of nuclear weapons, as well as building missile bases, radar stations and dumps for the disposal of radioactive waste. Could the reason the CIA wanted to be in the Sanctuary have something to do with China's nuclear arsenal?

Jack's third and last guess also involved the Chinese, and was the least comfortable proposition of all. It was that the Chinese intended to take advantage of the crisis between India and Pakistan to invade Nepal through Tibet, just as the Soviet Union had invaded Afghanistan back in 1979.

Jack would gladly have assisted any operation dedicated to preventing a war in India, or one that might frustrate any Chinese military ambitions in the region. But mostly he just felt irritated that he and his expedition colleagues were being used.

Having been on previous expeditions with Mac, Jutta, and the sirdar, he felt little reason to distrust any of them. Swift was beyond reproach, for obvious reasons. So Jack reserved his particular scrutiny for Tsering, Jameson, Cody, Warner, and Boyd, thinking it was only a matter of time before one of them would say something that might give himself away.

And when he did, Jack would be ready for him.

126

Ten

'Philosophy will clip an Angel's wings,
Conquer all mysteries by rule and line,
Empty the haunted air, and gnomed mine – .'

John Keats

Almost as soon as Lincoln Warner and Byron Cody arrived at ABC, the weather closed in. As dusk fell for a second time on the small group of people camped on the glacier basin, near white-out conditions prevailed and the wind built up in fury until it was a howling, almost animate gale.

Emerging from the shaft that led down to the appropriately named Hotel Snowland, Byron Cody found the wind literally taking his breath away. Even through his pioneer's beard it felt like a sandblasting machine against his face and he was glad that someone had thoughtfully erected a rope handrail between the lodge and the clamshell.

'What a night,' he muttered and fired a flashlight in front of him, picking out the various surrounding supply dumps tied down with ground sheets, that were shaking in the wind, as if the earth was racked by a violent fever, and then picking out the clamshell itself.

A sound like a footfall made him stop on the rope and point the powerful beam of light around the camp site. He peered into the gloomy blizzard to see if the mysterious noise would come again.

'Is someone there?' he shouted.

But there was nothing. Taking hold of the rope again, he bent into the wind and carried on walking to the clamshell. It was a distance of less than twenty metres but by the time he had covered it, wearing a Berghaus fleece and a pair of thick ski-pants, Cody felt quite numb with cold.

The first person he spoke to as he came through the airlock door was Jack.

'I thought I heard something out there,' he said, rubbing his hands together and shivering.

'Oh? Want me to come and take a look?'

Cody shrugged. He didn't relish the idea of going back outside and hunting around for something in the storm.

'No, I guess it was nothing,' he said, grinning nervously. 'Airy nothing. Except perhaps my own imagination. How easy is a bush suppos'd a bear! Or maybe a yeti. Ever since I could read I've been afraid of the dark and believe me I was a precociously early reader. This place is rather spooky in the dark. It's got me jumpy already.'

'The wind blows all kinds of shit around up here,' said Jack. 'Some of it right through your head.'

'It's a hell of a night though,' shivered Cody. 'If it's like this down here then what the hell's it like up on the south face of Annapurna?'

Jack grimaced. 'A hell of a long way from comfortable.'

'You tried to climb that sonofabitch, didn't you?'

'Tried and failed, Byron. And there's no son that comes into it. It's just a bitch, all the way. Annapurna means Goddess of Bountiful Harvests. It may have been someone's idea of a goddess, but it sure isn't mine.'

Cody sniffed the air like a hungry dog. 'What's for dinner?'

Jack grinned and jabbed a thumb back across his shoulder.

'Microwave's over there. Help yourself to an MRE.'

While the porters stayed wrapped up in their sleeping bags in the Annapurna Sanctuary Lodge, getting an early night after their exertions, the team and the two Sherpa leaders had gathered under the clamshell to have their evening meal, listen to the radio, and talk. Chairs and tables had been borrowed from the lodges and with the temperature inside the inflatable building a reasonably warm twelve degrees Centigrade, the team sat around eating their MREs and trying to ignore the storm outside on the glacier. Now and then they would hear an especially loud, howitzer-sized gust of wind and someone would emit a quiet whistle and lay a hand on the fabric of the clamshell, wondering how it managed to hold up against the storm.

As if to compensate for the inhospitable weather, everyone went

128

out of their way to be pleasant to each other, although it was clear that the altitude had already left one or two members of the team feeling restless and irritable. Boyd produced a bottle of bourbon and it was not long before they started to debate the subject of their expedition.

'I don't figure he'll come tonight,' said Cody. 'Not in this storm at any rate.' He took off the rimless glasses that lent him his Karl-Marx-in-the-British-Library look, and started to clean them vigorously.

'Who?' asked Jutta.

'The yeti, of course.'

Boyd laughed scornfully and knocked back his drink. He said, 'I don't figure he'll come at all,' and poured himself another generous shot.

Quickly the team divided itself into three groups of opinion: Swift, Jack, Byron Cody, Dougal MacDougall, Hurké Gurung and Ang Tsering, who all believed in the existence of the creature; Jutta Henze, Miles Jameson and Lincoln Warner, who were all agnostics; and Boyd, who dismissed the yeti as a traveller's tale or, at best, some kind of local phenomenon for which there would prove to be a perfectly rational explanation.

'I don't see anything particularly irrational about believing that these mountains might be home to an undiscovered type of great ape,' said Cody. 'I must say I find that possibility a great deal more likely than some of the other explanations I've heard for the yeti. Freak atmospheric conditions, giant sloths and lemurs, and that kind of thing.'

'You know, I'm a little surprised at you people,' said Boyd, absently brushing his short moustache with the edge of a forefinger. 'I thought you were scientists. But this – '

He moved off his moustache and started to rub his bullet-shaped head with apparent exasperation.

'I didn't say anything back in Khat, when you told me that you were hunting something more than just a few old bones. But frankly I think you're all on a wild goose chase.'

'Have you ever been on a wild goose chase?' asked Lincoln Warner. Underneath the clamshell his deep voice sounded like Darth Vader's.

'I can't say I have,' admitted Boyd.

'Back in Wisconsin, we used to see a lot of Canada geese. Me and

129

my daddy used to hunt them sometimes. Dumbest bird I ever saw. Driven by greed and not much brain.' He grinned a dazzling white smile and wagged a long dark poker of a finger at Boyd. 'Therefore my friend, speaking as someone who *has* been on a wild goose chase, I have to tell you that it's not half as difficult as it sounds. Those birds were easier to shoot than an empty beer bottle.'

Swift was silent for a moment. Back in Washington she had quite liked Boyd. But in Khatmandu, he had made a half-hearted pass at her in the hotel after a night on the beers and Swift, who had had a few drinks herself, told Boyd that there was more chance of her sleeping with a yak than there was of her going to bed with him. Now, out here, his scepticism struck her as plain rude, not to mention potentially demoralising for the team as a whole. She wondered if there was something personal in this mockery of their aims. If in some small-minded way he wasn't getting back at her for turning him down so abruptly and with such crushing sarcasm.

'You know, I've been collecting old bones, as you put it, for quite a while now,' she said calmly. 'Ever since I was a child. I was never much interested in collecting stamps, or coins or whatever. I could never see the point of that kind of collection. I used to say that collecting fossils, especially human fossils, was the one kind of collection in which the proximity of individual artefacts could create a greater meaning. Well, Jon, here I think the point is that there's a possibility that we have the chance of finding, for want of a better phrase, a living collection. Maybe a living specimen. The search for a new truth often starts out as the most unlikely proposition. But I don't see how that endeavour can be described as a wild goose chase.'

Boyd shrugged and shook his head as if dissatisfied with his earlier figure of speech. 'A wild man chase, then.' He smirked. 'I dunno. Something crazy at any rate.' It was clear that he hadn't really been listening to what Swift had said.

Swift decided that perhaps Boyd had just drunk too much bourbon.

'So what would you say to the two people sitting here who have actually seen a yeti?' she asked. 'Jack and the sirdar.'

'Jesus, I dunno,' said Boyd and laughed. 'H-A-D, maybe.' He meant high-altitude deterioration.

'Excuse me, sahib,' said Gurung. 'But I am born in these mountains.'

'Sherpas need oxygen too,' said Boyd.

'Only not as much as the rest of us,' said Jack.

'Okay then, Hurké, answer me this,' Boyd persisted. 'When you went to the summit of Everest, was it with or without oxygen?'

'Yes, you are right, sahib. First time of ascending, it was with oxygen. The second time of ascending, with Jack sahib, it was without oxygen please. But the point is significantly made. Even Sherpas can see through things funny. And though I am most awfully sure that I saw what I saw, maybe Boyd sahib is being too polite to be stating the obvious, which is that many Sherpas are very superstitious fellows.'

Boyd nodded his approval.

'Good for you, Hurké,' he said and refilled the sirdar's glass.

For a moment none of them spoke. Then something struck the outside of the clamshell with a thud. Even Jack jumped a little and, anticipating the question, shook his head and said:

'Piece of ice probably. The wind throws all sorts of shit around up here. As soon as they bring up that chicken wire from Chomrong, we'll build a fence. Just in case.'

'Just in case of what?' laughed Boyd. 'A yeti comes cold calling?'

Jack smiled patiently.

'Just in case of avalanches. That's another reason we didn't choose to pitch down at MBC. Some of that snow on the face of Machhapuchhare looked treacherous.'

He had good reason to be nervous of avalanches on Machhapuchhare, but he felt he hardly needed to expand on his caution.

'H-A-D,' MacDougall snorted angrily. 'That's just a lot of bollocks and I'll tell you for why. Because I'm bloody sure you couldn't count what happened to me as a hallucination, pal, and that's because I didn't see a bloody thing. But I heard something though. Oh aye, of that I'm quite sure, no mistake.'

'This was on Nuptse, wasn't it, Mac?' said Swift. There was hardly a single report of an encounter with a yeti that she had not committed to the memory of her laptop and with which she was not now familiar.

MacDougall nodded. 'Nuptse, yes,' he said.

'Nuptse is one of the foothills of Everest,' Jack said for the benefit of those who were not climbers.

'At nearly eight thousand metres, it's a hell of a foothill, is that no right, Jack?'

'Right.'

'Aye, well early one morning, we were maybe up at about five and

131

a half thousand metres or so, I awoke to hear someone moving around outside our tent. I mean, proper footsteps like, y'know? Sort of slow and deliberate. Anyway at first I thought it was Jack. He and Didier had been leading and I figured they must have reached the summit early and come back down. So I called out to him. I says, Jack, is that you? No answer. So I calls him again. What, are you deaf or something, you Yank bastard? How did you get on? Did you make it? Still no bloody answer. So, I'm zipped up inside my bivvy, right? And I'm thinking to myself, what the hell's going on here? Because now I start to hear whoever it is outside opening up rucksacks and going through our gear. And for a moment, I think, Christ, we've got a bloody thief on our hands. I really can't believe it, y'know? We're five and a half thousand metres up the side of Nuptse and there's some bastard tryin' to rip us off.

'So now I start yellin' away like a bastard, telling this thievin' shite what I'm going to do to him when I get my hands on him. But just as I'm about to unzip the tent, I suddenly stop like, because I hear something that doesn't sound anything like a man breathing in and out. It's something a lot bigger than a man. Know what I mean? Like it's maybe not a man at all. And at the same time as that happens I get this musky sort of stink in my nostrils. Like an animal, y'know?'

'I get it,' said Boyd, interrupting. 'You're saying that whatever it was, the smell was abominable, right?'

MacDougall shot Boyd a homicidal look as the other man started to chuckle at his own joke.

'Aye, maybe that's right,' he said through gritted and carious teeth. 'Anyway, the next minute whatever the bastard is, it takes off. I mean really runs, and on two feet. Fast too. Very fast. Well now I'm scared. And the guy I'm sharin' the tent with, he's heard it too and he's as feared as I am. But I open the flap anyway and have a wee look out. So then. Whatever it is has vamoosed, right? No tracks, nuthin'. It was too rocky I guess. But the kit – '

Mac shivered visibly.

'It still gives me the heeby-jeebies thinkin' about it, even now. The kit, right? The kit is all spread out on the snow, as neatly as if you had laid it out on your bed for an army inspection. And on the rucksacks, wee buckles had been opened. Not broken, or chewed or anything, mind. In fact there's nuthin' damaged at all. But the buckles have just been unfastened. No animal could have done it.

Except maybe some kind of ape or monkey. Nuthin' with claws anyway. This was a job for fingers.'

Mac shook his head and stuck his small hand inside the pocket of his fleece.

'I took a picture of the scene, just as I found it. Come to think of it, probably a whole roll of film. But this one was the best. For obvious reasons I've been keeping it on me since I came on this bloody tour.'

Swift had already seen Mac's picture. Like his story it would appear in the book she was planning to write about the yeti. Even if they didn't actually find a living specimen, the skull had given her more than enough material to make some informed guesses.

Mac fixed Boyd with an accusing stare, and handed him the photograph as if daring the other man to contradict him now.

'A picture, mind? Not a hallucination. Not high-altitude deterioration. Not a Hammer horror movie. A bloody photograph.'

Mac jabbed a finger at the photograph Boyd was holding, his pale face reddening as if someone had plugged him into the Semath Johnson-Mathey fuel cell.

'You tell me what kind of hallucination could have laid out my kit like that, pal? You just tell me that.'

Another piece of ice hit the clamshell, making everyone jump with fright once again.

'Can I see that picture?' Jameson asked Boyd when he had looked at it for a few moments.

'Perhaps a langur monkey,' said Boyd, handing him the photo.

'Langur monkey, my ass,' snarled Mac. 'This was a big animal.'

'It was you yourself who said that it could have been a monkey,' argued Boyd. 'And by your own admission you never actually saw it, so you can't be sure that it was a big animal any more than a small one.'

'I believe you, Mac,' said Jameson, clapping the Scotsman on the back. 'I've never heard of a langur that was more than a metre high.'

'Me neither,' echoed Cody.

'Nor for that matter have I heard of one that strayed very far from the forest. A langur up a mountain that high would be easy meat for a snow leopard.'

For some of those who were gathered under the clamshell, Jameson's Zimbabwean accent, which sounded to an untrained ear exactly like a South African accent, was sometimes so strong that they had to strain hard to understand what he was saying. Swift thought it was another reason he and Mac seemed to get along so well. Mac's accent was equally strong and, on occasion, equally unintelligible. Their close friendship was as ineffable as it was hard to understand.

'You're Scotch, aren't you, Mac?' said Boyd.

'The word is Scottish,' he snarled. 'Scotch is something you drink, you daft Yank so-and-so.'

'Good point,' said Boyd, refilling Mac's glass and then his own. 'I was just wondering if you also happened to believe in the Loch Ness monster.'

'Not everyone from Scotland believes in the Loch Ness monster any more than all Yanks believe in Santa Claus.'

Mac snatched a packet of cigarettes out of his fleece breast pocket and lit one with an angry snap of his lighter.

Boyd raised his hands peaceably.

'Hey, what the hell do I know? Me, I don't even believe in evolution. If you ask me, it's all there in the Bible.'

'The Bible?' Mac laughed harshly. 'The Loch Ness monster and the yeti look bloody ordinary compared to what's in the bloody Bible. Christ, I've read kids' comics that seemed more probable than the Bible.'

'You don't believe in evolution?' Jack raised his eyebrows. 'That's a strange thing for a geologist to say.'

'Recent research into the age of the earth has produced evidence that our planet may be a lot younger than the Darwinists have argued,' said Boyd. 'Perhaps as young as 175,000 years. Many geologists, myself included, believe that only a catastrophist model of development can account for the way the earth is now. And that many of the important assumptions on which Darwinism rests may be wrong.'

'Darwin has been killed dozens of times,' smiled Swift. 'And yet still he refuses to lie down and be buried. With views like yours, Jon, I'm not surprised you chose to become a climatologist.'

'As it happens you're right,' he said. 'Except that I didn't exactly choose to become a climatologist. I was kind of forced into it. Because of the perceived heresy of my geological views. In my opinion, contemporary Darwinists are no less intolerant than the Spanish Inquisition.'

Byron Cody cleared his throat in an effort to head off disagreement.

'Perhaps, under the circumstances,' he said, nodding his head, and grinning, 'it would be best if we left this discussion for another time?'

Cody kept on nodding his head and grinning affably. It seemed a suitably simian kind of behaviour for the Berkeley primatologist.

Swift looked around the clamshell, at the faces of her team. Cody was right. Morale would not be well served if they had some kind of argument now, albeit a scientific one. Perhaps, she thought, as the person most responsible for bringing everyone here, I ought to say something, formally, to them all.

'Okay, let me tell you why I think that our expedition stands a reasonable chance of proving that the yeti exists, where others have failed, most notably the British expedition sponsored by the *Daily Mail* in 1953. They chose the Sherpa district of Sola Khumbu in north-eastern Nepal, to make their search.'

'It's near Everest,' said Jack. 'Rough country.'

'This isn't exactly the Hamptons,' said Lincoln Warner, as the wind reached a new crescendo.

'No, that's true,' said Swift. 'But I believe they were unsuccessful for a number of reasons, not the least of these being that this was over forty years ago, and the Himalayas were more of a mystery than they are today. We're much better equipped to find the creature than they were back in 1953.'

'And how,' murmured Jack.

'I also think that some of those other expeditions must have failed because they came at the wrong time of year. Remember this is most likely a very shy animal. Probably much more shy than a giant panda or a mountain gorilla.'

'A gorilla,' said Cody, 'will go a long way to avoid making contact with human beings.'

'During the spring, summer and fall months,' Swift continued, 'the animal might just stay higher up, away from the tourists. Perhaps it's only during the winter that the creature feels bold enough to venture lower down. When there are very few tourists. And of course now, with the tourist industry in Nepal dead on its feet because of the threatened war in the Punjab, it could be that the Himalayas are as quiet as they've been in over fifty years. Perhaps since people like us started coming, which might just be

135

the best thing this expedition has going for it.'

'It's only a good thing so long as they don't do it,' said Warner. 'So long as those assholes don't start throwing nukes about.' He shook his head nervously. 'No telling what might happen then. Might not just be the yeti's ass that's hard to find. Might be ours too.'

'Which makes it fortunate,' she said patiently, 'that they have a cooling-off period. Our window. Three months. Enough time to make a thorough search of the area, and then get out and go home.' She paused and glanced at Jack.

'But there's another factor that may give us an advantage. The Nepalese authorities think we have come here to search for fossils on Annapurna. But as some of you already know, we are in fact going to centre our search on a different mountain altogether. Machhapuchhare. Or Fish Tail Peak as some climbers call it. Machhapuchhare and its surrounding area are forbidden to climbers but since we're not actually planning to go very far up the mountain, probably no higher than about four and a half to five thousand metres, we believe that we're not so much breaking this injunction as bending it a little in the name of science. We're going to be searching an area that we know no one has ever searched before, but where there have been three separate sightings of the yeti during the last twenty-five years. And several others within the Sanctuary itself, not to mention the bones that Jack found on the slopes of Annapurna.

'It may seem like an enormous piece of optimism to just turn up here and expect to find a yeti, especially when you think about how long the creature must have remained undiscovered. But when you add all of the factors I've mentioned together, I consider that we stand an excellent chance of success. Better than anyone before us. And don't forget that by discovering the skull only two kilometres or so from where we are now, Jack has already come up with more evidence of the existence of this creature than was ever found before.

'Ladies and gentlemen, if we don't find it,' Swift added finally, 'then I don't think anyone will find it.'

Jack and Swift were the last to leave the clamshell that first night. After the others had gone to bed, the two stayed up with no other purpose than to be alone. At Swift's suggestion Jack had agreed that they should bunk separately, accepting her argument that they needed to be completely focused on the expedition and that any intimacy between them could only be a distraction. So he was surprised when she put her arms around his waist and hugged him tight.

'I can't believe we're actually here,' she told him. 'Thanks, Jack. Without you it wouldn't have been possible.'

'I wish I could say it felt good to be back here,' he confessed. 'But the place makes me nervous. Like there's something I'm not doing. Maybe it's the fact that I know I'm not going to be doing any climbing. It's weird, but I'd feel a little more relaxed if I knew I was going back up that south-west face tomorrow morning. I guess it's like a motor racing driver going to a Grand Prix knowing he's not going to be driving.'

He shook his head and smiled at what he had just said. He almost convinced himself.

'That was a good speech you made, Swift.'

'You think so? I felt I needed to say something after that asshole Boyd started mouthing off about not believing in the yeti.'

'He's not so bad. You two just rub each other up the wrong way.'

'Maybe. You didn't think I sounded a little too much like a candidate? Say anything to get elected, y'know?'

'You believed what you were saying, didn't you?'

'Oh sure. But y'know . . . did they?'

Jack shrugged. 'Sometimes when you're leading an expedition like this, you have to say whatever you can to keep people on your side. Doesn't matter if people believe what you say or not. They need to see that you believe it. That's what leadership is about. That makes it the right thing to do.'

Swift nodded silently. Then she groaned and squeezed her temples.

'Headache?'

'Mmmm. I don't know whether it's the altitude or that bourbon.'

'Probably the altitude. You should drink plenty of water before you go to bed.'

She yawned. 'Maybe I'll be acclimatised in the morning.'

Jack laughed.

'I doubt it. Full acclimatisation to a height takes seven weeks. If you don't feel better in the morning we'll give you some Lasix.'

'If you don't mind me saying Doctor, that sounds a little hit and miss.'

137

'Up here there are really no hard and fast rules,' he explained. 'Everyone will have to find out what works best for him- or herself. Right now, a good night's sleep is probably just the ticket. If I were you I'd take a couple of Seconal and go to bed.'

'Okay,' she smiled. 'I'm convinced.'

They pulled on their stormproof outer clothing and ventured out into the freezing night and a wind so strong it almost bowled Swift off her feet. Eyes closed against the wind she held on to Jack's clothing for support. He shouted something at her, but whatever he said was borne quickly down the glacier in the general maelstrom of sound and air. After several laborious minutes' walk along the rope handrail they reached the open snow shaft that led straight down to the lodges. Jack motioned her to go first and then followed her down the ladder.

At the bottom of the shaft, Swift kissed him goodnight before going into her cold dark room. Having taken a Seconal with a large glass of water as Jack had instructed, she removed her outer layer once again and then climbed up on to her bunk and into her sleeping bag, feeling a little like a premature burial in a story by Edgar Allan Poe. Jutta Henze, lying on the bunk below, was already asleep, apparently untroubled by any of the feelings of claustrophobia that Swift found herself trying to overcome. As she waited for the sleeping pill to take effect, she listened to the wind and tried to distinguish the many different sounds she could hear in it: the roll of kettledrums; a large bath towel pegged securely to a washing line; distant gunfire – El Alamein; a newspaper shaken and folded in half; a train rushing past an empty platform. The Himalayan wind it seemed was a living thing of air, and could even become a voice: a crying child, a screaming peacock, or a soul in limbo; and sometimes, if she tried really hard, she could hear the howl of a mythical ape-man of the mountains . . .

Eleven

'I was impressed and mystified by these prints. But my Sherpas looked and had no doubt. Sonam Tensing, a highly sensible fellow who I have known for many years, said "That is the Yeti." I have an open mind. I have formed no opinion. But my Sherpas looked and had no doubt.'

Sir Eric Shipton

The day dawned brightly after the stormy night, with a sky as blue as the Buddha's eyes and the sun turning snow and rock to precious gold. But any feeling of warmth was purely aesthetic for the wind still blew periodically in short, buffeting gusts that were cold enough to finish a sentence, close a watery eye, or turn a back, and helped to keep the outside temperature down well below zero.

Jack was one of the first out of the lodges to inspect the campsite for damage. The northern edge of the clamshell was buried in snow as were several boxes of stores too large to have gone down the shafts and into the lodges, but otherwise everything seemed to have survived intact. Jack took a deep, euphoric lungful of frost-chilled air, as if here, in one of the world's most incredible glacier basins, life's breath had a special sweetness for him.

To his left, forming the southern portal of the Sanctuary, was Hiunchuli; at six thousand four hundred metres, one of the smaller peaks of the Annapurna group. It was, he thought, a shapely looking mountain, reminding him most of the head and beak of some enormous bird of prey: spindrift blew off the summit like a crest of snow-white feathers and a sharp wing of an ice-ridge curled towards Modi Peak, also known as Annapurna South.

Jack was still enjoying the air and the scenery when he heard a shout from further up the glacier basin, at the foot of the Hiunchuli ridge. Shielding his eyes against the blinding glare of the sun on the snow, for he was not yet wearing shades, Jack saw a figure waving at him. Lifting the small Leica binoculars from the cord around his neck to his eyes, he saw a camera tripod and realised that the figure was MacDougall.

Jack waved back and started towards him.

An excited-looking Mac met Jack half-way, by when it was obvious to the American what it was that had so thrilled the small Scotsman for, leading down the otherwise pristine slope of the ice-ridge, well beyond where Mac might have walked himself, and leading east around the campsite towards the Sanctuary's exit, like a long black zipper, was a trail of footprints in the snow.

'Has anyone else been out this morning? One of the Sherpas maybe.'

'No, I was the first,' insisted Mac. 'I wanted to come out and catch the sun on film as it came up over the mountains. And there they were.'

They walked back towards the line of tracks.

'For a moment I thought they were my own footprints, and then, when I saw how far up they went, I realised they couldn't be.'

The two men stopped just short of the trail. Jack dropped down on one knee to take a closer look as Mac snatched the lens cap off his Nikon and began to fire off shots.

'What do you think, Jack? It looks like it, doesn't it?'

'Could be, Mac.'

'Isn't it brilliant? I mean we've only just got here, and now this. It's like winning the lottery on your first bloody go.' He glanced at the f-stop on his camera and then at Jack. 'Whatever it was came right over the ridge and virtually straight through our camp.'

'Maybe Cody heard something last night after all.'

'Yes, of course. I'd forgotten that.' Mac shot some more film. 'Thank Christ for all that snow. The whole Sanctuary's like wet concrete. Just look at these tracks. They're perfect. Couldn't make a better picture if I'd styled and art-directed it myself.'

Jack lifted the GPS radio up from his breast and tilted his head towards the microphone. It was the sirdar who answered.

'Hurké? What's everyone doing right now?'

'Breakfast, sahib.'

140

'Well, tell them to finish their Cheerios and get their asses out here. And someone had better bring a tape measure. We've found some tracks. It looks like we almost had ourselves a visitor last night.'

Miles Jameson extended the tape measure across the length of one of the tracks in the snow, a tiny yellow metallic bridge over a pear-shaped crevasse.

'Thirty five and a half centimetres long,' he said to Swift, who was taking notes. Still holding the tape measure in place, he leaned back to let Mac take some detailed photographs for scale.

'Brilliant,' chuckled the Scotsman.

'None of the porters would come and look,' said Jutta. 'Are they frightened, Tsering?'

'Certainly, memsahib,' said the assistant sirdar. 'They are all rather superstitious, I'm afraid, and believe that to see a yeti or even hear one call signifies a bad omen. Do not be surprised if some foolish ceremony is now performed to ward off any bad luck.' He shrugged apologetically. 'Such is the character of my people.'

'If they're like this now,' said Swift, 'what will they be like if we're lucky enough to capture a living specimen?'

'American dollars can overcome any amount of potential bad luck,' replied Tsering.

'Now you're talking,' said Boyd.

Jameson probed the track with the tip of the measure and said, 'Depth, about thirty to thirty-eight centimetres.'

He squinted inside the indentation like a golfer sizing up a putt, trying to determine a contour. Then he moved on to the next track and did the same.

'It's hard to get a clear view,' he said.

Swift started to take notes again.

'The snow has tumbled into each hole. But generally speaking, it's a fairly long footprint with short toes and a longish big toe. Not as broad a footprint as I might have expected, but there are definitely no claw marks, and I'm one hundred per cent certain that this is not a bear track. It's hard to be more specific but it certainly looks like some kind of higher anthropoid at any rate.'

There were several whoops of excitement. Mac punched the air in triumph. Jutta hugged Lincoln Warner.

'What a great start,' said Swift. 'This is better than we could have hoped.'

141

'These look exactly like Shipton's photographs of the tracks he found on Everest's Menlung Glacier,' observed Mac. 'For that matter, they're the same as the ones Don Whillans photographed on Annapurna.' He chuckled delightedly. 'Christ, we've only just got here, eh?'

The sirdar squatted over the footprints for a moment, smoking thoughtfully.

'Please, sahib,' he said, flinging his cigarette away after a moment, and holding his hand out to Miles Jameson. 'May I take the Stanley Metro please?'

Realising that Hurké Gurung was talking about the tape measure, Jameson handed it over and watched him measure the distance between the footprints. Finally, the sirdar stood up and planted his own Berghaus boot in one track and then another.

'Good King Wenceslas,' joked Warner.

Gurung wobbled his head from side to side, as if uncertain about something, and said, 'Maybe almost two metres. And not very heavy. I think pretty small yeti. Maybe not full-grown. Or maybe female.'

'Do you hear that?' Mac demanded triumphantly of Jon Boyd, who stood and watched the forensic examination of the tracks with an amused, detached interest. 'The man said a yeti. Not a langur monkey. Not even the bloody Loch Ness monster. A yeti.'

'If you say so, Mac,' said Boyd. 'But like you say, it's still early days.'

'A young one or a female,' Swift repeated.

'*Hajur*, memsahib. It could be.'

'We won't know until we track it,' said Jack.

'The question is, which way?' remarked Jameson.

'How do you mean?'

'The tracks lead from a source. Do we follow the animal, or do we trace the tracks back to the source?'

Jack followed Jameson's eyes up the icy ridge connecting Hiunchuli with Annapurna South, from where the tracks had originated. The sky was still clear but the gusts of wind carrying gossamer sails of spindrift snow were so strong that they seemed to promise yet more bad weather.

'One is usually inclined to follow the tracks back to the source,' said Jameson.

'I figured on us all being here at ABC and becoming used to being above four thousand metres for a couple of days before we started going up any higher,' said Jack. 'It's about twelve to fifteen hundred metres to the top of that ridge. Hard going if you're not properly acclimatised.' He shook his head. 'Besides, the tracks lead towards Machhapuchhare and our major search area. So I guess that settles it. On this occasion I think you'd better follow the animal. Swift, Hurké, Miles? The three of you had better get going before it snows again and you lose the trail.'

'Aren't you coming?' said Swift.

'We can't all go. Besides, there are plenty of things that need to be done here.'

The sirdar nodded.

'Jack is right, memsahib. Make better hunter to be small party.'

Jameson straightened and spoke to the sirdar in Nepali.

'*Huncha. Kahile jaane?*'

'*Turantai*, Jameson sahib. Right away.'

'Good,' said the Zimbabwean, and smiled at Swift. 'Right then. I'd better go and get my gear together.'

Everyone began to trudge back towards the camp site, Jameson, Swift and Hurké outpacing the others in their eagerness to get started, leaving Mac behind to take yet more pictures. Jack walked slowly abreast with Warner, Boyd and Cody.

'You mentioned some things that needed to be done,' said Boyd. 'Anything I can help with?'

'Well,' said Jack, 'if that chicken wire arrives today, I thought I'd make a start on the avalanche barriers. Thanks for the offer, but the Sherpas will help. You might as well get started on finding your core samples.'

'Thanks, I think I will.'

'It was an avalanche up there that wiped out you and your buddy, wasn't it, Jack?' said Warner. 'There was something in *National Geographic* about it.'

'That's right.'

'Must have been terrifying for you. I can't imagine what it would be like, to be caught up there in an avalanche. Not that I would be.' The black American shook his head warily. In his brightly coloured wraparound sunglasses and expensively furred parka he looked like some kind of rap-artist. 'I like my big feet on flat ground.'

'It's hard to be sure, but I always reckoned that the actual avalanche was caused by a meteorite.'

'A meteorite, eh?' said Boyd. 'Interesting.'

'I've always wondered if that's how life got started on this planet,' said Warner. 'A few molecules on a piece of intergalactic rock? Did you know that the earliest reports of meteoritic phenomena are recorded on Egyptian papyrus, around 2000 BC?'

Warner turned towards Boyd.

'No offence intended,' he said.

'None taken,' said Boyd. 'Actually, I've always been interested in meteorites myself.'

'If it was a meteorite you were lucky, Jack,' said Warner. 'The one at the Hayden Planetarium in New York weighs thirty tons. Any idea where yours might have come down?'

'Are you thinking of looking for a souvenir?' laughed Boyd. 'Thirty tonnes of rock is a lot of excess baggage to take back to the States.'

'I was just curious.'

'Hard to be sure,' admitted Jack. 'But I had the idea that it came down behind us, somewhere on the glacier to the south of us.' He pointed in front of them, along the line of strange new tracks, beyond ABC, towards the entrance to the Sanctuary itself. 'That way. Towards Machhapuchhare.'

'Fish Tail Peak, eh?' mused Cody 'Yes, it does kind of look like one, doesn't it? What is that? About six or six and a half thousand?'

'Six thousand nine hundred and ninety-two,' said Jack.

'One hell of a walk, anyway,' Boyd guffawed.

'Technically speaking, it's not a particularly difficult climb.'

'They really believe that it's a holy mountain?' said Warner. 'The sacred home of the gods and all that jazz?'

'They do believe it,' affirmed Jack.

'That kind of stuff hardly seems possible in this day and age.'

'The longer you stay here,' said Jack, 'the more it will seem possible.'

The use of drugs for the restraint and immobilisation of wild animals was routine for Miles Jameson. During his time at the Los Angeles Zoo, Jameson had drugged everything, from an Indian elephant to an axolotl. He had used many of the chemical agents in his arsenal for two decades, almost as long as they had been around. But his preferred system for delivering a chemical restraint – a blowpipe – had been around for much longer. Working in the zoo,

144

Jameson had most often used a blowpipe that had been presented to him by some Ecuadorean Indians on one of his many specimen-hunting trips to Central America: a two-metre length of hollowed bamboo, the blowpipe had an effective range of fifteen to twenty metres, offering silent projection-anaesthesia with minimum trauma upon impact. Jameson had brought the blowpipe with him to the Chitwan National Park. But faced with the task of immobilising an animal in the high winds of the Himalayas, and over large distances, Jameson thought he would have little choice but to use a rifle.

As well as a selection of modified air pistols for the general use of members of the expedition, he had brought two pairs of Palmer Cap-Chur projector guns up from Chitwan. The first pair were two long-range rifles powered by compressed carbon dioxide, with a range of thirty-two metres. But it was to the second pair of guns that Jameson was trusting the most: these were two extra long-range Zuluarms rifles, each of them utilising a modified over-and-under combination of 0.22 calibre rifle and twenty-eight gauge shotgun, powered by percussion caps and accurate up to seventy-five metres. The Zuluarms rifle fired a special Cap-Chur aluminium-bodied syringe that was not dissimilar to the kind that Jameson used in his Ecuadorean blowpipe.

The choice of chemical restraint was more problematic. Liquid injected with excessive pressure could tear muscle. Worse, it was often fifteen or twenty minutes before complete immobilisation was effected – perhaps longer in the freezing conditions of the Himalayas – by which time an animal could be lost and, unassisted, might even die from respiratory depression. Most complicated of all was the calculation of a safe but effective dose for an animal that Jameson had neither seen nor knew anything about.

With great apes in the LA Zoo, he had always favoured the use of Ketamine Hydrochloride. The one side-effect of Ketamine was the hallucinations it induced, of which Jameson had personal experience having once accidentally injected himself with a dose intended for a chimpanzee.

Ketamine dosage in great apes was 2–3 milligrammes per kilogramme of body weight. Miles had little alternative but to guess the weight of the creature as in the neighbourhood of two hundred to hundred and twenty-five kilos based on the descriptions given by Jack and the sirdar of a yeti as being about a third larger than a big silverback gorilla. But following the sirdar's examination of the tracks and his pronounced opinion that this was a smaller yeti they were tracking, he had also prepared a Cap-Chur syringe containing a much weaker dose.

Before leaving ABC, Jameson checked the massive squeeze cage he and some Sherpas had assembled the previous day. If they were lucky enough to capture a live specimen this was where it would be kept. Transporting it there, on a stretcher, would be rather less simple, and he thought that, weather permitting, they might just have to call in the helicopter.

Jameson selected the Zuluarms, inserted a percussion cap into the rifle barrel, and a weaker-strength Cap-Chur syringe into the shotgun barrel. Then he slipped the safety catch on, pocketed a couple of spare syringes, which were plugged at the tip, collected his binoculars, slung the rifle over his shoulder, and went up the ladder of the lodge to find Swift and the sirdar.

Twelve

'The great tragedy of Science – the slaying of a beautiful hypothesis by an ugly fact.'

T.H. Huxley

The yeti, or whatever animal it was, had headed straight down the valley towards the site of what in summer was MBC – Machhapuch- hare Base Camp where, at the foot of Shiva's special mountain, two or three lodges were also buried under several metres of snow. Four hundred and twenty-five metres lower down than ABC, it was a trek of about one and a half hours. The tracks were easy to follow and seemed almost human in their apparent single-mindedness, observing an almost straight line until, after over an hour of walk- ing, the sirdar pointed to some marks in the snow where the crea- ture had apparently sat down upon a rock.

'Yeti, him get tired,' he laughed.

'I know just how he feels,' Swift said wearily.

'Are you okay, memsahib?'

'Nothing I can't handle, Hurké.'

'Maybe he stopped for a cigarette,' Jameson suggested and light- ing one for himself shook the packet at the sirdar.

'Yeti is Marlboro man too, eh?' He shook his head at the offered cigarette. 'But better no time to waste, Jameson sahib. Weather will change soon I think. Not good for us. Not good for trail. Only good for yeti.'

He pointed up the valley from where they had just come.

'Jesus,' said Swift. 'I didn't notice that.'

When they had started walking the sky had been bright blue. Only

147

fifteen minutes before she had looked up and seen a few clouds beginning to surround the sun like grey wolves drawn to the heat of a campfire. Now she saw a mist following them down so that it was impossible to see more than a hundred metres back up the trail. The effect was an eerie one for it was almost as if the mist was trailing them, just as they themselves were trailing the mysterious creature.

'Weather change very quick in Himalaya,' said the sirdar, and started walking again.

Another thirty minutes of walking took them past Machhapuch-hare.

'Perhaps the yeti knows that it's forbidden to climb Machhapuch-hare,' laughed Miles Jameson. 'Just like the rest of us.'

'I had the same thought,' smiled Swift.

'I'm just glad we don't have to start climbing again. I don't think we'd have got very far up that mountain today.'

The trail soon brought them to the Sanctuary's exit and, crossing several streams that flowed too fast to freeze, they passed through a gully that ran alongside a sparse wood. Sometimes Swift lost sight of the tracks altogether as the creature jumped over streams, or used yak ledges inside the gully, yet somehow the sirdar always managed to divine where the tracks were to be found. But finally, as the mist engulfed them like a cold shroud and they could scarcely see each other, even he lost the trail.

'*Ek chhin, ek chhin,*' he muttered as his keen Gurkha's eyes hunted across the snow-covered ground. 'One moment please, sahibs. *Kun dishaa? Kun dishaa?*'

'What direction?' said Jameson, translating for Swift's benefit.

'*Huncha,*' said the sirdar, straightening to face them once again. 'You wait here please. I look around, maybe ten, maybe fifteen minutes. Try find trail then come back here, *huncha?*'

'*Huncha,*' nodded Jameson.

The sirdar placed the palms of his woollen gloved hands together in front of his face, as if to pray.

'*Namaskaar,*' he said.

'*Namaste,*' said Jameson, returning the gesture.

The sirdar walked quickly away.

'Please do not wander off, sahibs,' he called over his shoulder. 'Sherpa know country, even in fog, even in white-out. But danger-ous for sahibs.'

A second later he had disappeared like a ghost.

148

Jameson lit another cigarette and kicked uncertainly at the snow beneath his feet. Swift blew her nose and then shivered.

'I guess he knows what he's doing,' said Swift.

'He's a good man,' said Jameson and unslung the rifle.

'I must say I wouldn't fancy trying to get back up to ABC without him.' She looked around uncomfortably. 'This weather's pure . . . Wilkie Collins.'

'English writer, is that?'

Swift nodded.

'It's a bastard, isn't it? Chances are that if we do stumble across a yeti, we'll be too close for me to use the rifle. Anything closer than twenty metres and the whole syringe might cause a fracture, or even drive straight through its body. I wish I'd thought to bring along one of the pistols.'

'Is that possible? I mean that you might injure it?'

'For sure, yes.' Jameson puffed impatiently. 'But even if I did manage to dart the beast, I'm not sure I want to go chasing after it in these sort of conditions. I mean, some sort of chase is mandatory. We could break a leg, or worse. No, the more I think about it – '

Jameson broke the gun in half, removed the syringe, corked its quill-like tip carefully, and then pocketed it.

'Just in case I'm tempted,' he explained.

Swift nodded. 'I think you're absolutely right.'

It was then that they heard a shout from somewhere up ahead. The sirdar had found something.

'*U yahaa*,' he called. 'Over here, sahibs.'

Jameson yelled back: '*Haani aau-dai chhau*.'

He and Swift started down the gully in the direction of the sirdar's voice.

'It would be just our bastard luck, wouldn't it?' said Jameson. 'If we came across one now.'

Boyd let the search party of three get about half an hour ahead up the trail of strange footsteps and then set out along the same south-easterly bearing. From time to time he stopped and appeared to check his position with the aid of a handheld electronic device. Along the way he considered the nature of the animal the other three were tracking. It amazed him that there were scientists who could subscribe to this kind of wishful thinking. Even if there was some sort of creature it had remained virtually undetected throughout human

149

history. And they just expected to be able to roll up and find it. He assumed there would be some rational explanation for the strange tracks and one that did not include the abominable snowman. A bear perhaps. Or even a giant Himalayan eagle. He still recalled the fright he had received when coming upon one of these rare birds on the trek up from Chomrong. How much like an ape it had looked from behind as it squatted on the ground. Even the huge footprints left by this enormous bird of prey had looked to be the kind that would be easily mistaken for those of a giant ape. The more he thought about it, the more he was sure that it would turn out to be an eagle after all. Possibly even the same eagle. The thought made him laugh out loud and he almost wished he could have been there if and when they ever caught up with whatever it was.

Still laughing he stopped, dropped his rucksack and prepared to take a core sample.

The mist was lifting as quickly as it had descended when Swift and Jameson mounted the crest of the gully and, where the stream of the Modi Khola widened, they came upon a small range of signposts that indicated a holy place.

Here they found a Tarch, a little wigwam of rag and paper banners that fluttered at the tip of long wooden poles, like so much washing left out to dry in the stiffening wind; a rock with some sacred symbols and mantras that were painted in green; and a small Chorten, which was a conical-shaped reliquary, built of red bricks and symbolising the four elements. Then they saw the sirdar.

Smiling apologetically he led them through the thinning mist along the river bed and pointed towards a spit of snow that extended into the fast-flowing river.

An extraordinary sight greeted their eyes. But it was not the one for which they had walked several kilometres.

There, his whole weight resting on hands that were firmly placed on a large flat rock, his brown body parallel to the snow-covered ground, with his long legs stretched out straight and his bare feet together, his long hair hanging down over his face in Medusa-like coils, and naked but for a small loincloth, was a man.

For a moment Swift and Jameson were too astounded to say anything. With the temperature at fifteen degrees Celsius below zero neither one of them had considered the possibility that the tracks in the snow might have been made by a bare human foot.

150

'Our yeti I think,' Jameson said finally. 'Boyd is going to love this when we tell him, the bastard.'

'Who is he?' an exasperated Swift demanded of the sirdar. 'And what's he doing here?'

'It is kind of a strange place to do your yoga exercises,' observed Jameson.

'Hindu Sadhu,' explained Hurké Gurung. 'A follower of the Lord Shiva.'

He pointed at a wooden trident that lay on the ground next to a thin discarded robe, as if this would mean something to them both.

'Had to stop here because of fog, just like us. Him practising *Tum-mo* yoga. Very good for heat preservation, not need any clothes.' The sirdar rubbed his stomach as if indicating that he was hungry. 'Him very warm on inside.'

'God, I'm freezing to death just looking at him,' admitted Jameson.

'Me too,' said Swift.

'This position called *Mayurasana*. But afraid not know English for *Mayura*.'

'A peacock,' said Jameson. He shrugged as if trying to judge the accuracy of the name. 'Yes, I suppose so. Before the peacock lifts up its trailing tail feathers to form a fan, the whole tail sticks out parallel to the ground.'

The sirdar continued to rub his stomach. 'Just so, sahib. Make very good belly muscles too.'

'I'll bet.'

'As *Mayura* kills snake, so *Mayura* kills poisons in body. Generate much heat. Just like Semath Johnson-Mathey fuel cell.'

Slowly the sadhu lowered his feet on to the snow and then adopted *Padmasana*, the lotus position.

Bowing several times, Hurké Gurung greeted the sadhu with a *namaste* and, when the heavily bearded ascetic returned the greeting, he began to speak to him.

'*O, daai. Namaste. Sadhuji, tapaa kahaa jaanu huncha? Bhannuhos?*'

The two men spoke for several minutes and throughout most of their conversation, the sirdar kept his hands pressed together, as if praying to the sadhu. At last, the sirdar turned toward the two Westerners.

'This is a most holy man,' he explained in tones of great reverence. 'He is the Swami Chandare, a Dasnami Sannyasin of the great

151

Lord Shiva. He has taken most strict vow of nothingness to put his mind to physical and spiritual disciplines.'

The swami nodded slowly as if he understood what the sirdar was saying.

'His life is spent walking around Machhapuchhare, which he says is the body of the Lord Shiva, the destroyer of all things, in order to make way for new creations. Formerly he was in India, to be near to another mountain. Shivling, it is called, which, he says – I am sorry, memsahib, to say such words in your presence – he says it is the thing of the Lord Shiva.'

The sirdar shook his head with mild disapproval and added, 'How, ever after, I have seen this mountain and it is only the sun's shadow on the mountain which is sometimes looking like a man's thing. *Huncha.* I have said to him that we are most scientifically minded people who have come to search for yeti and the swami now asks, Why are you wishing to find it, please?'

'Has the swami seen a yeti, Hurké?' said Swift.

'Oh yes please, memsahib. Once upon a time, while praying on lower slopes of Machhapuchhare, a yeti came along carrying a great stone under his mighty arm. The yeti look very fierce, very strong. But the Swami, he was not at all scared. Over years he has seen many times yeti but never harm come to him. Only because yeti know he mean no harm to yeti. Understand? Yeti even help Swami with *dhyana*. Jameson sahib, English *bhaasha maa kasari dhyana bhanchha?*'

'Meditation,' said Jameson.

'Meditation, yes,' nodded the sirdar. 'Swami, him say that yeti not speak to him, but very clever.'

The swami spoke again to Hurké Gurung.

'Swami asking why we want find yeti, again please.'

'Tell him that we mean the yeti no harm,' said Swift. 'We just want a chance to study it.'

'Then why bring this gun please?' said Gurung, translating the swami's reply.

Holding it by the fabric tail piece, Jameson took the Cap-Chur syringe out of his pocket, and breaking the gun in half demonstrated how it slid into the barrel. Then, removing it once more, he explained in fluent Nepali that his rifle only contained a small amount of sleeping draught, sufficient to immobilise the creature for an hour or less.

The swami closed his eyes for a moment and muttered something under his breath. When he spoke again, it was in English.

'To understand the intelligence of a yeti,' he said in a thin, reedy little voice, 'you must be twice as clever as he is. And this is a very clever being. How else would he have avoided capture and study for so long? Are you twice as intelligent, or merely twice as arrogant?'

Swift and Jameson exchanged a look of surprise.

'You speak English,' Swift said.

'Since I am speaking it already, you cannot mean me to treat that remark as a question. And as a remark it is of course redundant. Why should you be surprised? Under our constitution, which is the lengthiest written constitution in the world, English is one of India's official languages. With no definite date set for its abandonment. Before becoming as you see me now, I was a lawyer.'

'Just like Gandhi,' murmured Jameson.

'In that and in that alone,' returned the swami. 'So what is it about the yeti that you hope to learn?'

'We hope that by learning about the yeti, we may learn more about ourselves,' said Swift.

The swami sighed wearily.

'He who has understanding is careful and ever pure, reaches the end of the journey from which he never returns. But it is natural to search as you do. From where do we come? By what power do we live? Where do we find rest? Beyond senses are their objects and beyond these is the mind and beyond that is pure reason. To know the answers to these questions however is not always a source of much comfort and satisfaction, for beyond reason is the spirit in Man.

'Science shifts Man away from the centre of the Universe. Is it not so? Shifts him so far away that he feels small and insignificant. There is a truth, yes? But not a very satisfactory one. Strive for the highest and be in the light, but the path is as narrow as the edge of a razor and difficult to tread. We are all of us fascinated by physical ties of ancestry. Is it not so? In the West people try to find that which was lost through their family trees. But why is so much forgotten? Why is it difficult? Why are there so few of us who can follow our lines of descent? Perhaps it was not meant to be. Perhaps it is better after all to live in ignorance of such things.'

'I can't believe that it's good to live in ignorance of anything,' said Swift.

153

'Once,' said the swami, 'there was a man who tried to search out his ancestors. Along the way he discovered that the woman who was his mother was in fact his aunt, and that the woman he had always known as his aunt was in fact his mother. Having found much more than he had bargained for the man became very angry with both women and sent them away. Now he has neither a mother nor an aunt. Shake the branches of a complacent-looking tree, if you wish. Fruit may indeed fall into your lap. You may even be nourished by it. But do not be surprised if the branch breaks off in your hand.' The swami giggled. 'The tree of life has many such surprises. Your words and your minds go to Him, but they reach Him not and return. Know the thinker, not the thought.'

So saying the swami stood up, collected his robe and gathered it around his bony shoulders, picked up his staff and set off once again, leaving behind the now mockingly familiar prints of his bare feet in the snow.

'What an extraordinary man,' said Swift, as they watched the swami go.

'Yes, he is rather impressive,' said Jameson.

'Oh yes, sahib. A most holy and religious man.'

Swift grunted. 'That's not what I meant.'

'Oh? What did you mean?'

'The Universe is exactly the way it should be if there is no super-natural design, no purpose, just complete indifference. To me it seems quite extraordinary that we should try and equip it with any meaning other than a purely scientific one.'

'Swift, you're much too elemental,' chuckled Jameson. 'If the gods do intervene it's because we need to believe we're more than just a few atoms. It's what distinguishes human nature from the rest of nature.'

Disappointed that the tracks had led them to nothing, Swift shrugged, hardly caring to argue with him.

'Come on,' she sighed. 'We'd better be getting back to camp.'

Thirteen

'The most beautiful thing we can experience is the mysterious.
It is the source of all true art and science.'

Albert Einstein

Three weeks went by, and with no sightings of the yeti or its tracks
the high spirits that had characterised the first full day on the glacier began slowly to evaporate. As the expedition team learned to
appreciate the enormous size of the Sanctuary and became aware
of its many hazards, not the least of these being the extreme
weather, the scale of the task they had set themselves began to
dawn on them. Swift did her best to remain optimistic but, as the
third week gave way to the fourth, even she started to have misgiv-
ings that they might never find her living fossil, Esau. So it was to
revive her own confidence as much as anyone else's that she told the
sirdar to announce to all the Sherpas that she would pay a bonus of
fifty US dollars to the man who discovered a genuine yeti track.
Efforts among the Sherpas were redoubled but proved useless and
with each succeeding day the expedition grew more and more
demoralised.

Jack had come to believe that the expedition was attempting to
cover too much ground and decided to establish another camp, on
the slopes of Machhapuchhare, on a site he had selected through
his binoculars and named Advance Camp One. While Jutta and
Cody were to go with Ang Tsering and make a reconnaissance in a
valley close to Annapurna III that they had yet to explore, Jack
would lead Swift, Mac and Jameson up the lower slopes of
Machhapuchhare, to establish a camp where they might stay for

155

some days at a time. Warner would stay back at ABC, while Boyd was to be left to look for core samples on his own.

'We'll need a camp that's higher up,' Jack announced, with a nod in the direction of the now familiar Fish Tail. 'Chances are we'll be doing much of our searching up that way. The place I have in mind is the little island of rock you can see further down the glacier on the lower slopes of Machhapuchhare. It's what we mountaineers call a Rognon. In this snow it's going to be heavy-going, to say nothing of the higher altitude. The extra six hundred metres are going to seem like three thousand.

'I thought you said we were acclimatised already,' objected Swift.

Jack laughed. 'To just over four thousand metres, yes. Not to nearly five thousand. But this is what it's all about, folks. No sooner have you got used to one altitude than you go higher and start the whole lousy process all over again.'

He pointed after the four Sherpas, led by Hurké Gurung, who were already making steady progress down the glacier in the knee-deep snow, despite the loads they carried on their backs. To Swift they looked like tiny flies crawling over a newly iced cake.

'Come on,' said Jack. 'The sooner we get going the sooner we can come back again.'

The morning was fine but Jack's party made slow work of following the Sherpas, who were soon out of sight in an ice field. They had marked the route with bamboo flag-poles and the party had no problem trailing them. By the time they reached a series of jagged looking ice-towers however, Swift and Jameson were feeling the effects of altitude and had been forced to take some of the acetazolamide tablets that Jutta Henze had provided for this eventuality. These dehydrated the user by making him, or her, want to urinate, and Swift was subjected to the uncomfortable experience of squatting to pee underneath icicles that hung from one of the ice-towers like the enormous fangs of some prehistoric monster.

Jack called out to her from behind another serac.

'You can sure pick a spot, I'll say that for you, Swift. One of those toothpicks falls, you're the sharp end of Dracula, honey.'

Swift finished quickly and joined the others at the beginning of a corridor that the sirdar had marked to lead them through the seracs. A little way behind them, where Jack was standing, she could see the yawning black hole of an enormous crevasse and she began to realise just how hazardous the area really was. Surrounded by a maze of precarious looking ice-towers, thorn-sharp icicles, and hidden chasms, Swift thought the place looked almost as if it had been created by some vindictive snow queen to impede their progress.

It had been a difficult year for Sherpas and porters. Because of the Indo-Pakistan war, few visitors were flying to Delhi from the West and with few direct flights to Khatmandu, tourism in Nepal had all but collapsed. Money was short. Things were as bad as Hurké Gurung could remember in all the time he had been guiding climbing expeditions in the Himalayas.

He had thought that the presence of the scientific expedition to the Annapurna Sanctuary and, more importantly, their plentiful supply of US dollars would have made those Nepalese lucky enough to find work grateful to their employers and hence more pliable. Instead the sirdar discovered that it had produced exactly the opposite effect, with every man determined to screw every last cent and perk that was going from the Americans. Several times he had found himself embarrassed by the apparently churlish demands of his fellow countrymen – demands that he was obliged, reluctantly, to put to Jack sahib: more cigarettes, more sweatshirts, more woollen pullovers, more Dachstein mitts, more fleece jackets, more woollen hats, and better footwear – in short, more of everything that could later be sold for hard currency. Hurké was very aware of how desperate the plight of his people had become, for they depended on tourist dollars to give them a small improvement in their otherwise subsistence-level living standard. He knew how rich all Westerners were in comparison. But he felt compromised, remembering the friendship and admiration he had for the man who had once saved his life. It was difficult to make extra demands of such a man, especially when the truth was that the rest of the Sherpas were acutely nervous of the object of their expedition, and potentially unreliable.

When it was a matter of plodding through deep snow at altitudes of over seven and a half thousand metres while carrying loads of three and a half kilogrammes or more, the sirdar believed that his men lacked for nothing in courage and strength. But yetis were a different story. Just the sound of a yeti – the loud whistling noise like the plaintiff call of a big bird of prey – was enough to put them in fear of their lives.

As one of the bravest and toughest of Sherpas, the so-called

'Tigers', Hurké Gurung was not himself afraid. And on the rare occasions when he did feel fear of something – usually a storm, or a route up a mountain – he did not show it. That was what being a sirdar meant.

Mac had climbed on to a bank of snow and was looking through binoculars towards the lower slopes of Machhapuchhare on the other side of the forest of ice.

'No sign of them yet.'

Jack got on the radio.

'Hurké, this is Jack. Come in please, over?'

There was a brief pause and then they all heard the calm voice of the sirdar.

'Receiving you loud and clear, Jack sahib.'

'How's the route through the glacier coming?'

'We are through, sahib. It's not very straight. But no other way could be found. Maybe you will see better way. But I think it is not as bad as the ice fall near Everest.'

'Well that's good to know.'

Jack released the talk button on the radio.

'Friend of mine was killed on that ice fall,' he said and spat into the crevasse.

'Now he tells us,' said Jameson. Raising his eyebrows, he added, 'Still, this does look like the kind of place you'd expect to see a yeti.'

'A yeti's probably got too much sense to hang around in a place like this,' said Mac.

'Mac's right,' agreed Jack. 'Time we were moving. This place gives me the creeps.'

Mac stayed where he was on the bank of snow, still looking through the binoculars.

'Come on, Mac.'

'Just a minute,' he growled irritably. He lowered the binoculars and, frowning, stared across the ice barrier towards Machhapuchhare's lower slopes. 'Probably nothing.'

'What is it?' said Swift.

Mac raised the binoculars again. 'Shouldn't they be just about to start up the mountain, towards the Rognon?'

Jack was climbing up on the snow bank beside the Scotsman. 'Yes, they should.'

'Then what are those?'

158

Mac handed him the binoculars and pointed. 'Just below the crest of the Rognon,' he said quietly. 'Around two hundred metres above the ice fall. See them?'

Jack followed the line of Mac's arm and was just able to pick out two tiny black dots standing motionless on the approach slope of the holy mountain.

'They've stopped now,' said Mac. 'But I'll swear they were moving until a moment ago.'

'I've got them,' said Jack. 'Are you sure? They look like a couple of rocks to me.'

'Course I'm bloody sure.'

'Wait a minute. You're right. They are moving.' He twisted the focus bezel, trying to improve the clarity of his view. 'It can't be the Sherpas. Even the sirdar's not that quick.'

'The Sherpas are going up,' said Mac. Throwing down his glove he began to quickly fit a long zoom lens on to the body of his camera. 'Those two look like they're coming down.'

Swift tore a monocular out of her rucksack and, taking Jack's outstretched hand, climbed up on to the snow bank beside him. She pointed it towards the Rognon.

'Yes, I see them,' she said excitedly.

Her heart gave a leap as one of the two tiny figures started to move quickly downhill, springing from one leg to the other through deep snow.

'Christ,' breathed Jack. 'Look at that thing move.'

Mac tried to focus his long lens on the distant slope.

Jameson called the sirdar on his own radio.

'Hurké? This is Jameson.'

'Go ahead Jameson, sahib.'

'We're looking through the field glasses at the slope immediately above you. There appear to be two figures coming down towards you from the upper slopes of Machhapuchhare.'

'I not see anything, Jack sahib. But the sun is in my eyes.'

'Whatever it is looks bloody powerful,' said Mac, holding down the shutter button. The power-wind on his camera sounded like a tiny robot in perpetual motion.

'Mac, there's no whatever about it,' Swift insisted. 'They just have to be yetis.'

'Yes,' yelled Mac. His triumph echoed around the seracs, drowning out what Jameson was saying to the sirdar. Mac snatched out the roll of film and fumbled another one into the camera body. 'Christ, I hope these bloody pictures enlarge all right.'

'Say again please?' said the sirdar.

Jameson repeated himself in Nepali.

'*Haami her-chhau dui wataa yeti, timiharu ukaado maathi*,' he said.

'That just has to be some kind of great ape,' said Mac. 'It can certainly move all right.'

'The other one's moving as well now,' said Swift. 'They seem to be heading straight for the ice field and the Sherpas.'

Aware of some kind of commotion at the sirdar's end, Jameson pressed his talk button and said:

'*Ke bhayo*, Hurké? What's the matter?'

Now he could hear the raised voices of the other Sherpas and then the sirdar shouting.

'*Roknu, roknu*. Stop. *Aaunu yahaa*. Come here. *Hera. Hera!*'

'Hurké, come in please. What the hell's going on there?'

For a moment he heard a whistling noise that he thought might be feedback between his own radio and Jack's and he glanced around to see that Jack was holding the binoculars again.

The whistling noise came across the radio again and this time he recognised it for what it was. Not radio feedback. But like a big seabird, wheeling over a windswept harbour. It was the sound of a large mammal.

When the Sherpas overheard Jameson telling Hurké Gurung on the radio that two yetis were descending the slope of the mountain and heading towards the ice field, they were terrified. Terror quickly gave way to panic as they heard the snow man's distinctive call echo among the ice-towers.

Hurké Gurung shouted at them to stay where they were and even cursed them as cowards. But by then they had already dumped their loads and turned on their heels, running back the way they had come.

The ice field below Machhapuchhare, like the larger one at the foot of Annapurna, was a frozen cataract, a river whose source was to be found on the slopes of the mountain itself. Entering this frozen chaos was like walking into a minefield – something you did only with extreme care. Anyone foolish enough to rush into such a lethal obstacle did so at his immediate peril, as the many deaths in ice falls throughout the Himalayas had proved.

The first man to run was Narendra, the son of one of the other

Sherpas back at ABC – a Tiger named Ngati. The last the sirdar saw of Narendra was when he darted across instead of around a space marked by three bamboo poles. It was not fifteen minutes since Hurké had probed the snow covering the space with one of the poles and guessed at the existence of a hidden crevasse. His guess had been a good one and as soon as he ran on to the snow, Narendra disappeared screaming into the unseen chasm below.

The man behind, Ang Dawa, seeing Narendra fall to his death, veered abruptly to his right and barged into a tall and precariously balanced pinnacle of ice. The next second, Hurké heard a dull crump and several tons of snow and ice engulfed Dawa and two others, Wang Chuk and Jang Po. A fifth man, Danu, leapt out of the fatal path of the falling serac only to find that his almost superhuman jump had brought him to the lip of yet another crevasse. For a brief second he swung his arms like a windmill as he tried to regain his balance before his feet slipped from under him and, emitting a cry of horror that lasted for several seconds after he too disappeared from sight, the man fell to his death.

Trembling, sick to his stomach, the sirdar sat down heavily on the snow and watched helplessly as a huge cloud of ice particles, like the vapour from some enormous explosion, mushroomed above the fallen tower and then slowly dissipated.

Jack's voice on the radio jolted him from his stunned contemplation of the disaster that had befallen his men.

'Hurké? Come in please. It's Jack.'

'Jack sahib.'

'Are you okay?'

'Not okay, sahib. The men are dead. They ran away, sahib. They ran back into the ice field and now – '

He stopped talking and looked around. A loud, vocalised sound on the slope above him, like a series of sustained belches, followed by some harsher, staccato grunts that sounded like the pigs feeding in his village, and then a sharp whistle, reminded the sirdar why the others had run away in the first place.

'How many did he say were dead?'

'Five men,' said Jack, grimly.

'Jesus Christ. Five?'

'Hurké? Are you still there? Come in please. This is Jack calling. Over?'

The radio stayed silent for a moment.

'What the hell's the matter with him? Why doesn't he answer? Hurké? Come in please.'

Then Jack heard a whisper.

'Jack sahib, shut up please. Don't say anything at all for my pity's sake. They're here.'

Swift jumped down from the snow bank and started along the trail marked by the unfortunate party of Sherpas.

'Come on,' she said. 'There's no time to lose.'

With long stooping strides, their powerful arms hanging down by their sides, the two creatures came down the slope of the mountain and were about to enter the ice field when they caught sight of the sirdar, and stopped. No more than thirty metres separated the two yetis from Hurké Gurung. The first and only other time he had seen a yeti it had been at a distance of at least a hundred metres with the animal moving away at speed. but now he was close enough to see that each creature was a big male, at least two metres high, very thickset and the general shape of a human being, like a gorilla, but covered in short and reddish-brown hair that was more like an orang-utan. The head was very large and pointed, the face bare and flatter than a man's, although not so flat as an ape's.

Instinct told the sirdar to remain quiet and still, for it was plain that the yetis were both immensely strong and he had the impression that he had only to make a sudden move and they would tear him apart. The sirdar desperately wanted to run away. But even if he did manage to get a few metres' start on them, what then? His only escape route was back through the ice field and the way that had been marked with bamboo poles was now a shambles. It seemed certain that running away, he could only end up like the rest of the Sherpas, buried under a tower of ice blocks, or falling down a hidden crevasse. So he remained where he was, feeling more terror than he had ever felt before, and prayed to every god he knew that the two yetis might lose interest in him and move on.

Fourteen

'. . . a monkey converted to Buddhism lived as a hermit in the mountains, and was loved and married by a demonness; their offspring also had long hair and tails, and these were the mi-teh kang-mi, the "man-thing of the snows" – the yeti.'

Peter Matthiessen

Lincoln Warner looked at all the computers and laboratory equipment that had been set up under the clamshell, feeling irritable. He thought of the numerous facilities that were available to him in this remote part of the world – mapping, linkage, gene expression, DNA sequencing, remote spectroscopy, microphotometry, quantitative fluorescent imaging, and many more besides – and let out a sigh. He was bored. In the three weeks he had spent in the Sanctuary he had set up the Gel Analysis software and checked the concentrations of his DNA and RNA isolation reagents. The rest of the time he had occupied himself with playing chess on the computer, listening to music on his CD Walkman, reading books, walking on the glacier, and generally hoping that the rest of his colleagues might make the zoological find of the century that would provide him with some material to work on. But he was beginning to think the odds were surely stacked against something so remarkable. Probably the best they were going to come up with were a few minutes of film shot from a distance of several hundred metres that might or might not show some kind of Himalayan anthropoid. He was beginning to regret not having resisted the pressure on him that he should come. The chances were that he would see out the duration of the expedition having improved his chess game and not much else. About the

163

only thing he had achieved so far had been his mastery of the PASS program.

Written by one of his colleagues at Georgetown University in Washington DC, the Phylogenetic Analysis and Simulation Software was a method of predicting how evolutionary trees were joined together through their mitochondrial chromosomes and how these DNA connections might be affected by changes in environment. Back in 1987 Berkeley biochemists had announced to the scientific world how their studies of DNA had revealed that all human beings shared common ancestry with a single African female who had lived some two hundred thousand years ago – the so-called Mitochondrial Eve. But Lincoln Warner had come to suspect that humans were once possessed of more than one kind of DNA and that there was little real evidence for the assumption that Eve must have been an African. He was even sceptical as to one of the most fundamental of anthropological tenets: that the human species had possessed one single origin. Evolution, it was always argued, did not work any other way: new species would only become established through unique speciation events. Lincoln Warner was not so sure, and the more he toyed with the large number of theoretical evolutionary possibilities that were made available through the PASS program, the more he supported the concept of multi-regional evolution.

One environmental possibility posed by the PASS program was the so-called holocaust mutation scenario: would a flow of new harmful mutations resulting from some sort of nuclear catastrophe damage the basic genetic structure of the human species forever? Warner hoped that neither he nor his friend in Washington would ever find out.

Catching sight of his own reflection in the empty black screen of his desktop computer he shook his head sadly. The chin beard he had grown in the month he had been in the Sanctuary was, he decided, not working. It may have helped to keep his face warm outside, but it itched terribly. It would have to go.

Warner glanced at his wristwatch and saw that it was time to call the search parties. As the only member of the team remaining at ABC it was his job to keep an eye on the weather station and make sure that everyone was kept up to date with his readings.

He pulled on his expensive fur-lined Parka jacket and went outside to where the anemometer was whirling round in the almost continual wind like the blades of a tiny helicopter. He pressed a few keys on the weatherproof-keyboard and noted down the readings that were displayed digitally on the cigarette packet-sized display screen. It looked as though the high pressure that had brought a blue sky to the Himalayas was set to continue for a while and for once he would have good news to report.

Warner went back inside the clamshell and, shrugging off his jacket, sat down in front of the communications control centre that Boyd and Jack had rigged up in one corner.

Oblivious to the effect his routine radio-call would produce up on Machhapuchhare, Warner picked up the handset.

'ABC calling Hurké Gurung. ABC calling Hurké Gurung. Are you receiving me? Over?'

The sound of Hurké's radio shattered the frozen silence of the glacier like a hammer against a pane of glass, scaring the two yetis and compelling them instinctively to adopt their most defensive behaviour. Teeth bared and with deafening screams they charged their way down what remained of the slope, on two feet, straight to the sirdar who, believing his last moments had come and that he was about to be torn to pieces, made a *namaste* with his hands, bowed his head and sank slowly to his knees.

This submissive pose saved the sirdar's life.

The bigger of the two yetis, whose red hair was almost silver-coloured on his back, braked to a halt just over half a metre short of the kneeling figure of the Sherpa.

Hurké felt something torn from his jacket and, with eyes closed, he braced himself for a blow from an enormously powerful arm. But when, after several minutes, the two yetis stopped screaming and he found himself still unscathed, he felt able to risk opening first one eye and then the other.

Both creatures were crouched in front of him on all fours, like two enormous football players, the hair on each of their pointed head-crests fully erect, and their large yellow teeth fully exposed for maximum aggression. His eye met the enraged red iris of the smaller yeti and the creature roared its disapproval.

Once again, the sirdar closed his eyes and whispered a short prayer as he realised that in his terror of the yeti, he had soiled himself.

Gradually he became aware of the smell produced by the results of his own reflexive action. But it was as nothing compared to the strong smell of the yetis. As soon as they had charged him he had become aware of an overpoweringly pungent stink polluting the fresh mountain air, like the smell produced in a place where there were a great many cats. It was so strong he almost gagged and the sirdar wondered if this was not some kind of fear odour that had been secreted by the frightened yetis. He was certain that their fear was as nothing beside his own.

For a moment the smell seemed to grow more intense and, opening one eye a fraction again, he saw that the creature was now dropping dung. Disgust turned to horror as the yeti reached under its backside, caught the coil of dung before it hit the snow and consumed this fecal matter as if it had been the tastiest of morsels.

Hurké's gagging revulsion became a cough and the sound was enough to set the two yetis screaming hysterically in his face once more, only this time so close that he felt the heat of their breath and the sting of their spittle on his pale cheeks. But still they did not hit or bite him and gradually the sirdar began to think that they only meant to intimidate him. For the next thirty minutes the sirdar's slightest movement resulted in another bout of roaring to keep him cowed until the two creatures were absolutely sure that he posed no threat to them.

It was the longest thirty minutes of Hurké Gurung's life.

When at last the two yetis returned back up the slope of the mountain, towards the Rognon from where they had come, the sirdar offered up a prayer of thanks to the Lord Shiva for his deliverance.

He was still kneeling in prayer when Jack and the others found him.

Fifteen

'Talk of mysteries! Think of our life in nature – daily to be
shown matter, to come into contact with it – rocks, trees, wind
on our cheeks! the *solid* earth! the *actual* world! the *common*
sense! *Contact! Contact! Who* are we? *Where* are we?'

Henry Thoreau

Jack lit a cigarette and inserted it between the sirdar's bluish trembling lips. Inspecting the mangled radio that the yeti had torn from
Hurké's stormproof jacket, he said: 'Looks like this fella's got a hell
of a handshake. I'd say you had a pretty lucky escape, Hurké.'

The sirdar nodded silently, his face displaying a vexed and
quizzical expression, his brow furrowed almost apologetically. Jack
was shocked to see that there were tears welling up in his friend's
eyes. He wondered if these were tears of gratitude at having come
through the experience he had just finished describing to them, or
if they were tears for the men who had died in the ice field.

Hurké Gurung sucked noisily at the cigarette and for a moment
let the puff drift around his open mouth like gun smoke before trying to force a smile past his chattering teeth.

'You've had a bad shock,' Jameson told him. 'You ought to go
back to ABC.'

'There are five men dead,' said Jack. 'Perhaps we should all go
back to ABC.'

'Like hell we should,' said Swift, and pointed up the slope of the
Rognon and the forbidden, holy mountain behind it. 'Look at those
tracks. We might never get a better trail than that. Come on, Jack,
this time we know it's the real thing.'

'Not some local mountain Maharishi,' said Jameson. 'She's right, Jack.'

Jack glanced at Mac who was taking the sirdar's photograph. 'Mac? What do you say?'

Mac shrugged. 'I say we do what we planned. We carry all this gear up to the top of the Rognon. While two of us establish Camp One, the other two can follow the trail. The weather's good. So's the forecast. There's still plenty of daylight. The lady's right, Jack. We might never get a better chance. This is what we bloody came for.'

Jack asked the sirdar if he felt up to returning to ABC on his own. 'I think yes.'

'What about the families of those men who died?' asked Swift. 'Someone will have to tell them.'

'I will do it,' added the sirdar.

Jack caught Hurké Gurung's eye and looked awkward.

'You'd better make sure they're aware that it was running away that caused their deaths. Not the yetis,' he said. 'And you can tell them that they will receive the proper compensation.'

'I understand, sahib. And you must not be reproaching yourself. It was not your fault, Jack sahib. No more than last time. It is as you say. Sherpas should not have run away. But instinctively you would wish to do so. Yeti is a pretty terrifying fellow. And what is more, he is smelling abominable, just like Boyd sahib is saying to us.'

Mac sniffed the air suspiciously. There was still a faintly musky smell hanging around the area where they had found the sirdar.

'That's the smell I remember from Nuptse,' he said.

'And you say he ate his own dung?' asked Jameson.

The sirdar grimaced.

'Yeti very dirty fellow. Him eat his own shit, yes. Like very *raagako maasu* dinner.'

'That would certainly explain why no one has ever found any yeti excrement,' observed Swift.

'Most great apes are coprophagous,' explained Jameson. 'It enables the animal to absorb some extra nutrients beyond what is available in its normal diet. It's simply a matter of squeezing every possible mineral and vitamin out of the food it eats. If you see what I mean.'

'I'll remember that,' said Jack. 'Next time I'm hungry.'

'The fact that it had a shit at all would seem to indicate that the animal was probably as scared as poor old Hurké.'

168

The sirdar shifted awkwardly inside his trousers.

'I not think so, Jameson sahib. Besides I do not think yeti is an animal. He look much more like a man. Behave like ape, maybe. But teeth not as sharp. No big dog teeth. And face not as flat as ape. Before I see him up close, face to face, I think that yeti was an animal. But now I am no sure. He is, as people say, a snow man. And now I think that is why some Sherpas are calling yeti by a different name. *Teh* is the name of this creature, sahibs. *Yeh* is meaning rocky place. Yeti means rock creature. Only some Sherpas call this fellow *Maai-teh*. Miti. *Maai* means a man. So not *Yet-teh*, but *Maai-teh*. I think this maybe a better name for what I have seen. Miti. For he was like a very big man, sahibs. A very big man creature.'

The sirdar finished his cigarette and tossed the end into the nearest crevasse. Jack lit him another and then handed him his own radio. Turning to the others, he said:

'Okay, you asked for it. To the top of the Rognon is a straight pull of about three hundred metres. Not much more than a bit of simple hill walking if you were at sea level. But at almost five thousand metres it will seem a hell of a lot harder, believe me.'

At Jack's request the sirdar helped him to shoulder a large box that had been discarded by one of the dead Sherpas.

'And with a twenty-two-and-a-half kilogramme load on your back?' He grinned cruelly. 'Well let's say that you're about to have an object lesson in just how tough Hurké and his people have to be. Guys? You're going to learn what it takes to be a Sherpa.'

Half-way up the icing sugar slope, Swift stopped and tried to think beyond the endless effort of her ascent of Machhapuchhare's Rognon. She had not thought it possible to feel quite so exhausted and still force herself to go on. More than anything she wanted to drop the load off her aching back, only she knew that she would never have found the strength needed to pick it up again.

The one thing that kept her going was the certainty that she was close to finding her own particular holy grail. Esau. The zoological find of the century. And she was going to make it. It would be in every science magazine and in every newspaper. She might have smiled if she hadn't thought that the extra effort would cause her to have a heart attack. It was just a question of following Jack's route in the snow. All the way up the Rognon. Right to the top.

How did the Sherpas do it? How was it possible that people so much smaller than herself could carry such loads and still make faster progress than any Westerner burdened with not so much as a bumbag? Jack was right. A new respect for these tough little men could hardly be avoided: she felt it in her chest, in her thighs, in her shoulders, in her back every time she took another step. Her muscles felt as if they were saturated with lactic acid.

'Are you okay?'

Jack and MacDougall had long disappeared over the crest of the Rognon. It was Miles Jameson, about fifty metres up ahead of her.

'Yes,' she gasped. 'I'm just too tired to breathe, that's all.'

She waited until the throbbing in her head seemed to diminish a little and then slowly plodded on. The grind of hauling her load up the Rognon quickly drove all thoughts of the yeti out of her mind. And she had long since ceased to pay very much attention to the tracks that the two creatures had left during their own descent and ascent of the Rognon. She had only one thought now, and that was the desperately slow, tedious business of getting up Machhapuchhare's lowest slope.

When at last she reached the top, drenched in sweat, her lungs feeling as raw as if she had gargled with acid, she found Mac and Jack had already erected one of the Stormhaven tents. Jameson had set up a paraffin stove and was boiling water for some tea. Swift slumped down on to the snow and let Jack remove the dead weight from her shoulders. When the load was gone, she rolled to one side like a dead body.

'Proud of you,' said Jack. 'That was a hell of an effort you put in.'

Mute with fatigue, Swift nodded and lay back in the snow, staring up at the face of Machhapuchhare which, much closer now, towered over the Rognon like the ramparts of some enormous white castle. Something built by that mad King Ludwig of Bavaria. There was indeed a fairy-tale aspect to the mountain. As if it might indeed be magical. The peak was so sheer that only the actual summit was covered in snow, like the Paramount Pictures logo. Or was it Columbia? The biting Himalayan wind had airbrushed the snow so delicately that the peak seemed to be trying to tear itself from the greater mass below, but could not break away from the white membrane that held it fast like glue. Shiva's mountain looked so much more impressive on top of the Rognon than it did five kilometres away and six hundred metres further down the glacier at ABC. She closed her eyes and tried to imagine herself back home in her bed in Berkeley, or in a hot tub, but as Jack was already giving orders it was a short reverie.

'Mac? You and Miles stay here and finish making camp. As soon as we've had that tea Swift and I will push on after the yetis. We'll try and follow those tracks for a while, and then get back here before dark.'

Something bloody lying near her in the snow made her recoil with disgust. It was the corpse of a small furry animal, about forty-five centimetres long – and it had been eviscerated.

'Ugh, what's that?' she said.

Jameson gave it a cursory glance.

'Dead marmot. Eagle probably had it. Lucky him. There's not much meat in these mountains.'

Swift sat up slowly and took the cup of steaming tea that Miles had handed her. She wanted to say that someone else should go, that she was physically finished, and she might well have done, except that she knew she didn't know how to put up a tent. Besides, it had been her idea to push on after the yetis in the first place. Instead she said:

'We're spending the night here, Jack?'

'That's the general idea.'

Swift looked at the tent and frowned. After the luxuries of the snow-buried lodges and the heated clamshell, the Stormhaven tent looked as flimsy as a paper lantern. She sipped her tea noisily and stared back across the valley towards the octopus-like shape that was Annapurna. She saw that Jack was right. It might as well have been thirty kilometres. There was no way to track the yetis and get back to ABC before nightfall.

She finished her tea and searched the flat dip on top of the Rognon for the yeti tracks. It was then that she saw that there was more ice field between the Rognon and the foot of the mountain and that the tracks led straight into it.

'From here on we'll need crampons and ice-axes,' said Jack and hauling Swift's legs out straight in front of her, strapped two sets of lethal-looking yellow points on to the soles of her boots. Then he helped her to her feet.

'How do they feel?'

'My legs? Like they used to belong to someone else. Someone old and crippled.'

'I meant the crampons.'

171

Swift lifted one foot and then the other.

'Okay, I guess.'

'Let me know if they ball up under your foot, and we'll adjust them.'

He put the rubber-covered non-slip shaft of a DMM ice-axe into her gloved hand.

She hefted it experimentally and nodded, but the sight of Jack climbing into a chest harness and then collecting a slug of rope off the ground did nothing to allay a sudden sense of anxiety.

'What's this? Are you planning to give me a tow?' she asked hopefully as he passed the rope around her waist.

'Only if I have to.'

Expertly he tied a single figure of eight about a metre from the end of the rope and half a fisherman's knot back on to the main rope. Then he hooked it on to a karabiner that was hanging off the chest harness.

'The figure of eight will act as a stopper knot,' he explained. 'Just in case you need to stop suddenly.'

'Jack, it's not the stopping I need help with. It's the getting started. Tie me a knot that will make my legs move.' She shook her head with exasperation. 'Why the hell should I want to stop suddenly?'

Mac guffawed loudly.

'She doesn't bloody get it, Jack.'

'Get what?'

'It's in case you fall down a crevasse, darlin'.' Mac laughed again. 'That's the kind of bloody sudden stop he's on about. So you don't go all the way to the bottom!'

'Oh, great.' Swift swallowed a mixture of fear and injury. To her greater chagrin Mac suddenly produced a small compact camera and, still laughing, took her picture.

'One for the album that. Come on, darlin'. Have a bit of faith. Don't you know? Faith can move mountains.'

'Oh yeah?' She smiled thinly. 'To do what?'

Jack shouldered Jameson's Zuluarms rifle.

'Swift, you go first. That way if you do fall I can pull you out.'

'Very reassuring.'

He shouldered his rucksack and then handed her a coil of spare rope.

'Here,' he said. 'You can carry this. Now just take it nice and easy.

Keep in the yetis' tracks. Chances are they have a better idea of where the concealed hazards are than we do.'

Swift adjusted her sungoggles, zipped up her stormjacket and sighed uncomfortably.

'Why do I feel like I'm being staked out for something?' she grumbled and set off towards an ice corridor that ran through the upper part of the glacier to the point where it was divided into two by a ridge running down from the centre of the rock face.

The second search party were exploring a valley to the north-east of ABC that led up to Annapurna III when Lincoln Warner radioed them with the news that five Sherpas had been killed and two yetis sighted.

'I don't suppose there's a chance that any of those men could still be alive?' said Cody.

Jutta shook her head. 'People don't normally come out of a crevasse alive. It's like falling off a cliff.'

'It's too bad this had to happen. What's the normal procedure, Tsering? Do we go back, try and help to recover the bodies?'

The young assistant sirdar shook his head slowly.

'I doubt that such a thing would be possible. Indeed it might well cost the lives of yet more men. But what better place of burial could a Sherpa have than to lie in the snow and ice where he fell? There will be a time for formal ceremonies. But it is not now, and you will find, Cody sahib, that those who survive will behave with dignity and make no excessive show of the grief they feel.'

Cody nodded politely but thought Ang Tsering was a pompous ass. He disliked the assistant sirdar, thinking him conceited and could not understand why Jutta seemed so keen to help him improve his German. Or perhaps it was just that like many of her race, she felt an English-speaking world to be a slap in the face of a German one. Either way he was tired of hearing the proper way to order a meal, or to count, or to ask for a hotel room in German. Even Tsering, he suspected, was showing signs of a general weariness with things Teutonic.

Tsering walked on a short way, to the top of the slope they were standing on. Warner's radio message had interrupted them in the act of identifying this slope from the map as Gandharba Chuli, a long ridge that slowly ascended towards the more precipitate heights of Machhapuchhare where the other team was headed.

173

Cody sighed.

'He's a moody son of a bitch.'

Immediately Cody regretted having said it, expecting Jutta to leap to the Sherpa's defence and point out that five of Tsering's fellow Sherpas had just lost their lives. Instead he found her agreeing with him.

'I keep trying to be nice to him, but I know what you mean.'

'I shouldn't have said that. Five of his people were just killed.'

Jutta shrugged. 'But I think his mood was like this before we found out about those others,' she said. 'His mood is always not good.'

'I think I prefer the company of apes to someone like Ang Tsering,' he said. 'I don't mean to be racist or anything. It's just that –'

Jutta smiled. 'Don't apologise. I know what you mean. Have you always worked with apes?'

'Oh, I've done everything with apes. Everything except mate with one. And believe me it wasn't for lack of offers. Female gorillas can be very insistent. Back in the Seventies some friends of mine in the CIA even tried to enlist my help in setting up a programme to exploit large primates for the military. Teaching chimps to drive car bombs. Training gorillas for jungle warfare, that kind of thing.' Noting the look of shock on Jutta's face he added quickly, 'Not that I agreed to do it, of course.'

Jutta nodded her approval.

'So what do we do now?' he asked. 'I guess if they've sighted two yetis there's not much need for us to go gallivanting off down this end of the Sanctuary.'

Tsering was waving at them to come up the slope.

'Now what's he want?' grumbled Cody.

They trailed up the slope after the assistant sirdar and found him staring down the valley through an ancient pair of binoculars. Silently Tsering pointed into the distance. His keen eyes had spotted something – a tiny figure in the distance heading up the valley, towards Tarke Kang, the Glacier Dome.

Both Cody and Jutta found their own field glasses and pointed them at the figure. For a moment they thought that the Sanctuary must be teeming with yetis until, a little further to the north, they saw two little black triangles. They were tents.

It was another camp.

*

174

Running between the two branches of the glacier, the corridor was marked by snow walls to their right and icy rubble to their left, and the route brought them nearer to the sheer cliff that had impeded the perennial progress of the eroding ice. Overawed by the proximity of the mountain and the uncanny silence, Swift walked in the tracks of the two yetis as she had been advised, with the caution of one who half-expected their creators suddenly to appear from behind a heap of snow and to attack her with all the ferocity of a tiger defending its territory.

But there was something else too. An uncomfortable feeling that they were being observed: that they themselves were being tracked. And so far from ABC, in such inhospitable and overwhelming surroundings, Swift realised that she was afraid. A couple of times she had to stop and look around, just to make sure that Jack was still roped to her, for the glacier and the mountain and the nature of their quest had reduced them both to silence.

When, after an hour's walking she stopped a third time, it was not because of her fear of finding herself left alone in such a place but because the tracks suddenly deviated from the main corridor and led three metres up and over the glacier wall to their left.

Catching her up, Jack glanced up at the icy wall and instinctively picking out a route, quickly climbed up to the top of it.

'Maybe they thought they were being followed,' she said, only half-joking.

Searching for the trail, Jack grunted. Then finding it again, and seeing where it led, he said: 'You could be right at that. You'd better come up and see this for yourself.'

Worried less about falling than about the ice wall collapsing on top of her, he sat down and, trying to spread the load of his body on the icy platform, kept the rope taut until she was sitting alongside him. Helping her on to her feet, he said, 'Be careful now. The glacier's very broken up here and one false step, you could find yourself – '

'I know, I know,' she said irritably, for by now she was feeling very tired. 'I'm history.'

'That's right. Pure theory. No fossil.'

He turned carefully and led her across a short slope of jumbled ice and snow, to where the tracks ended at the curling blue and white lip of an enormous crevasse.

Gingerly they approached the edge and with a growing sense of bafflement stared first across the gaping black chasm and then into the frozen resonance of its hidden depths.

'I don't understand,' said Swift, searching around her feet. 'The tracks stop right here on the very edge. Did they jump across, do you think? It must be six metres.'

'Seven and a half,' admitted Jack.

Finding his binoculars, he surveyed the opposite side of the crevasse. There were no tracks to be seen and the snow on the far side looked as pristine as if it had been manufactured for a magazine advertisement. Jack shook his head.

'Is this the Twilight Zone, or what? Not even a fingerprint.'

'Could their tracks have been somehow covered up by something. Maybe more snow?'

'On just one side of the crevasse? That's a little too peculiar, even for the Himalayas.' He looked all around them as if searching for some kind of clue. 'It's like they just disappeared.'

'We both know that isn't possible.'

'Chasing around after a myth and a legend, who knows what's possible and what isn't?'

'As I see it, there are just two possibilities. One, they jumped into the crevasse.'

'Like lemmings, you mean,' shrugged Jack. 'Suicide.'

'Two, they're smarter than we thought. Perhaps they sensed they were being followed and somehow they backtracked, Indian style, placing their feet in their own tracks.' She shrugged. 'I don't know. But there has to be a logical explanation.'

Jack nodded.

'Either way we've got zip,' he said. 'We might as well go back.' He tried to unhook the radio from his jacket, but found it was stuck under the chest harness buckle. Jack unclipped it and tugged the radio free. 'I'll let them know we're coming.'

Swift did not disagree. Her headache was no better, but not wishing to take any more Acetazolamide she had decided to try and walk through the pain. Keen to be returning to Camp One and a lower altitude where her headache might improve, she retreated from the lip of the crevasse and then turned too quickly, spiking her other crampon's binding.

'Let me do it,' said Jack. Momentarily pausing in his attempt to rebuckle the harness, he bent forward to free her binding, but Swift had already automatically lifted one foot clear of her boot and,

176

tired, simply lost her balance. The next second both feet had disappeared from underneath her and she hit the ice, landing heavily on her hip.

She felt no pain. What little discomfort there was became instantly absorbed by the realisation that she was still sliding. Failing to hear what Jack shouted to her, she turned instinctively on to her stomach, which merely seemed to accelerate the speed of her descent and, as she perceived that she would fall into the crevasse, she felt her heart leap back up the slope as if by its very motion it might help to propel her forward again.

The scream leaving her chapped lips became instantly amplified as she found herself swallowed up in a great blue-black void of snow and ice.

Marching into the ill-equipped little camp, Cody, Jutta and Ang Tsering were met by a dog – not the kind of cur that Cody had grown used to seeing in Nepal, but a reasonable-looking animal that was wearing a proper collar. Upon hearing the dog start to bark, a powerful-looking Asian/Oriental emerged from one of the dirty-looking tents. Ang Tsering pressed his hands together in a courteous way, bowed slightly and began to speak to the man.

'*Namaste, aaraamai hunuhunchha?*'

The man said nothing.

'*Tapaai nepaali hunuhunchha?*' said Tsering, bowing once more. When the man shook his head, Tsering added, '*Tapaaiko ghar kahaa chha?* Where do you come from, please?'

The man grunted and said, '*Chin.*'

'*Achchhaa.*'

Tsering turned to Jutta and Cody. 'He is Chinese.' Then he shook his head. 'I don't speak Chinese.'

'I speak a bit,' said Cody, and stepping forward he tried a little Mandarin.

'*Ni hao,*' he said smiling. '*Nin hao Byron. Wo Xing Cody. Nin gui xing?*'

'*Wo xing Chen,*' growled the Chinese, still none too friendly.

'*Wo shi meigno,*' said Cody. '*Ni zuò shénme gōngzuò?*' What do you do?

The Chinese frowned and thought for a moment.

'*Wo bu dong,*' he said finally. I don't understand. '*Qing ni zài shuo yíbiàn?*' Would you say that again please?

'*Keyi,*' said Cody. Sure.

Other men had appeared now. Cody counted four. Three of them regarded Tsering and the two Westerners with obvious suspicion, but the fourth advanced and bowed politely.

'*Nin hao*,' said the fourth man. 'Yes, I speak English. Welcome.'

'Excellent,' said Cody. 'We're scientists. We're based further up the glacier, near Annapurna.'

'We are also scientists,' said the Chinese. 'Make weather prediction.' He struggled to add, 'Meteorology, yes?'

'Is that so?' said Cody. 'One of the members of our expedition is a meteorologist. This is Doctor Henze.'

Jutta smiled and said, 'Would you like some American cigarettes?' She opened her jacket and offered around a packet of Marlboro.

'*Xiangyan*,' breathed the English speaker with keen appreciation. 'Yes, please. We have run out.'

'Sure,' said Cody. '*Xiangyan*, y'know?'

'Keep the pack,' said Jutta.

'That is very kind of you,' said the English speaker.

The other men came nearer and shyly accepted Jutta's cigarettes, which she lit with a stormproof lighter.

'We thought we were the only people up here,' said Cody. 'How many of you are there?'

'Just small team. Six of us is all. You like *cha*?'

'*Cha*,' said Jutta. '*Cha* would be good.'

They stayed drinking tea for about half an hour before making their excuses, promising to come again with whisky and more cigarettes, and their own party's meteorologist.

'It's nice to know we're not the only ones up here,' said Cody as they waved goodbye.

'What do you make of them?' Cody asked Tsering as they walked back towards MBC and the place where they would turn west in the direction of ABC.

'They've no Sherpas,' said Tsering.

'Yes, I wondered about that,' said Jutta.

'If they had hired Sherpas I would have heard about it. In which case they may be in my country without proper permission. The border with Tibet is less than forty kilometres to the north. I think they are Chinese army soldiers.'

'Deserters, maybe?' suggested Jutta. 'I didn't see any guns.'

'Deserters don't normally have a satellite dish,' said Cody.

178

Sixteen

'It was on all fours and it was bounding along very quickly across the snow, heading for the shelter of the cliffs. That was the point at which I thought, That thing is an ape or ape-like creature.'

Chris Bonington

The second that Swift disappeared over the edge of the crevasse Jack threw himself on to the ice before the rope could yank him after her. He was hardly surprised that she should have been unable to stop her slide. He had yelled at her to lie on her back and dig in with her crampons and her ice-axe, but self-arrest was not an easy technique to master. Like most mountaincraft it needed practice. As a young climber he had learned ice-axe braking on a concave slope, with a safe run-out and sufficient time to perfect the skill. He fell feet first, on his back and rolled towards the hand holding the axe head rather than towards the spike. As he started to bring his own weight to bear on the pick and to spread his legs, trying to dig the toes of the crampons into the ice to add to the braking effect of the axe, Swift hit the end of the rope.

Jack gritted his teeth as the sudden impact of her weight threatened to snatch the ice-axe out of his grasp. With arms at full stretch he pressed his face against the ice and prayed that the muscles in his arms and shoulders would take the strain. And that the unbuckled chest harness would stay on – it was only his rucksack that had stopped the harness being torn off his shoulders when Swift fell.

When at last he stopped moving and risked looking back over his shoulder he saw that his feet were just under a metre short of the crevasse. Another second and they would have both been dead.

From inside the crevasse he heard Swift's screams grow quieter as she struggled to gain control of her fear. He took a deep breath and called out to her.

'Swift? Are you okay?'

There was a long pause until finally she said in a nearly inaudible voice:

'Yes, I think so.'

Jack cursed his own stupidity, telling himself he should never have unbuckled the harness without first having secured them both to a separate rope-anchor, and that he should never have made her walk up from the Rognon. It would have been better to have taken Miles or Mac. She had been more tired than he had thought.

He looked under his chest, searching for the radio to call for help from the other two at Camp One. But the radio was gone. He had been about to call them at Camp One when she fell and must have dropped it. Looking desperately around he saw that it had fallen on the ice several metres away, next to Swift's own ice-axe, and well out of reach.

He would have to pull her up by himself. Now if the harness could only hold long enough for him to be able to get the rope securely in his hands . . . as if awoken by this very thought, the karabiner holding the rope began to slip over his shoulder, pressing down the padded strap of his rucksack.

'Okay, don't lose it. I'm going to try and get you out of there.'

For what seemed like an eternity Swift just hung there, turning on the rope, eyes closed and hardly daring to look up for fear that she should find Jack slowly dragged down into the crevasse after her. But when she felt herself drawn several centimetres up the crevasse, Swift opened her eyes.

Gradually her sight adjusted to the frigid gloom and her immediate thoughts upon seeing the cold abyss beneath her redundant feet were to do with the breaking strength, elongation, elasticity, impact force, number of falls sustainable, and water absorption inability of the rope holding her up. She had seen enough movies to have in her mind's eye a picture of a rope slowly fraying on the edge of the crevasse above her as Jack struggled to pull her up before it finally snapped.

180

Trying to clear her head of these images, she attempted to help Jack by telling him how much rope he would have to haul and perceived that she had fallen about six metres down inside the chasm. With this came the realisation that it would probably take him as long as an hour to haul her out of there.

'Jack? I'm about six metres down,' she reported loudly, her voice already sounding like it belonged to something dead, a plangent soul lost in that unfathomed and space. 'Is there anything you want me to do?'

Slowly, he began to draw himself towards the head of his ice-axe and further away from the edge of the crevasse. The dead weight on the rope's end was almost too much for him and the karabiner was now half-way down his arm but, gradually, he got his head level with the shovel-like end of the axe that was the adze. When he was quite certain that he was secure he twisted out the pick and then swung it at arm's length, hammering it fast into the ice above his head, before drawing himself up the length of the shaft once again.

Jack repeated this manoeuvre until there were at least six metres between himself and the crevasse. Only then did he slowly turn on to his back and feel around for the rope, ready to begin the laboriously slow, back-breaking task of hauling Swift up and out of the crevasse.

The very next moment he felt something separate under his shoulder. Like buttons popping on a shirt.

The harness was of a type that enhanced the safety of climbers when a large rucksack was being carried as it helped prevent a climber from inverting in the event of a fall. Buckled securely, the load of a climber's weight was evenly spread around the whole harness. But with the whole weight of the rope holding Swift brought to bear on only one half of the harness, the integrity of the stitching on the flat webbing shoulder-strap could only last a short while.

Jack guessed in an instant what was happening. Desperately he lunged for the rope and missed. He cried out as the strap holding the karabiner unfolded like a tiny fist, and the rope holding Swift disappeared into the crevasse.

She heard him shout something but the actual words were lost as, distinguishing yet more of her dark and cheerless surroundings, she was suddenly falling again.

Her scream had hardly time to leave her lips before she landed, almost immediately grasping what must have become of the two yetis before something hit her head. Seeing it was the karabiner that had been attached to Jack's harness, along with the rest of the rope that had been holding her up, she started to sense just how narrow was the escape she had enjoyed.

As narrow as the ledge she had landed on.

Another metre or so further along the crevasse and she would surely have missed it altogether. Inside the curling lip of the crevasse, about nine metres down the throat of the chasm, she was sitting on a long twisting shelf covered in ice and snow that bore the same tracks as the glacier outside; a natural mountain path that led hundreds of metres away into the shadows. The two yetis must have been aware of the existence of the shelf, for it was plain to her that they must have jumped from the edge of the crevasse straight down into the very darkest part of the fissure – a prodigious leap that would, she knew, have challenged the instincts of even the most resourceful and intelligent of wild animals.

Jack's head appeared over the edge of the crevasse, shouting her name in a voice hoarsened with fear.

'It's okay,' she called to him. 'I'm okay. There's a kind of ledge here about a metre wide. I'm sitting on it.'

'Thank God.'

'Now we know what happened to the yetis,' she said.

Jack started to laugh.

Pressing herself back against the wall of the crevasse she stood up slowly, her trembling legs reminding her of how close she had come to dying. A cold sweat and sudden wave of nausea followed.

'You okay?'

'I think so. I couldn't have fallen more than about three metres from where I was. I'm about nine metres down.'

'That's a hell of a jump,' observed Jack.

Realising what had happened to the two yetis was enough to make Swift understand a little of how these legendary creatures had managed to evade observation and capture for so long. If they could make such a jump on to an invisible rock ledge, what other physical feats might they also be capable of?

'Can you throw the rope up to me?'

Straight away Swift wrestled off her knapsack and the coil of rope and took out a Mini-Maglite for there was a peculiar atmosphere in the half light of the crevasse she hoped to quickly dispel. Shining the powerful beam of the Maglite ahead of her she saw the ledge – over a metre wide where she stood, but narrowing as it snaked away into the darkness – and the tracks. They would have to come back later, perhaps the following day, and continue tracking the yetis. It was impossible to lose the trail for there was clearly only one way to go and that was along and inside the crevasse.

She put away the Maglite, uncoiled the rope, measured out a length, and mentally rehearsed the act of throwing it up.

'I don't think so,' she reported. 'There's not enough room.'

Looking up at the top of the crevasse and the narrow aperture of blue sky beyond, Swift waited to hear what Jack would suggest next and shivered. In her fear she had paid no attention to how bitterly cold it was in there.

'What do we do now?' she called to him.

'Good question,' said Jack and, retreating from the edge of the crevasse went to fetch the radio.

As soon as he picked it up he saw there was no LCD on its tiny grey screen and realised that there was no signal. Somehow the aerial had become detached when the radio hit the hard ice. Jack scanned the edge of the crevasse but the squat black rubber teat that provided the radio signal was nowhere to be seen.

'Shit.'

That was the thing about equipment failure. One failure usually occasioned another.

A glance at his watch and then the sky reminded him of what he already knew. There was no time to walk down to Camp One and then come back again with Mac and Jameson before dark. He knew how cold it could get inside a crevasse. Bad enough in daylight, but in darkness it would be like a butcher's deep freeze. Seeing Swift's ice-axe on the ground he picked it up, certain now that with two ice-axes he had no alternative but to climb down into the crevasse, collect the rope himself, and climb back up again.

Jack found himself retching as he realised he was going to have to do what he had hoped to avoid at least until he was better prepared.

He was going to have to climb on a sheer wall of ice, without ropes, with only his crampons and the two ice-axes to aid him. It would be as near to being back up Annapurna as he could imagine.

*

Jutta, Cody and Ang Tsering returned to ABC to find Boyd laying out cylindrical specimens of ice that he had obtained from the glacier using a portable drill bit, on a special groundsheet. The specimens, called cores, were almost two metres long and seven or eight centimetres in diametre, and each one was attached by a couple of wires to a small digital computer. When Boyd saw the three coming he stopped what he was doing and stood up and adopted a sombre-looking expression.

'You heard what happened, huh?' he said. 'About those poor guys?'

They nodded.

'Gee, I'm sorry, Tsering. Naturally my organisation will pay its share of expenses. Y'know? Ceremonies. Compensation. Whatever.'

'Thank you, sahib.'

'At least the sirdar is okay. According to Link he's on his way back down here.'

They went back into the clamshell and found Warner had already boiled a kettle.

'I heard you coming,' he said. 'Coffee anyone?'

'Coffee. Great.'

'How is your own work coming along?' Jutta asked Boyd pleasantly.

'Okay, I guess.'

'You know,' said Warner. 'I thought you had to drill real deep to get core samples.'

'Not for these cores. These are only supposed to relate to the last thousand years. The really deep stuff we already did in the Antarctic. Most of it offshore too. On the Amery Ice Shelf, off the Lambert Glacier we went five hundred metres deep, and ten thousand years back in time.'

Boyd took hold of the steaming mug being passed to him by Warner and sipped it with noisy enthusiasm.

'Thanks a lot. But great news for you guys, huh? I hear Hurké saw not one but two fancy-dress costumes. Hey, Link, maybe now you can do some work?'

'I sure hope so. I'm getting kind of bored.'

Tsering frowned and shook his head. 'Two fancy-dress costumes? I do not understand, sahib –'

'It's just Boyd's weird sense of humour,' explained Jutta. 'He means two yetis.'

184

'We saw something interesting ourselves,' said Cody. Something that might interest you, Boyd. You being a meteorologist 'n' all.'

'Climatologist,' insisted Boyd. 'Meteorology's different.'

'Some fellow scientists. A small team of Chinese meteorologists. Just six kind of ragged-looking guys.'

'You don't say?'

'Where was this?' said Warner. 'I thought we were the only people up here.'

'Only Tsering thinks maybe they were Chinese army deserters,' added Cody. 'On account of how they didn't have any Sherpas.'

'If they had hired porters in Kat, I would have heard about it.' Tsering sounded adamant.

'Maybe they're an invasion force,' laughed Cody. 'From Tibet.'

'Where was this?' repeated Warner.

'The valley above MBC,' said Jutta. 'The one that runs towards Tarke Kang. They're camped at the foot of Fluted Peak.'

'And you spoke to them?' said Warner.

'Yes,' said Jutta. 'Byron speaks some Chinese.'

'Some.'

'Where'd you learn that, Byron?' enquired Boyd.

'In Vietnam. For a while I was in Special Forces. Interrogating prisoners, that kind of thing.'

'No kidding,' said Boyd. 'Torture any?'

Cody snorted a contemptuous sort of laugh and shook his head.

'Special Forces. Wow. Did they say what kind of meteorology they were doing?'

'No. But I said we'd go back sometime. Bring them some cigarettes and whisky. We could maybe find out what they were up to?'

'Maybe we could at that.'

'I'd be very surprised if they were still there when we went back,' said Tsering. 'I'd be very surprised if they didn't just pack up and leave the minute we left their camp.'

'You know your trouble, Tsering?' said Boyd. 'You have no faith in your fellow men.'

*

185

> HUSTLER. GUESS WHAT? WE'VE GOT COMPANY.
> THERE IS A CHINESE ENCAMPMENT IN THE AREA,
> 83°75 EAST OF GREENWICH, 28°45 NORTH. ONE OF
> OUR SHERPAS BELIEVES THAT THEY MAY BE
> DESERTERS. ON THE OTHER HAND THEY MAY BE A
> PARTY OF HOSTILES INTENT ON TREADING UPON OUR
> TOES. MY OWN INCLINATION IS TO ASSUME THE
> LATTER AND TAKE THEM OUT OF THE PICTURE
> STRAIGHTAWAY. PLEASE ADVISE. YOURS, CASTORP.

Jack took a deep breath and knelt down at the edge of the crevasse. He felt as if he should have prayed. He wanted to confess his sins, ask for courage, and seek guidance as to some other way of rescuing Swift, all at the same time. He badly did not want to do what he was about to do. His stomach felt as sour as if he had swallowed vinegar, while his heart was beating so quickly he thought he must be on the edge of a cardiac arrest.

Come on. Get a grip on yourself. She'll freeze to death if you leave her down there.

He twisted round carefully and chopped at the ice with each ice-axe. Only when he was entirely satisfied with the holds did he complete the turn, lower his legs into the crevasse like a man slipping into a swimming pool, and then hack at the wall beneath him with the double-front points of his crampons.

It wasn't the first time he had made a free climb on an ice wall and Jack was aware of all of the hazards, which were mostly dependent on the ice quality. Toe points could pull out. The ice could split. Even worse, ice could shatter under the blow of an ice-axe and the whole shard could carry you on a one-way toboggan ride. It was fortunate that the picks on the two ice-axes were slim enough to permit easy penetration and yet sharp enough along their top edges to help extraction. Hardest of all was the technique of ice-axe climbing in reverse. Having found a couple of good handholds, you had first to pull out of the ice one toe and then one pick, lower your body until your hand was at the very end of the fixed axe shaft, and then hammer in with the other axe, and kick in with the other toe. It was as nerve-racking a way of coming down a wall as any human being could have devised.

Nine metres was not so far. Except that if he did fall off the blue-green wall of the ice-encrusted rock Jack knew it would be fatal. He knew his weight and the angle of his body would carry him over the edge of the shelf and into the depths of the crevasse. With such a climb there was no margin for error.

Bryan Perrins sat down at his desk, glanced at the *Post*, and then threw it into the bin. He preferred the *City Paper*, a free alternative weekly with better gossip and arts coverage. Perrins liked going to the movies, and the *Post* – not so much resting on its laurels as sleeping under them – never seemed to have the same amount of movie reviews as the *City*. He switched on his computer and stared out of the window at the Potomac river, wondering if he might get a chance to go to the American Film Institute at the weekend and see something from the early Hitchcock season they were running. *Vertigo*, maybe – one of his favourites. The thought of vertiginous heights made him think of the Himalayas and he called up HUSTLER's e-mail and checked to see if there was something in the tray from CASTORP.

The news that there was a Chinese army encampment in the Annapurna Sanctuary did not particularly surprise him. The Agency had been expecting something of the kind from the Chinese. What surprised Perrins more was the alacrity with which CASTORP offered to dispose of the Chinese, without any attempt to verify his own suggestion that there was a possibility that the Chinese were actually deserters. Perrins saw little point in authorising a surgical strike unless it was necessary and straight away e-mailed CASTORP to do nothing until the Agency had organised an aerial surveillance of the Chinese position. Then he contacted the NOR and Reichhardt, who agreed to organise an overflight by a U2R from an airforce base in Saudi Arabia. The U2R's on-board computers would be able to gather the signals picked up from the site of the Chinese camp twenty-seven thousand metres below on the Annapurna Sanctuary, and then beam them via satellite back to Langley. The signals could then be analysed and evaluated before being passed up to Perrins with a recommendation.

Swift shone the Maglite up the wall as Jack descended into darkness, uttering only the odd word of encouragement so as not to distract him. But when, about half-way down, he stopped moving altogether she realised that something had gone wrong.

'Jack? Are you okay?'

187

He was motionless so that he looked like a statue high on the wall of some strange cathedral chapel, a saint or an angel, frozen in the act of some weird benediction.

That was it. He was frozen with fear.

'Jack?'

'Shutup, shutup, shutup.'

Swift heard the panic in the echoing voice from above and with no pleasure she knew she must be right.

'Jack, listen to me. Listen. You're more than half-way down. Just take your time.'

He did not move. He said nothing. All she could hear was the sound of his breathing, as fast as if he was running a marathon.

She paused, wondering what to say next. If he didn't make it, she wouldn't make it either. Things were that simple. Whatever words she said to him now, they would probably be the most important things she would ever say.

'Jack? I don't know if this is the right time or place. Maybe if we get out of this, we'll laugh about it afterwards. But we'll both know this was still the truth. What I said. What I'm saying. I love you, Jack. In my way I always have. After this is all over I don't want us ever to be apart again. This is a little like a balcony scene from Shakespeare, except that it's me who should be up there, and you down here. But I mean what I'm saying, Jack. So you can't stop now. You just can't. You have to climb down here so that you can tell me you love me and so that we can go on with the rest of our lives. Do you understand?'

Swift stopped speaking and waited a long moment. Then, slowly, like something that was dead coming to life again – a mummy from a Pharaoh's tomb – he moved first his arm, then his leg, and resumed his descent.

When he reached the shelf at last, they held each other in silence for as long as Jack perceived that their situation allowed.

'Thanks,' he said, releasing her from his strong embrace. 'I really lost it up there. You were pretty good, the way you talked me down.'

'I meant every word of it.'

He nodded, picked up the rope, and began to tie it around his waist. 'I know you did,' he said. 'If I'd had any doubt about that, I'd probably still be up there.' He glanced up at the deepening blue pennant of sky that flagged the entrance to the crevasse. 'Be easier going up than coming down, I guess.'

'All the same, I think you'd better take this with you.' She kissed him hard on the mouth. 'Just in case you should start to slow down.'

Jack turned towards the wall and got ready to climb again.

'Wait,' she said. 'You haven't told me you loved me yet.'

'No?' He grinned back at her. 'Well get ready to watch a man in love climb this wall.'

CASTORP. SENIOR SPEAR, SENIOR RUBY, AND SENIOR SCAN COMINT.ELINT. SOURCES INDICATE THAT THE CHINESE SOLDIERS AT THE SANCTUARY POSITION YOU DESCRIBED IN YOUR LAST MESSAGE ARE INDEED PEOPLE'S ARMY SOLDIERS. ALTHOUGH THEIR PRESENCE IN NEPAL IS TECHNICALLY ILLEGAL, THEIR PURPOSE WOULD APPEAR TO BE THE CAPTURE AND APPREHENSION OF GENUINE DESERTERS FROM SAME ARMY; AND TO THIS EXTENT SUCH MINOR INCURSIONS ARE QUITE USUAL. THEY ARE TOLERATED BY THE NEPALESE GOVERNMENT WHO HAVE NO WISH TO UPSET THE CHINESE AUTHORITIES, NOR TO ENCOURAGE ILLEGAL EMIGRATION TO THEIR ALREADY POOR COUNTRY. AS A RESULT, THERE IS NO NECESSITY TO TAKE ANY ACTION AS YOUR MISSION IS NOT COMPROMISED BY THEIR PRESENCE. HUSTLER.

When Swift and Jack got back to Camp One, exhausted and ravenously hungry, it was already dusk. Mac and Jameson had prepared them a meal of beef stew and rice pudding with tinned fruit. Wrapped up warm in their sleeping bags, Mac and Jameson smoked cigarettes, drank whisky, listening as the pair wolfed down their food and related the events of the day.

'And you reckon the yetis just jumped nine metres straight over the edge?'

'No doubt about it,' Swift said. 'There were tracks all over the shelf.'

'That's what I call a bloody leap of faith,' said Mac.

'The shelf goes straight up and into the mountain. It's the best kind of trail we could have. I mean, there are no tracks to blow away. We just follow the shelf to the end. What do you say, Jack?'

Jack nodded. 'But we'll need one of Boyd's survival suits. It gets pretty cold inside a crevasse.'

189

'Don't remind me,' Swift shivered. 'It was like a tomb in there.'

'Very nearly was, by the sound of it,' said Mac. He unzipped his sleeping bag and crawled towards the door of the tent.

'I'm just going outside,' he announced with mock solemnity. 'I may be some time.'

Jack nodded at the bottle of scotch by Jameson. 'I could use a drink.'

'Of course.' Jameson reached to pour him a drink. 'Swift?'

'No thanks. Haven't you had enough?'

'You don't understand,' smiled Jameson. 'There's a reason why we're drinking.'

'Who needs reasons?' said Jack.

'It's because we're so close to the rock face.' Jameson lowered his voice. 'Mac thinks that we're right in the way of an avalanche. Sorry, a bloody avalanche. He says that if we're engulfed he doesn't want to know anything about it.'

Jack shrugged and sipped his whisky. 'Maybe he's right. And it tastes a lot better than a Seconal.'

'Well, I certainly won't need a Seconal to put me to sleep tonight,' said Swift. 'Avalanche or not. I could sleep on the point of a sword.'

Removing only her boots and her stormproof outer shell, Swift crawled into her sleeping bag and zippered up. Mac came back into the tent with the news that it had started to snow.

'Just what we bloody need,' he said. 'More bloody snow. If you ask me, the weather's closing in a bit. I wouldn't be at all surprised – '

Jameson's radio interrupted him, sounding like the tent's forgotten guest.

'Hello, Jack. This is Link. Come in please. Over.'

'About time they bloody called,' grumbled Mac.

Jack picked up the radio and pressed the call button.

'Hello ABC, this is Jack at Machhapuchhare Camp One. You're loud and clear. Over.'

He waited a moment and then heard Link's voice again.

'How's things?'

'Fine. Link? Did Hurké make it back all right?'

'Affirmative. Jutta's given him something to help him sleep. He seemed badly shaken up. Won't say much about it though. Says he doesn't want to scare the rest of the boys.'

'Good thinking. How'd they take it? The loss of those men this morning?'

190

'Not good. But nothing I don't think can't be fixed.'

'Good. Is Jon Boyd there?'

'Wait a second.'

'Hi, Jack. This is Jon.'

'Jon. Those SCE suits you were talking about. I'd like to try one of them out tomorrow. Can you get some of the boys to carry one up first thing tomorrow? Plus the rest of the Camp One gear.'

'Sure thing.'

'And plenty of rope too.'

'Going climbing?'

'Not exactly. I'm going down a crevasse. And it gets very cold and dark in there.'

'You going after those Sherpa bodies?'

'No. I'm going to follow the yeti trail. That's where they went.'

'Okay, Jack. Well, you'll find all the instructions for use of the suit in the box. Just like a kid's toy. Try and remember one thing though. Your environment lasts twelve hours and no more. After that, no heat, no light, no voice coms, nuthin'. You copy?'

'Yes. I've got that.'

'Hey, I nearly forgot to tell you. The B team found another expedition in the Sanctuary. Bunch of Chinese meteorologists. Only Ang Tsering reckons they might be Chinese army deserters.'

'That's interesting.'

'Cody wants to drop by and say hello again.'

'Tell him to be careful. How's the weather station looking? It's started to snow up here.'

'We're clear down here. Temperature's dropping like a stone. But the pressure looks not too bad. Set to continue fine I'd say.'

'Good. Well that's all from us, I guess. Say hello to everyone.'

'For sure.'

'Over and out.'

Jack tossed the radio on to the groundsheet.

'Chinese army, eh?' he said. 'What do you make of that?'

'I'd say Tsering was probably right,' said Jameson.

'I wonder,' said Jack.

Jameson finished his drink and then lit another cigarette. He studied the smoking end for a moment and then said:

'What do you make of this, then, chaps? I've noticed that the physical process of smoking seems to make breathing easier up here. My theory is that the general lack of oxygen makes you *think*

191

about breathing, which normally is an involuntary process, and that the thinking about it consequently engenders a slight feeling of suffocation. Back down at sea level breathing seems to be effortless because carbon dioxide stimulates the nerve centres that only make it seem that way. Okay? But as well as the lack of oxygen at altitude, there is also a lack of carbon dioxide. This is the clever part: somehow the cigarette smoke is able to substitute for carbon dioxide normally present in the human body and therefore stimulate involuntary breathing in the normal way. I have noticed that the effect of one cigarette can last as long as a couple of hours.'

Mac laughed with obvious delight.

'That would also explain why nearly all of the Sherpas smoke like bloody chimneys,' said the Scotsman.

'Precisely, Mac.'

'Who knows? Maybe the bloody yetis smoke too,' said Mac. 'It might explain why they're so quick up these bloody hillsides.' He cackled loudly. 'When you're next looking for a sponsor to bring us all back here, you'll just have to ask the lads at Philip Morris. What do you think of that, eh, Swift?'

But Swift was already fast asleep.

In the moonlight CASTORP stood looking through a pair of night-sight binoculars at the Chinese encampment. It all looked innocent enough: a huddle of heavy canvas storm-tents, a pile of stores – respectably civilian, and the satellite dish. Soldiers hunting deserters hardly needed to bring along a satellite dish. Snow began to give way beneath him, obliging him to shift his stance. It felt uncertain underfoot. Dangerous even. He had an idea.

CASTORP returned the binoculars to his rucksack and unfolding an entrenching tool started to dig a pit as deep as the surface layer of snow with a vertical back wall. He straightened for a moment, catching his breath. It had been quite a hike down from ABC in the dark. Then he cut away a chimney about thirty centimetres deep on one side of the wall before adding a V-shaped slot on the other side, exposing an isolated block of snow about thirty centimetres wide. Lastly he thrust his shovel down the back of the block and pulled gently outwards, using only a small amount of leverage. The block suddenly sheared away along the contact face and immediately he stopped pulling. The shearing block of snow indicated that the slope was in a very unstable condition. He wondered if the Chinese soldiers had even bothered to make the same rudimentary field test as he had done, and decided they couldn't have done. They would hardly have pitched their camp there if they had. On the other hand maybe they'd been there for a while. It was a smaller valley than at ABC and there had been quite a bit of snow of late. Still, he thought, there was no point in leaving it to chance. And it wasn't as if HUSTLER had expressly forbidden him to take any action.

Wiping his brow he allowed himself a small smile of contempt for the people back in Washington. What did they know about the people in the camp below? He was the man on the ground. He should never have told HUSTLER in the first place. He should just have gone ahead and told HUSTLER afterwards. This was his call. He was best placed to read the situation. When you perceived a threat you didn't wait for it to develop. You took action.

From his rucksack he removed a couple of small explosive charges and placed them carefully and at regular intervals along the ridge above the Chinese camp. He found himself singing.

'Good King Wenceslas looked out,
On the feast of Stephen,
When the snow lay round about,
Deep and crisp and even.'

CASTORP trudged back down the valley on to some safe ground and, hardly hesitating, detonated the charges with a small remote control. Snow muffled the sound of the little explosions, each of them sounding no louder than a hand clap. At first the snow hardly moved and he wondered if he might have miscalculated. But gradually the whole slope, one enormous slab of snow and ice, began to move, like a mess of porridge pouring out of a pot. Quickly it increased in speed and volume until it was a deafening tidal wave, a mushrooming tonnage of cloud and cold debris, like a tall building from which the foundations had been blown away.

When the avalanche was over and the airborne powder had cleared, the moonlit valley looked as peaceful as a Christmas card scene and it was as if the Chinese camp had never existed. The man turned away and heading back towards ABC he sang again:

'Brightly shone the moon that night,
Though the frost was cruel,
When a poor man came in sight,
Gathering winter fu-el.'

193

Seventeen

'Of all the wonders, none is more wonderful than man.'

Sophocles

Bitterly cold, Swift awoke to find Jack's gloved hand held over her mouth. It was still dark and she could hardly see his face, only felt his hot breath, still smelling of whisky, as he whispered:

'We've got company.'

She sat up abruptly, almost bumping heads with Mac or Jameson – she wasn't sure which – and, with breath held, listened carefully.

It had stopped snowing. Even the wind had dropped. Outside the tent, the snow had frozen solid under the Himalayan night's hard frost. She could hear the snow crunching underfoot as whatever it was moved around Camp One.

'Is it someone come up from ABC?' she whispered hopefully.

'Too far and too dangerous,' said Jack. 'It would be suicide to try and come up here in the dark.'

'What about those Chinese?'

'Ditto. They're just as far away. No, this is something else.'

Jameson had found his pistol and was trying to load it with a syringe dart. The footsteps were coming closer to the tent.

'This isn't so easy in the dark,' he whispered.

'Take the gun,' said Jack. 'The gun's still loaded.'

'Too powerful. Can you and Mac handle the flashlights? I'll only have a chance for one shot and I want to make it – '

Jameson stopped to listen to a loud sniffing noise as the creature outside the tent inhaled the cold night air.

'The stew,' Swift whispered. 'It smells the beef stew.'

194

'Connoisseur eh?' said Jameson. 'Good for him.' He slid the syringe into the barrel of the pistol and closed the breech. 'Ready.'

Something batted the wall of the tent which then bulged as for a moment a large body pressed up against it. Swift felt her heart miss a beat as she detected a pungent animal smell.

Now the creature struck the wall again, only this time the sound was accompanied by the rattle of some mess tins. It had found what it was looking for: the remains of the beef stew.

Swift would hardly have thought it possible to feel a chill of fear on top of the cold she already felt, but her hair was rising on her scalp as if her skin had recognised first what her ears and her brain were slower to register. There really was a big animal out there.

'I'd better go first,' said Mac, swallowing loudly. But he did not move. He was held back by a loud ripping sound. Claws. The creature was tearing open the back of the tent next to Swift's head with claws that were as sharp as razors. Swift thought back to the sirdar's description of the yetis. She could not remember him saying anything about them having sharp claws. Was it possible that these higher anthropoids might have long and sharp fingernails? By Hurké Gurung's account, they seemed to lack nothing else in aggression.

'I don't think you'll have to go outside,' she hissed back at him. 'Whatever it is is coming in.'

'It's coming in,' Jack repeated. 'Christ, she's right.'

The ripping sound grew louder as the creature's claws scored several wide tears in the orange material of the Stormhaven tent. Swift caught sight of something through a slash and as coolly as she was able, said:

'Better let it make a decent hole first, Miles. You wouldn't want to shoot the tent.'

'Get ready to switch on those flashlights,' said Jameson.

Moonlight slashed into the tent followed by a wave of cold air and then something animal hit Swift's nostrils, only more powerfully this time.

'Hold it,' she said through teeth that were chattering with fear and cold. Her heart felt as if it had stopped pumping blood to her head. She tensed herself, waiting for the inevitable moment when the creature would be inside.

A low growl rumbled through the tent, then followed another, more furious rip of claws and a gaping hole appeared in the slashed-

195

to-ribbons nylon wall, big enough to have allowed Swift to crawl out. Or something else to crawl in. For a moment she could see nothing but the snow on the ground outside the tent. In the moonlight something moved, slowly at first, and then picking up speed. There was a louder growl and the shadowy form became something more substantial as what looked like a head pushed through the pennants of nylon that trailed across the hole in the tent. Suddenly an almost luminous yellow eye met Swift's own.

'Now,' she said, 'now,' and dropped her head flat against the groundsheet so as to avoid being shot herself.

Flashlight filled the tent a second before Jameson pulled the trigger. There was a short coughing noise, like the sound of a cross-bow being fired, as the carbon dioxide cylinder in the pistol discharged its chemical restraint, then a loud, quite inhuman roar as the creature recoiled first from the light and then from the dull pain of the dart. Then they heard something running lightly over the frozen crust of the snow.

They all scrambled to find an exit.

'Did you get it?' said Jack.

'I think so.'

'I hope so,' said Swift.

Mac was laughing almost hysterically.

'Those teeth. The size of those bloody teeth. That was all I could see. Christ, I'm shaking. Where's my bloody camera?'

'It's not as big as I thought,' said Jameson.

'That's because you weren't right beside it,' said Swift.

Jack was first out, shining his own flashlight around the top of the Rognon, looking for some sign of the creature. Near the corridor something was still running, its breathing stertorously loud and laboured.

'It's heading back down the ice corridor,' he shouted. 'Towards the mountain.'

Swift felt a pang of regret. If it jumps in the crevasse when it's still full of dope she thought, it will be killed.

Mac, camera in hand, was by Jack's side now. He fired off several shots and the Rognon was illuminated with flashgun light, as if by lightning. Swift and Jameson joined them on the Rognon, collecting equipment and preparing to give chase. Jameson brought the Zuluarms rifle in case he needed to make a second, more distant shot.

Forty-five metres away the creature roared again as the

Ketamine Hydrochloride in the dart syringe began to take effect. It was a roar Jameson seemed to recognise, like the voice of an old friend.

'That's no anthropoid,' he said, first to himself, and then, more loudly, to the others. His keen eyes caught the tired flick of a long, well-muscled tail as the creature staggered down the corridor towards the rock face.

'Stay back,' he yelled. 'Jesus Christ, that's a cat. A big cat.'

Feet splayed, its head lower than its shoulders, the big cat faced its pursuers and growled indignantly. Almost two metres long, with a long thick tail that looked like a fur wrap, the cat had a coat of pale grey fur with dark rosette-like markings.

'Be very careful,' Jameson warned the others. 'He still might have some fight left in him.'

'What is it?' asked Swift as the four of them walked slowly towards the cat, which was now rapidly succumbing to the analgesic. 'Some kind of mountain lion?'

The cat sat down as if resigned to its fate.

'That is one of the rarest animals in the world,' said Jameson. '*Panthera uncia*. A snow leopard. I never ever thought I'd see one. Mostly they stay across the border in Tibet. There the people believe that some of the great Lamas turn themselves into snow leopards to get around the mountains or escape from their enemies.'

Grunting, as if in assent to what Jameson had just said, the snow leopard lay down on its side. A slow flick of the tail and a profound sigh were enough to persuade Jameson that it was now safe to approach.

'Maybe this is a Lama on the run from the Chinese commies,' said Mac.

'Look at the size of those pugs,' said Jameson, the veterinarian in him smiling in admiration of the animal.

'He's a real beauty all right,' agreed Mac, and took a photograph.

'A male,' said Jameson. 'Must weigh well over forty-five kilogrammes.'

The syringe had lodged deep in the animal's rich pale fur in the muscle mass just below the left shoulder. Jameson knelt down by the leopard and gently withdrew the dart. The animal's eyes remained open and the vertical pupils fixed. Now there was hardly any breath at all.

197

'Is he going to be all right?' Swift asked anxiously. 'The eyes – he looks like he's dying.'

'Ketamine does that,' said Jameson. 'The eyelids stay open.'

The leopard swallowed noisily.

'I think he'll be fine. In half an hour or so he'll probably try and get up again. All the same, I think I'll stay here and keep an eye on him, just in case. I wouldn't care to have the death of the world's rarest big cat on my conscience. The rest of you might as well go back to camp. Lucky we erected both tents, eh?'

'Well if it's that rare a beast I want to get some good pictures.' Mac walked around the creature and then knelt down to get a good shot of the leopard's handsome-looking head. 'You just stay there, Miles. I'll get you as well.'

Jack, turning on his heel, stopped as something else ran across the snow.

'Did you hear that?' he said.

Jameson stood up and looked around.

A dark shadow slipped behind a block of ice.

'Another leopard?'

'Could be.'

He and Jack waved their Maglites across the Rognon and in the blink of an eye it was as if the snow-covered rocks had magically come to life. Startled by the sight, Mac uttered a short exclamation of fear and moved closer to the other three. Several pairs of eyes, each like two green moons in the darkness, stared unflinching into one Maglite's powerful beam.

'Timber wolves,' said Jameson.

He counted as many as eight, each the size of a small pony and the colour of the sheerest granite underneath a light spray of powdered snow. The biggest and darkest of the pack, who was also the nearest, yawned hungrily, spread out his paws and dropped a big black nose to the ice in search of scent. Jameson realised that he was sniffing for blood, asking himself if a kill had been made. At the same time he guessed the probable chain of events that had led these animals to the top of the Rognon.

'They must have been hunting the leopard,' he said.

'A wolf beating up a leopard?' said Mac. 'That doesn't sound very likely.'

'Don't you believe it. I've seen a medium-sized wolf bite through the bars of a cage designed to house rabid domestic dogs. They're extraordinarily powerful. And back in Zimbabwe, it's common enough for a pack of hyenas to take on a lion and drive it off a kill.'

'Cut the *National Geographic* video,' said Jack, 'and tell us what we do now. I don't like the look of these bastards.'

Jameson unslung the Zuluarms, broke open the rifle barrel to remove the Cap-Chur syringe, but left the percussion cap in the shotgun barrel.

'They don't seem at all afraid of us,' remarked Swift as another wolf appeared on top of a block of ice.

'I expect they've not seen men much before,' said Jack. 'If it comes to that I've never seen wolves in this part of the Himalayas.'

'Fire the gun, for Christ's sake,' urged Mac.

'You're the one who's afraid of avalanches,' Jameson said pointedly. 'How about it, Jack? Is it safe?'

Jack looked up at the rock face above them. They were probably far enough away to survive any ordinary avalanche. But one caused by gunshots? That was harder to call.

'What's the alternative?' he said. 'Will they attack?'

'As long as we all stick together, they probably won't risk it. But we can hardly stay out here all night.'

'How about this?' said Jack. 'We all link arms in a square and head back towards the camp. There's fire there. We can scare them off with that.'

'What about the leopard?' said Jameson. 'We can hardly leave him to get eaten.'

'Do you have a better idea?'

'No.'

'Right then. Let's do it.'

They linked arms and formed a square, with Jameson walking backwards to protect their rear. The wolves watched them for a moment and then, growling loudly, one of them snapped at Jack's leg. He kicked the wolf away and called a halt.

'That puts paid to that idea.'

'I didn't much like it anyway,' observed Jameson.

Jack looked again at the rock face. There were maybe a couple of thousand tonnes of snow up there. But now there seemed to be any alternative.

'Okay, use the gun.'

Jameson didn't needed asking twice. The big leader was closing in on him with a look of real purpose. He levelled the rifle straight at the wolf's head and fired. On top of the Rognon, the gun sounded like a howitzer.

With a yelp of fright the wolf sprang back and trotted away, with the others scattered ahead of him. Jack glanced up the rock face and then back at the wolves.

'Another,' he said.

Jameson loaded another cap and fired again to hurry the pack on its way. The gunshot seemed almost to bang against the rock face as if daring the snow to break. But this time the wolves ran with an even greater sense of urgency.

'Thank God for that,' breathed Mac. 'For a minute there I thought I was some evil mutt's breakfast.'

'Poor bastards,' said Jameson. 'They might have tracked the leopard for as much as a hundred kilometres.'

'I know the feeling,' said Swift. 'This time I really thought we were going to be lucky, y'know?'

'This time we *were* lucky,' said Jameson. He loaded another cap and gazed over the Rognon, but the wolves had gone.

'I mean, with the yeti.'

'Sure,' said Jameson. 'But you're a hunter. You'll have to learn patience if you're going to pull off this expedition, y'know?'

Jack glanced at his wristwatch and then at the drugged cat.

'Five o'clock. Sun'll be up soon.'

'Cup of tea anyone?' said Mac. 'I could use a brew after all that excitement.'

'I'm going to wait here for a while,' said Jameson. 'See this chap safely back on his feet in case Mowgli's brothers come round again.'

Jack stretched lazily.

'It's back to bed for me. There's not much we can do until the Sherpas get here with one of Boyd's space suits.'

It was mid-morning by the time the Sherpas from ABC, led by Ang Tsering, reached Camp One. They were accompanied, at protracted length, by Byron Cody and Jutta Henze. Their ascent had been without incident although in the whirl of the bitter wind and spindrift, the end of Byron Cody's nose had succumbed to frostbite, while his feet felt quite frozen. Almost as soon as he had removed his small rucksack, Jutta Henze took him into the undamaged tent where she covered his nose with a dressing, to keep it warm as much

200

as anything, handed him some antibiotics, and then administered an intravenous shot of low-molecular dextran.

He emerged from the tent yawning as widely as any gorilla he had ever studied.

'You should have stayed in bed,' Jack told him.

'I'm sorry,' he said. 'But I didn't get much sleep last night.'

'I thought you wanted to go and visit with those Chinese,' said Jameson.

'Tsering's right. They were probably deserters. Besides, I didn't want to miss anything up here.'

'I think you'd miss the end of your nose,' remarked Jutta. 'If it doesn't improve today you'll have to go down to base camp and have some oxygen and an anti-coagulant.'

'Where's Hurké?' Jack asked Jutta. 'I was counting on him being here.'

'He wanted to come, of course. But I made him stay. He's had quite a shock. It's on his mind what happened and his mind needs to be on the mountain if he's going to be up here.'

Unequal to the task of arguing with the German, Jack nodded. There was something about her tone of voice that sounded so common-sensical, so matter-of-fact that he could only agree with her decision that Ang Tsering should lead the Sherpas up to Camp One.

'He'll come up later this afternoon. But only if he's one hundred per cent.'

'Good thinking, Jutta. You're absolutely right. A mistake up here is nearly always fatal.'

He found Ang Tsering enjoying his sixth or seventh mug of Tibetan tea with Mac. Sherpas always drank large quantities of tea, aware that exhaustion on the mountain was more often due to the want of body fluids. Brewed with salt and butter, Tibetan tea was an acquired taste that Jack had never acquired. That Mac should seem to enjoy the stuff almost as much as the Sherpa seemed quite unaccountable.

'Delicious,' grinned the Scotsman, and smacked his lips with relish.

'As soon as you think the boys are ready, we'll get going down the corridor,' Jack told Tsering.

The assistant sirdar nodded slowly and took one of Mac's cigarettes.

201

'Were there any problems with them this morning?'

'Naturally,' said Tsering, puffing his cigarette into life with the help of Mac's flame-thrower of a lighter. 'The loss of so many close friends confirms them in their expectations that looking for a yeti is just the same thing as looking for trouble. They burned some incense before leaving ABC. And several times on our way we had to stop for prayers. No doubt they were asking the gods for the good health to spend the extra hard currency that Boyd sahib has given everyone in order to stay on.'

'He did that, huh?' Jack nodded. Boyd may have been a harsh critic of their mission, but there was no denying his capabilities. Not to mention his willingness to put his hand in his pocket and buy their way out of what could easily have proven to be a potential crisis with the porterage. Up here, when the porters went home, an expedition was finished.

'New notes too,' added Tsering. 'The boys prefer new notes, of course. Boyd knows that. I tell you, one might think that Boyd was printing them himself, such is the quantity of dollar bills at his disposal. It is just as well that we are an honest people. If I were Boyd I'd be afraid that someone would try and rob me.'

'I wouldn't worry about Boyd,' Jack told him. 'I reckon Boyd can look after himself.'

Behind the ruined tent, Jack stripped naked and took a quick snow bath, scrubbing himself clean with handfuls of snow. After drying himself vigorously, he donned the special underwear; then Mac and Jameson helped him to climb into the single-piece suit through an access hatch that was revealed when the backpack, with its Antarctic life-support system, was swung open on its rubberised seal. After the arm and leg lengths had been adjusted to Jack's height, the metal bayonet fittings of two air-conditioning hoses were locked on to their receptacles on the front of the suit. Then came hoses for the water-warmed underwear: the water, heated in the backpack, was designed to circulate through a tiny network of microscopic tubes woven into the material. Jameson and Mac locked each hose into place according to the suit's simple instructions.

'This is like arming Achilles,' said Jameson, handing Jack a clear bubble helmet that was made of photochromic plastic to reflect any strong sunlight.

'Don't you think it would make better sense if someone went with you?' said Swift. 'After all, there are two suits.'

'No,' said Jack. 'This is just a reconnaissance. It makes no sense at all to risk the lives of two people down there. I'm going to follow the shelf along the inside of the crevasse, see where it leads and then come straight back.'

Jack crowned himself with the helmet and while Jameson and Mac locked it on to the suit, he checked his helmet's hot mike through the small control unit he wore on his chest. This also provided display readings for the backpack.

Mac spoke into the suit's outside microphone that allowed the wearer to pick up ambient sound.

'Hadn't you better turn on your life support?'

'Good idea,' said Jack and, flicking another switch, started the tiny pumps and fans in his backpack and heard the reassuring whirr of the micro-machinery that would help to keep him warm in the freezing depths of the crevasse.

'Gloves are a bit stiff,' he said flexing his fingers. 'But everything else feels fine. I'm warming up now. Man, this feels good. I could sure have used this last night. It was a cold one up here. Hold on. What's this? There appears to be a loose pipe. Can you see? Next to my cheek.'

'That's your drinking water,' Mac advised.

Jack turned his head inside his helmet and found that the plastic pipe slipped neatly into his mouth. He sucked and tasted cool water.

'They seem to have thought of everything.'

Mac nodded down at Jack's genitals and shook his head.

'Not everything,' he said. 'If you want a piss you have to go in the suit. Or take it off. Your choice.'

Jack felt air blowing past his face as the suit gently inflated, and then stamped his boot to check the grip of his crampons.

'I don't think I could climb in this,' he said. 'At least not a big wall like the south-west face. But I reckon it would keep you alive in real weather.'

'According to the instructions,' said Mac, 'the helmet will illuminate automatically when you enter somewhere dark. The lamp on top is controlled manually, with the switch next to your radio control. There are two bulbs. Carbide for standard use and when you want to conserve battery life, and halogen when you want the extra power.'

Mac pointed to the control panel on the front of the suit.

'The other display is a compass and position finder. Allows you to use a satellite navigation system to tell precisely where you are on the earth's surface to within fifty metres. Assuming you wanted to deviate from the route inside the crevasse, all you would have to do would be to input the co-ordinates of where you wanted to go and the device would give you precise compass headings.'

'Got it.'

The Sherpas greeted Jack like excited schoolboys, pointing at him and laughing. One of them, a man named Kusaang, grinned and made a great show of offering Jack a cigarette, and with good nature Jack made a show of taking one, realising that he could not smoke it, and then tucking it behind the hose-pipe on his helmet, much to their apparent delight.

'Okay, folks, show's over. Let's get this expedition on the road.' Jack collected his ice-axe and began to walk slowly towards the ice corridor.

Picking up piles of rope, aluminium ladders, a tent, guns, camera equipment, food, and rucksacks, the rest of them followed.

While some of the Sherpas were putting up a tent in the corridor, Jack waited for Mac to hook the rope on to the karabinier on his waist-harness.

'You're safer camped down here than right next to the crevasse, I'd have thought,' said Jack. It would be from this tent that the rest of the team would stay in contact with him by radio. 'More sheltered too.'

'Don't worry about us,' said Mac. 'We'll be fine. As soon as you're gone, we're opening the whisky.'

Standing on the opposite side of the corridor, Swift raised the radio to her mouth.

'Jack, this is Swift. Can you hear me okay?'

'Loud and clear.'

As soon as Mac had moved out of the way Jameson stepped in to strap a holster around Jack's waist and to give him a hypodermic pistol.

'There's one in it, okay? It packs quite a dose so don't for Christ's sake shoot yourself.'

Jack tried to place his trigger finger inside the guard and found there was only just room and no more.

'I don't suppose the fingers of these gloves were made for guns,' he said, and holstered the gun before mounting the ladder that Tsering had fixed to the wall of the corridor with ice-screws and some wire. 'Wish me luck.'

At the top of the ladder, Jack stepped on to the wall, and turned to look back down at them all.

'Jack,' said Swift. 'Please be careful. If something happened to you –'

'Sure, you'd never forgive yourself.'

Then he waved once and disappeared from their sight as he walked down the gentle slope towards the crevasse.

Tsering and Mac, holding on to the end of Jack's rope, nodded at Swift.

'Taking in,' she said. 'Climb down when you're ready.'

Jack sat down carefully at the lip of the crevasse and hammered in his ice-axe.

'Slack,' he said and slowly eased himself over the side, searching for the shelf in the almost unfathomable depths below him.

Eighteen

'In the Treasure House of the Great Snow.'

Joe Tasker

As Jack descended into the darkness he switched on the standard light on top of his helmet, turning the blue ice a fantastic shade of yellow in front of his face. It was like being lowered into the frozen stomach of an enormous alien animal, seemingly long dead. The tiny trickle of meltwater running down the walls, caused by the heat from his suit, felt like an ominous sign that the alien's digestive juices were already stimulated by the presence of this explorer. And now that he was inside the crevasse he could see how much wider it was than on the outside. From one wall to the other was distance of at least eighteen metres, with the bottom of the crevasse hundreds, perhaps even thousands, of metres below.

Once, when climbing Everest, he had been obliged to cross a crevasse that had required five aluminium ladders tied end to end, in order to span it. The ice field, with as many as thirty of these aluminium bridges, had been one of the most dangerous things about climbing Everest. In a way the darkness below your feet helped: the height of any potential fall, and hence the danger, remained an unknown quantity. But now he thought he might never walk across one of those sagging ladder-bridges again. As his feet touched the shelf he looked up at the blue Danube of sky above his head and saw just how hazardous crossing a monster crevasse like this one might really be. To say nothing of leaping blindly on to a hidden shelf. A leap of faith was what Mac had called it; and that was what it was. Imagining the two yetis making such a jump gave him a new respect

206

for the capacity of these legendary creatures to survive and to remain elusive.

'Okay, I'm down,' he said. 'You can cut me some slack now.'

'Okay,' said Swift.

Jack paused for a moment, pulled the rope towards him and then unclipped the waist harness karabinier from the rope. He had no idea just how far he might have to walk and there was always a danger that a rope dragging behind him might snag or even freeze, and cause him to trip. Better to trust to his crampons and his ice-axe.

'Untying now.'

He turned to face the route. There was no doubt about this. To his left the shelf petered out underneath a series of enormous stalactites that descended into the darkness like so many organ pipes. He switched momentarily to the halogen light. To his right, the shelf was so well-defined that it looked almost like a proper pathway and what he could see of the route at the limit of the beam, some twenty or twenty-five metres in front of him, appeared to be straightforward enough. Here and there layers of ice and snow were marked by bands of what he took to be volcanic ash, creating fantastic shapes and patterns.

'Boyd would love this,' he said, slightly overawed by the character of his surroundings. 'Weirdest-looking ice I've seen.'

Switching back to the carbide light, he started to walk.

'Right then. Here I go, feeling like one of the Seven Dwarfs.'

'Which one?' asked Swift.

'Dopey, I guess. I must be dopey to do this, mustn't I?'

'You said it,' said Mac.

'Thanks, Grumpy. Thank goodness for water-heated underwear anyway. So far this isn't so bad. Not much more than a trek.'

The shelf led straight for about a hundred metres, then started to bend left. Above him the opening of the crevasse began to narrow. Jack checked the compass reading on the suit's control panel.

'From here the route bears west. There's a bit of a descending slope. The weirdest thing though. The ice on the wall is so finely marked it looks like the skin of some kind of animal.'

Without the crampons attached to his boots he could never have maintained any kind of pace. He walked another couple of hundred metres, using the ice-axe as a walking stick, with the pick end in his gloved left hand, nearest the drop, and the spike in the icy shelf underfoot. The angle of the shelf meant that he was tilted towards the wall, with his empty hand pressed almost continually against its icy surface to balance himself. After another five or six hundred metres, the sky vanished altogether as the crevasse closed up overhead and grew nearer his helmet. To Jack's experienced Himalayan eye the top of the great chasm appeared to have been partly filled by an avalanche.

'Well, that's the last of the daylight. From now on we're in the hall of the mountain king. Wait a minute,' he added. 'What's that?'

There was something leaning down over the shelf. At first he thought it was a stalactite. His steps faltered as he tried to make it out in the gloom. Then he stopped walking altogether. Was it his own imagination, or was there something vaguely human-looking up ahead? He switched to the halogen to get a better view and thought that he could make out a head and an arm. Whatever it was seemed almost to be waiting for him.

'There's something up ahead.'

'Jack,' said Swift. 'Please be careful.'

'I'm taking the pistol out, just in case.'

Unholstering the hypodermic pistol he started slowly forward again.

'I can see what looks like a head, and an arm,' he reported. 'Nothing's moving though.'

'Jack? This is Miles. Remember you're only accurate up to fifteen metres. And there's enough dope in the shot to fell a yak.'

'I hope so,' breathed Jack. 'Because the words BB-gun and rhinoceros spring to mind.'

'As soon as you get a clear shot, Jack.'

'Okay, it's definitely human-looking. Jesus, it's big too. About two, two and a half metres tall. Still not moving though. And no sound from it either. It's maybe twenty or twenty-five metres away. I need to get closer.'

'Jack, this is Byron. If the creature behaves as much like a gorilla as Hurké's description seemed to suggest, then it will quite probably remain quite still for a while and then charge.'

Considerably apprehensive now, Jack stopped in his tracks.

'What the hell does that mean? Do I stay still myself, or what?'

'It's probably curious about you. Try not to touch your chest. It might think that you're chestbeating. Great apes think of that as a signal for excitement or alarm.'

'Excitement or alarm, eh?' Inside the SCE suit and partly

208

amplified by the hot mike just below his Adam's apple, his own heart sounded like a set of bongo drums. 'I don't know where you got that idea.'

'Just – just don't do anything sudden.'

'Right.'

Jack inched his way forwards, holding the gun in front of him like a talisman. He hoped he would not have to rely on the ice-axe for protection. But if and until the Ketamine took effect it was either that or lie down on the ground and try and stab at the yeti with the chromoly steel tips of his crampons.

'Nearly in range,' he said, levelling the pistol and taking aim at what he perceived to be the creature's shoulder. At least if it charged now he could hardly avoid hitting his target.

'Nineteen metres . . . Eighteen . . . still no movement or sound. . . maybe this thing thinks I can't see it. . . seventeen metres . . .'

'You're going too quickly, Jack,' said Cody. 'Stand still for a moment.'

Jack stopped. He had a better view now. The creature looked much more human than he had supposed. Somehow this was not what he had imagined at all. Certainly this creature looked very different from the one he had seen at a distance on Everest's North Col.

And yet there was also something more sinister about it too. The lack of all movement gave the creature a much more terrifying aspect.

'Hardly like an ape at all,' he said. 'Still not moving. This is strange.'

'Jack, this is Miles. Seventeen metres is okay if you're aiming at a stationary target. But aim a little high.'

'Stationary isn't the word. Maybe it's asleep.'

'Jack, this is Byron again. I think you should go back. I really don't like the sound of it. This is classic defensive behaviour among mountain gorillas. They lure you on. Go back, please.'

'Just a bit closer, I think.'

'Now, Jack, now,' said Miles.

At less than seventeen metres Jack fired. He saw the dart strike the figure's exposed shoulder, but to his surprise the creature remained completely motionless and silent, as if it had felt nothing.

'There's something wrong,' he told the people up on the ice

corridor. 'I've fired and I can even see the dart sticking out of a shoulder, but nothing's happening.'

'It can take several minutes to take –'

'No, no. I mean it's like it didn't feel anything.'

'If it has a really thick hide and as much body fat as you might need to survive in these mountains, it may feel only minimal trauma,' said Jameson. 'Could be no more than a flea-bite to an animal that size.'

'Hold on. I'm going to have a closer look.'

'Jack, no,' protested Swift.

Coming closer now, Jack frowned and said, 'I think this is going to be okay. Whatever it is looks like it has been dead for some time.'

Near enough to reach out and touch it now, Jack holstered the pistol and started to brush some of the snow and ice away. The head lolled slowly backwards. The mosaic of snow-covered hair quite fair underneath. The mouth, slightly open to reveal a row of nicotine-stained gap teeth. And the eyes still open in a face that looked almost alive. Blue eyes. Staring at him now. Like someone. . .

Jack yelled with horror and started back against the ice wall.

'What is it, Jack,' said the voice in his helmet. 'Jack, are you okay?'

Nauseated by what he had found and trembling with shock, Jack slumped down on the icy shelf and took a deep unsteady breath of the warm air circulating inside his helmet. If he could have touched his face he would have wiped the cold sweat that had suddenly broken out on his brow. He felt like he had been punched in the stomach. It all came rushing back to him. The last few seconds before the avalanche that had swept him off the mountain face; and killed his old friend and climbing companion. There he was, hanging upside down above the ledge, held tight by the packed snow and ice that had dumped him there, months before.

Like a lost glove.

Jack rose numbly to his feet and brushed some of the leprous snow away from his friend's dead face. He hardly looked dead. His skin was unmarked, with not even a bruise. Rather he looked as if he was keeping very still for a photograph with a long exposure. As if he might only have to beat his arms against his side to pump some life into himself. As if, at any moment, he might pluck some of the many white plectrums of ice from his beard and speak.

210

Finally Jack himself spoke, answering the insistent clamour of voices in his helmet.

'Didier,' he sighed.

Sitting in the storm tent in the ice corridor up on top of the glacier, Byron Cody shrugged.

'Who's Didier?' he asked.

'Didier Lauren,' said Swift. 'He was killed in an avalanche the last time he and Jack came up here. The same avalanche that shovelled Jack into the cave where he found Esau must also have dropped Didier into that crevasse.'

'Jesus,' said Jameson. 'What a terribly lonely way to go.'

'You knew him too, didn't you, Mac?' said Swift.

Mac grunted his assent and incinerated the end of a cigarette, with a bitter lack of enjoyment.

'He wouldn't be the first of my friends to die in these mountains. And he probably won't be the last.'

'But to be here all that time,' said Cody. 'In the snow.'

'I also knew Didier,' said Jutta. 'He was a fine mountaineer. Poor Jack, to find him again like that.'

'Jack?' said Swift. 'Are you okay?'

'You're not going to believe this,' Jack said angrily. 'His wristwatch and ring are gone.'

'Maybe he lost them during the avalanche,' she suggested.

'It was his sponsorship watch. A Rolex Oyster Explorer. We both went to London to get them before coming out here. The watch is virtually unbreakable. And that ring always looked tight on his finger. Besides, he was wearing gloves.'

Byron Cody thought for a moment, remembering the deep curiosity exhibited by mountain gorillas concerning foreign objects. He picked up his radio and said: 'Jack, this is Byron. It's just a thought, but quite often a gorilla I was working with would steal my car keys or my glasses. Or any shiny object. It could be that one of the yetis took Didier's watch.'

'So now it will know when it's time to come and scare the shit out of me, huh?'

'Jack, this is Miles. Look, forget the watch for a moment. That was your only hypodermic dart. I want you to remove it from your friend's body and take a look at it.'

'Okay, but what's the point?'

'The point is this. When the syringe strikes the target, pressure

211

against the hub of the syringe pushes a tiny weight in the back of the charge against a small spring. The sharp tip of the weight penetrates a seal, setting off the charge and driving the plunger forward to discharge the drug. It's quite possible that because Didier's body is probably frozen solid none of the above happened. And that the Ketamine is still in the syringe. Do you see?'

Jack tugged the Cap-Chur syringe out of his friend's shoulder and scrutinised it carefully in the yellow carbide light. Wearing gloves and a helmet, there was little he could tell about the condition of the dart except that it looked much the same as before. He reported as much on the radio to Miles Jameson.

'Reload the pistol with it anyway,' said Jameson. 'It might be better than nothing.'

'Perhaps you ought to come back now,' said Swift.

Jack checked the readings displayed on the SCE suit's control unit. He had been inside the crevasse for about an hour. There was still plenty of power, at least ten hours' worth remaining in his backpack.

'Negative. I'm going on for a while longer. There's plenty of juice left in the suit, and I'm feeling fine. Besides, the point of this space walk is not to capture a yeti but to try and track them to whatever it is you call a great ape's lair.'

'It's called a nest,' said Cody.

Jack picked up his ice-axe and started to walk again, silently promising Didier that whatever happened he would not leave him there.

'Tell the boys to put that stretcher together. On my way back I'm going to carry him out.'

HUSTLER. THE CHINESE ISSUE IS NOW ACADEMIC I'M AFRAID. THIS MORNING I WENT TO CHECK UP ON THEM AND FOUND THAT AN AVALANCHE HAD WIPED OUT THEIR CAMP. OOPS. THERE WERE NO SURVIVORS. STILL, IT'S PROBABLY JUST AS WELL. DESPITE WHAT YOU SAID I HAD A BAD FEELING ABOUT THOSE SLOPES. MEANWHILE I HAVE WALKED FROM ONE END OF THIS SANCTUARY TO THE OTHER, BUT STILL NO LUCK. CASTORP.

212

Eager to be doing something, Miles Jameson and Jutta Henze went outside the tent and assembled the Bell split rescue stretcher themselves. Constructed from square section reinforced steel and fitted with a headguard, leg and chest restraints, and plastic ski-runners, it had been intended that the Bell could be used to transport a chemically restrained yeti back to ABC with the help of a helicopter from Pokhara.

'I had hoped we'd be needing this for a yeti,' remarked Jutta. 'Not another body.'

'We'll catch one yet,' said Jameson.

'You're an optimist, I think.'

'Hunting wild animals, my dear Jutta, you have to be. But I would have thought the same was true of people like you. Mountaineers.' Nodding at Annapurna's implacable south face, he explained, 'I mean, you'd have to be an optimist to think you stood a chance of climbing that.'

Jutta shook her head.

'No, I am a pessimist. In a place like this, optimism can easily get you killed. My husband was an optimist, as you say. He pushed himself too hard. But there is nothing you can do to change this kind of person. Jack is the same. He knows he is lucky to be alive after the last time, but he cannot be different. He would not want to be different.'

Sensing that she was in danger of becoming morbid, Jutta smiled brightly.

'I hope you are right, Miles. To find this animal would be really something, wouldn't it?'

'Yes. It would be like discovering a live dinosaur somewhere.'

'More interesting than that, surely. None of us is related to a cold-blooded animal. At least, not closely.' She grinned mischievously. 'Except Jon Boyd perhaps. He is not optimistic about our chances.'

'Yes, I'd really like to catch a yeti, if only to see the look on Boyd's face when we pulled it out of the net.'

'Or better still, when we put him in the net with a yeti.'

Jameson's eyes narrowed. 'I wonder,' he murmured.

'He could hardly deny it.'

But Jameson's mind was already on something else.

He left the stretcher and climbed the ladder to the top of the ice wall.

'Where are you going?'

'To take another look at that crevasse. I might just have an idea. Are the boys bringing the rest of the gear this afternoon?'

'Yes. What kind of an idea?'

'Let's just call it my Magic Johnson.'

The crevasse was completely dark now. Picking his way carefully along the shelf, with only the light on top of his helmet to illuminate the way ahead, the roof above Jack's head became solid ice, a vaulted roof of tiny cones, like the sound baffles in a studio or concert hall, or like crystals of salt or sugar magnified many hundreds of times. Jack decided that a yeti's sight must be better than a human being's – an observation he put to Byron Cody over the radio.

'That's interesting, Jack,' said the primatologist. 'The rest of the great apes, without exception, are diurnal creatures. So a yeti would be quite unusual if it was nocturnal. On the other hand, with no large predators to threaten him at night, a yeti may have evolved to take advantage of that fact. Perhaps even to become something of a predator himself.'

'Well that's a comforting thought to a man walking in darkness,' said Jack. 'But it might also explain why so few yetis are seen by men.'

'There's another possibility,' said Swift. 'Yeti may have become nocturnal specifically to avoid contact with man. If some of those Sherpa stories are true, man may indeed have been the yeti's principal enemy.'

Hearing Swift's theory reminded Jack of a grisly trophy he had once seen on his expedition to climb Everest.

'There's a small Buddhist temple at Pangboche,' he explained. 'In the foothills of Everest. For a few rupees, the Lama will show you what is claimed to be the scalp of a yeti. And also at Khungjung, in the same area. That's three hundred kilometres away. But if things don't work out here. . .'

The shelf rose steeply in front of him and bent round sharply to the right. Steep enough to require the aid of handholds, maybe even a few ice-screws. On one side the wall was completely smooth, while on the other there was just the chasm disappearing into the darkness below. With his ice-axe he struck at the floor of the shelf and found the chrome molybdenum head bouncing off rock-hard ice.

214

The wall proved no less durable. He tried to hammer in an ice-screw, and then a peg, but with no result.

'Looks like I'm going to have to climb some,' he said. 'Only I'm damned if I can see how. I've never seen ice this hard before.'

Sliding the axe beneath his belt and returning hammer and screw to his bum bag, Jack reached forwards and ran his hands up and down the wall. Finally he found something. Between the sloping floor of the shelf and the wall was a gap of about five centimetres. Just enough room to employ the same sophisticated mountaineering technique he had used to get up the National Geographic building. Called laybacking, the technique involved bending forward, holding on to the narrow underside of the wall with the tips of his fingers and then climbing up on the very points of his crampons.

'I'll say one thing for those hairy guys,' he grunted as he tried to climb in a series of fluid, continuous movements between one resting place and the next. 'There's nothing wrong with their mountaincraft. Of course, getting back down this little slope – is going to be – even more fun than climbing up.'

Turning the corner he reached the top, panting after his great effort, and an extraordinary sight now met his eyes.

He was standing at the beginning of an enormous cavern whose icy walls rose far above his head and dimly reflected the light from a distant disc of blue sky. About a hundred metres across an assault course of medium-sized ice blocks and mini fissures was the cavern's exit, an enormous portal of ice whose wind-blown shape resembled an eighteen-metre-high figure of eight. Beyond the portal was a remarkable scene. A strange gigantic company of pinnacles rose, gleaming white in the late afternoon sun and enclosing, like some smaller, more exclusive sanctuary, not white ice, but snowy green.

'I've found something,' he told the others. 'I must have come out on the other side of the Sanctuary, on the eastern side of Machhapuchhare.'

He stepped from one block to another, like a beachcomber crossing the rocks on a seashore inlet, and finally stepped on to a floor strewn with loose moraine – the debris carried down and deposited by the glacier – upon which an inadequate path had already been stamped. Sensing some new discovery, he started to walk quickly towards the cavern's legendary-looking exit.

215

'There's a tiny valley here. No more than about one and a half square kilometres. And hidden by a small circle of peaks. It looks incredibly well sheltered. There seems to be vegetation. Yes. This is fantastic. I wish you could see this. I've never seen anything quite like it.'

Emerging from the figure-of-eight exit, he found himself at the edge of a dense forest of pine trees and giant rhododendrons. He had heard of such high-altitude forests in other more remote countries bordering Nepal, like Sikkim and Zanskar, but not in this particular part of the mountains. There were times when Jack thought he knew all there was to be known about the Himalayas, but this was not one of them. Full of wonder at what he could see, he tried to describe the sight on the radio.

'There's Himalayan silver fir, birch, juniper trees, and some coniferous shrubs I've never seen before. And the rhododendrons are just incredible. I've seen them ten metres high. But these must be fifteen. Densely packed too. This looks more like rain forest than an Alpine zone.

He glanced up at the sky, the photochromic plastic in his helmet darkening in the sunlight, and caught sight of a large bird of prey – a Himalayan vulture he thought – as it wheeled high above the valley, searching for food.

Something scampered across the ground near his feet. A small mouse hare, almost tame.

'There's animal life here too. I just saw a rabbit. If the yeti has a natural habitat, I'm certain this just has to be it. Swift, this is it.'

'Jack, this is Byron. I hate to be a party pooper, but once again I advise extreme caution. If this habitat is as much like the rain forest as you say, then it might be best to suppose that yeti will behave like any mountain gorilla. Blundering through tall vegetation in that space suit could be very dangerous. Especially if the yetis have any young ones with them. Also if the yetis have learned to treat Man as an enemy then it might be safer to assume that they will defend their habitat aggressively. Jack, on no account should you try and find a nest. Mountain gorillas commonly post sentries to keep a lookout for the rest of the group. The chances are that they've probably seen you already, but won't react unless you look like you're about to pose an immediate threat.'

'Whatever you say, Byron, you're the expert. Only it seems a shame to go back now, having come so far.'

'Just bear Hurké Gurung's experience in mind.'

'Good point.'

A whistle, as loud as any construction worker's, echoed through the forest, as if simultaneously confirming what Cody had said.

'Did you hear that?' Jack asked.

'We heard it,' confirmed Cody. 'Now get the hell out of there.'

'On my way.'

Reluctantly, Jack turned to go back the way he had come. Not that it would have been easy to go any further anyway. The rhododendron forest looked so impenetrable that he would have needed a jungle knife – a khukuri – to hack his way through it.

Another whistle, louder this time. Did that mean a yeti was coming closer? No matter. He was going anyway. Already he was stepping on to the medial moraine that led back into the ice cavern.

He glanced down at the control panel. Eight hours of power left. More than enough to make it back up to the surface. Hearing a rustling sound Jack felt his heart stir uncomfortably inside his chest, as if protesting its unease, and he turned to face the forest again. There was movement in the giant rhododendron bushes and for the first time since his arrival on the edge of the forest he felt alarm. Now he was glad that he had taken Cody's advice. It would have been foolish to have gone blundering into the forest. Jack turned on his heel and hearing what might just have been the sound of chestbeating, he carried on walking with quickened footsteps. Alarm was being overtaken by fear now. The sooner he was out of there the better. The next time he came he would bring Jameson and a gun and a net. Several guns probably.

Another chestbeat. Like the sound of coconuts tumbling out of a sack and on to the ground. Or a big drill working on a distant wall. Once again he picked up his pace. He was almost running now. Stumbling a little on the loose moraine – the crampons were not suited to this kind of terrain, and he knew he ought to have removed them – he glanced down at the ground to check his footing. And as he moved a little further away from daylight, the carbide lamp on top of his helmet switched on automatically, illuminating the high ceiling, and some roaring demon hurtling towards him out of the darkness of the cavern ahead.

Jack heard someone yell 'Shit,' and then groaned as the collision knocked all the breath out of his body and carried him backwards on to the ground, like the most powerful football tackle imaginable.

217

A sharp stabbing pain in his ribs was followed by a more protracted torment as the tornado of arms and legs mauled him powerfully for about ten or twelve metres back across the floor towards the forest, and then something bit him hard. The last thing he was aware of was being wrestled through the rhododendrons, down a short gradient, and another excruciating flash of teeth.

Nineteen

'Remember your humanity and forget the rest.'
        Bertrand Russell and Albert Einstein, *Manifesto*

Inside the tent in the ice corridor Cody, Swift, Jameson, Jutta, Mac and Tsering faced each other grimly. They had all heard the loud roars that had accompanied Jack's own yells of fright and pain in the seconds before his radio had stopped working. Swift was still trying to re-establish communications.

'Jack, come in please. Are you all right?'

'One of the yetis must have charged him,' said Cody, stroking his long beard agitatedly.

'That's what it sounded like,' affirmed Mac.

'Probably bowled him over.'

'Can you hear me?'

Swift released the talk button and waited a moment, but there was just static and the wind outside. She tossed the radio aside and collected her face in the palms of her hands as she tried to control her first instinct, which was to let out a loud wail of despair.

'I got nailed by a mountain gorilla once myself,' said Cody. 'It was my own fault. I violated normal gorilla protocol. This was in Kigezi Gorilla sanctuary. A big silverback, a four-hundred-pounder, broke my collarbone and damn near bit through my femoral artery. I've still got the scars. There's one – '

'Look,' said Swift, interrupting him. 'What are we going to do about Jack?'

'I'd say that one of us is going to have to go and get him,' said Mac.

219

'Yes, but which one?' said Swift.

'Well obviously it can't be you, darlin'. This is no job for a woman.'

Instinctively Swift started to argue her own candidacy and then realised that she was probably the least qualified of any of them.

'Unless the woman also happens to be a doctor and a mountaineer,' said Jutta. 'I can see nobody who is better suited to this job than me.'

'Suppose you have to carry him,' objected Mac. 'Could you carry him?'

'Whoever goes should know the correct way to approach large primates,' said Cody.

'You've got frostbite,' said Jutta. 'It can't be you. That much is certain.'

'Who said only one person can go?' said Jameson. 'Why not two? With the Bell stretcher. Two makes more sense, surely?'

'There's only one environment suit up here,' said Mac. 'In a couple of hours it will be dark and it's going to get very cold in that crevasse. Without a suit, it's doubtful anyone would make it.'

'Mac's right,' said Jutta. 'Only one person can go.'

'And that's me,' added the Scotsman.

'You?' said Jutta. 'You're smaller than me.'

'Smaller, but stronger.'

'Aren't you confusing strength with aggression?' said the German. 'I'm as strong as you and a superior mountaineer. If his injuries are as bad as Byron's were, he'll need proper medical attention. Perhaps urgently. There's no telling how long he will last without it.'

'Assuming his suit's not damaged he might last the night,' said Mac.

'After those sound effects?' said Cody. 'That's a pretty big assumption considering his radio no longer works. It sounded like he got hit by the whole front line of the Forty-niners. Including Joe Montana.'

There were shouts outside the tent as another group of Sherpas arrived from ABC bearing more stores and equipment. They were led by the sirdar. He bent down and squeezed into the tent, still steaming from his exertions. The sky looked grey and it had started to snow again.

Jameson told him what had happened to Jack.

The sirdar listened carefully and without emotion. He thought

220

for a moment, nodded and then said, '*Me jaanchhu,* Jameson sahib. I want to go get him. Jack sahib is Hurké Gurung's friend and one time, two maybe three years ago, him save Hurké's life. So please, sahib, there can be no argument about who is to go and bring help to him. If the situation was other way, it would be Jack sahib who come and get me. That is how it is. Also, this is my country and I have been closer to yeti than any person here. Also I am best mountaineer. Even know some first aid. No question about it. I am going. *Bujhina?* As soon as I have drunk cha and put on these special clothes that will make me look like a spaceman I will go and fetch my friend Jack sahib.'

The sirdar's strong unsmiling face held such an expression of grim determination that there was no one who felt able to challenge his claim to the rescue mission. Jameson exchanged a look with Swift who nodded back at him.

'Okay,' Jameson told the sirdar. 'Job's yours.'

'*Hajur. Pugna kati samay laagcha?*'

'We think it should take you about three hours at the most. It's a more or less straight route along the shelf inside the crevasse.'

Hurké glanced at his Casio sportswatch and then outside the tent. The weather had deteriorated even in the few minutes since he and the Sherpas had come up from the Rognon. The sky was grey and it was starting to snow a little.

'Be dark by then. And there is maybe bad weather to come. As soon as I am in crevasse, rest of team should go back down to Camp One. Not stay here.'

'He's right,' said Mac. 'I'd better go and organise the boys.'

'Mac sahib. Before you go. *Mero tasbir khichnukos? Laai ke bhaanchha?*' He shrugged apologetically. 'Could you take my picture please?'

'Sure,' said Mac, and lifting the Nikon that was nearly always hanging on a strap around his neck, he quickly took the sirdar's portrait.

'Thank you, sahib. It is for wife and son. In case anything happens to make problems. You would see that they get it, yes?'

'Of course. But don't be bloody silly. Nothing is going to happen to you.'

'Yes, sahib.'

'I'll go and fetch that suit for you,' said Swift and followed Mac outside.

*

221

Jameson went to find Ang Tsering.

'The gear the sirdar and the boys just brought up,' he asked. 'Where is it?'

Tsering pointed to several thirty-kilogramme loads that were still roped up for carrying.

'But we must go back down. The sirdar has said so.'

Jameson examined one of the loads and then another. He seemed to find what he was looking for and clapped his hands together purposefully.

'Yes, yes. But before we leave there's something I want to organise first.'

'And what is that, sahib?'

'A surprise.' Jameson looked excited. 'Can't understand why I didn't think of this before. Seems the perfectly logical thing to do really. But there we are. You can't always be omniscient. Tell me, Tsering, do you know how to fix an ice-screw, or a dead man anchor.'

Tsering shook his head. 'I regret no, sahib.'

'Never mind. I'll show you.'

'This dead man anchor? Is it for Jack's friend, Didier sahib? Is this the surprise?'

'Christ no. It's to keep the surprise secure.'

Bryan Perrins had asked Chaz Mustilli to come to his office. Mustilli was in charge of assigning field personnel and had recommended CASTORP for the job in the Himalayas. Like Perrins, Mustilli had also formed the conclusion that the Chinese soldiers had been murdered by CASTORP. Mustilli was a thick-set man, with a Kojak head and an expensive-looking pipe he sucked often but only ever smoked in his own office. As he handed the DDI a file on CASTORP and sat down, he looked uncomfortable, even depressed.

Perrins noted Mustilli's expression and assumed the worst. But he let him go ahead with his explanation.

'I did what you asked, Bryan. I started to look into CASTORP's background. And it would seem that we – um – somehow overlooked his most recent psychological profile. Unfortunately the person who did the evaluation went sick soon after it was done and, well, the long and the short of it is that we just didn't know about it when we recommended CASTORP for this mission. The report has only just turned up. I mean he seemed to be perfectly well qualified. Of

222

course, if we had known what we now know then, we'd probably have recommended someone else.'

Perrins nodded slowly.

'And what does this tardy bit of psychological evaluation have to say about our man in Himalaya?' He laughed at his own little joke. 'I mean, it's not good, right?'

'There is some evidence of recent psychological problems.'

'Chaz, your face tells me that much. Tell me something I don't know. Tell me what the shrink said.'

'Apparently his thoughts and deeds no longer meet the demands of reality. He is probably suffering from some kind of psychosis.'

'Well we can't afford to recall him. He's the only card we have to play. No, the question is how to control him.' Perrins stood up and went to the window. 'You've been reading his reports, Chaz. Do you think he killed those Chinese?'

'Yes, I do.' Mustilli sucked noisily on his empty pipe as if he had been using an inhaler. 'You know, it won't necessarily stop him from getting the job done.'

'I think you're right, Chaz. No, I'm just worried what might happen if any of those poor fucking scientists happen to get in our psycho's way. There's no telling what he might do. I'll send him an e-mail. Try and put him on the straight and narrow.'

Arriving back at ABC after another day walking around the glacier, Boyd found only a couple of Sherpas hanging around in their snow-bound hotel and, underneath the clamshell, Lincoln Warner composing an electronic message on his computer.

'Thank God for e-mail,' grumbled the tall black man. 'Otherwise I think I might go mad up here.'

'You more than most,' murmured Boyd. 'Who's it from?'

'What?'

'The message.'

'Oh, just some students,' he said vaguely. 'From time to time, I zap some information about our expedition to a classroom in Washington.'

'Nice of you.'

Boyd wondered exactly what it was that Warner actually did all day. He rarely ventured out into the Sanctuary, except for the walk he took regularly at around three o'clock in the afternoon. He seemed to spend the rest of his time sitting in front of his screen.

The one time Warner had let him get near enough to see what he was doing it had turned out he was playing some kind of interactive computer game.

'Hey, Link, where the hell is everyone? This place looks like it's a public holiday.'

Warner clicked his mouse to mail the message via the satellite and turned on his chair.

'Nearly everyone's up at Camp One. Seems like Jack found the place where the yetis are holed up.'

'Hey, no shit?'

'No shit.'

'So why the face like Bela Lugosi? This means you guys are going to be famous, doesn't it?'

'They lost radio contact with Jack after what sounded like an attack. He could be hurt.'

'An attack? By one of the monsters?'

Warner winced uncomfortably. 'Yes. If you want to put it that way.' Boyd reminded him most of Kent in *King Lear*. Someone who mistook being blunt for wit.

'That's too bad. Anything we can do?'

'No. Apparently not. The sirdar's gone to rescue him. We hope.'

Boyd nodded judicially. 'He's a good man. If anyone can save Jack's ass, it's the sirdar.'

He hauled off his windproof jacket and dropped it on to the floor.

'It looks like I was wrong, doesn't it? What do you think it is – this yeti? Some kind of great ape, huh?'

'I'd say that some kind of great ape was probably the most likely scenario.'

Boyd poured himself a coffee from a Beverage Butler that stood on a table and sat down opposite Warner, nursing the steaming mug in his cold hands.

'Yessir, you and some of these other scientists are going to be famous.'

Warner rubbed his smooth chin thoughtfully. The beard was gone now, but he was missing its tactile comfort. Stroking it had made him feel more relaxed somehow. Like being your own dog.

'If we live that long.'

'How's that?'

'I was listening to the Voice of America on the radio a little while ago. It seems that the cooling-off period between India and Pakistan

224

may be coming to a premature end. Several Muslim countries have stated that they will declare war on India if it should attack Pakistan. An act of religious solidarity, they said. They've already sent troops and equipment. I'm beginning to think that it might become rather difficult to get out of here.'

'Oh, is that all?' Boyd looked and sounded unimpressed.

'You sound like you don't believe the war is a possibility, Jon.'

'They haven't had one yet, have they? Look, if there is a war it isn't going to be about troops and equipment,' said Boyd. 'It's going to be about a failure of deterrence. If one of them thinks that they can get away with a strike. Right?'

'Maybe. But where exactly will that leave us? That's what I'd like to know. The Indian border is not so very far away.'

Boyd drained his coffee cup and lit a cigarette.

'Beginning to get to you, huh?' he said. 'The proximity?'

'I don't mind admitting it.'

'Maybe you know something I don't. All those radio broadcasts you listen to. You're probably a lot better informed about the situation than I am. But frankly, Link, I wouldn't let it bother me.'

'No? Even a nominal nuclear case scenario is likely to have some kind of effect on the world's weather system.'

'Not really my area,' said Boyd. 'Solid fuel emissions are more likely to screw things up for us back home than a few nukes down here.'

'But Delhi. That's where we flew into on the way to Kat. That's just six hundred and fifty kilometres away. If Delhi is nuked . . .'

'If Delhi is nuked then we'll just have to find another way to fly home, is all. Calcutta probably. No way Pakistan can reach Calcutta. It's just too far for their missiles.' He laughed. 'Of course if we happened to be back in Delhi at the time, now that would be different. That would be unfortunate.' He kept on laughing as he expanded on the possibility. 'Especially if you had also happened to have evidence that proved the existence of the Abominable Snowman.'

'I seem to recall you saying that there was no telling what might happen if they started throwing nukes around.'

'I was just – ' Boyd smiled ruefully. 'Y'know, playing devil's advocate. My honest opinion? It's like Swifty said. This whole international situation's been a big bonus for us. The whole world is shit scared of what's been happening on the Indian subcontinent. We've got the place to ourselves. For a team of scientists, what could be better than that?'

225

'Apart from those Chinese up near MBC.'

'Funny thing about them. They're gone. I was up that way earlier and there's not a sign of them. I reckon Ang Tsering was on the button. They must have been deserters. Probably skedaddled as soon as Cody and Jutta were out of there. You ask me those two people are lucky they're still alive.'

Boyd poured himself another coffee and laughed at Warner's gloomy expression.

'Hey, come on, lighten up. You must have known what you were getting into when you came up here?'

'I guess I didn't really give it much thought.'

'That Swift,' laughed Boyd. 'She can be pretty damned persuasive when she wants to be.'

'Something like that.'

'I thought so. She's a good-looking girl. Not much she couldn't persuade me to do, if she put her mind to it. If she put her body into it as well then. . .' Boyd shook his head as he tried to conjure an image of what he might be capable of doing in the carnal cause of Swift's body.

Warner grinned back at him uncomfortably. Generally more comfortable with women than men, he especially disliked this kind of locker-room talk.

'Hell, for a night with her, I think I might even take a shot at the south-west face,' declared Boyd.

The other man felt his cheek muscles harden with irritation but tried to keep his smile going. Boyd was developing a real knack of knowing how to annoy him. Wondering if he had the same effect on everyone else, Warner turned and fixed his eyes on the roof of the clamshell and spoke as if he could not bear to look at Boyd.

'She is very attractive, isn't she?'

'You want my advice? Don't even think about it. Stop scaring the shit out of yourself with what's on the radio and pray that they can capture one of those ape-men.'

'Okay. Yes, I'll do that.'

'Now then. What do you say we find some of those ready-to-eat meals a good bottle of scotch, and have ourselves a real dinner? Me, I could eat a horse.'

226

Twenty

'There are demon haunted worlds, regions of utter darkness.'
The Upanishads

Jack Furness lay on the ground in the rhododendron forest, drifting slowly back to consciousness. He was tired and wanted only to sleep. Shifting his position he felt the pain in his left shoulder from where he had been bitten and almost fainted again. His whole body ached from head to toe as if he'd been thrown around by one of those television wrestlers. Thrown around, slammed, stamped on, clotheslined, suplexed and half-strangled. There was a terrible throbbing pain in his head, so bad it made him feel sick. Inside the SCE suit however it was at least still warm. Warm enough to make him want to go back to sleep, to forget the pain.

To forget the extraordinary-looking creature that had been the cause of his pain.

He pushed himself up on one elbow, opened his eyes, groaned and rolled on to his back – slowly, in case the wild man of this high Himalayan forest should think he still he posed some kind of threat and attack again. If it was even still on the scene. Jack looked around, trying to get his bearings and wondering what they must be thinking in Camp Two on the ice-corridor. They must have heard the attack.

'Hello, this is Jack calling Camp Two, are you receiving me, over.'

He was lying on a gentle gradient that was covered with low, spiny shrubs. Above him soared the tops of the trees and the giant rhododendrons, and although the daylight was beginning to fade fast, he could now see that the forest concealed a deep depression and that

227

the valley was more probably the bowl of an extinct volcano. It would certainly have explained the apparent fertility of the soil. It would also have explained why the forest was so uniquely sheltered.

'Hello, Swift, this is Jack. Can you hear me? Over.'

He sat up and, feeling sick again, dropped his head between his knees. Feeling a stabbing pain in his left side as he tried to take a deep breath, he concluded that at least one of his ribs was cracked or broken. Added to the injury he had sustained to his left shoulder, this meant that the only really comfortable position for his left arm was pressed close to his side. Thus, partly disabled, he lifted up his head and gently thumped the side of his helmet hoping to restore the communications connection that had been lost sometime during the attack. He found the water pipe pressing against his cheek and, turning his head towards it, took a long cool drink.

'Is anyone reading me? Over.'

It was no good. He tried to imagine what they would be thinking. Did they think he was dead? Would they attempt a rescue? It was imperative he re-establish radio contact. As soon as he could get back up the slope and into the comparative safety of the crevasse, he would have to try and take off the suit and check out all the connections. He could hear a bird singing somewhere, and the sound of the wind stirring the bushes around him, so the hot mike was also working.

At first he saw only dense foliage ahead of him. But here and there, between thick, leathery evergreen leaves each as big as a baseball glove, he could see patches of a different colour. A dark, reddish brown colour.

They were moving patches of colour.

He stared, both fascinated and terrified.

Curious, they stared back.

There were maybe fifteen or twenty of them. They were sitting further down the same gradient, less than fifteen metres away, eating rhododendron leaves and a fungus like a giant mushroom that grew in quantity on the bark of a tree.

'Holy shit,' said Jack.

They behaved like apes, and yet they were also something more. Their brows were ape-like but there, he thought, the similarity ended, for the yetis' faces were quite hairless and flesh-coloured, like a young chimpanzee's, and featured a small but very definite-looking nose. Their mouths were different too: smaller than a

228

gorilla's and yet seemingly more articulate. Mostly they just belched with apparent contentedness, or grunted like a pig, or uttered raspy expirations of noise that sounded like chuckles. But occasionally one would lean towards another and, still looking straight at Jack, utter a more complicated set of belched vocalisations that seemed to require some labial dexterity – sounds that resembled the barking, guttural remarks of a man whose larynx had been removed. Jack felt his ears burning. Maybe he was imagining it, but for all the world it looked like the yetis were talking about him.

'Swift, Cody? I wish you could see this. It's fantastic.'

A sense of awe did not blind Jack to the gravity of his situation. It was still possible that the yetis might kill him. And in only a few hours his power pack would run out leaving him without heat. With the outside temperature already dropping as dusk approached and snow filling the air above the treetops, he would probably freeze to death. He had to get out of there.

Cautiously Jack dug his heels into the soft, black volcanic earth and pushed himself gently half a metre back up the hill.

His movement produced a variety of reactions among the group of yetis.

Some craned their necks to obtain a better view of him, while others, chattering amongst themselves, stood up. A female holding an infant turned her back to him protectively. Nearest of all, an adult male, easily recognisable by his enormous size and silver-red torso, watched him intensely for a moment and then uttered a deafening roar.

Jack remained still for a moment, waiting for them to settle down again. When he thought it was safe he repeated the manoeuvre. It had become sufficiently gloomy underneath the leaf cover of the forest for the light on top of his helmet to switch itself on automatically. Momentarily dazzled by the carbide lamp, the big male rose on long bowed legs – much longer than a gorilla's – to his full height. Jack guessed him to be over two metres in height. The male took a deep breath and leaning towards Jack, roared with even greater volume and ferocity.

'Wraaagh!'

It was as intimidating a display of hominoid power and aggression as Jack had ever witnessed and he could well understand how Hurké could have lost control of his bowels.

229

'Okay, you made your point. You don't like the light. No problem.'
Jack quickly turned the carbide lamp off and stayed quite still.

But now that he was on his feet, the big male yeti was apparently set on underlining his dominance over Jack and the rest of the group, and flinging his long shaggy arms above his head, he roared again.

'Wraaagh!'

'Okay, okay. I hear you. You're the bossman.'

Advancing towards Jack, the yeti walked quite unlike any ape he had ever seen, not with the upper part of his hugely-muscled body, brachiating on the knuckles of his hub-cap-sized hands, but upright, with all of his weight on his legs, his head held high in the cold mountain air, like a man. Jack thought Bossman must have weighed all of a hundred and eighty kilogrammes and the crest on his head was as high as a Norman helmet. He was the most magnificent animal, if animal he was, Jack had ever seen.

Jack realised that Bossman might possibly also be the last thing that he would ever see. He pressed his head against his knees, bracing himself for the mighty blow he felt certain was coming. At best it would be a blow that knocked him senseless again.

Instead the yeti merely stood over him like some ancient Greek Titan intent on storming heaven, roared once more, and then stomped back to his original position, where he sat down again on his enormous backside. But while Bossman's silver-red back was temporarily turned, Jack managed to push himself further back up the gradient.

Painfully he glanced back over his good shoulder and saw that he had only about three metres to go to reach the line where the forest ended and the ice cavern began. Although his shoulder and side hurt, his legs felt fine and he thought he might have stood up and climbed what remained of the crater's slope had he dared to turn his back on the yetis. Instead he dug his heels into the earth and the shrubs and pushed himself up.

His hand touched something flat and reflective. It was not a piece of flat stone as he first thought, but a piece of plastic, a layered grid of what looked like photo voltaic cells. Jack felt around his helmet to see if something had come loose even though the object looked too big to have . . .

The second attack came from directly behind him.

Jack yelled out with fright as two enormous hands clasped his helmet like a basketball, lifting him clear off his feet. There must have been another big silverback male squatting behind him at the top of the crater all along, possibly the same yeti that had attacked him in the first place. For a moment Jack hung there, grappling with the roaring yeti's vice-like grip as he made a futile attempt to free himself. Suddenly the creature gave his helmet a sharp twist, just as if it had intended to break Jack's neck, and for one terrifying moment he had a close view of the yeti's cavernous mouth with its large tartar-covered teeth. The teeth had looked harmless enough on the skull he had given to Swift. And yet they were undoubtedly the same size as the ones now snapping at his throat.

Seconds later Jack fell to the ground, but without his helmet. That remained in the yeti's hands. His attacker roared with satisfaction, perhaps imagining that it had decapitated its victim, and then hurled the helmet back into the ice cave.

Jack told himself to play dead. It was now his only chance if the creature was not to finish him off. He had heard about Alaskan grizzly bears that would leave you alone if they thought you were dead, but Jack was aware that this would require a control over his own body and its thresholds of pain he no longer possessed.

There was just one chance he might make a more convincing corpse.

Jack hauled Jameson's hypodermic pistol from its holster.

For a split second he thought of shooting the yeti only something told him that the two or three minutes required for the drug to take effect on such a large creature would be all it needed to kill him. If indeed there was any drug in the syringe at all. And if there was no drug he would surely just aggravate the beast even further. It was his best chance and he knew it. He pointed the pistol at the inside of his thigh and pulled the trigger.

The hypodermic dart struck its close target with the cold sharp sting of a large snake. Jack cursed and fought his automatic instinct to pull out the dart.

'Damn you, Miles,' he thought. The dart hurt, whatever Jameson said about painless anesthesia, the dart hurt.

In half an hour it would be dark. In another half hour – if the drug worked – he might be able to crawl away unseen.

The big silverback male – surely even bigger than Number One – swept a rhododendron bush out of its path and advanced on Jack

231

as he waited, desperately, for the Ketamine Hydrochloride to deliver its mercifully analgesic effect.

The sirdar, being a former Gurkha naik, or sergeant, and a member of a tribe that lived in a part of Nepal always more strongly influenced by India, was a Hindu. But many of the Sherpas, including Ang Tsering, were Buddhists of Tibetan stock. Like most Nepalese, Hurké Gurung was scrupulously tolerant of Buddhists, just as they were of Hindus, and indeed Nepalese Hindus were quite Buddhist in their relaxed interpretation of the caste system. So before beginning his rescue mission, the sirdar was happy to accept a blessing from Pertemba, a Sherpa who in a previous incarnation, it was said, had been a Tibetan Lama. Hurké also accepted the loan of a little image of the Green Tara, who took precedence among all the queens of Tibetan mythology and who, he was promised, would protect him from all harm that might befall him. Another man tied a piece of yellow thread around the sirdar's neck for good luck.

Hurké Gurung was touched by the devotion shown by his men and decided that it could only be the case that they felt he had represented them well as far as the *bideshis* were concerned. But he preferred to put his own faith in Ganesh, the elephant-headed god of wisdom and the remover of obstacles; and if the occasion arose, Pashupati, a benevolent form of Shiva, and the Lord of Beasts.

Uttering silent prayers to these two Hindu deities, and with fond thoughts of his wife and their son, the sirdar was lowered into the crevasse and on to the shelf leading to what the rest of the Sherpas were already calling the *pabitra ban* – the Holy Forest.

Jack had wrongly supposed that the Ketamine Hydrochloride would render him unconscious. He experienced the effect of the drug most noticeably as a lessening of the pain in his shoulder and side, and then, as a creeping paralysis of all his major muscle groups. He had quite forgotten that the drug had only an immobilising effect; that he would become insensitive to external stimulation; that his eyelids would remain open in a semblance of death; but that he would remain fully conscious. So he could not even blink when the yeti, crashing through the undergrowth after him, picked up a rotten log as big as a filing cabinet, and raised it in the air with the apparent intention of crushing him underneath.

Instead, seemingly influenced by Jack's complete immobility, the

232

creature sat down on its haunches only away from Jack's head and allowed the log to roll harmlessly back down its enormous shoulders and on to the ground. Bending forward, the yeti searched the fixed expression in Jack's eyes for any signs of life.

Jack could only meet his penetrating stare and sense a sharp consciousness behind the amber-coloured eyes. Surely, he thought, this was no ordinary ape. This was a highly intelligent creature, with an awareness of the world that seemed quite uncharacteristic of any ordinary animal.

Another more painful indication of the creature's intelligence immediately followed, for with an insight that seemed quite uncanny, it poked Jack hard against his injured ribs with one long cigar-tube of a forefinger. It was as well he had thought to restrain himself chemically, he told himself. But for the anaesthetising effect of the Ketamine he would undoubtedly have yelled with pain, with a probably fatal result.

Gradually the yeti began to relax and glance around to its companions with the smug delight of one who had defeated an opponent. It even seemed – he was quite sure this could only be the drug – that the creature was laughing: a deep, unpleasant, alien kind of laugh that sounded like one of the giants he had been thinking of earlier. Cronus or Hyperion. A contemptuous belly laugh born of enormous strength and size such as the Cyclops Polyphemus might have uttered before eating six members of Ulysses's crew.

But if he had thought that the yeti might now leave him alone, Jack was soon made aware of this mistake, for the creature took him by the ankle and began to drag him back down the slope towards the rest of the group like some kind of trophy, as if he wished somehow to emphasise his dominance of the rest by his victory over the strange interloper.

The others slapped the ground with clear delight and whooped and roared their admiration of the yeti that Jack assumed was the real Number One, for even Bossman seemed subdued when Number One was on the scene.

Number One howled, made a snatching sign with its long, ramrod fingers, as if plucking the head of a flower, and then put the fingers to his mouth, repeating the action several times as if it contained a meaning, and eliciting from the rest of the group many grunts of approval.

Other yetis signed back. It looked like sign language.

Jack did not know much about linguistics beyond what he had seen on PBS, or read in the *New Yorker*. He was aware that some chimpanzees, Washoe for one, had been taught a rudimentary form of communication. He was also aware that there was considerable debate as to whether or not such communication implied thought and/or emotions. But this looked like something much more tangible. A sign language that they themselves had originated and not one taught by humans. Or was this just another hallucination? If so it was a very general one, for the impression he had was of all the yetis communicating with each other and with some dexterity too.

Something squeaked.

Not the baby yeti as he had first thought, but a smaller creature, about a half a metre long, covered with thick fur and with a distinctive squat build. It was a Himalayan marmot. One of the pendulously-breasted yeti females was holding the creature in her hand.

An absurd idea that this might be some kind of pet was immediately rejected when the female took the squeaking marmot by the leg and, wielding it like a slingshot, banged it hard against the side of a tree, killing it instantly. For a moment she seemed to examine the marmot's stomach fur until Jack saw the blood on her strong fingers and realised that she had disembowelled it and was now eating the innards. Her meal over, the female yeti flung away the gutted furry carcass as if it had been an empty sweet wrapper.

A vague memory of the eviscerated marmot they had seen on top of the Rognon, and of an article in *National Geographic* devoted to a group of meat-eating chimpanzees, was quickly replaced by a sense of dread as to the meaning of the yeti sign language.

Dread turned to horror as Number One ripped the control panel off the front of Jack's SCE suit and started to chew at it experimentally.

The yetis were carnivores.

They were planning to eat him. And to eat him alive.

Twenty-one

'This survival of the fittest which I have here sought to express in mechanical terms, is that which Mr. Darwin has called "natural selection", or the preservation of favoured races in the struggle for life.'

Herbert Spencer

As soon as Hurké Gurung was in the crevasse, the team, with the exception of Jameson and the Sherpas, prepared to start back for Camp One.

The sky was gun-metal grey and full of snow and the wind was already blowing fiercely.

'Where are you going?' Swift asked Jameson as he mounted the ladder that led up on to the wall next to the crevasse.

'Won't be long. Something I want to do first with the boys. You carry on.'

Swift eyed the spade-shaped alloy plates dangling from a fistful of wires he was holding.

'What are those? What are you up to, Miles?' she asked suspiciously

Grinning maniacally, the Zimbabwean started to climb the aluminium ladder.

'Ask no questions,' he said from the top of the wall. 'I hope all will become clear in due course. Trust me.'

Tsering and some of the other Sherpas were already working under a floodlight in the jumble of ice and snow that led down to the black hole now containing their sirdar. Out of the shelter of the corridor the wind was stronger and Jameson had to shout to make himself heard.

'Did you put those ice-screws in, like I showed you?' he asked Tsering. 'At six-metre intervals?'

'Yes, sahib.'

'The lugs should lie flush with the surface,' he said, bending over to inspect one. 'That looks good.' Experimentally he slipped the point of his ice-axe into the lug and turned it.

'They're all tight,' Tsering said wearily. He still had no idea what the *janaawar daaktar* had in mind.

'Good, good.'

Jameson pointed to a large canvas bag that the Sherpas had carried up ABC.

'Now then, inside the bag is a net. We're going to secure it inside the crevasse.'

'Will the yeti not tear it?' asked Tsering. 'The sirdar said the yeti was very strong.'

'Not this net. It's a cargo net. Same sort as they use to lift things out of the holds of ships. I last used this net to trap a wild musk-ox. And believe me, if it was strong enough for a musk-ox, I think it should be strong enough for a yeti. We'll secure one side of the net to the lugs and the other to the dead man anchors I need to place on the other side.'

'Yes, sahib. We have roped some ladders together as you asked, but – '

'Then I'd better rope up.'

Jameson was already tying a rope around his own waist.

' – but in this wind it is dangerous, sahib. Perhaps it would be better to wait until morning.'

'And miss a night's hunting? Nonsense.'

He waited until Tsering had tied the other end to one of the ice-screws and around himself, and then jerked his head down the slope.

'Come on. I want this all fixed before it gets dark.'

They walked further along the edge of the crevasse, towards the several sections of aluminium ladders that now spanned it in a rickety-looking banana-shaped drawbridge. Jameson stood for a moment and then pronounced it a fine piece of engineering, although it was hardly level: the slope on the other side of the crevasse meant that the bridge had a camber that tilted sickeningly to one side.

'Good work, boys,' said Jameson. 'Okay, take up the rope.'

Tsering and the others collected the rope and watched as the white Zimbabwean placed one foot on the first rung of the ladder, making sure that it slotted comfortably between the points of his crampons. Each was glad he would not be asked to cross the bridge. Rope or no rope, there was no doubting Jameson's courage.

Adrenalin racing through his legs, Jameson moved on with the steadiness and utter concentration of a high-wire walker. He had no idea how deep the chasm below him was and felt just as glad he couldn't really see into it. Sometimes it was better to live in ignorance. His footsteps faltered only once and that was when he reached the middle, where the two ladders had been tied end to end with knots of rope that were Gordian in their size and complexity. As he lifted his foot over one of these, the ladder wobbled alarmingly and then sagged under his weight. For a brief moment Jameson had a vision of himself standing between the two separating halves of the makeshift bridge, like a man who finds himself on a splitting floe of ice; but he just as soon regained his nerve and carried on, reaching the other side with a loud exclamation of relief.

Straight away he set about placing the dead man anchors, embedding each spade-shaped plate in the snow in such a way that its entire surface could resist movement when a load was applied to the wires: pulling on the wires had the effect of bedding the anchors further into the snow. When Jameson was satisfied that these were secure he hauled the cargo net over the crevasse. Next, he tied the rope to the anchors and then to a series of screwgate karabiners that were attached to the net. Last of all he adjusted the height of the net so that it lay just below the lip of the crevasse, immediately above the hidden shelf on to which the yetis were wont to jump.

'Do you see?' Jameson shouted redundantly. 'When a yeti jumps on to the ledge, we'll have him.'

Jameson walked back along the far side of the crevasse to the ladder bridge and waved to Ang Tsering.

'Okay, throw me a line,' he said.

The rope securing him during his first walk across the bridge had been used to haul the net over and then to position it inside the crevasse.

Tsering looked around the ground and then shouted to one of the Sherpas.

'*Dori kahaa chha?*'

Looking crestfallen, a man named Nyima walked back up the

slope and disappeared over the top of the wall of the ice corridor.

'He's gone to fetch some more rope,' Tsering explained.

Jameson nodded patiently, once again preparing himself mentally to cross the void.

A minute or two passed and then the Sherpa returned, bowed to the assistant sirdar, and said that there was no more rope. Tsering began to curse Nyima loudly and told him to go down to Camp One and fetch some.

'Look, never mind,' said Jameson. 'There's no time to go back down. I'll have to do it without.'

Tsering looked appalled.

'But, sahib. It is dangerous. Suppose you fell?'

Jameson picked up the rope that had been used to lower the ladder across the crevasse like a drawbridge, intending to use it as a makeshift banister, and placed a foot on the ladder.

'Then I suppose I'll have to try and hold on to this,' he said coolly, and started to walk.

Gingerly, like a man stepping through a minefield, Jameson made his way across the ladder, pausing only once, to wait until a powerful gust of wind had died away.

Reaching the other side, he brushed aside Nyima's apologies and Tsering's continued praise for the ingenuity of his trap.

'Yes indeed,' said Tsering. 'The yeti will get a real surprise.'

From his rucksack, Jameson removed a long cylindrical-looking object and began to attach it to one of the ropes supporting the net.

'And what is this, sahib?'

'This?' Jameson grinned another manic-looking smile. 'This might just turn out to be my early morning wake-up call.'

Still paralysed by the Ketamine, Jack lay listening to the chatter of the yetis, waiting helplessly for Number One to rip his guts out with his teeth and fingers. Chewing the control box investigatively, the yeti appeared to be in no real hurry and Jack decided that his main hope of survival now lay in the taste of the plastic box. If Number One was persuaded that the rest of Jack's body was equally unappetizing then its late dinner might be cancelled.

Number One stopped chewing and broke the box into two pieces as if it had been a stick of bread. Appetite gave way to curiosity as the yeti began to pick the chips and wires out of the box.

Jack found small consolation in the sight. He felt like a teddy

238

bear which at any moment might find its stomach ripped open by some inquisitive child in search of the source of its growl.

Another big silverback, the one Jack recognised as Bossman, walked stoopingly towards Jack's supine body eliciting a warning bark from Number One. Ignoring the obvious warning, Bossman sat down and began to tug at Jack's boot. This time Number One flung the control box aside, strutted over and, separated only by a small tree, sat down immediately beside Bossman, and ignored him with studious care. But it seemed plain from the reaction of the rest of the group that something was going to happen, something violent: all the yetis fell silent.

Suddenly Bossman slapped down the tree between himself and Number One, tore off a useful-looking branch and stood up, brandishing it like a club. Number One needed no more provocation. Roaring angrily, he too stood up, and Jack saw that not only was he at least a foot bigger than Bossman but also that he was armed with Jack's ice-axe.

It was fortunate for Bossman that Number One struck him with the shovel-like adze instead of the sharper and more lethal pick. The blow landed on Bossman's shoulder and instantly Bossman began to retreat towards Jack, screaming hysterically.

For several anxious seconds Jack thought he would find himself trampled to death by the huge feet of the defeated yeti. Instead his whole head was suddenly drenched with Bossman's noxious-smelling urine as real fear caused the creature to lose control over its capacious bladder.

His eyes, ears, nose and mouth filled with the yeti's piss, Jack swallowed involuntarily – Ketamine allowed the normal pharyngeal-laryngeal reflexes – as Bossman fled downhill, far out of Number One's way.

Number One turned to face the rest of the group, his crest and head hair erect, barking excitedly and still brandishing Jack's ice-axe as if seeking to draw out any other potential challenges to his leadership. A few seconds later he charged into the midst of the group, grabbed a young female by her neck hair as she knelt submissively in front of him and then, pig-grunting with annoyance, began to mate with her as if simultaneously demonstrating his dominance over the rest of his harem.

A minute or two passed and then Number One sat down again, staring scornfully at the rest of the group, and began eating the leaves of a rhododendron bush.

Jack realised that Number One had forgotten about him. Reeking of Bossman's urine, his eyes stinging from the acids it contained, Jack prayed for deliverance and tried to recall exactly how long the snow leopard had remained drugged after Miles Jameson had fired his dart. He thought it had been an hour. Yet he also had an uncomfortable memory of Jameson mentioning that recovery periods of as long as five hours were not uncommon. Jack decided that he must have been lying there for not much more than thirty minutes. Perhaps fifty minutes had passed since the first attack. He felt his eyelids flutter. Did that mean he was tired and wanted to sleep? Or that he was recovering the use of his muscles? He tried to blink and succeeded. He was recovering. The realisation made his heart leap within his chest. With it returned the pain in his ribs. And the big silverback.

Smacking his lips hungrily, Number One sat down beside Jack's head and sniffed at him, apparently undeterred by the stench of urine. Then he reached inside the suit and curled a big walking-stick handle of a forefinger underneath the neck of Jack's water-warmed underwear. Fascinated by the elastic collar and the way it snapped back against Jack's chest every time it was released, the yeti managed to amuse itself in this way for the best part of two or three precious minutes. With every passing second Jack was starting to regain feeling in his body. He wanted to maintain control until the very last possible moment. To obtain the maximum possible shock value. Because if the yeti thought he was dead, then maybe he could use that to his advantage. Seeing the corpse of a defeated enemy spring back into life might surprise Number One just long enough for Jack to make his escape. It wasn't much of a plan, but it would have to do. Clenching his buttocks, flexing his calf muscles, wriggling his toes, Jack prepared to come back from the dead.

With bared teeth Number One leaned towards Jack's throat.

It would have to be now.

Jack scrambled to his feet, yelling at the top of his voice.

'Bastard!'

Number One recoiled, voiding a stream of diarrheic dung on to the ground before running away through the undergrowth.

With a series of grunts, barks, and ear-piercing screams the rest of the group followed him, crashing through the rhododendron forest, flattening small trees and breaking through bushes in their desperation to be away from whatever it was that had frightened a yeti of Number One's power and status.

Unsteady on his feet and feeling nauseous again – he was uncertain if this was due to his injuries, the drug, or to the yeti urine he had swallowed – Jack staggered back up the gradient and through the forest towards the ice cavern. Arriving laboriously at the top, he was violently sick, causing such a pain in his injured side that he collapsed on to the icy floor and almost passed out. On his hands and knees he forced himself to go on. There was no time to lose. Oddly he still felt warm although he could not see how the SCE suit could be working and attributed the continued heat of his body to the Ketamine. Perhaps, he reasoned, one of the side-effects of Ketamine anesthesia was heat production. He had no idea how long such a state might last but with the air temperature already well below zero and still falling, it was now imperative that he keep moving. At least there was no wind to cope with inside the cavern.

Jack reached the figure of eight and feeling a little stronger, he stood up and took a few paces forward, at the same time kicking something the size of a rock but also somehow hollow. It was his helmet. At least now he could conserve some precious body heat, even if the means of generating it were no longer functioning. He put on the helmet, plugged it into the redundant life-support unit he still wore on his back and started to pick his way slowly back across the ice blocks that covered the cavern floor. His water pipe was gone, but miraculously the carbide light on top of the helmet still worked – although not the halogen – prompting him to wonder how he would have managed the route back along the shelf in total darkness. The yellow carbide lamp illuminated the difficulty he now faced in getting back down the icy slope that led on to the shelf, twisting round into the darkness of the crevasse like a helter-skelter. With only one good shoulder it would be impossible to lay-back his way down; and without the ice-axe to brake his slide, the journey down might easily end at the unfathomed bottom of the crevasse.

Jack sat down on his backside and braced himself. He took as deep a breath as the pain in his ribs allowed and then launched himself down the icy slope.

The sirdar stepped carefully along the shelf inside the crevasse,

241

keeping as close to the wall as his own overriding sense of urgency permitted. He tried to keep his mind on the route in front of him but, isolated inside the SCE suit and alone in the darkness, his thoughts returned to Jack and how the American had saved his own life.

It had been six years before. There had been an accident on Lhotse, the fourth-highest mountain in the world. A rockstep on the south-western ridge. Having helped Jack and Didier to establish a camp from which they hoped to conquer the summit, Hurké and another climber, an Englishman named Thompson, had been descending a snow ridge between six thousand four hundred and six thousand seven hundred metres when they slipped and fell. Thompson had been killed. Although badly concussed, Hurké had managed to use his ice-axe to brake his fall but as a result had suffered severe lacerations to his hands. Jack had abseiled down to him and in doing so had almost been killed himself – once when a peg had come out of the hard granite wall, and again when he was struck by a small rock fall.

There was no getting away from it. But for Jack sahib, he would still be on that mountainside.

Hurké's radio crackled. It was Jameson. Inside the sirdar's helmet he sounded like the voice of his own conscience. Or maybe the Lord Shiva himself. Hurké stopped to take a rest.

'Hurké, how are you coming along?'

'Good, thank you, Jameson sahib. But this is a bad place. I would not be surprised to see writing on this wall. There is a destiny here.'

'If that's so, then I'm sure you must be earning good points for your karma,' advised Jameson. 'Like the sadhu we saw. Remember?'

'Yes, I remember.'

The sirdar wasn't sure if he believed in karma and the wheel of rebirth very much. He had seen too many people killed in the mountains to accept the idea that an unfulfilled karma would bind him yet more closely to a continuing cycle of birth, death and rebirth. His belief in friendship seemed stronger.

'I just wanted to warn you about something for when you come back,' said Jameson. 'I've left a net over the mouth of the crevasse. Just in case another yeti should decide to drop in. You wouldn't want one following you, would you?'

Hurké cast his mind back to the ice field and his encounter with the two yetis.

242

'No indeed, sahib.'

'Anyway, let me know when you're on your way back. Won't take long to shift it out of your way. Half an hour at the most.'

'Yes, sahib. Thank you.'

'That's all. Cheerio.'

Hurké smiled and walked on. He liked the way Jameson had spoken to him. The *agreji* made it seem as if it was a foregone conclusion that the sirdar would be coming back.

'*Saathi, pheri bhetaulaa,*' he said to himself. Friend, I hope we meet again.

'Oh shit.'

Jack realised that he was sliding too fast. Leaning back against the slope meant that he only succeeded in streamlining himself. He felt like some kind of winter sports athlete. The ones wrapped in skin-tight rubber wet suits. Lugeing. He yelled with fright as the slope turned and the crevasse raced towards him.

At the last second, when he was certain he was about to cannon over the edge of the precipice, Jack pointed his toes, and dug into the ice with the points of his crampons. Such was his desperation to stop and, as a corollary, so strong was the downward force he exerted on the crampons that one of them immediately broke off his boot and disappeared painfully under his body and then behind his head. Ignoring the cramp that now racked the backs of his legs, Jack gouged hard at the ice with the other remaining crampon.

Too hard . . .

His foot stopped dead, but his body kept on travelling and he found himself catapulted forwards as if he had been thrown over the handlebars of a suddenly braking motorcycle. He had a brief, heart-infarcting view of the depths of the crevasse before the shelf came rushing towards him and, knowing that he was about to hit flat rock, he tried to break his fall with his forearms.

Safety never felt so hard.

With all the wind knocked out of him and the pain in his ribs now multiplied tenfold, Jack heard something groan horribly in the darkness, followed by a whistling in his ears that grew louder as he slipped into an abyss of unconsciousness darker and deeper even than the place he was in.

Twenty-two

'. . . would it be too bold to imagine, that all warm-blooded animals have arisen from one living filament which the Great First Cause endowed with animality . . .'

Erasmus Darwin

It was one of Mac's fondest axioms that forecasting in the Himalayas was an unpredictable science, especially when you were trying to forecast the weather. By the time Jameson and the Sherpas had followed the rest of the team down to Camp One on top of the Machhapuchhare Rognon, the threatened storm that had driven everyone from the ice corridor had cleared with a rapidity worthy of the most capricious mountain deity. Jameson crawled into the largest of the tents and found Swift cooking some beef consommé on the primus stove.

'Want some? This has got sherry in it.'

'Sherry. Good Lord, at last I'm back in civilisation. I can hardly wait.'

Cody, wearing his Petzl headlamp and looking like a coal miner, was already inside his sleeping bag and reading *Seven Pillars of Wisdom*.

'Seems an odd choice of reading up here,' remarked Jameson.

'All of the books I brought have absolutely nothing to do with mountains, snow, or apes,' explained the primatologist. 'Most of all apes. Just reading about the desert helps make me feel warm again.'

'Yes,' agreed Jameson. 'This billet isn't quite up to the standard of the clamshell, is it?'

'Boyd's making us soft,' grumbled Mac. Radio in hand, he was keeping in touch with the sirdar's progress inside the crevasse.

'Where's Jutta?' Jameson said to no one in particular.

'Inside one of the other tents,' said Swift. 'Asleep.' She handed Jameson a mug full of steaming consommé. 'As soon as I've had some of this soup, I'm off to bed myself.'

Jameson nodded with loud enthusiasm. 'This is good.'

'Any more of that?' asked Mac.

Swift opened another can, emptied it into the saucepan and then poured in some sherry. She replaced the saucepan on top of a primus flame, and stirred the mixture thoughtfully. They had all overheard Jameson's conversation with the sirdar. She admired his persistence. Jameson was as worried about Jack as everyone else, she had no doubt of it. But that did not stop him from having the main object of the expedition at the forefront of his mind. It was only this kind of dogged determination that would give them any chance of success.

'Will it work, do you think?' she asked him. 'Your trap?'

'Never can tell,' he said. 'Best thing you can do with any trap is to try and forget all about it.' Jameson shrugged. 'Let's wait and see, shall we?'

When she had finished her own soup and eaten a whole chocolate bar without feeling any guilt – something she could never have done back in California – Swift went into the tent where Jutta was sleeping and crept into the empty sleeping bag beside her. Inside the third tent the Sherpas were talking quietly and the pungent smell of their cigarettes and their *cha* prickled her nostrils. With her head propped on her rucksack and wearing her headlamp, she found her own paperback copy of *Little Dorrit* and tried to read a few pages before going to sleep. The Marshalsea, Bleeding Heart Yard and the Circumlocution Office were the principal features of a landscape that was very different from the one she inhabited now. She did her best to give herself up to Dickens's world of prisons, real and metaphysical, and felt her eyes closing . . .

She sat up with a start, aware that a very loud noise had summoned her from sleep, and found Jutta, similarly disturbed, already lacing up her boots. The echo of the sound still hung above the Machhapuchhare Rognon like a cannon-shot.

'What on earth was that?' said Swift.

245

'It sounded like a bomb going off,' said Jutta, pulling on her wind-proof. Crawling out of the tent, she immediately took on a pink glow as if she had started to catch fire.

Jutta was looking up at the sky, her russet-coloured face now a pink carnation of wonder.

'It looks like some kind of distress flare.'

'Who could be in distress?' said Swift, following her outside.

A pink flare hung over the Rognon like a shooting star, dyeing the snow the colour of candy floss. Mac's own bad-tempered face looked as if he had spent too long on the beach. Or drunk too much, which would have been more likely.

'What the bloody hell's going on?' he said testily.

Miles Jameson was grinning excitedly.

'I can't believe it,' he shouted, his accent suddenly thicker than usual. 'Christ, we've done it. We've sodding well done it, man.'

He hugged Mac, and then Jutta and Swift in turn.

'We've caught one. We've caught ourselves a yeti.' He stared up at the sky as if he was witnessing a scarlet epiphany.

'Are you sure?' asked Cody, ill-tempered from interrupted sleep. 'Only it seems to me that we've caught everything but a cold on this expedition so far.'

'Quite sure,' insisted Jameson. 'It would have to be something pretty big to set that rocket off. Bigger than a leopard, or a wolf, that's for sure. And I don't think there are likely to be many yaks at this altitude.' He laughed and then hugged Cody. 'Take my word for it. This time we've really caught one. We've caught a yeti. We're in the history books, my friend. You're going to be famous, damn you.'

Hurké Gurung saw a small yellow spot of light on the shelf ahead of him and knew that he had found Jack. He was lying face down at the bottom of an icy slope that curled away into the darkness like the yellow hat of a *Gelugpa* monk. He seemed to be unconscious.

Hurké knelt beside his old friend and, noticing the blood on his shoulder, turned him carefully on to his own lap. The pain of being moved, and the bright light from the sirdar's own halogen lamp, brought Jack back to consciousness.

'Hurké Gurung calling Camp One. Come in please. Over.'

'Go ahead, Hurké,' said Mac.

'I've found Jack sahib.'

246

'Is he okay?'

'I think so, yes. Alive, for sure.'

'Miles thinks he's caught a snowman,' said Mac. 'He'll want to organise a helicopter to take it down to ABC. If Jack is injured, then we could call in a rescue now. Kill two birds with one stone. Can you advise, over?'

'*Huncha, huncha*. Wait a moment please.'

Hurké took off Jack's helmet. Groaning and rolling his head from side to side Jack blinked several times, like someone awakening after a long sleep. The sirdar blinked too, so powerful was the odour coming off his friend's hair.

'Jack sahib, how are you please?'

'Hurké? Is that you?'

'Yes, sahib. It is me.'

Seeing that Jack's drinking water pipe was missing, the sirdar leaned closer and fed his own between Jack's pale lips.

Jack drank some water, coughed painfully and then shivered. 'Cold. Broke some ribs I think.'

His teeth began to chatter: inside the resonance of the crevasse, the sirdar thought they sounded like one of the other sahibs typing something on his laptop computer.

'Let's get the hell out of here, Hurké, before I freeze to death.'

'Can you walk, sahib?'

'Probably.' He sat up, wincing visibly. 'Either way it's too cold not to. My fingertips have gone hard. Frostnip, I'd say. Couple of stops short of frostbite. But don't worry, it won't stop me. Here, give me a hand up.'

The sirdar replaced their helmets and then assisted Jack to stand. The shelf was too narrow for them to go two abreast and it was plain to see that Jack would have to go unaided. Or be carried on Hurké's back. The sirdar knew the American well enough to be aware that this second alternative was not worth mentioning. If Jack said he could probably walk, then he could.

'Mac, sahib, this is Hurké. Jack sahib is walking, but thinks he has broken ribs. And frostbite very possibly also. I think you should call in rescue helicopter now.'

'That's good, Hurké. Thanks a lot. Keep us informed of your progress, will you?'

'*Huncha*.'

Hurké unwrapped a length of rope, tied it around Jack's waist

247

and then his own, indicating that Jack should go first. That way if he stumbled and fell there would be a better chance of catching him. Jack nodded and turned unsteadily to face the long route back along the shelf. Slowly, painfully, he started to walk.

The team from Camp One were still just under a kilometre away from the crevasse when they began to hear the screams and hoots of the trapped creature. Neither Jameson nor Cody had ever encountered animal sounds like these before and this only made them more certain that they had caught a yeti and not a wolf or another snow leopard. The screams were shrill and prolonged emissions of sound that seemed more expressive of alarm, whereas the hoots, although just as plaintive, were more suggestive of some kind of communication.

'Jesus,' said Mac. 'Sounds like my ex. She used to complain a bit herself.'

'Hoo-hooo-hoooo-hooooo!'

'That's the damnedest sound,' Cody observed as, puffing loudly, he tried to keep up with the rest of the team. 'I can't wait to record and play these noises in conjunction with a vibraliser.'

'Let's hope it didn't injure itself during capture,' said Swift.

Dawn was breaking by the time they reached the ladder that led up the wall of the ice corridor to the crevasse. A faint orange glow was appearing over the eastern edge of the sanctuary like some distant conflagration. Nearer to the gigantic mass of mountain everything was the flat blue-grey colour of a warship.

Jameson taped a Maglite to the barrel of the Zuluarms rifle, which he loaded with a cap and a dart. Next he tied a rope around his waist, handed the end to Tsering and one of the other Sherpas, and started to climb the ladder up the corridor wall.

'Hoo-hoooo-hoooo-hoooo!'

The series of hoots started at a low pitch and became louder as they became longer. To Swift the animal sounded like a very large owl.

'If that's a cry for help,' said Cody, 'then it's just possible another animal might hear it and come to investigate. What I mean to say is that Jack and the sirdar might find themselves followed along that ledge.'

Swift shook her head.

'I don't think so,' she said. 'Think about it, Byron. This is just an entrance. A yeti could jump into this crevasse, but it would have to have the jumping ability of a flea to be able to jump out. There has to be another exit from that Alpine forest. Possibly over the mountain ridge. Or another crevasse, another tunnel we don't know about.'

Still monitoring the sirdar's progress back along the shelf, Mac went ahead and asked him how far he had left to go.

'We have come past the body of Didier, the poor fellow,' reported Hurké. 'Maybe an hour or so walk is ahead. Possibly more. Jack is very slow. Over.'

'They're still at least an hour away,' Mac shouted up to Jameson who had reached the top of the ladder. And then to one of the Sherpas. 'Nyima? You'd better break out some flares. That helicopter will be here by then. We'll need a signal.'

'Hoo-hoooo-hooooo-hooooo!'

Jameson gave a thumbs-up sign to Mac. Then, unslinging his rifle, he approached the edge of the crevasse. Kneeling down he pointed the barrel of the gun and the beam of the torch into the darkness below. The restraining ropes shifted violently as the beam touched the net's big shaggy red-haired captive, causing it to begin a near interminable series of hoots. Jameson felt a small quiver of excitement as he made out the distinct white of one terrified eye.

He lifted the gun to his shoulder and ranging across the yeti's writhing body tried to select a mass of muscle that might make a suitable target, using the eye as an original point of reference. Presented with a clear view of the yeti's neck where there was little chance of chemical absorption taking place, he dropped the barrel and, squeezing the trigger, fired the dart neatly into what he hoped would turn out to be the creature's shoulder. For several moments after he had fired, Jameson kept the Maglite under the gun barrel pointed at the dart to make sure the yeti did not try and pull it out.

Gradually, the screams grew quieter and finally the creature became silent. Jameson stood up and climbed back to the top of the ladder, smiling broadly.

'We've got a live one.'

There were several cheers. Even the Sherpas, initially nervous at the yeti's strange calls, looked pleased.

Swift thought: Let Jack be okay and the expedition's triumph would be complete.

*

Jameson glanced at his watch and then looked up at the sky. He and Mac and a couple of Sherpas faced Swift, Tsering and the others from the far side of the crevasse.

'You'd better light that flare now,' he told Tsering. 'Let's hope the chopper gets here soon. I'd rather not give the yeti any more dope until I've had a chance to take a quick look at him.'

'Yes, sahib.'

The flare Tsering ignited was yellow – the colour to indicate a rescue position. The signal smoke rose into the early morning sky like some mountaintop sacrifice.

The Sherpas heard it first, their keen ears less affected by the high altitude than the Europeans' and the Americans'. A distant chugging in the air. A minute or two later a French-built Allouette came into view, doodling itself on to the white horizon, a black dot becoming a spot on its way to being a smudge. Specially designed for high-altitude rescue work, the Royal Nepal Airlines Corporation chopper arrived from the south, flying at the very edge of its five-thousand-metre ceiling. The pilot, a young Nepalese named Bishnu, was already on the radio, giving the expedition call sign and asking if the yellow smoke was theirs.

'That's it,' Jameson told him. 'Over.'

'What do you want me to do? Over.'

'Do you have ski pads?'

'Ski pads, yes. But I can't see a landing site. There's nowhere suitable. Do you want us to lower you a line? Over.'

'Negative. What I want you to do is this. Come in as low as you can over the crevasse. We'll hook an animal on to the pads. It's in a large cargo net, so there shouldn't be any problem. Then I want you to lift it up under my instructions so that I can get a better look at it before we go back down to our campsite. There's a rocky outcrop on Machhapuchhare to the south of here. A sort of Rognon. You may have seen it. Over.'

'I saw it.'

'You can land there and wait for an injured man to be brought out of the crevasse. Then, when we've picked up the injured man, we'll fly him and the animal back up to Annapurna Base Camp, together with myself, the expedition doctor and whoever else there might be room for. Over.'

'Okay, this is your shout. And your bond. Over.'

Since the RNAC never flew any missions without written assur-

250

ance of payment and this paperwork could take several days, the office in Khatmandu had posted a twenty-five-thousand-dollar bond to cover all airlifts and rescues at the outset of the expedition. Each flight up from Pokhara cost at least a thousand dollars.

The Allouette made several looping turns, dropping fast and began to lower itself towards the crevasse, the nearly solid silver disc of the extra-wide rotors glinting in the rising sun like some giant-sized halo. The tents in the corridor began to stir against the mechanised wind. Snow billowed in the stiffening downdraft. Under Jameson's experienced direction, the Allouette dropped towards the crevasse in a series of lurching drops and halts until it was no more than three metres above the chasm. Meanwhile, Mac, Tsering and the Sherpas had taken hold of the net and were hauling the captured creature up to the surface. Jameson took hold of one section of the cargo net, paused for a moment as he radioed the pilot to come down several more centimetres, and then neatly hooked the net on to one of the helicopter's ski pads. He repeated the manoeuvre and then climbed aboard the ski pads himself to ride the chopper across to the other side of the crevasse, where he and Tsering hooked the rest of the net on to the other pad.

Slowly the chopper began to rise again, and the yeti appeared over the lip of the crevasse, its shaggy red hair blowing through the spaces in the cargo net. Only when Jameson had checked the netting to see if the creature had torn any holes that might allow it to fall from the helicopter did he take the hand of the co-pilot and climb up into the body of the chopper.

The Allouette's interior revealed the helicopter was an ancient one, resembling an old bus, with just one seat – the pilot's – and a bare steel panel floor. As soon as Jameson was aboard, the co-pilot shouted, '*Bhitra.*' The pilot replied with a thumbs-up sign and returned his attention to what view there was to be had through the perspex bubble in which he sat. It was cracked and starbursted in so many places that it seemed to Jameson to be almost opaque. The helicopter began to ease upwards, more quickly now, and Jameson glanced anxiously out of the open door to check on the yeti as the chopper curled up and away from the crevasse and the ice corridor.

'Is that what I think it is?' asked the co-pilot.

'Yes, it is,' said Jameson.

'*Hajur? Hudaina. . .*'

'*Chha, hernuhos.*'

251

The co-pilot looked out the door again.

'*Aoho,*' said the co-pilot with eyes that were large first with amazement, then with laughter.

'*Ke bhayo?*' asked Jameson.

'Sir, the yeti,' giggled the co-pilot. 'It is married.'

Jameson frowned and looked out of the doorway. A strange-looking hand was poking out of the net. It was larger than a gorilla's hand, stronger, with longer fingers, and he noticed that the tip of one of these was adorned with Didier Lauren's gold ring.

Half an hour went by. Then the sirdar was on the radio, reporting that he and Jack were back at the rope. Straight away Jutta Henze descended into the crevasse with a casualty bag and the Bell stretcher. With the helicopter already returning from the Rognon she had no time to examine Jack properly, but it was plain to see that he was already suffering from the effects of hypothermia.

'We'll have you back under the clamshell at ABC in no time,' she said zipping him into the bag. 'You should be pleased. We got what we came for. We've captured a yeti.'

Jack smiled weakly.

'That's good news. I just hope it's friendlier than the one I met earlier.'

'It's quite docile at the moment,' she said, attaching him to the stretcher with a length of nylon tape so as to avoid putting any pressure on his injuries.

'Good,' said Jack. 'Because I'm not up to any more wrestling today.'

This time the Allouette winched down a line. Expertly Jutta set about the task of securing herself and her patient to the cable.

A few minutes later she and Jack were flying down to Camp One.

Alone with the drugged yeti on top of the Rognon, Miles Jameson removed the dart from its shoulder and began to examine the creature in anticipation of giving it another shot. Almost two metres long, the yeti resembled an enormous furry rug he had spread out on the snow. Producing a stethoscope from the medical bag in his rucksack, Jameson began to search the creature's enormous torso for a heartbeat. Satisfied with what he heard he snatched the stethoscope from his ears and bent closer to the yeti's head. It seemed to be breathing steadily but Jameson had a laryngoscope to make sure that nothing had been regurgitated during the restraining procedure that might be aspirated. The animals he had treated in zoos were rare and expensive and he had learned not to take any chances. But there was none could have been rarer than the animal he was examining now.

The yeti's swallowing reflexes were apparently unaffected by its experience. But the sun was shining brightly now, and with the yeti's eyelids fixed open there was a danger of corneal ulceration from prolonged exposure to the reflected light on the snow, so Jameson applied an ophthalmic ointment into its conjunctival sacs. As he finished this treatment, the yeti twitched convulsively, prompting Jameson to administer 0.25 milligrams of diazepam in a separate intravenous injection prior to redosing the creature with more Ketamine.

In the distance he heard the lawnmower-like sound of the helicopter coming back and he stood up in anticipation. The yeti twitched again. It was not exactly a seizure but still it made Jameson feel a little anxious. The diazepam ought to have lowered the animal's threshold for any convulsive stimulation. He cursed out loud. This was the problem using drugs on animals he had never even seen before. It went against every established veterinarian practice. For a second his own heart flopped around in his chest and he found himself dropping quickly on to his knees again as he noticed something else. Underneath the place where the yeti was lying, there was fresh blood in the snow.

Eclipsing the sun for one brief moment, the Allouette spiralled down on to the Rognon like a sycamore seed. One of the tent flaps tore open and flapped violently back and forth, a furious semaphore signifying nothing in the general maelstrom of air and snow. Except perhaps Jameson's anxiety.

On the pilot's signal he ran towards the helicopter and Jutta who was sitting on the metal floor beside the stretcher bearing Jack.

'You'd better come and take a look,' he yelled above the sound of the rotors. 'There's something wrong – '

'What's the problem?'

'I'd say we have a pregnant yeti on our hands,' said Jameson. 'And worse, one that's about to go into labour too. Ketamine Hydrochloride isn't supposed to cross the placenta. I mean I've never known it to produce abortion in pregnant animals before. But then

I never used it on a yeti before.'

Jutta jumped down from the chopper and ran towards the yeti, ripping off her gloves. Noting the blood, she dropped on to her knees beside it and quickly pressed her bare hands to the creature's abdomen.

'It could be her first,' she said. 'Which might be why you didn't notice it earlier. But you're right. Her womb is as tight as a drum. And if she is premature and her baby is delivered out here, it will die for sure.'

'Then there's no time to lose,' he said, gathering up the net and securing all the four corners to one karabiner. 'We have to get her back up to ABC right away.'

Flying back to ABC, Jameson and Jutta spoke to Byron Cody still at Camp Two on the radio.

'What can you tell us about the primate birthing process?' Jameson asked him.

'You're kidding.'

'I wish I was. We're worried that she's going to miscarry.'

'Jesus. Well, with experienced gorilla females it tends to be an overnight thing. They kind of know when it's about to happen and go off and make a nest. I've only seen it happen once and that was in captivity. But when it does happen you can expect the actual birth to be quick. To be frank with you, it's not a hell of a lot different from human beings. Standard forty weeks from the first day of the last normal menstrual period.'

'I hope so,' said Jutta.

'I wish I was there,' said Cody.

'So do I. But as soon as we've taken the yeti off the chopper at ABC, Jutta thinks the chopper should fly on down to the American hospital in Khat. Jack not in the best of shape.'

Jack, who was still conscious inside the casualty bag and feeling a little more comfortable now, said, 'No way am I going down to Khat. Not now that we've found this animal. This is what I've risked my neck for. And you want to dump me in Khat just when things are about to get really interesting? No way.'

'You need to be in a hospital, Jack,' protested Jutta. 'With proper facilities. You could have some internal injuries.'

'I'll take my chances,' insisted Jack. 'If that yeti is about to give birth you can't afford not to have Cody at ABC with you. He's the

254

primate expert. Besides, I'm in better shape than I look. I'll be all right in a few days. You see if I'm not right.'

Jutta exchanged a look with Miles Jameson.

'I suppose that if we need to we can always airlift you out later on,' she admitted.

'That's settled then,' said Jack, and closed his eyes.

'Did you hear all that?' Jameson asked Cody. 'It looks like you're going to get a lift back down after all.'

'Well I'll be damned,' said Boyd when he saw what was in the net underneath the helicopter. Along with Lincoln Warner and the two Sherpas still at ABC, Boyd helped to unhook the net from the ski pads and then dropped down on to his haunches beside the beast while the chopper set down a few metres away. He looked at the drugged animal for a moment and then stroked its thick fur, winding some of the greasy reddish brown hair through his fingers. It felt oily to the touch, like the lanolin in a sheep's fleece.

Jutta and Jameson jumped down from the helicopter and slid out the stretcher bearing Jack. As soon as they were clear, the helicopter took off, heading back up the glacier to collect the rest of the team.

Boyd helped Jameson carry Jack into the clamshell.

'Anyone who wants to say I told you so, go right ahead,' said Boyd.

'Told you so,' croaked Jack.

'Attaboy, Jack. How are you feeling?'

'Tired.'

'Is this the guy that beat you up?'

'His kid sister. And she's in labour.'

'No shit.'

Lincoln Warner followed them through the door and, at Jutta's direction, began to push together two dining tables end to end.

'What's this? The delivery room?' asked Boyd.

'Looks that way,' said Warner.

Jameson and Boyd, having transferred Jack to a camp bed, went off with the empty stretcher to collect the yeti and bring it under the clamshell. The minute the yeti was lying on the tables, Jameson started to search its abdomen with his stethoscope, looking for a second heartbeat.

'I was never at a birth before,' admitted Boyd.

'Me neither,' said Jack.

'Everybody has been present during a birth, at least once,' Jutta remarked tartly. Swiftly she performed an endotracheal intubation and then attached the tube to a cylinder of oxygen.

'Hey, Boyd,' said Jack. 'Light me a cigarette, will you?'

'Sure thing.' Boyd lit two and fed one between Jack's lips. 'There you go. Gee, this is just like MASH.'

Jutta looked around angrily.

'No smoking in here,' she yelled.

'Sorry,' said Boyd, and extinguished both cigarettes with a shrug of apology. 'I forgot.'

'If you want to help, Jon, you can help Jack to undress. I shall want to examine his injuries as soon as we're finished here. And you can give him a hot drink with whisky in it.'

'Sure thing.'

'The heartbeat,' said Jameson, snatching off his stethoscope. 'I've got it.'

'Good,' said Jutta and pressed her hands on to the yeti's abdomen. 'Okay, let's see if we can time these contractions. Ready?'

Jameson nodded and lifting his wrist stared closely at his Breitling wristwatch.

'Contraction,' said Jutta.

'Right,' said Jameson, pressing one of the bezels on his watch. 'She looks well dilated.'

Jutta peered down between the animal's legs.

'There's more bleeding too,' she said. 'You know if this was a human baby, I'd probably be thinking about performing an episiotomy.'

'We have no idea if this is full-term or not. Anything less than thirty-two weeks her baby won't be viable anyway, so it won't matter if the skull is injured or not. Besides, delivery forceps aren't exactly the sort of thing you bring along on a trip to the Himalayas.'

'I was thinking that we could maybe improvise something,' suggested Jutta. 'The cook boys have some large serving spoons.'

'You mean like a victis. Yes, that might work.' Jameson glanced around the clamshell and caught Warner's eye.

The other man needed no prompting.

'I'll see what I can do,' he said and quickly left the clamshell.

There was a long pause before Jutta reported another contraction.

'Four minutes,' said Jameson.

256

'I think we still have a little time,' she said. 'I'd better go and take a look at Jack.'

Jutta washed her hands and pulled on some polythene gloves. Boyd, helping Jack to sip a hot drink, stood up to allow Jutta to sit down and examine him.

As a doctor working with mountaineers, Jutta had seen a lot of contusions and knew that fit men in their prime of life bruised less easily than anyone else. But Jack's whole body was the black and blue colour of a housefly and he looked to her to be as bruised as she had ever seen a man. She made him spit into a tissue to check his sputum for any internal bleeding and, seeing none, she then looked more closely at his ribs, running her fingers over the covering tissues.

'You're lucky,' she said. 'The ribs are probably just cracked. Of course I'd prefer you to have an X-ray, but from the look of you it doesn't seem as if there's been injury to any deeper structures. We'll need to strap you up a bit, but rib injuries are less liable to infection.' Shifting her attention to the bite on his shoulder, she added, 'Which is more than I can say for your shoulder. That's a nasty-looking bite. It will have to be cleaned and dressed immediately. And I'll need to give you a tetanus shot.'

'Contraction,' reported Jameson.

When Jutta had bandaged Jack's ribs tightly, Boyd helped her to turn him over so that she could stab a hypodermic into his buttock. Then, while she dressed the bite, she questioned him closely about his freezing injuries, trying to distinguish frostbite from the two less serious conditions of frostnip and frostnumb. Concluding that it was too early to be sure, she gave him some antibiotics to prevent any infection, zipped him up in the warm casualty bag, and placed an oxygen mask over his nose and mouth.

'Will these do?'

Lincoln Warner came back into the clamshell brandishing two long-handled spoons. He handed them to Jutta, who laid her fist in the bowl of one spoon and nodded.

'I'd say that was about the size of a child's head. What do you think, Miles?'

Jameson took one of the spoons and shrugged.

'I suppose so. You're the doctor.'

'Yes, and that's why you're going to deliver this baby.'

'Me?'

'You're the veterinarian. You're going to be the expert on yetis, not me.'

'Since you put it like that. I suppose it should be me.'

'I'll help.'

Outside the clamshell a faint growl in the air announced the return of the Allouette with the other members of the expedition from Camp Two.

'I still think you should go back down in the helicopter, Jack.'

Jack shook his head.

'I'm feeling better already,' he said.

Twenty-three

'Ancestors are rare, descendants are common.'

Richard Dawkins

The helicopter set down five passengers: Swift, Cody, Mac, Hurké Gurung, and Ang Tsering. With no room on the Allouette for the rest of the Sherpas, they were descending from Camp Two, in the Machhapuchhare ice corridor, on foot. As soon as its passengers were clear, the helicopter's rotors picked up speed, beating the air hypnotically. Then it backed into the sky, tail first, like some great dragonfly, and by the time Swift and the rest had reached the clamshell, it was no more than a distant hum on the horizon.

Mac was the first through the airlock door. Already bristling with cameras, the little Scotsman immediately began to set up the video camera on a tripod, close to the delivery table where he thought he could get the best shots. Swift and Cody followed closely behind. With only a glance in the yeti's direction, Swift went straight over to Jack and knelt down beside him. He looked drawn and pale.

'How are you doing?' she asked. 'You had us worried back there.'

She pulled the oxygen mask a few centimetres off his face so that he could answer.

'See if you can persuade him that he needs to be in a hospital,' Jutta said over her shoulder.

'How about it, Jack?' said Swift. 'Jutta says you need to be in hospital.'

'I'm a little tired,' he whispered, on the edge of sleep. 'And I ache a bit. But I'm really okay.' He smiled weakly. 'If it was you, would you leave now? With a living specimen under your nose?'

259

'I guess not,' she admitted 'My God, Jack, we've actually done it. We've actually got a yeti.'

'Then you'd better not waste any time,' he said drifting off to sleep. 'Get to it . . .'

Swift got up and stood at Jutta's shoulder.

'I've given him something to help him sleep,' she said. 'I'd feel better if he could have an X-ray. His ribs have had a beating. And he's got a bad bite. If he doesn't show any marked improvement after sleep, I'm sending for the chopper again, and I don't care what he says.'

Swift nodded silently. She walked around the table, arms folded about her, rapt in thought, hardly daring to believe the evidence of her own eyes. This was her first proper view of the yeti close up and her immediate impression was that it was magnificent-looking, with a nobility about the head and face that was quite unlike the many artist's impressions of the creature she had seen in her extensive computer archive. She was reminded of the difference between the early illustrations of Neanderthal as hulking subhumans of low intelligence, and more recent computerised makeovers that had grafted images of living humans on to Neanderthal skulls, producing handsome intelligent-looking faces that you might have seen on any subway. She picked up one of the hands, examining the big leathery palm almost as if she expected to be able to deduce the creature's character and temperament before proceeding to divine its fortune. The yeti was wearing Didier's ring, on the very end of its smallest finger.

'Now we know what happened to Didier's ring,' she said with a smile, before adding, 'But I don't think he'd mind. She's beautiful.'

Cody agreed, following her round the table. 'Isn't she? She's the classic ape somatotype – a little like a gorilla-sized orang. Bigger than a gorilla, of course. But that face. It's a much more human-looking physiognomy. This ape has a proper nose, with none of the outstanding nasal troughs that characterise a gorilla's features. . .'

Cody hesitated to step in front of Mac's camera lens.

'Keep talking, Byron,' said Mac. 'I'm getting all this down on videotape.'

Jutta glanced over her shoulder at Mac and his video camera and said, 'I wouldn't stand there if I were you, Mac.'

'Why the bloody hell not?' Mac frowned. 'This is going to be an important film of record. Byron's first thoughts about the snowman could be important. I'm not in your way.'

'No but – '

'Still not – '

Jameson had been about to tell Jutta that he thought the baby's head was still not engaged in the yeti's pelvis when suddenly a large quantity of amniotic fluid, the so-called birth waters, made a dramatic exit from the still anaesthetised creature's vagina, drenching Jameson, Jutta, Mac, and Mac's camera.

Having anticipated some kind of membrane rupture, Jutta was able to ignore what had happened and immediately check the yeti's cervix which she found was now fully dilated. But soaked from head to foot, Mac was beside himself with rage and disgust, much to everyone else's amusement.

'That's just bloody great,' he bellowed. 'Look at me. I'm covered in this shit.'

'I told you not to stand there,' murmured Jutta, amid general guffaws of laughter. She glanced at Jameson.

'Can you see any meconium in the liquor?'

Jameson nodded. 'Some,' he said and placing the ends of his stethoscope in his ears, he listened once again for a heartbeat. 'Seems rather slower than it was.'

'– like something out of *Aliens*,' grumbled Mac, wiping down his camera.

'You're lucky it wasn't outside,' said Swift. 'Or you'd now be frozen solid.'

The yeti moved its head, prompting Jameson to administer another, smaller shot.

'She's going into the second stage of labour,' he said. 'Last thing we need now is her regaining consciousness.'

'Not to mention the use of those arms,' said Cody. 'Probably she'd kill us and then kill her baby.'

'How's she breathing?' Jameson asked Jutta.

The German checked the ambu resuscitation bag.

'Normal.'

Jameson checked the baby's heartbeat once again.

'Slower still,' he said. 'You were right, Jutta. It's looking very much as if we're going to need those spoons after all.'

Like Boyd, Swift too had never seen any kind of birth, except on television, which somehow hardly counted. Watching Miles

261

Jameson and Jutta Henze as they helped to deliver the yeti baby, she thought it was probably not so very different from human birth. There was even the guy with the video camera getting it all down on tape for posterity like a proud father. But she had not expected to feel quite so emotionally involved in the spectacle. She wondered if they all felt the same.

Lincoln Warner was pacing up and down the clamshell looking for all the world like an expectant father. Hurké Gurung and Ang Tsering were nervously smoking cigarettes in the airlock doorway and keeping their distance. The yeti labour looked distinctly human to them, and therefore something from which they would normally have been excluded by the women. Byron Cody was standing a short distance away from the delivery table, his arms tightly folded in front of his chest as if he didn't quite trust his hands to behave calmly. Even Boyd, his scepticism gratifyingly silenced, was chewing his fingernails anxiously.

A forceps delivery. Swift knew the phrase to mean something hazardous, with a greater risk of damage to the baby, as well as the not inconsiderable risk to the mother. As Jameson confirmed the position of the baby's head with his fingers, and prepared to insert the first cup of his makeshift forceps, Swift discovered she could hardly bear to watch.

Miles Jameson had never used a pair of forceps before, let alone a pair that had been improvised from a Himalayan kitchen. At the Los Angeles Zoo he'd been involved in the births of many animals, even done a couple of Caesarean sections with some of the more valuable specimens, but what he was now doing seemed uncomfortably similar to the birth of a human baby. He kept wishing he could cede control of the labour to Jutta, but she told him that he was doing fine and that she would make a midwife out of him yet.

Gently he guided the first spoon alongside the baby's head, using his fingers to check that it passed smoothly and easily between the head and the side wall of the yeti's vagina. Then he inserted the second spoon and only when he was satisfied that the cups of the spoons were correctly applied did he gather the two handles together.

'Here goes,' he said. 'Are you ready with those scissors?'

'Ready,' said Jutta and snipped the air attentively.

Slowly, Jameson started to pull, maintaining traction for about thirty seconds after which he relaxed for a moment and then began again. Each pull brought the baby's head lower down the yeti mother's pelvis until eventually the perineum was distended and Jameson ordered Jutta to perform the episiotomy. Jutta stepped in to the table and began to cut.

The muscles of the yeti's perineum were so strong that they were almost rigid and Jutta had to use every ounce of strength in her forearm to close the sharp scissors on them. Nevertheless the operation was quickly performed and the perineum neatly incised in the mid-line. As soon as Jutta finished cutting, Jameson was able to extend the baby's head on its neck so that its small and wrinkled face could extend over the vaginal wall and the perineum.

'Here comes the head,' he said.

Immediately he removed the forceps and having cleaned the baby's nose, mouth and eyes with a sterile swab, he set about aspirating the throat and mouth with a small piece of plastic tubing that had been improvised from Jack's discarded SCE suit.

Boyd watched him spit several times on the floor and grimaced. 'I don't know how you can do that. Jesus, it spoils my dinner just watching you.'

'We're almost there now,' said Jameson, hardly conscious that Boyd had said anything.

'Nobody's asking you to watch,' Swift said irritably, suddenly feeling a powerful sense of sorority with the labouring female in the face of such stupid male disgust. 'You're the one who said this was just a hallucination, remember?'

'You're right,' said Boyd. 'I was out of line, I admit it.' He smiled amiably. 'Hey, I'm just glad she's not a single mother, y'know?'

Swift looked puzzled.

'I mean, she's wearing a gold ring,' explained Boyd. 'How come?'

Swift explained what had happened to Didier Lauren and how the yeti must have taken the ring from his dead finger.

'Primates have a fascination for shiny objects,' added Cody. 'In that respect they're just like children.'

'Is that so?'

The rest of the delivery was easy and minutes later, Jameson laid the yeti baby on the still sedated mother's abdomen. Already breathing normally, the baby lay there and twitched a little, its head looking distinctly pointed, and its thick hair plastered down on to its body by the vernix. Gradually as the blue skin colour disappeared, the baby grasped its mother's fur with two small fists and, grimacing angrily, it uttered a short cry.

'Wow,' muttered Boyd. 'Eraserhead.'

'Wonderful,' said Mac, quickly thumbing another roll of film into his stills camera.

'It's a male,' said Jameson, and clamped the umbilical cord with a bulldog clip.

Swift stepped forward to take a closer look at the newborn yeti baby.

'Isn't he sweet . . . ?' she smiled.

Jameson severed the umbilical and then began to pull on the cord that remained inside the mother's body, trying to hasten the placenta out of the uterus.

'What are we going to call him?' he grunted.

'You delivered him,' said Swift. 'You should name him.'

'That's right,' said Jutta. 'It's your call.'

'By the way,' said Cody. 'Congratulations. I think you did a fine job.'

Jameson fell silent for a moment as the placenta was finally expelled into his hands. As soon as the placenta had been expelled, Jutta began to repair the episiotomy, carefully suturing the posterior wall of the yeti's vagina with a few stitches.

'Here, Link,' said Jameson. 'I imagine you'll want to have this.'

'You bet I do,' said Warner and holding out a plastic bucket, took possession of the yeti placenta.

For Lincoln Warner this was the most exciting moment of all, the moment he had been waiting for, when he could finally go to work on a specimen of the baby's blood. It was easily collected from the cord attached to the placenta simply by removing the clamp. He showed the contents of the bucket to Swift with delight.

'Well, now I can get started,' he said. 'At last.' And straight away he sat down at his makeshift lab table and began to prepare some slides.

'I was wondering,' Boyd said to Cody. 'What do you suppose happens to the placenta and the cord in the natural state? I mean, in the wild a yeti won't have Miles and Jutta to help. So how does Junior get separated from the cord?'

'The mother eats it of course,' said Cody. 'There are dietary, possibly even antibiotic benefits to be gained from eating it.'

Boyd affected a queasy look and turned away.

264

'I thought of a name,' said Jameson. 'Esau. I vote we call him Esau. That's what you called the skull Jack found, isn't it, Swift? When you started to think about this expedition?'

'Esau,' she repeated. 'I like that.'

'Means we've got a name for his mother too,' said Jameson. 'Esau was the son of Rebecca and Isaac.'

'Let's hope Isaac doesn't come looking for them both,' said Mac. 'He might be none too pleased.'

'Like it or not,' said Jameson. 'We're stuck with her for a couple of days. We can't let her go until those stitches are out. As soon as she starts to come round we're going to have to give her a local anaesthetic just so as she doesn't try and take them out herself.'

'Are you finished now, Miles?' asked Cody.

'I think so, yes.'

'Only I'd like to examine her in more detail before she wakes up again. Swift? What do you say?'

'Try and stop me.'

HUSTLER. HEY, WHAT DO YOU KNOW? THEY FOUND A YETI. NO KIDDING, THEY REALLY DID FIND ONE. IT LOOKS LIKE DOCTOR JEKYLL AFTER HE'D HAD THAT ALL-IMPORTANT LITTLE DRINK, Y'KNOW? EXCEPT THAT IT'S A FEMALE. THEY GAVE HER A NAME: REBECCA. NOW IF THAT WASN'T INCREDIBLE ENOUGH, IT'S JUST POSSIBLE THAT THE YETI IS GOING TO HELP UNCLE SAM OUT. I HAVE YET TO RUN A SMALL TEST ON HER TO MAKE SURE OF THIS, BUT I DON'T THINK I'M PUTTING MY BIG FOOT IN IT HERE WHEN I SAY THAT I THINK WE MIGHT JUST BE NEARLY THERE. UNTIL THEN BE COOL. CASTORP.

When Perrins read CASTORP's latest message he groaned and picked up the telephone.

'Chaz? It's Bryan. Check the in-tray from CASTORP. I think our man has completely flipped his lid.'

Twenty-four

'In my beginning is my end.'

T.S.Eliot

SUMMARIES OF FINDINGS FROM THE EXAMINATIONS OF
TWO YETIS

REBECCA
Fully grown female anthropoid, age unknown, examined in the
Annapurna Sanctuary, Nepal, by Professor Byron J. Cody and
Doctor Stella A. Swift of the University of California at Berkeley,
following the delivery of a baby, Esau, by Doctor Miles Jameson and
Doctor Jutta Henze.
EXTERNAL EXAMINATION:
Weight approximately 140kg (300lb). Height approximately 186cm
(6ft 6in). Accompanying sketch shows body dimensions. Although
smaller in circumference than a typical gorilla 78–89cm (30–35in)
the yeti's head 71cm (28in) is roughly 1½ times higher above the
ear, being over 17cm (6.75in) high. Doubtless this large head height
is needed for masticatory muscles sufficiently powerful to move the
enormous lower jaw. Nevertheless, position of cranial crests confirms earlier observation that creature holds head in an upright
position and, as a corollary, may be taken as prima-facie physical
evidence of bipedalism. Quite pronounced nose, with small cartil-
age. No external parasites were found. Mammary glands in active
phase, and when squeezed produced a great deal of milk. Some
evidence of anemia indicated by pale pink colour of gums, although
no dental caries were to be found. Large calluses on right palm

266

seemed to indicate that Rebecca favours the use of this particular hand. Old scar tissue on left-hand side of neck, about fourteen centimetres long, possibly from a fight. More recent scar tissue on the right femur. General physical condition appeared to be good. Upper and lower body musculature quite noticeable, especially Rebecca's legs which were extraordinarily thick and massive, as might have been expected of a mountain-dwelling simian. Body itself covered with thick, foxy red-brown hair, about six centimetres long, quite oily to the touch and revealing itself to be completely waterproof. Most remarkable of all are the creature's feet, 1½ times as long as those of the largest gorilla. The heel is noticeably massive, as is the hallux, or big toe, which is typically prehensile and doubtless well-adapted both for support and for gripping bare rock.
INTERNAL EXAMINATION:
Genitalia bear a close resemblance to those of a gorilla. Placenta (weight 1140 grams) a shiny, bluish colour, with maternal surface divided into a dozen brownish-coloured segments, and generally healthy-looking.
HISTOLOGY:
Blood group O, rhesus negative.

ESAU
Newborn baby male yeti anthropoid, examined immediately after birth of baby by same personnel, under same conditions.
EXTERNAL EXAMINATION:
Esau weighed 6.84kg (15.16lb), length approximately 68.5cm (26in). Accompanying sketch shows body dimensions. Muscle tone after delivery was extremely good. Body temperature approximately 36.6°C (98°F.) Heart rate was over 100bpm. Respiratory effort, strong and regular. Reflexes, strong. Colour, dark. Put to his mother's breast soon after birth, Esau displayed strong and rapid sucking reflex.
HISTOLOGY:
Blood group P, rhesus negative.

Jameson said that the clamshell was as warm as any incubator and that if Esau had been premature it offered him the best chance of survival before being released back into the wild. So while Swift and Cody examined Rebecca and her infant, Jameson and Ang Tsering went outside where they took the squeeze cage to pieces and then reassembled it underneath the clamshell. Constructed of heavy-duty steel bars and galvanised sheeting, welded at the seams to prevent an animal from tearing it off by inserting a claw underneath a seam, the cage had been originally designed to confine a bear. While it allowed Rebecca room to stand up or lie down at full stretch, it also allowed Jameson, by means of a wall of bars that could be moved in or out with a simple winding mechanism, to squeeze her into a position wherein she might be easily injected. As soon as the squeeze cage was erected under the clamshell, four Sherpas lifted Rebecca off the delivery table, and carried her inside. Already recovering from the effects of the Ketamine, she turned on to her stomach and tried to sit up.

Holding baby Esau, Jameson squatted in the open doorway of the cage and waited until he judged it safe to hand him over to his mother. Too soon and Jameson risked a still stupefied Rebecca rolling on top of her baby and perhaps crushing him to death. Byron Cody said that with wild mountain gorillas this happened all the time. But too late and Jameson risked her rejecting Esau altogether. In the event Rebecca solved the problem for him when she made a sharp teeth-clacking sound and, leaning forward, politely held out her hands to receive her baby.

'Watch her now,' Cody advised. 'These animals can be real smart. It could be a trick to persuade you that she's more interested in getting her baby than in killing you.'

Carefully Jameson handed Esau over and then retreated from the cage, closing the steel-barred door gently behind him. Immediately Rebecca drew Esau to her breast and started to feed him.

'Well that's a relief,' he said.

Cody caught the look of implied criticism in Swift's eyes.

'Okay, okay. I'm being over-cautious,' he admitted. 'But, hey it happens. It doesn't do to underestimate a creature like this.'

They watched Rebecca and Esau as feeding gave way to a period of intense grooming.

'Who knows?' said Cody. 'He might actually be better off with us for a few days, than with his own group.'

'How's that?' said Jameson.

'Among large primates, infanticide is quite common. With some adults it's virtually a reproduction strategy. Killing an infant sired by a competitive male makes the mother become fertile again. Means the killer now has a chance of siring offspring himself.'

'Macho males,' snorted Swift. 'It's the same the world over.'

268

'You know it beats me how the human species ever got itself going,' said Boyd. 'I'm surprised we're not as rare as the giant panda. I'd eat any kid of mine in seconds. Anyone mind if we have those cigarettes now? Doc? What do you say?'

'No, go right ahead. I'm sorry I shouted at you.'

'You were quite right to.' Boyd lit one for himself and for Jack, but Jack was asleep, so he gave it to Cody instead.

Rebecca started to vocalise a series of low moans.

'What's the matter with her?' said Boyd.

'I imagine she's hungry,' said Jameson. 'It's been a while since she ate anything.'

'That's a point,' said Swift. 'What are we going to feed her? What exactly do yetis eat?'

'I always fed the primates who were in my care on muesli,' said Cody. 'I brought several large bags of the stuff in case we got lucky.'

He went outside the clamshell for a couple of minutes and when he came back he was carrying a five-kilo bag of unsweetened whole wheat, dried fruit and nuts. He pushed the bag through the bars of the squeeze cage, tore open the top, and then threw a handful of muesli at Rebecca's stomach.

Rebecca barked back, almost as if she had been questioning Jameson. She picked one of the seeds off her stomach, scrutinised it like a bum checking a coin, and then put it into her mouth.

A minute passed before Rebecca drew the bag of muesli towards her, gouged out a large handful and then slowly allowed it to pour on to the scoop of her extended lower lip. After chewing for several minutes she began to emit a soft, purring sound that resembled the rumbling of a large stomach.

Jameson grinned happily. 'I think she likes it, don't you?'

'Now I've really seen everything,' Boyd grumbled on his way to the clamshell door. 'Someone who actually enjoys eating that stuff.'

CASTORP. CONGRATULATIONS ON YOUR YETI. DON'T THINK WE'RE BEING SCEPTICAL, BUT WE'D APPRECIATE A LITTLE FURTHER ELUCIDATION ON HOW YOU THINK AN ABOMINABLE SNOWMAN CAN HELP WITH YOUR MISSION. ALSO, YOU'D BETTER CHECK THE REUTERS ONLINE. THE NEWS IN YOUR PART OF THE WORLD JUST GOT WORSE. HUSTLER.

269

Lying on the camp bed, covered in sweat, Jack awoke with a start. He seemed to have been asleep forever. His body ached from head to toe, but he reminded himself that this was a good sign. At least he could feel his toes again. At least he had been spared frostbite. And there was something else they all seemed to have been spared.

The guy from the CIA had never shown his hand. Had whoever it was ever really posed a threat to them? It seemed unlikely. Now he wondered why he had ever been so bothered by it. Having survived his experience in the yeti forest, it hardly seemed important.

Jack lifted his wrist up to his face, wondering what time it was and then remembered that Jutta had removed his Rolex to take his pulse and blood pressure. Was it light or dark? Inside the clamshell it was hard to know if it was day or night until someone came through the airlock door. But no one did. They were all sitting in one corner, huddled round the radio, like something from a Norman Rockwell painting. The family listening together. It seemed odd that they were paying no attention to Rebecca and her baby Esau. For a moment he listened quietly as they all talked above the sound of the crackling receiver.

'Are you getting anything?' Cody asked Boyd. 'Anything at all?'

Jack thought Cody sounded anxious about something.

'Nothing but interference,' Boyd said dully and let out a loud sigh. 'No, it's gone now. I'll check the e-mail. See if there's anything coming through there.'

'It couldn't have been a mistake,' said Jutta. 'Could it?'

'I don't think so,' said Swift. 'Not on Voice of America.'

'Shit,' said Warner. 'When it was the Punjab, that didn't seem quite so bad. I mean, it's hundreds of kilometres away, right? But this? This puts us right smack in the middle of things.'

'Selfish, but none the less an accurate assessment of our current situation,' observed Byron Cody, pulling his long full beard nervously through his hands like a length of rope. 'Let's just hope that commonsense will prevail.'

There followed a long silence.

Jack coughed. 'Could I have a glass of water please?'

Swift collected a bottle and a paper cup and went over to the camp bed. She drew up a chair, poured out some water and helped him to drink.

'Thanks.'

'Some more?'

270

'Yes.'

'How are you feeling?'

'Better. How long have I been asleep?'

'Quite a while. Almost twenty-four hours.' This time she handed him the cup of water and he drank it himself. 'Jutta gave you something.'

'I figured as much. Is it morning or night?'

Swift glanced at her own watch. 'Seven o'clock at night.'

He noticed the grim look on her face.

'What's the matter? Has something happened? Has something happened to the yeti?'

'There was just some bad news on the radio.'

'Bad news? What kind of bad news?'

'To do with the Indians and the Pakistanis.'

'They haven't – ?'

'Not yet,' she said grimly. 'If things weren't bad enough already we just heard that China and Russia have lined up behind the two protagonists. Apparently China has declared that it will intervene militarily on Pakistan's behalf should they be attacked by India. In response the Russians have said that if China attacks India then they will attack China. What's more, it seems as if there may have been some kind of missile launch by one side or the other. Nothing is confirmed yet but we could be right at the centre of a nuclear war that's about to go off.'

'That's awkward,' said Jack. 'It would appear that our expedition's window just got broken.'

Swift nodded unhappily.

'I don't understand,' said Jutta. 'Why should China decide to support Pakistan? Or Russia decide to support India?'

'China and India have always been rivals,' said Boyd. 'India only went for the bomb after China exploded its first device in 1964. Two years after they'd fought a border war which the Chinese won. Meanwhile the old Soviet Union was arming the Indians because they were just happy to have an ally against the Chinese. The Russians had their own little border war going with the Chinese, in Manchuria. Pakistan is an Islamic country that has helped many of the former Soviet Union's own Islamic republics to try and break away from Russian control. It's natural that the Russians should be opposed to Pakistan. And so it goes.'

'I'm sorry,' Swift said quietly. 'This is all my fault. I should never

271

have brought any of you up here. If I hadn't been so – '

'Cut it out,' said Cody, interrupting her. 'We all knew the risks we were taking when we signed on for this expedition.' He looked pointedly at Lincoln Warner, as if daring the other man to contradict him. 'Besides, we found what we were looking for.'

'Maybe so,' said Warner. 'But shouldn't we now be thinking about getting out of here? I mean, what are we doing just sitting around, waiting for something to happen?'

'Where do you suggest that we go?' said Boyd. 'You said yourself, we're right in the middle of things. Up here may actually be safer than any of the places we could go to. Delhi, Calcutta, Dacca, maybe even Hong Kong. Temporarily at least, this could be as safe as anywhere else.'

'Boyd's right,' croaked Jack. 'We should stay put and hope it blows over.'

'Isn't that just the problem?' said Warner. 'The fall-out. It might very well blow over us. It might have happened already and we just don't know about it.'

'Again,' said Cody, 'selfish but accurate. Link? Have you ever thought of working for the American State Department?'

'At this kind of height, we'd probably be okay,' said Boyd. 'Anyway, we'd know if there had been.'

'How's that?' said Warner.

'We'd know if there had been any kind of nuclear exchange in this region,' explained Boyd, 'because an electromagnetic pulse would have been generated by the blasts, affecting all semiconductor devices. Radios, computers, telecommunications, you name it. Kind of like a lightning strike, except much more rapid. The radio may be a little temperamental right now. Probably some bad weather on the way. But we're still getting e-mail. I just got a letter from my girlfriend. There's still a world outside, folks.' He chuckled unpleasantly. 'At least for the time being.'

Twenty-five

'Now I am become Death, the destroyer of worlds.'

The *Bhagavad Gita*

The standard perspective on the nuclear security of the Indian sub-continent was that a failure of deterrence would be the most likely cause of any nuclear conflict between India and Pakistan. Consequently, this received far more attention as a possible path to war than what the strategic analysts termed – with typical massive understatement – *inadvertence*. But even then, ran the conventional wisdom, inadvertence could in itself prevent a crisis from escalating. Command and control dysfunctions and other non-rational factors that might cause two countries to blunder into war would, it was argued, actually motivate rational statesmen and -women to step back from the abyss of fully fledged nuclear war.

Such thinking was fine during the Cold War when the two principal antagonists, the United States and the Soviet Union, had been enemies for only a few decades. It counted for nothing when applied to an essentially religious conflict that was at least twelve centuries old. Moreover, religious faith was, by its very definition, irrational. When presidents and prime ministers took advice from their joint chiefs of staff, things promised to turn out better than when they accepted the recommendations of their respective gods.

Even before the cooling-off period brokered by the American Secretary of State, both the Indian and Pakistani Governments had brought all their strategic and tactical forces to a state of maximum readiness: unlock codes had been distributed, targets assigned, contingent times of future launches designated – so that if the enemy

273

did attack, one code word would be all that was required to order a retaliatory strike. To further safeguard against the threat of state decapitation, given the vulnerability of centralised command and control systems, each side had disseminated its code word to the two commanders in the field so that they might employ nuclear missiles at their discretion, provided they were needed to repulse an attack and provided the commander was unable to receive direct orders from his head of state. It was this essentially irresolvable dilemma of control, added to the intervention of the Russians and the Chinese on opposite sides of the Indian subcontinent conflict, that now brought the world to the edge of the nuclear abyss.

The new crisis began simply enough, with a not uncommon event in the Pakistani capital city of Islamabad – a power cut caused by a gang of negligent workmen. In itself this would not have done very much to affect the city's communications; however, the sudden return of the electricity supply caused a massive power surge in the computers controlling the Islamabad telephone exchange and this resulted in the loss of all outgoing and incoming trunks for several hours.

During this same period, potential safeguards reached a critical point and broke down when the Indian Navy fired an unarmed practice missile, an SS-N-8 with a range of nine thousand kilometres, from one of its Charlie 1 class nuclear-powered submarines that, despite the cooling-off period, was continuing a blockade of the city of Karachi from the Bay of Bengal. The missile had been aimed at the regular practice target site in the Great Indian Desert. But soon after launch, the missile veered sharply to the north and could not be destroyed by the submarine's safety officer. It eventually hit an empty factory building on the outskirts of Karachi, Pakistan's largest city, several hundred kilometres off course, killing two men. Immediately the Khairpur regional governor put out a statement to the effect that a missile had hit Karachi, but that it had failed to go off. Unable to find further clarification from Islamabad because of the problems in the local telephone exchange, the commander in the field, General Mohammed Ali Ishaq Khan, assumed that a nuclear missile had also been launched against the capital city and had annihilated it. After a short hesitation he ordered that Pakistan's own M9 surface-to-surface ballistic missiles be prepared for immediate launch. Twelve missiles using a combination of fixed site and mobile launchers, each carrying a crude twenty-kiloton

274

uranium device twice as powerful as the bomb that destroyed Hiroshima, were armed and readied for use. With an effective range of just six hundred kilometres, they were targeted at the Indian cities of Ludhiana, Jodphur, Ajmer, Jaipur, Agra, Amritsar, Ahmadabad, Delhi, New Delhi, Faridabad, Ghaziabad, and Moradabad.

But before ordering the launch of Pakistan's missiles, General Khan prayed. And while he waited for an answer the world covered its eyes.

Hundreds of kilometres away in the Himalayas no one said very much. There was little that could be said. Everyone was worried.

Swift's first feelings on the renewed crisis were those of guilt that she had exposed her colleagues to such a risk, but these quickly yielded to a sense and outrage that, in the age of knot theory, laser fusion, space time, gender therapy and chaos, there were still people who could do such things in the name of the stupid and tyrannical fables of religion.

Some members of the team, however, did hoist a few prayers to the blue sky above the Sanctuary. Others drank a lot and tried to put the events out of their minds. Mostly they tried to forget what was happening by immersing themselves in the scientific work they had come to do. Boyd sectioned his samples. Jutta nursed Jack. Cody, Swift and Jameson studied the yetis, and Mac took their photographs. None of them worked harder than Lincoln Warner. But his dedication to the task before him was only partly explained by his desire to forget about being at the centre of a potential nuclear war. He was, quite simply, now the one who had the most with which to occupy himself.

The molecular biologist buried himself in his work on Rebecca's protein chemistry. Underneath the clamshell, hardly noticing the deteriorating weather, he rarely moved from the small laboratory he had created for himself. Completing separations, isolating DNA, staining gels, analysing spots and blots, performing optical density calibrations, and compiling data. It all helped to detach him from the horror of what might occur. At the same time the irony of the situation was not lost on him. There he was, devoting himself to the general cause of discovering man's origins, while not eight hundred kilometres away, Man was apparently set on destroying his own future.

275

He felt grateful for the literal isolation and separateness of what he was doing. Purifying high-quality plasmid DNA to an absolute minimum. Separating DNA from RNA, cellular proteins and other impurities. There was no doubt about it: molecules were a great way to keep your head together. And molecular phylogeny, as the drawing of evolutionary family trees from biochemical data was called, was as much of a sanctuary as the glacier on which the clamshell was erected.

Despite the fact that he was working in one of the most inaccessible places on earth, Warner was equipped with the very latest biochemical hard- and software. The techniques he was using were a thousand times more sophisticated than those that had been available to Sarich and Wilson, Berkeley's two *wünderkinds* of molecular anthropology, back in the Sixties. Warner's work involved analysing not just nucleotide sequences but the yeti's DNA structure itself. He had more faith in the idea that whole genome DNA changed at a uniform average rate than any serum albumins. DNA hybridisation was a technique that involved the analysis of not just one blood protein or gene, but all of an organism's information-carrying genetic material.

Generally speaking, Warner had no argument with the results Sarich and Wilson had found with regard to the DNA differences between apes and human beings. He still remained impressed by the simple fact that the chimpanzee, the gorilla and Man shared ninety-eight point four per cent of their DNA. But unlike Sarich and Wilson he assumed a more distant divergence between Man and apes, at around seven to nine million years ago. And he had his own view of Man's evolutionary tree.

The standard version in most textbooks depicted the human line as something separate from the common ancestor of the gorilla and the chimpanzee.The molecular evidence as argued by Sarich and Wilson, however, placed Man, chimp, and gorilla together, with no human ancestor that was not also an ancestor of the chimp and the gorilla. Lincoln Warner had argued, however, that humans were once possessed of more than one kind of DNA, and that the human species had enjoyed a double origin: African and Asian.

Now, as he faced the UV image of Rebecca's DNA on the colour monitor, adjusting the brightness, and performing edge enhancement with his mouse, things were looking very different from what he had imagined. So different that at first he thought he must have

276

made a mistake and went back to run the whole gel documentation program again, to make doubly sure of his results. Satisfied at last with the image, he clicked on the mouse, storing the final picture on the hard disk, and then ordered up a thermal print for his notes.

He was going to need a little time to consider the implications of what his DNA analysis had thrown up. Meanwhile, he fed the data into the Phylogenetic Analysis and Simulation Software program to see what the computer itself might extrapolate from his apparently extraordinary discovery.

The threat of nuclear war seemed to herald a storm as bad as any of the old Himalayan hands – Mac, Jutta and the sirdar – could remember. The temperature dropped while the wind, touching speeds of well over a hundred and sixty kilometres per hour, howled through the Sanctuary as if in homage to the larger, man-made energy that might at any time be unleashed upon the whole sub-continent. Even the clamshell groaned and shook under the force of the wind, making its human occupants ever more nervous and irritable.

By the third morning of the storm, in whiteout conditions that made even the shortest walk between the clamshell and the hotels hazardous, relationships among the expedition team were strained to breaking point.

'Hoo-hooo-hoooo-hoooo!'

Cody, who was recording all Rebecca's sounds, nodded apprecia-tively and turned off his machine.

'You know, Swift, Rebecca has over a dozen different kinds of sound,' he said. 'And that doesn't include her vocalisations. If we had another adult we might actually be able to record them all in detail. And if I had a more powerful microphone than the thing on this Walkman I might be able to pick up some of the noises she makes to Esau.'

Nursing Esau, Rebecca would frequently cuddle him and emit a number of whispered sounds into his face. But sometimes she moved her lips as well in a simulacrum of human speech, and it looked to everyone as if she might be talking to her baby.

'Jesus, listen to him,' grumbled Boyd, staring at the game of sol-itaire he was playing on his laptop computer. He did not find Cody's enthusiasm for the yetis in the least bit infectious. 'He wants two of these monsters. As if it doesn't smell bad enough in here already.'

Swift was about to offer some caustic remark at Boyd's expense and then checked herself, realising that for once she agreed with him. Rebecca had developed diarrhoea, and despite the fact that the squeeze cage was cleaned several times a day, the smell was sometimes overpoweringly bad.

'What do you expect an abominable snowman to smell like,' laughed Mac who was busy labelling his films.

Jameson, reading a book, looked up and said: 'She can't help it.'

'The rest of us go outside,' persisted Boyd. 'Why can't she?'

'As soon as her stitches are healed', said Jameson, 'we'll have to let her go. But until then we owe it to her and to Esau to keep a close eye on them. After all, they didn't ask to be captured.'

'When will that be?' demanded Boyd.

Jameson looked enquiringly at Jutta.

'Perhaps tomorrow,' she said.

'Hoo-hoooo-hooooo-hooooo!'

Boyd left off his game of solitaire and began to pace around the cage.

'I think I'll have gone crazy by then. Can't you tell her to shut up. I thought Jack said that the yetis knew sign language. I mean, what's the sign for shut your goddamn mouth?'

Jack swung his legs off the camp bed and sat up slowly.

'They do sign,' he said. 'I saw them.'

'Oh, I don't doubt it,' said Cody, his enthusiasm undiminished by Boyd's ill-tempered remarks. 'I've tried to sign to her but without success. I expect it's just that the signs she knows belong to a different convention, that's all.'

He put down his tape recorder and stretched wearily.

'I guess that's enough for one day,' he said, and collecting his well-thumbed paperback copy of *Seven Pillars of Wisdom*, he returned his mind to Lawrence and the revolt in the desert.

Boyd stopped his pacing and began to search for something in his rucksack.

Swift stood up from the circle of chairs that were grouped around the cage and went to sit beside Jack.

'How are you feeling?' she asked him.

'A lot better, thanks. You know, Boyd's right. It does stink in here. I don't think I'll ever get the stink of them out of my nostrils.'

'That's for sure,' said Boyd. Glancing round the clamshell he saw that nobody was paying Rebecca any attention. Cody was now deep inside his book. Warner was working on his desktop PC. Jutta was listening to some music on her personal stereo. The sirdar was looking at an old magazine and drinking a cup of his disgusting *cha*. Boyd nodded to himself. This was the opportunity he had been waiting for. He stepped closer to the cage and almost absently began to pass the small electronic box he had collected from his rucksack up and down the fur on Rebecca's back. About the size of a photographer's lightmeter, the device was a radiometer, a sophisticated kind of Geiger counter. On the lowest range setting, the radiometer was picking up a very small reading from Rebecca's fur. As if she might have come into contact with something radioactive. He put his arm through the bars of the cage, bringing the radiometer as close to Rebecca's hands as he dared. This time the needle flickered significantly.

Cody glanced up from his book and caught sight of the electronic device in Boyd's hands.

'Jon? What is that you're holding there?' he asked.

Boyd took his eyes off the radiometer for only a second, but it was all the time Rebecca needed to snatch it away. She barked excitedly and, turning her back on Boyd, began to examine the radiometer with interest.

'Damn it,' scowled Boyd. Not that it really mattered. He had the answer to his question. He smiled at Cody. 'She really does like shiny things, doesn't she? A regular mocking bird.'

Cody got up from his chair and leaned towards the edge of the cage, trying to see exactly what it was that Rebecca had stolen.

'What is that thing?'

Swift, leaving Jack's bedside, and walked tentatively towards the cage. Boyd was looking shifty and uncomfortable as if he had just been caught doing something of which he was slightly ashamed.

'Oh, it's just a radiometer,' he shrugged. 'I wanted to take a base reading from us all, just in case the nukes do go off and I have to start checking everyone for radiation levels.'

'That's very noble of you,' said Swift. 'But I can't say that I've noticed you checking anyone.'

'Maybe not everyone.'

Swift pursed her lips and raised her eyebrows. Folding her arms defensively, she stood in front of Boyd and looked him squarely in the eye.

'Or maybe not anyone.'

Boyd grinned at her and shook his head as if in pity. 'Swifty. Really. Now why do you say that?'

'I don't know,' she said. 'Just a feeling I have about you, Boyd. It's the same feeling I get when I walk under a ladder.'

'Do *you* have a suspicious mind? Every time it thinks something it wants to read you your rights first.' Aware that everyone was watching him now, Boyd kept grinning, as if the persistence of his smile would prove his innocence. 'Cabin fever,' he added. 'That's what it is. Cabin fever. The gold prospectors used to get it in the Yukon.'

'C'mon will you, Swift?' said Jack, coming to Boyd's aid. 'Why are you riding him? What's wrong with a little planning ahead? Boyd's right. If the bombs do start going off it *would* be useful to know if we ended up showing some signs of contamination.'

'Isn't it Boyd who's always saying we'll be safe up here?' she returned. 'So why the need for any reading at all?'

'Speaking for myself,' said Jutta. 'I'd like to know if I was contaminated or not.'

'Okay,' said Swift. 'So would I.' She stared back at Boyd. 'Tell us. What was the result? Of these checks you performed on us all? Sorry, on only some of us.'

Boyd glanced into the cage and saw that Rebecca had the radiometer in her mouth and was now chewing it gently. He shook his head.

'It was nothing. I mean, hardly significant. Just the normal you'd expect from people who been at quite a high altitude.' He grinned. 'You know, we're a lot nearer space up here. And space is radioactive.'

'Hoo-hoooo-hoooo-hoooo!'

Deciding that she couldn't eat it, Rebecca threw Boyd's radiometer out of her cage. It spun across the floor of the clamshell towards Swift, colliding with her boot.

Swift bent down, retrieved the unit, wiped it free of Rebecca's saliva and then stood up wearing a disbelieving smile.

'Let's just see now, shall we?' She glanced at the radiometer. 'A few toothmarks, but it seems undamaged. I think I know how to work one of these things. It's kind of like a Geiger counter without the exciting science fiction sound effects, isn't it?'

Depressing the control button she passed the radiometer over her own torso and then over Jack's.

'You're right, Boyd. Nothing so far.'

280

Boyd watched her take a reading from everyone under the clamshell. There seemed no point in losing his temper over what she was doing.

Now she was checking Jutta, Warner and then Jameson, and all the time shaking her head.

'Swift? I think you're being very insulting about this,' Boyd said patiently.

She waved the unit in front of the sirdar, Mac and Jameson. 'Guys? You're clean too.' Quickly she checked Boyd himself. 'Now you, Boyd. No reading? Well that's a relief.'

'It's like I was saying,' said Boyd. 'It was just a precaution. A base reading. Like a control sample. Just to check the thing was working properly.'

Gently he tried to take the radiometer from her but Swift was already pushing it through the bars of the squeeze cage.

'Wait a minute, we mustn't forget Rebecca, must we?'

This time the needle on the radiometer flickered.

'What do you know? Rebecca seems to be giving off ionising radiation. Only a small amount. Not much. But it's there all right. The question is why, when none of the rest of us is showing a reading? Perhaps you have a theory about that, Boyd?'

'I really couldn't say. Look, I only just remembered I had this little machine.' Boyd was looking apologetic. 'It's like I say. I wanted to check us out. I just didn't want to alarm anyone, that's all. Radioactivity is a scary thing. People go funny around it. I should have explained what I was doing. I'm sorry.'

'You know it's a pity this little machine can't detect lies as easily as it picks up ionisations,' said Swift. 'Anywhere near your mouth and I bet it'd go right off the scale.'

'Swift,' protested Jameson.

'He's right, you know,' said Boyd, his smile waning, and his face colouring a little. 'You're way out of line. You should hear yourself.'

'Can I see that thing?' asked Cody.

Swift handed him the radiometer.

'Go ahead, Byron. Check her yourself.'

Cody checked the radiometer against the luminous dial of his wristwatch. The needle flickered slightly as he approached the squeeze cage.

'Maybe it's because Rebecca's been more in the open air than the rest of us,' Jameson offered by way of explanation. 'I believe that granite is mildly radioactive.'

'Boyd's the geologist,' said Swift. 'Let's ask him.'

'That sounds like a reasonable hypothesis,' agreed Boyd.

Rebecca stared at Cody and shifted slowly on her behind as he returned with the machine.

'Hey, it's okay, okay,' he said to her soothingly.

'You know, it's a funny thing,' said Swift. 'The skull that Jack brought back to Berkeley? From a cave somewhere up on the rock face.' She shrugged. 'Professor Stewart Ray Sacher ran all kinds of tests on it in the lab. It wasn't in the least bit radioactive.'

Nodding and speaking gently, Cody pushed his own arm through the bars and took his own reading. Rebecca was nodding back at him.

'Okay, it's okay.'

'Perhaps some kind of tektite field,' said Warner. 'Or a small uranium deposit.'

'Again, another reasonable hypothesis,' said Boyd.

'So why lie about it?'

Boyd shook his head with exasperation. 'Lie about what? For Christ's sake. Jesus, what is going on with you, Swifty?' He punched the palm of his hand. 'Altitude sickness. That must be it. Maybe you should take something.'

'Altitude sickness?' Swift grinned. 'Maybe that's why I'm seeing Rebecca now. Wasn't that your first theory to account for the yeti, Boyd? When we first arrived? And stop calling me Swifty.'

Next to the squeeze cage, Cody frowned as he seemed to see an expression of enquiry in Rebecca's calm-looking face. The radiometer needle moved with greater speed than it had done next to his watch.

'There's no doubt about it,' he said. 'She's showing a reading.'

Rebecca gave an excited bounce on her behind. She was puckering her lips.

'. . .Crazy bitch you are,' Boyd muttered.

'Don't worry, Rebecca. Everything's okay.'

'Oh-oh-oh.'

The sound was simian enough, half bark, half chuckle even. It was the second sound that took everyone by surprise. Even Boyd.

'Keh-keh-keh.'

Cody felt the hair rising on his head and face.

'Bloody hell,' whispered Mac.

Jutta was standing up. Warner too.

'Oh-keh! Oh-keh! Oh-keh!'

'She's talking,' breathed Swift. 'Rebecca can talk.'

'Oh-keh! Oh-keh!'

'Okay,' repeated a delighted Cody. 'Okay!'

'Oh man,' breathed Jack.

'Precisely,' said Swift.

Twenty-six

'If a lion could talk, we could not understand him.'

Ludwig Wittgenstein

Boyd had left the clamshell, almost unnoticed now in all the excitement, and returned to his lodge. Jack, Jutta, Warner and the sirdar watched fascinated as Swift, Cody and Jameson spoke to Rebecca, encouraging her to try another word. Mac was hurriedly reloading the video camera with another Hi-8 cassette.

'Let's see how you are with some breakfast,' said Swift and offered Rebecca a bowl of muesli. 'Food,' Swift pronounced clearly. 'Food.'

Hugging Esau closely, Rebecca clicked her teeth and remained obstinately silent, even when she took the bowl from Swift's outstretched hand.

'No one's ever been able to do more than teach an ape a few voiceless approximations of words,' said Cody. 'Of course there are anatomical restrictions of a large primate's vocal tract that prevent it from talking. But they can understand words easily enough. Apes seem to have at least a receptive competence for language if not an expressive one.'

Swift recalled the virtual reality model of fossil Esau's brain that Joanna Giardino had created back at UCMC in San Francisco, and the small but distinct Broca's area they had found. Paul Broca was chiefly remembered for establishing, that destruction of a small area of brain matter not much larger than a silver dollar made a person unable to speak.

'Food.' Swift repeated the word several times, using different

284

intonations: surprise, delight, questioning and tempting. 'Food.'

But as well as discovering that the expression of ideas through words could be established in this area, Broca had also been a palaeoanthropologist of note, being the first to describe Cro-Magnon and Aurignacian, or Palaeolithic Man. It was Broca who had lent the new science of anthropology its whole critical method.

'Hoo-hooo-hoooo-hoooo!'

'She's certainly got the right vowel sound,' Jameson said hopefully.

'But not the diphthong,' said Cody. 'Maybe it was just coincidence after all.'

'Like hell it was,' said Swift. 'Come on, Byron. We all know exactly what we heard. Didn't we, Rebecca?' Swift put some of the dry muesli into her mouth and, chewing, began to rub her stomach contentedly. 'Food. You say it. Food.'

Rebecca put a handful of muesli into her own mouth and began to crunch it loudly.

'Just look at that face,' said Warner. 'Do you think if Descartes had seen Rebecca he might have arrived at a different conclusion?' He glanced uncertainly at Jutta and Mac and added, 'He said that animals are unable to think. That they are machines without a soul, mind or consciousness. The animal mind is like a clock made up of wheels and springs.'

'It's possible,' said Cody. 'But the fact is that if Rebecca was a human – say a feral human – we would probably have a similar difficulty in teaching her to talk. For apes, just as much as us, infancy is the time of maximum social learning. If you haven't acquired language by the time you're aged nine or ten, then it's probably too late.'

Swift realised that back in Berkeley she had said much the same thing to her class. But faced with the real-life situation she felt rather differently about it. She anticipated a vicarious satisfaction in proving Cody, and her earlier self, wrong.

'Give her a chance, will you?' said Swift. 'Food, fooo-oood.'

Rebecca turned her head away. She had a bored, slightly sad air about her as if wishing that she and her baby Esau could be elsewhere. Sighing loudly, she scratched herself for a moment and, catching Swift's eye, took another handful of muesli.

'Food,' nodded Swift.

Rebecca started to nod back, almost as if she was agreeing with

285

Swift. Swallowing. she tucked her lower lip behind her front teeth and started to blow.

'Now what's she doing?' said Cody.

'If you ask me,' said Jack, 'she's trying your diphthong.'

It was true. Rebecca's blowing noise was starting to sound more like an 'f' sound.

'You're right,' Swift said triumphantly. 'She is.'

'Ffffff-oooooo – '

'I can hardly believe my ears,' said Cody.

'Food,' said Swift. 'That's it.'

'Fffff-oooo – '

'C'mon, you can do it. Foo-oood.'

Rebecca started to nod again.

'Fooo-ooo-dah! Foooo-oooo-dah!'

Swift clapped her hands excitedly, much to Rebecca's obvious delight.

'Good girl,' said Swift.

'Incredible,' admitted Cody.

Swift glanced around anxiously at Mac, whose eye was still pressed close to the viewfinder of his video camera.

'Mac? Tell me you're getting this.'

'Ffff-ooooo-dah!'

'Every fff-uckin' diphthong,' he growled. 'Whatever that might be.'

'Foo-ooo-dah!'

'Christ, it's getting like bloody Oliver Twist in here.'

Swift kept on applauding.

'Okay, that's a good girl.'

'Oh-keh! Oh-keh!'

'It's no accident she became a teacher,' said Jack.

'How about that?' breathed Cody. 'Rebecca has doubled her vocabulary in less than an hour. I just wish we had more time to study her. Maybe we can see how many words she can learn. Is the learning method vocal? Or is it facial? Swift, we have to have more time.'

'Foo-ooo-dah!'

'Good girl,' said Swift. 'You're right, Byron. We need more time. Miles?'

Jameson shrugged.

'Sure. But we can't hold on to her forever. It wouldn't be fair.'

286

'Maybe we can find out why she's radioactive while we're at it,' said Swift.

Mac laughed. 'Great idea. Go ahead and ask her.'

'I meant – ' Swift frowned, then laughed. She was too excited to dispute with Mac. 'You know what I meant. I meant that maybe we can find out why Boyd tried to bullshit us about it.'

'Where is he anyway?' said Mac.

'He went back to the lodge,' said Warner.

'I'm not surprised,' said Jutta. 'You were rather hard on him, Swift.'

'Foo-ooo-dah! Oh-keh!'

'It would seem that Rebecca is already demonstrating a readiness to master the basic elements of syntax,' said Cody.

'If Boyd can master it, then I'm sure Rebecca can,' said Swift.

Jack laughed out loud and then hugged his ribs with regret.

'Don't. It hurts when I laugh.'

'I'd still like to know why he lied about this whole radioactive thing.'

'I've been thinking about that,' Jack said painfully. 'And I've just remembered something. Something that might just explain it.'

HUSTLER. I WAS RIGHT. THE YETI CAN HELP US. I BELIEVE WE ARE GETTING VERY CLOSE NOW. BUT AT THE SAME TIME WE NOW HAVE A SERIOUS PROBLEM HERE. A CONFLICT OF INTEREST SITUATION WHICH I ASSUME YOU WOULD WANT RESOLVED IN OUR FAVOUR. I WAS AFRAID SOMETHING LIKE THIS MIGHT OCCUR. FOR THE SAKE OF MY MISSION AND THE NATIONAL SECURITY OF THE UNITED STATES I HAVE NOW CONCLUDED THAT MY COLLEAGUES HERE IN THE SANCTUARY MAY HAVE BECOME EXPENDABLE. BELIEVE ME I'VE TRIED TO BE ACCOMMODATING, BUT I CAN ONLY GO SO FAR. NATURALLY I'LL TRY TO LIMIT THE DAMAGE, BUT IT SEEMS CLEAR NOW THAT THEY WILL OPPOSE ME AND THAT I WILL HAVE TO MAKE AN EXAMPLE OF ONE OF THEM. POUR ENCOURAGER LES AUTRES. CASTORP.

'Just before Rebecca's team leader attacked me, I found something

287

on the forest floor. Really I only got half a look at it. And then the attack put it right out of my mind until now. You see, I have some solar panels on the roof of my house back in Danville. Well this thing I found on the forest floor looked just like a piece of one of those solar panels. I remember wondering if it could have come off my SCE suit when I got clipped the first time. Only it couldn't have done. It was too big and flat.'

'So if it didn't come off your suit, then what did it come off?' asked Swift.

'Not someone else's roof, that's for sure,' said Cody.

Jack rubbed his jaw thoughtfully as something else seemed to occur to him now.

'Actually, I figure that whatever it was must have landed there,' said Jack.

'Landed there?' said Mac. 'You mean like a bloody spaceship?'

'Yes. Why not? Just before the avalanche that killed Didier we both believed that we heard something in the sky. We thought it must have been a meteorite. But meteorites aren't the only flying objects that fall to earth. And they're certainly not solar-powered. It just came to me, just now. It must have been some kind of satellite. Perhaps even a military one. You know, like a spy satellite. At the very least some kind of satellite that it might be important to retrieve. That would explain how we suddenly got the funding for the whole expedition when the National Geographic Society had already turned us down. Of course. That's why Boyd is here. He's their man. That's their angle. His job must be to retrieve this satellite.'

'Whose man?' asked Warner. 'Who are we talking about?'

'The CIA.'

'Oh, come on, Jack. We're getting a little carried away here, aren't we?' said Warner.

'No, it all makes perfect sense.' He looked around uncomfortably. 'You're sure he's in his lodge?'

Jutta nodded.

'But I don't understand why a satellite would cause Rebecca to be mildly radioactive,' she said.

'Well I'm no space engineer. But I do know that with some satellites solar cells are only half the story. There has to be some kind of secondary power source, for when the satellite is eclipsed by the earth. Especially one that includes the two poles. The power necessary for one of these is quite considerable. I dunno. Some kind of nuclear reactor perhaps.'

'Not by Uncle Sam,' said Warner. 'We don't build that kind of satellite. Not these days. We're environmentally friendly since Skylab fell to earth back in 1979. Besides, then you wouldn't need the solar panels. No, I expect it's probably some kind of thermo-nuclear generator, perhaps heated by a small radio-isotope. It needn't be any bigger than the kind of thing you'd get in an X-ray machine. I'd have thought that would be more than enough to give Rebecca a reading.'

'Especially if she handled it,' added Cody. 'We know she likes shiny objects. She's got Didier's ring, right?'

'Look, there's an easy way we can check my theory,' said Jack. 'The gloves I was wearing when you carried me back in here. Does anyone know where they are?'

The sirdar walked over to a pile of discarded clothing that was heaped at the edge of the clamshell.

'They are here, Jack sahib.' He rummaged in the pile and then held the gloves aloft triumphantly.

'Of course I only had my hand on it for a moment or two.'

Jack took the right-hand glove, with which he had handled the shard of solar panel, and put it on.

'Give me a reading on that thing, will you, Byron?'

Cody picked up the radiometer and held it over the glove. The needle moved.

'It's reading,' said Cody. 'The same reading I got on Rebecca.'

'QED,' said Jack. He took the glove off, and threw it back with the rest of the suit.

'So what do we do here?' said Mac.

'I don't know,' said Jack.

'Why don't we ask him about it?' said Jutta. 'Boyd, I mean. When he comes back here.'

'Okay,' said Swift, searching the faces of her colleagues. 'Are we all agreed? We'll ask him when he gets back in here.'

'Heee-rrrr,' said Rebecca breaking the tension.

Everyone smiled.

'Rebecca shows a remarkable propensity to develop her linguistic skills,' observed Cody. 'And to extend them quite spontaneously. Her ability to adapt to a situation is impressive to say the least. I wonder just what she might be capable of.'

Lincoln Warner, who had been silent for a while, cleared his throat loudly.

'Actually,' he said, 'I might be able to answer that. She might be capable of doing just about anything we can do. There's something about Rebecca I think you ought to know. Something remarkable.'

CASTORP. WE ARE PLEASED THAT YOU THINK YOU MAY BE ABOUT TO COMPLETE YOUR MISSION, BUT AT THE SAME TIME WE HAVE STRONGLY ROOTED OBJECTIONS TO ANY COURSE OF ACTION THAT MIGHT RESULT IN YOUR HARMING ANY OF THE SCIENTISTS WHO HAVE BEEN YOUR UNWITTING HOSTS. YOUR MISSION WILL BE REGARDED AS A FAILURE IF IT INVOLVES THE DEATHS OF ANY AMERICAN CITIZENS. MOREOVER, THIS OFFICE AND THIS OFFICE ONLY WILL DETERMINE ISSUES OF NATIONAL SECURITY AS THEY AFFECT THE UNITED STATES. PLEASE ACKNOWLEDGE BY RETURN IMMEDIATELY UPON RECEIPT OF THIS E-MAIL TO INDICATE YOUR COMPLIANCE. HUSTLER.

Bryan Perrins and Chaz Mustilli sat in Perrins's office and waited for CASTORP to acknowledge their last message. The configuration of the CIA's e-mail server meant that they knew CASTORP had already collected the message from his in-tray. But fifteen minutes passed and still he did not acknowledge his compliance. Perrins turned to his desktop PC and typed another e-mail, demanding that CASTORP acknowledge. This time Perrins's message remained uncollected.

'I reckon he must have collected the last message and turned off his laptop,' said Mustilli.

'That's what I think,' agreed Perrins. 'Shit.' He shook his head. 'Is there anything we can we do? To protect those people?'

'I can't think of anything.'

'Damn it, Chaz, we've got to do something. We can't let him just murder them.'

'Maybe we could try calling the Royal Nepal Police. See if they could send a detachment of men up there to protect them.'

'Do it.'

'But you know,' added Mustilli, 'if there is a nuclear war down there, he might turn out to be the least of their problems.'

'And if there's not a war?'

Chaz sucked hard on his empty pipe.

'I'll make that call.'

Twenty-seven

'This thing of darkness I acknowledge mine.'

William Shakespeare

In the Sanctuary the wind seemed finally to have blown itself out. Underneath the dark canopy, Lincoln Warner looked vaguely troubled by what he had to relate.

'Most of our DNA doesn't add up to very much,' he said. 'Molecules that once had a function are now lost. For example when we had gills or used our tails to hang on to branches. It's like finding a key for a lock in a door to a house that no longer exists. Except that there are thousands of such doors. The main molecules that concern us are to do with the long chains of amino acids we call proteins. Haemoglobin for one. That's made up of two amino acid chains each described by a single bit of DNA. A single gene, if you like. Okay, that's something you can't see. But genes influence how you are seen, what you look like.

'Now take a human being and a chimpanzee. Only one point six per cent of our DNA differs from chimp DNA. Although as a matter of interest, that doesn't include those genes that describe our haemoglobin. You'd be right if you said that it's different genes that prevent a chimp from speaking like we do. We don't actually know which genes they are. All we can say with any certainty is that they're part of that elusive one point six per cent difference I was just talking about. Just think of that for a moment. Ninety-eight point four per cent of our genes are normal chimp genes. And that one point six per cent difference? Why it's less than that between two species of gibbons. Nought point six per cent less to be exact.

292

'The chimp is our closest living relative. Up to now, scientists like me have found only five out of a grand total of thirteen hundred amino acids that are actually different. Three of them are in an enzyme called carbonic anhydrase. One is in a muscle protein called myoglobin; and the fifth is in a haemoglobin chain called the delta chain.

'So here's the first part of the news. That enzyme called carbonic anhydrase? Rebecca has only two of those particular amino acids different from us, not three. And the delta chain? It's the same. So what we have here, very crudely, is an animal – and I use the word with some caution – an animal that is different from us in its DNA by less than one per cent. Which makes Rebecca and her species our closest living relative, not the chimpanzee.'

'That's fantastic, Link,' said Swift.

'I'm not finished. Not by a long way. Some of you will be familiar with the idea of using differences in protein chemistry as a kind of molecular clock. A protein can be used as a marker, determining a mutation from the main evolutionary branch. To cut a long story short by a few million years, it's generally assumed that *Homo sapiens* split from chimpanzees about five million years ago. Personally I've always thought it was rather more distant than that. About seven to nine million years ago. But whatever the time span, it's clear to me that *Homo sapiens* and *Homo vertex*, as I propose that we shall call the yeti, demonstrate a much more recent separation. Perhaps as recently as the beginning of the Pleistocene epoch, some million years ago, before the last great periods of glaciation. It could even be that the pre-glacial period, at the end of the Pliocene epoch, may date the mutation.

'Only I don't speak of the mutation that has resulted in Man, but rather the other way round. Until I get back to my laboratory, it's hard for me to be more precise about this. However my early findings indicate that the yeti's ancestor split from Man's ancestor and that, given the mutation was in all likelihood occasioned by a dramatic change in the world's temperature, then we should regard *Homo vertex*, the yeti, as the younger of the two species. Far from being some kind of missing link that reinforces Man's privileged status in the evolutionary scheme of things, we can probably regard the yeti as no less of an inevitable being than ourselves. You can't argue with the molecules, folks. However we may wish to view it otherwise, we can no longer view *Homo sapiens* as the ultimate living being on earth.

'Now all of this might not mean very much except for the nuclear war that threatens this part of the world, perhaps even the whole planet, and the climatic conditions that might easily result from it.'

'What is certain is that a climatic catastrophe would result from even a nominal thermonuclear war between the superpowers. All of the post-holocaust environmental consequences would cause sunlight to be absorbed by the dust in the atmosphere, the atmosphere to be heated rather than the earth itself, and the earth's surface to be cooled. A study by a number of scientists including Carl Sagan demonstrated that severe and prolonged low temperatures would follow even a small thermonuclear war. What they called a "nuclear winter". Even a one-degree cooling in the world's temperature would nearly eliminate wheat-growing in Canada. But a worst-case nuclear scenario might result in a temperature drop of between twelve and fifteen degrees Centigrade. In short, it would bring on another ice age.

'I have a computer program which predicts how DNA connections and evolutionary trees might be affected by environmental changes. It was designed to take account of climatic differences between continents. But I was interested in what it might say about the environmental changes provoked by a nuclear war. And what it says is that in the event of one hundred major Chinese and former Warsaw pact cities being destroyed, a nuclear winter would ensue within a few months, lasting for at least a year, during which period the only major anthropoid to survive would be *Homo vertex*. Already well adapted to almost permanent Arctic conditions, the yeti might very well inherit the earth, and Man might find himself as extinct a species as the dinosaurs. Within another million years, according to the same computer predictive sequence, the yeti could conceivably have evolved to become the dominant life form on this planet.'

Lincoln Warner stopped talking. His eyes flicked across the faces of his small audience in search of some reaction. They looked stunned by what he had told them and, pursing his lips, Warner threw up his hands as if both confirming that he had finished and that he was as surprised by his own findings as they were. It added a demagogic touch to what he had just said.

'You can't argue with the molecules,' he said again, by way of epilogue.

'So much for Man's God-given stewardship of the earth,' remarked Cody.

'Amen,' said Swift.

'Someone saying their prayers?'

It was Boyd, back under the clamshell and wearing one of the SCE suits. In one hand he has holding a helmet. And in the other he was holding a gun.

'Are you planning on using that thing?' asked Jack.

'If I have to,' said Boyd. 'But please don't make me shoot one of you just in order to prove that I'm serious, Jack.'

'That'll be a first,' said Swift. 'You never made much of an impression as a scientist. But go ahead with the good manners if it makes you feel any better about yourself. You'll still look like a cheap hood with a gun in his hand. What are you anyway? Some kind of government agent?'

'Something like that, yes.'

'Didn't they tell you? Or were you just too dumb to ask?'

Boyd put down his helmet and, grinning unpleasantly, took a step towards her.

'You and that smart mouth, Swifty. Think you're Katharine Hepburn, huh? Well I never did like redheads much.'

For a moment she thought he was going to shoot her. Then he started to say something, but before he had uttered more than one syllable the ever-present grin had disappeared and he slapped her hard, a backhand blow that knocked Swift off her feet and sent her sprawling on the clamshell floor.

Intending to grab the hand holding the gun, Miles Jameson darted forward only to find the barrel of Boyd's automatic shoved painfully under his ribs. Their eyes met for only a second, long enough for Jameson to relax and return his weight on to the back foot.

In his last e-mail, Hustler had only said that he wasn't to kill any American citizens. He hadn't said a thing about not killing the citizens of Zimbabwe. Boyd made a tut-tutting noise and pulled the trigger.

Under the clamshell the noise of the shot left everyone's ears ringing like a tuning fork. Rebecca started to scream. Boyd let her. She was too important to his plans for him to kill her. Jameson hung on to Boyd's arm for a moment, like a blind man. He and Boyd were the only two still standing. Thoroughly cowed, most of the team gradually picked themselves up from the crouching, protective poses

295

they had adopted on the floor, as equally slowly, Jameson collapsed. Swift stayed where she was, still stunned by the ferocity of Boyd's blow. Jutta crawled towards Jameson, in a futile bid to stem the blood that was trickling from his side. His legs jerked convulsively and then he was gone.

'He's dead,' she said quietly when at last Rebecca stopped screaming.

'You bloody bastard,' said Mac.

'You know it's a pity it had to be Miles,' said Boyd. 'I rather liked him. A bit stiff sometimes. But I really did like him.'

Smiling bitterly he wagged a finger at Swift who was sitting up and cradling her jaw with her hand.

'It only goes to show,' said Boyd. 'You never can tell. I was sure it was going to be you I'd have to kill, Swifty. But when it came down to it, I just couldn't do it. Don't ask me why. Don't even thank me. And believe me, I shan't hesitate to do it again. I'm kind of warmed up now.

'Okay people, I think it would be best if everyone went over to the other side of the clamshell. Just in case we have any more unfortunate accidents involving handguns.'

Jutta helped Swift to her feet as Boyd waved the gun impatiently.

'Come on, come on.'

'You won't get away with this, Boyd,' said Jack.

'This? This?' He laughed. 'You don't even know what *this* is all about.' He paused as something seemed to occur to him. 'No, that's not quite true, is it, Jack? After all it was you who guessed about the satellite.'

Noting the look of surprise on all their faces, he permitted himself a smug little smile.

'I heard you talking while I was lying on my bunk. The clamshell is bugged, of course. You don't think I'd let you talk about me behind my back without listening in on what you had to say, do you? That's not nice.' He sighed. 'I don't mind telling you, I thought I was never going to find that bird. But it was you, Jack. You who told me where to find it, for which I owe you my thanks.' He smiled thinly. 'Thanks. I'm very grateful to you.'

Covered in Jameson's blood, Jutta shook her head and said tearfully:

'Why is this satellite so important that you had to kill him? Why?'

Boyd crouched down and glanced out of the airlock door.

296

'The storm is beginning to blow over. But it will be a little while yet before I can leave you folks and finish my job.' He stepped forward and drawing up a chair straddled it, leaning on the back. 'I guess I can tell you. And me, well you wouldn't know it, Jutta, but I'm a natural born storyteller.'

'It's like Jack said. A spy satellite. A bird, as we prefer to call them. A Keyhole Eleven, for obvious see-through-your-bathroom-door reasons. Codename Peary. Same as the explorer. The bird was to occupy a polar orbit along a seventy-five degree line of longitude obtaining fine-grained strategic intelligence of specific sites in India, Pakistan and the People's Republic of China. In short to monitor the developing situation in the North Indian theatre.

'However, on completion of its low-orbit mission, instead of boosting to a higher orbit at thirty-five thousand kilometres, the bird began slipping closer to the earth's atmosphere. Whoops. We wondered about that. The usual did-it-fall-or-was-it-pushed kind of question? Finally the eggheads decided that it had been affected by recent sunspot activity. Caused an overload in the bird's solar power cells. You were right about that too, Jack boy. Solar cells supported by a small thermonuclear generator. You're really a very clever man, for a rock rat. Anyway, the overload caused the computer to mis-cue both imaging and the boost to higher orbit. The sunspots also acted to increase the density of the uppermost part of the earth's atmosphere. But when the density increases, so does the friction acting on the bird. With the result that the bird effectively tripped and fell. Computer forecasts led us to believe that re-entry would take place in a non-hazardous location somewhere on the Antarctic continent. That's where I was at the time. Got myself all ready to go find it. But it turned out that periodically the bird tumbled sideways along its orbit, with the result that the air drag factor soared and the decay rate increased by fifteen or twenty times. So instead of coming down in the Antarctic it came down somewhere else and it came down early. Whoops again.

'Our earliest guess as to the location was along the original orbital line. We tracked the automatic distress signals on the existing frequency as long as we could, but lost contact as the satellite entered Nepalese air space. We figured somewhere in the Himalayas. But where? Sent up a few spy planes to try and spot it. No dice. Finally we got our best lead from guess where? *National*

297

Geographic magazine. A little article about Jack boy and his partner swept off the mountain in an avalanche caused by a meteorite, on or about the exact time we calculated our bird was in the sky. Wouldn't you just believe it? Five-hundred-million dollar aircraft overflying the whole of Nepal looking for a missing satellite, and this is where we find it. In a lousy magazine article. Eeeeeh! One in the eye for the folks at the Pentagon.

'But hey, I'm missing the best bit part of the story. You see what made the situation so urgent was that before re-entry, Peary's onboard computer downloaded all the reconnaissance imagery it had collected to our tracking complex at Cheyenne Mountain. Now they discovered that the same malfunction caused the computer to photograph not nuclear missile and airforce bases in India and Pakistan and their respective states of readiness, but strategic sites in countries antipodean to the Indian subcontinent along the same line of longitude. By which I mean Canada and the United States. Double jeopardy. Our own spy satellite ends up spying on us. What made this major pain in the ass even worse was the fact that Peary was designed for reuse. In other words, it would not burn up on re-entry. And with the probability existing that the on-board computer systems were still in possession of our own strategic intelligence this made it imperative that we find and destroy the bird as quickly as possible. Major fuckin' problem. Coming down so close to the Chinese border, during the current political situation, well you can guess the panic that affected people back in Washington. Imagine what would happen if the slopes could target all our sites. That kind of thing. So you see how it is.'

Boyd stood up and went over to the door again, to glance out and check the weather.

'So all this time,' said Warner, 'instead of looking for core samples from the glacier . . .'

'That's right, Link. I've been looking for some trace of a satellite.'

'But why didn't you throw your lot in with us?' said Jack. 'For God's sake. We're on the same side. Aren't we?'

'Nominally, yes. But ask yourself this question. What would have happened if my mission and yours came into a conflict of interest? Your new species versus my own satellite. We wouldn't have gotten along at all. No, it wouldn't have worked. My mission had – has – absolute priority, at all times. Whatever the circumstances. I can't see Doctor Swift going along with that, can you? Isn't that right,

Swifty? You're not about to allow any kind of risk to your precious new species, are you?'

'What are you talking about?' Swift said dully.

Boyd looked awkward.

'I can hardly tuck that bird under my arm and take it home to Washington, now can I? It weighed the best part of eighteen hundred kilogrammes when it was launched. A little less now, I should think. But still, heavy. No, I have to blow it up. Even if that means a few of Rebecca's brothers and sisters getting in the way.'

'You bastard,' said Swift.

'See? That's what I mean by a conflict of interest. I don't mean any harm to come to – what did you call them, Link?'

'*Homo vertex*. It means Peak Dwelling Man.'

'Oh-keh! Oh-keh!'

'Yeah. That's nice. Even Rebecca sounds as if she likes it. Fact is, I don't mean Mr and Mrs Peak Dwelling Man any harm. But if they get in the way it will be too bad, y'know? Maybe they'll get lucky. Maybe they will be somewhere else when it goes off. There are issues of national security here that I don't expect you to be concerned about. Besides, it will only be a small explosion. It's not like I'm planning to destroy the whole of your hidden forest, Jack. Shouldn't need more than two and a half kilogrammes of plastic.'

'But why do you have to blow it up?' asked Cody. 'There must be some easy way to fry the satellite's computer banks and wipe out the information that it has gathered? I could probably do it for you.'

'Nice idea, Byron. But you still don't get it,' said Boyd. 'Retrieving the pictures of Uncle Sam's backyard – that's only half the point of the exercise. There's a lot of classified intelligence-gathering technology on that bird. And I mean state-of-the-art. It's not the kind of tin thing you want to leave lying around for someone to find and take to pieces. We really can't afford to give those slope scientists a leg up for their own spy satellites. So, when I find it, I have to make sure that it's completely destroyed.'

'Wait a minute,' said Warner. 'You said there was a small thermonuclear generator, on board, right?'

'S'right. Powered by a radio-isotope, just like Jack said. Jack, you're in the wrong business. You should be doing my job.'

'Now hold on a second,' insisted Warner. 'If you blow that up, it could be disastrous. Even a small explosion could be environmentally disastrous.'

'Fooo-oooo-ooo-duh!'

'Yeah, I heard you before.'

'No, no, you're not listening to me. This is something different, don't you see? The explosion would disperse the radioactive isotope right across the hidden valley the yetis inhabit like ... like an aerosol, poisoning them and their whole environment. What kind of isotope is it, do you know?'

Boyd shook his head irritably. He was beginning to regret this whole conversation. The weather was almost clear now. It was time to be setting off.

'No matter,' said Warner. 'Even if you were to assume that the isotope is not Plutonium, say the weakest kind of isotope, like Cobalt 60, with a half life of only five years, an explosion would make the whole valley quite uninhabitable, by anyone or anything.'

'C'mon. Give me a break.'

'No, really. Everything would die, Boyd. And if it turned out to be something like Plutonium 239, then you'd be talking about a half life of twenty-four thousand years. Either way you simply can't do it. You know there's just a chance that this part of the world is so high up that it might escape the fall-out from all those bombs. Don't you think it deserves a chance. . . ?'

Boyd picked up his helmet. 'I've heard enough – '

'I don't think you have.' Warner was becoming agitated. 'You say you were listening to our conversation with your bug? Well were you? Didn't you hear what I had to say about this creature? This creature is much closer to us than a mere cousin like the chimpanzee. Boyd. This is like your brother, for God's sake.'

'You know? I never did like my brother much. He lives in Wisconsin too. If you see my meaning, friend.'

'Please listen to him,' implored Swift. 'What you're proposing. It would be like murder.'

Boyd grinned wolfishly and then nodded down at Jameson's lifeless body.

'As you may just have noticed, Swifty, I don't really have a problem with that concept.'

'Worse than murder. Genocide.'

'Storm's over. I gotta be moving.'

'The storm will have wiped out the trail,' said Cody. 'No one's going to take you there. To the Alpine forest. We'd rather die first.'

'That so?'

300

Boyd pointed the gun straight at Cody, then at Jutta, then at Jack, and then at Swift.

'I do believe you would die to protect these apes,' he laughed. 'How about that? Lucky for you I'm just kidding.' He tapped the side of his head with the barrel of his gun. 'Lucky for you one of the porters already told me the way to go. Lucky for you I also figured out who my best guide is going to be. Someone who won't mind leading me straight there. I won't even need to wave my gun.'

'And who might that be?' demanded Swift.

'Someone who's been lots of times,' said Boyd. 'Rebecca, that's who. Who better than her to lead me to this little hidden valley of yours?'

Twenty-eight

'Am I my brother's keeper?'

Genesis 4:9

Boyd was looking pleased with himself.

'Reckon I'll just take my time and follow her tracks. Shouldn't be too hard in all this fresh snow. By the way, you can forget trying to call anyone on the radio, or on e-mail. I already fixed the satellite mast.'

'You'll never make it by yourself,' said Jack. 'We'll come after you.'

'I wouldn't advise it,' said Boyd. 'I've been trained. You've no idea how much I can do by myself. And you may have noticed, I have a skill with this thing. I'll be carrying a rifle too. That's a rifle with a telescopic sight, and real bullets, not hypodermic syringes. I see one of you people coming after me, I'll blow you away. 'Sides, I already thought of a way to keep you all in here. Short of killing you all, that is. Only first I gotta show our hairy friends the way out of here.'

Stepping back into the airlock door, he threw open the outer section to reveal sunshine and a blue sky.

'Whoooa,' he said, taking a deep, almost euphoric breath. 'Get a lungful of that air. Looks like it's gonna be a nice day.'

Holding the gun at arm's length, Boyd came back into the clamshell and approached the squeeze cage.

'Nobody try anything,' he said, stepping over Jameson's body. 'Unless you want to cuddle up to your friend on the floor. If you want to feel heroic, sing the Stars and Stripes. C'mon, back up all of you.'

302

'D'you think it's a good idea, just letting a wild animal loose in here,' said Cody. 'It could be dangerous. Remember what happened to Jack.'

'I'm the one with the gun,' said Boyd, and drew the bolts on the cage. 'Remember what happened to Miles.'

He opened the door and then moved away.

'You know, I hate to see a beautiful animal in a cage.'

For a moment Rebecca remained seated in the corner of the cage, eating mouthfuls of muesli and feeding Esau, and showing no inclination to escape from her captivity. But gradually she became aware that something had changed in her circumstances, and pressing her infant close to her breast, and grunting gently, she stood up.

'Oh-keh! Oh-keh!'

'That's the girl,' said Boyd. 'Time you took a little walk around the yard, Cheeta.'

Slowly Rebecca emerged from the squeeze cage. She stared apprehensively at Jameson and, squatting down beside him, wiped some blood on to her finger and then into her mouth. The taste brought a frown to her features, as if she recognised that something was wrong. She prodded Jameson for some signs of life, and finding none, uttered a quiet whimper and then walked fearfully towards the open doorway. Swaying one way and then the other, like a caged elephant, she looked around, as if she half expected someone to try and stop her from leaving.

'Oh-keh! Oh-keh!'

Swift met the yeti's penetrating stare and nodded.

'Okay,' she said, and raised her hand in farewell. 'Okay.'

Rebecca turned towards the door, already uttering an increasingly loud series of hoots. Then she was gone.

Boyd nodded with satisfaction.

'There, that wasn't so bad, was it? I don't think she's dangerous at all.'

He followed her to the doorway.

'Like I say, don't anyone think of leaving the clamshell. Not unless you think you can stay one step ahead of a speeding bullet.'

Swift started to curse him and then checked herself as she saw a sudden ray of hope. Standing outside the clamshell, apparently unseen by Boyd, and armed with a pistol, was Ang Tsering.

*

Tsering must have heard the gunshot that had killed Jameson, must have seen Boyd was holding a gun on them. Swift thought that he must have found a gun somewhere in Boyd's lodge and that he would surely shoot or attempt to disarm Boyd as soon as he could. Even when the assistant sirdar was only a metre or so behind Boyd, Swift still expected him to step forward and hit the American smartly over the head; right up until the moment that Boyd started speaking to Tsering without even turning round, as if he had always known the Nepalese was there. As if he didn't need to worry about him. As if they were working together.

'The yeti is already moving up towards the ice field,' said Tsering.

'Good. Okay, you know what to do. Any of them steps out from under the clamshell, shoot them. You should be comfortable enough in here,' said Boyd, and with a final cheery wave, zipped up the airlock door behind him.

'Goodbye,' he shouted and then dropped the outside flap to seal the entrance.

The sirdar turned immediately towards Jack, brought his hands together in a *namaste*, bowed and said, 'I am sorry, Jack sahib. How it is happening I don't know. I thought Ang Tsering was good man, good assistant sirdar. I pick him. *Yo saap. Yo bhiringi*. It is my fault, Jack sahib. *Malaai ris*, Jack sahib. *Malaai dukha*.'

Jack shook his head.

'Forget it, Hurké. It's not your fault. The question is, what are we going to do about it? Do you think he'd really shoot if one of us went outside now?'

Hurké Gurung moved his head from side to side in an expression of uncertainty.

'I am not sure at all,' he said finally. 'It is a terrible thing to do murder in my country. Tsering is not a very religious man. For him to kill someone, I think he would require very much money. Enough perhaps to leave Nepal for good. He has always wanted to go and live in America, I think.'

'Boyd's certainly not short of money,' said Jack. 'And his people could probably fix something with the State Department.'

'*Ke garne*, Jack? What is to be done?' He shook his head sadly. 'Perhaps, I am thinking he would kill one of you *bideshi*, because you are foreigners. He is a most resentful fellow I think. Always he has been most troublesome for more money, and for more equipment, always more. A real *saaglo*. But me? Perhaps he will be having more respect for me, because I am sirdar. For him, I am *maalik*. He will have to have *maanu* for me. And maybe more than a little fear too. Like some *pahelo* cowardly fellow.'

Jutta picked up Jameson's jacket and covered his face. Then she stood up and shook her head.

'I think you're wrong,' she said. 'I think I'm the one who he would find hardest to kill. After all the help I've given him – ' Jutta checked her irritation.

'The memsahib is right, of course,' said Hurké. 'Perhaps if the memsahib was to engage Ang Tsering in conversation, then I might come at him from behind.'

'Aren't you forgetting something?' sighed Swift. 'There's only one way out of this damned tent. And it's made of Kevlar too. Not exactly your average tent material.' She punched the wall experimentally. 'Not even a snow leopard could tear through this. This stuff's virtually bullet-proof.'

Hurké Gurung dived into his rucksack and came up with his Nepalese knife, the boomerang-shaped *khukuri*. He drew the forty-five-centimetre-long hatchet-blade from its hard leather scabbard and hefted it confidently.

'Pardon for contradiction, memsahib,' he said. 'But this will do the job. Maybe bullet-proof, yes. But bullet-proof not knife-proof. *Khukuri*. From when I was a Gurkha. Cut through anything. Very sharp. Even cut through Boyd sahib's clamshell.'

'Ang Tsering?' Jutta's tone was matter-of-fact, even friendly. 'Are you there? I need to talk to you, please.'

Hearing nothing, she repeated the question and began to unzip the interior door.

'I don't want to talk to you.'

'Well, I have to talk to you.'

'Didn't you hear what Mister Boyd told you? said Tsering. 'What he told me? That I was to shoot anyone who stepped outside of the tent.'

'Yes, but you and I are friends, Tsering. We've been friends since the beginning. That's why I helped you with your German.'

'I wouldn't place too much reliance on this help, Miss Henze,' insisted Tsering. 'And Mister Boyd is my friend now. He is helping me.'

'Well, maybe he is, but I can't believe you'd shoot me.'

'Be assured it would give me no pleasure. But I have my orders. Please stay inside the tent. There I can assure your safety.'

'Have you ever heard of the Hippocratic oath, Tsering?'

'Of course. It is an oath taken by doctors of medicine.'

'Well then, Jameson sahib has been shot,' she said. 'I need to fetch something from my medical bag in the lodge. Otherwise he will die.'

Jutta threw back the outside flap and still standing inside the doorway faced Ang Tsering. Smoking nervously and with an automatic pistol in his gloved hand he looked more uncomfortable than usual. Jutta wondered if he had ever held a gun before, if Boyd had even shown him how to use it.

'That is far enough please, memsahib. I do not wish to shoot you.'

She glanced down the blood-stained front of her body.

'As you can see, Jameson has already lost a lot of blood. He is quite likely to bleed to death unless I can help him.'

The assistant sirdar threw away his cigarette and rubbed a hand through his sea-urchin haircut frustratedly.

'So you can see I simply must have that bag. Perhaps one of the other Sherpas could fetch it for me.'

'No, this will not be possible. All of the Sherpas ran away as soon as they heard the shooting.'

Jutta heard a ripping sound inside the clamshell behind her, and knew that the sirdar must be nearly outside. She stepped out of the doorway and on to the snow. Looking down the glacier she saw the tracks in the snow. But the sun reflecting off the snow was too strong and Boyd was already invisible to her.

'Then either you must get my bag, or I will fetch it myself.'

Tsering backed away, levelling his gun at Jutta's head. Only now did he think to work the slide that pushed a bullet into the breach of the automatic.

Jutta smiled, realising that his familiarity with the gun was probably limited to television programmes.

'What about the safety catch?' she said.

Tsering glanced at the side of his weapon and then checked himself angrily.

'Don't patronise me,' he said and fired into the snow in front of Jutta's feet. 'You see? You see? I know what I'm doing and I will shoot. Believe me, memsahib. If you take one more step I will

306

have no choice but to shoot you in the leg. And who will help the doctor? Answer me that, please?'

'You'll have to kill me to stop me helping Jameson sahib,' she said.

'Why do you want to get yourself killed?' pleaded Tsering. 'You have been very kind to me. I do not wish it. Now please go back inside.'

Out of the corner of her eye, Jutta saw the sirdar stealthily approaching Tsering's back. She caught sight of the murderous expression on Hurké's face and the razor-sharp blade of the *khukuri* glittering in his hand like a bolt of lightning, and stopped her cry with her own hand.

Mistaking her gesture for fear, Tsering advanced towards her, still pointing his gun.

'Yes, you would do well to be afraid. I will do it, make no mistake. I care not if Miles Jameson sahib lives or dies. He is just another *bideshi* to me. Do you hear? Let him die. He should never have come in the first place. None of you should have come. You are all thieves. All of you.'

Tsering was shouting at her now, as if trying to convince himself that he could use the gun and shoot her if he had to.

'Now go back inside, you stupid woman,' he told her angrily. 'Or I will shoot you. Do you hear?'

The hand pointing the gun at her was shaking. Jutta retreated, thinking he might pull the trigger accidentally.

By now the sirdar was only about a metre behind Tsering, the *khukuri* held at shoulder level.

Jutta gasped. Surely he wouldn't actually use the knife.

A split second later Hurké Gurung raised the deadly knife high in the air and, catching the sun like a heliograph, it began its lethal arcing descent.

Involuntarily Jutta cried out and held up her hands to stop the sirdar.

Tsering thought she was pleading with him and sneered with contempt. She had taught him some German, that was all. So what did that matter? He did not even like the language. Only Boyd had actually offered him some money and an American passport. To live in America. That would really be something.

It was the last thought that passed through his head before the hatchet knife interrupted his thoughts.

Jutta's scream mixed with Tsering's own and then the sound of the gunshot as his forefinger pulled the trigger reflexively before the severed hand hit the bloodied snow.

Tsering fell back, his good hand holding the bloodied stump of his arm in front of his face as if hardly comprehending the fate of his missing hand.

'*Mero paakhuraa dukhyo*,' he groaned pitifully. '*Aspataallaai jachaaunua parchha.*'

'You can count yourself lucky it wasn't your head,' said the sirdar and spat into the snow in front of Tsering. '*Hajur?*'

'*Mero haat*,' whimpered Tsering. '*Mero haat.*'

Jutta brushed past the rest of the team now emerging from the clamshell doorway, to fetch her medical bag. There was probably no chance she could save the man's hand. Not with the radio out of action, and so far away from a hospital in Pokhara. But she could at least stop him from bleeding to death.

Ignoring Ang Tsering, the sirdar had limped a short way out of camp after the tracks left by Rebecca and then Boyd, and his keen eyes, slitted against the sun, were already searching for them on the upper part of the glacier. Of the yeti Rebecca there was no sign. But he was sure he could just make out a tiny figure on the edge of the ice field in front of Machhapuchhare. Looking round he found Jack standing beside him, holding a pair of binoculars, and pointed silently.

Jack nodded and found Boyd in his lenses. He was ahead of them by almost a full hour.

The sirdar's eyes followed several other sets of tracks that were leading from the camp in the same direction, south and out of the Sanctuary.

'The other Sherpas ran away,' he said.

Jack saw the tracks and nodded. Swift was kneeling down by the assistant sirdar's severed hand, separating the gun from the pale fingers.

'Can't say I blame them,' growled Jack and went over to her.

The gun was still cocked and ready to fire. She applied the safety catch and then, holding the hammer with both of her fingers, she pulled the trigger and eased the hammer carefully forward against the shielded firing pin. When the gun was safe, she looked up at Jack and said:

'I'm going after him.'

'Not on your own you're not. Take Hurké.'

Jack looked around for the sirdar and found him kneeling down in the snow, inspecting a bloody hole in the heel of his climbing boot. Tsering's loose shot.

'Forgive me, please, Jack sahib. But I think I have been shot with a bullet.'

They helped him to limp inside the clamshell where Jutta was already applying a tourniquet to Tsering's injured arm. Hurké sat down and allowed Jack to unlace his boot, grimacing with pain when the boot and then his sock were slipped off. There was plenty of blood and although it was clear to Jutta that the bullet had done no more than crease the fleshy part of the sirdar's heel, it was clear also that he would not be walking any great distance for several days.

Swift was already climbing into the SCE suit.

'I'm coming with you,' said Jack.

'You'll only slow me down,' she said, lifting her mane of red hair and tying it with an elastic band. 'You're hardly recovered from your last journey.'

Jack recognised the truth of this but, still reluctant to let her risk her life alone, he suggested Mac go instead.

'What about it, Mac?'

The Scotsman shrugged.

'The suit doesn't fit me,' he said. 'It's too bloody big.'

'What about the one Hurké wore?'

'She's wearing it,' he said.

'Look, Jack,' said Swift. 'Jutta's got her hands full here. Byron's too slow. Link's not acclimatised to anything above four thousand metres. Mac's too small. Hurké's injured, and so are you. That leaves me, in a hurry, with no time for all this bullshit.'

Jack nodded and then embraced her.

'Okay but there's one thing I've got to explain to you. And that's laybacking.' He told her about the curling slope at the end of the shelf, where the handhold was to be found and how to use it.

'Look, be careful,' he added. 'Remember what Boyd said. He's a professional. He's been trained for this kind of work.'

'What will you do,' asked Mac. 'if you do catch up with him?'

'Do? What do you think I'm going to do?' Swift's tone was almost scathing. 'I'm going to try to kill the sonofabitch.'

Twenty-nine

' . . . we shall eventually get to love the mountain for the very
fact that she has forced the utmost out of us, lifted us just for
one precious moment high above our ordinary life, and shown
us beauty of an austerity, power, and purity we should never
have known if we had not faced the mountain squarely and
battled strongly with her.'

Francis Younghusband

Emerging from the ice field – a hazardous experience that would
have left him considerably unnerved but for the yeti's tracks, for
much of the original route marked by the Sherpas had been obliterated by the storm – Boyd toiled up the slope towards the Rognon
and Camp One.

This was going to be easy, he told himself. A lot different from
the several weeks he had spent at the NRO as CIA liaison officer on
the satellite recovery programme, codename Bellerophon. That
had been like trying to find the proverbial needle in a haystack.
Harder than that. He remembered the complaints of one of the
desk analysts who were supposed to be putting him on the track of
the fallen bird:

'Worse than a needle in a haystack,' the guy had said. 'This isn't
proverbial. This is metaphysical. This is like trying to find angels on
the head of a pin. A country the size of Florida. Eight hundred kilometres of mountains, most of them unclimbed. Whole valleys completely unexplored. Shit, this was a closed country until 1951.'

Boyd pushed his ice-axe deep into the snow and stopped to take
a breather. That he had found the satellite at all now seemed even

310

more remarkable. Especially when he considered how inadequate to the task had been the NRO's much vaunted technical systems. He smiled to himself and glanced around to see if there was any sign of pursuit, uncertain as to how equal to his task Ang Tsering would be. But the ice field blocked his view. He would take another look when he reached the top of the Machhapuchhare Rognon.

He was hardly new to this, having established what the Director of Field Personnel, Chaz Mustilli, had termed 'a hallmark of accomplishment' in this kind of operation.

A hallmark of accomplishment. Boyd had liked the sound of that. When he had destroyed the satellite that would be another hallmark. Maybe even a medal. Certainly he would be paid a generous bonus and promoted a grade or two. The Agency was nothing if not grateful to its successful operatives. Eventually, when they saw the situation on the ground as he had seen it, they would surely understand why it had been necessary to kill one of the scientists, contrary to the order that he had been given. It was the kind of order you could only make if you were behind a desk back in Washington. Not the kind that applied in the field if you wanted to get the job done. That was all that mattered here, and if they didn't understand that then they had no business to be in charge of his mission in the first place. Sending him down here with a gun in his hand, what did they expect? There was no point in having a dog and wagging its tail yourself.

He pushed on, slowly and steadily, managing a reasonable speed, but still nothing to compare with Rebecca. Boyd was carrying only a light load. Just his rifle, a handheld radio wave detector to help him pinpoint the location of the satellite, some C4 plastique and some fuses, and the Satcom transceiver with which he was going to radio in his own rescue helicopter. But the climb up towards Machhapuchhare was still a hard, almost cathartic experience that made him appreciate the capabilities of the yeti, whose tracks lay clearly ahead of him like a series of tiny craters on some cold and forgotten planet.

It was too bad, he thought. Too bad if they would be poisoned by the effects of the exploded isotope as Warner had said. But he could not see any alternative. If the satellite was not destroyed, then someone else – the Chinese probably – might find it and use the information and the technology it was carrying against the USA. What were the lives of a few apes – albeit ones as rare as the yeti –

against the national security of the United States? There was none of them back at ABC who understood that. For that matter, there was none of them back in Washington who understood that.

He was beginning to feel the effect of the altitude. It was not that he felt breathless. It was just a general lassitude that worked on his legs like one of Jameson's immobilising drugs, so that he had to force himself to keep climbing when his body wanted to take a rest. And after a while, conscious that the lengths of his rest periods were growing longer than the work periods, he had to discipline himself, taking fifty steps before taking a rest. Finally he reached the top and collapsed into Camp One as exhausted as if he had climbed Machhapuchhare itself. Crawling into one of the tents, he closed his eyes and dropped into a light doze.

The physical effort of pursuit helped Swift to deflect her mind from the danger Boyd posed to the yetis and to her own person. For a while she reproached herself for taking him at face value, for not not being more suspicious of him from the very beginning. Was he really a geologist? A climatologist? He had seemed to know something about what he was supposed to be doing.

She was also aware of the irony of her situation. Just as she and Jack had concealed the true intention of the expedition from their sponsors, so Boyd had concealed his real intentions from her and everyone else. No wonder the expedition had been so well equipped. It was the US military that had been their supplier. And all of it in the name of national security and a missing spy satellite.

But it did not seem so strange to her that it should have landed in the Himalayas. Eight kilometres north of Khatmandu, near the small village of Budhanilkantha and the walled compound that marked the ancient site, was a recessed water-tank where lay the five-metre-long statue of an Indian god known as the Sleeping Vishnu. Even when she had first seen it, Swift had been struck by how much like some cryogenically suspended alien spaceman the Sleeping Vishnu had looked. Now even more so that she was aware of a missing spacecraft. It was almost as if Vishnu might have fallen to earth from the stricken satellite.

Swift had little regard for organised religion but if she had thought it could help her prevent Boyd from blowing up the satellite and poisoning the yetis' hidden valley she would offer perfume, flowers and a whole basketful of fruit to this sleeping god, the least bloody-minded of the principal Vedic deities.

Mindful of the fate that had befallen the four Sherpas in the ice field, Swift entered the precarious maze of ice and chasms telling herself that this was not a place to put haste ahead of caution. Boyd's trail was easy enough to follow. He himself had been wise enough to place his own feet in Rebecca's footprints wherever he could. Swift hoped she would come upon him underneath a fallen mass of ice, or find some evidence that he had disappeared into a crevasse. But in her fast-beating heart she knew to expect more of him. Jack was right. Boyd was a professional. Probably some kind of Special Forces type well-trained in this kind of terrain. He would not make an obvious mistake. Whereas she . . . she was only a lecturer at a university. Just thinking it made her feel inadequate to the task facing her. Apart from the odd skiing trip, the most hazardous thing she'd ever done was venture into a class with sex-mad morons like Todd Bartlett. She figured her best chance – perhaps her only chance – was that Boyd would hardly be expecting her, she might sneak up on him when he was placing the charge and shoot him in the back. Killing him would be the easy part after his cold-blooded murder of Miles Jameson.

Walking through this frozen, fragile landscape, Swift felt as alone as she had ever felt in her life. She wished she could have used the short-wave radio in her helmet to stay in touch with the rest of the team at ABC, for despite the loss of the main radio, the smaller, less powerful GPS units still worked. But that would only have alerted Boyd, who was on the same frequency, to the news that she was following him. So she observed radio silence and tried to forget the possibility that Boyd might be lying in wait just to make sure that he was not followed.

She turned quickly on her heel, her heart beating wildly as the hot mike on the SCE suit amplified a sound behind her, and was just in time to see a spectacular serac, as big as a house, collapse across the way she had just come. She felt goose bumps rising on her body as she realised how close she had been to being killed. For a moment she stood there, trembling inside her suit and listening to her voice reminding her of her own miraculous escape.

'You were bloody lucky, Swift,' she told herself. 'Jesus, you could have been under that lot. Now you have to go on. You've no choice, have you? You can hardly go back across that lot. Should be interesting on the return journey.'

313

When she stopped her nervous soliloquy, there was no sound except the occasional creak of the glacier as the sunlight grew stronger. Then she turned and took up the pursuit once again.

Boyd climbed down the ropes into the crevasse and stood on the shelf. He felt the cavernous dimensions of the chasm to his left, extending a few hundred metres below, and smiled in awe of the drop. He had never cared much for heights. Outside wasn't so bad. But inside made him feel distinctly claustral and sealed off. Like he was already in his casket. One slip here and he might be. He'd be bungee-jumping without the bungee.

Pressing himself closer to the wall he began to walk, slowly at first, hearing the ground harder under his cramponed feet than on the snow-covered surface up top. Ahead of him the shelf curved away into the shadowy distance like something he'd once seen in a Tarzan movie. It was small wonder that these creatures had remained hidden from the outside world for so long.

The route had a Gothic splendour about it and, but for the intense cold, Boyd half expected to find his way blocked by a marauding tribe of pygmy head-hunters. Other times the shelf narrowed and he was obliged to edge his way along with his back to the wall like some Wall Street type contemplating suicide from the top of a skyscraper on Black Friday.

As it grew darker, his head lamp came on and soon after that a large rocky overhang forced him to face the wall and side-step his way around like a spider. You had to hand it to Jack. But for the certainty that he had already followed the route successfully, Boyd would hardly have dared follow so precarious a path. Just as he thought things could hardly get more difficult he felt himself gasp with fright as he saw a distinctly simian outline standing on the shelf up ahead of him. It was Rebecca, waiting for him in the darkness in a crude-looking ambush.

Momentarily unnerved, Boyd backed away, at the same time unslinging his Colt Automatic Rifle, a short barrel, telescope-stock carbine version of the standard 5.56 millimetre M16A1 service rifle. It had an effective range of almost five hundred metres, but he still wished he had thought to bring along a night-sight. He raised his weapon to his shoulder and fired five times, blowing the creature's arm away into the darkness, and was disappointed that it didn't go howling after it.

314

Disappointed and then puzzled.

It was a minute or two before Boyd got near enough to work out that he'd wasted valuable ammunition on the frozen corpse of Jack Furness's former climbing partner. Boyd cursed himself. He'd known about this. Someone had explained how Rebecca had come to be wearing Didier's ring. He should have remembered. Now he wondered if he might have cause to regret entering the yetis' hidden valley with anything less than a full magazine.

Swift was barely down the ropes and standing gingerly on the half-frozen shelf, staring up at the narrow ribbon of blue above her head, when she heard the rolling, reverberating sound of distant shots.

Inside her head time was already ticking away like a metronome and, anxious not to waste precious moments by standing around trying to interpret the reason for the gunshots, she immediately started along the shelf.

Had Boyd caught up with Rebecca? Had Rebecca turned to attack him? Or had he shot her just for the hell of it? None of these three possibilities seemed very convincing and she was still trying to think of a fourth when she remembered Didier Lauren.

Swift realised that Boyd must have made the same mistake as Jack, and confused poor Didier's frozen corpse with that of a yeti waiting for him in the darkness. She smiled, aware that she now had a definite idea of exactly where Boyd was. Still about an hour ahead of her. But at least now she could be sure that Boyd was not preparing an ambush of his own.

Encouraged by her own conclusion, she quickened her pace, trying to channel her sudden optimism into energy. She did not feel brave. But there seemed to be little point in worrying about the huge drop to her left. Not when there was a whole primate species – the anthropological discovery of the century – at stake. Alone in the subterranean world of ice and rock she moved faster, trying to goad herself into hurrying when the conditions and the route warned her to go slowly, becoming angry with herself and with Boyd. She knew that she would have to keep hold of that anger if she was going to be able to point her gun at Boyd and pull the trigger.

Back at ABC, Warner surveyed the wreckage of the radio mast left by Boyd and shook his head.

'We're never going to fix that,' he said. 'Apart from our own individual radios, we're mute. Boyd must have a more powerful radio with him. He must be planning to arrange his own airlift or something.'

'One of us is going to have to walk down to Chomrong,' said Jack. 'Mac? Feel up to a walk? It shouldn't take you longer than a day or two. Sixteen kilometres downhill.'

'No problem.'

'I think there's a telephone at the Captain's Lodge. You could call the chopper in Pokhara and get them up here by tomorrow. And fetch some Royal Nepalese Police from Naksal. We can hardly stay here and do nothing.'

'On my way.'

'Shit.'

In the darkness of the crevasse, Boyd stood staring up at the route in front of him. Flat for a couple of kilometres, the shelf now rose steeply, bending round the wall like a spiral staircase. Except that there were no stairs.

Boyd struck at the surface of the slope with his ice-axe and found the ice as hard as steel.

'How the hell did you get up this, Jack?'

He punched the wall gently with his gloved fist.

'Come on, man, think. There has to be a way. You've come too far to let this hold you up. He did it. So can you. It's just a question of figuring out how, that's all.'

There was no other way he could go. That much was plain. Beyond the slope, the shelf petered out into a shattered rib of rock and the sheer face of the crevasse. He was stumped. There were no obvious handholds. Nor any pegs or screws he had left on the route. The wall looked as smooth as the face of his helmet.

'You're one hell of a climber, Jack boy, I'll say that much for you.'

After a frustrating ten minutes had elapsed, Boyd's headlamp finally picked out a broken crampon further up the slope. It was a reassuring sign that he had not been mistaken. Jack had indeed negotiated the slope. The broken crampon was eloquent evidence to the greater difficulty of the return journey. Presumably, he told himself, the yetis had another way out of the hidden valley. Perhaps a route that took them over the mountains. But that was in the future. Right now he had still to get up. He sat down to rest while he considered the problem.

316

'Come on, you dumb bastard,' he told himself. 'Do you want to spend the night here? Look again, there just has to be a way up.'

He raised his ice-axe and then hammered the ground in frustration. Then he saw it. A gap underneath the wall, no wider than about five centimetres. Just enough of an undercut to provide a good handhold if you had the nerve to try it. He would have to step up the wall with his fingers in the groove like a rope-walk up the side of a building. There was no other way.

Boyd stood up and tightened the strap of the Colt AR-15 to stop it from shifting on his back. Then he gripped the undercut and placed his cramponed feet on to the slope. This had to be the way Jack had done it. A real piece of mountaincraft. Not for nothing did people say that Jack Furness was one of the best in the world.

Well he was pretty good himself. You had to be good just to come through the Basic Underwater Demolition, SEAL training. Hell-week, they called it. Drownproofing followed by the toughest assault course in the world, when you had to scale the side of the high-rise wooden walls on San Diego Beach. Climbing along nothing more than two-by-fours bolted to the face of the wall. That required great strength in fingers and ankles too. If he could do BUD/S, he could do anything.

Once he had tried the technique, Boyd found that it was easier than he had imagined. But it was heavy going on the fingers of his gloves. And near the top he caught the sleeve of his SCE suit on an edge of the wall that was nearly razor-sharp, and ripped it badly.

When he was standing on flat ground once again, he inspected the damage.

'Shit.'

He was going to have to make a repair or risk a significant, perhaps even fatal, heat loss. But for a moment he allowed himself to feel impressed by his new surroundings – an enormous, open-ended cavern that looked as big as the Houston Astrodome. Just the kind of place that Tarzan would have fetched up on his way to recover some treasure.

Then he sat down against one of the icy walls, opened the control unit on his chest and removed a neatly packaged repair kit.

Swift didn't stop to look at Didier Lauren's mutilated corpse. The arm, shot away at the elbow, was sufficient confirmation that her earlier theory regarding the gunshots had been correct. And even

317

through the air conditioning system in her suit she could detect a distinct smell of cordite. She just kept on moving, as quickly as her crampons allowed, ignoring the fatigue that was creeping over her, with only the sound of her own breath inside the helmet for company.

Thirty minutes had passed.

She had arrived at the place Jack had told her about: at the spot where the ledge sloped up into the cavern. Now she was going to have to climb. What was the phrase Jack had used?

Laybacking.

It was, she considered, an inappropriate name for such an obviously strenuous technique. She had only to think of the word to see herself back in the lodge, lying on her bunk, wrapped up inside her sleeping bag, and sleeping for a very long time. Or, better still, back home, on her big brass bed in Berkeley. Now that was what she called laybacking. But not this awkward, crouching way of climbing Jack had described to her, that threatened to put her back out. It was fortunate she was so light and, being a natural climber – or so Jack had once tried to persuade her – within ten or fifteen minutes she had gained the top of the slope and entered the cavern that gave on to the hidden valley and the forest.

The sight took her breath away.

Jack had not exaggerated. It was indeed a magical-looking place. Well sheltered. Lush. The perfect spot for the world's newest and shyest ape species, if ape was what you called a creature whose DNA was just over half a per cent different from Man's own. Swift was no longer sure. All she knew for certain was that the yeti had to be protected. At whatever cost. She drew the automatic from her belt and advanced cautiously across the broken ice floor, towards the cavern's curiously shaped exit. There she stopped and, crouching down close to the wall, scanned the edge of the giant rhododendron forest and listened carefully.

The forest in front of her was silent. There was only the faint rustle of leaves and the groan of the cold Himalayan wind stirring the tops of the tall fir trees. There was a film she had seen, based on a book by James Hilton, a name for such a secret magical place: Shangri-La. It was true there were no monasteries in sight, and certainly the hidden valley offered no immediate prospect of eternal life. It would be as much as she could do to survive the next few

318

hours. But this looked and felt like somewhere special.

Swift removed her crampons. Then, slowly, she approached the tree line.

The forest remained silent.

She peered forward, through the enormous rhododendron leaves. Then, grabbing a branch for support, she began to move down a gentle gradient and waded into the thick vegetation. She came stealthily, acutely aware she was in as much danger from the yetis she was trying to protect as she was from the man who was threatening to kill them. Boyd had already demonstrated that he would not hesitate to use his gun to protect himself against the yetis. But could she? She kept on moving, always looking around her and ready for anything, she hoped. She was not afraid. Rather she felt a strange kind of exhilaration. Anthropology had never seemed so exciting.

But if she had hoped to track Boyd through the forest she was disappointed. There were no obvious clues as to the direction he had taken. Recalling a story that Byron Cody had told her about tracking mountain gorillas in Zaire, she dropped on to her belly and began to crawl through the undergrowth. Visual clues, he had told her, were often obscured by thick vegetation.

There was very little snow on the ground, so dense was the plant life. Ahead of her lay a short tunnel that was roofed by a fallen fir tree and walled by dense rhododendrons. She wormed her way inside it, grateful for the cover it seemed to afford, and hoping that her suit would not tear. Without its protective warmth she knew she would not live for very long in such low temperatures. At the far end of the tunnel, she stopped crawling and listened.

Nothing.

Where were the yetis? Where was Boyd? Was he here at all?

A powerful smell, similar to a stableful of horses, only stronger and more pungent, permeated the vegetation ahead of her. Inside her helmet she felt her nose wrinkle with disgust. It was the same stink she had smelt on Jack after the sirdar had brought him out of the crevasse and she wondered how much stronger it would have been had she not been partly shielded from it by her suit.

Swift looked around for dung deposits, having no wish to find herself crawling through the stuff and was surprised that there were none to be seen. It was a moment or two before she guessed the reason for the bad odour.

319

Fear. It was the smell of fear.

If yeti anatomy was anything like a gorilla's then the creature's axillary parts would have contained several layers of apocrine glands which were responsible for making this simple but highly effective means of olfactory communication. One yeti following the trail of another would have come across the scent and recognised the message: danger close by.

Was Boyd the danger?

With a growing sense of urgency, Swift kept on crawling until, from somewhere in the distance ahead of her, she heard the unmistakable sounds of a yeti hoot series followed by a gunshot.

Swift got to her feet and started to run in the direction of the sound.

Thirty

'Tread softly, for this is holy ground.
It may be, could we look with seeing eyes,
This spot we stand upon is paradise.'
                                    Christina Rossetti

Annapurna Base Camp was still. The air was the colour of sapphires, as if the gods had already purified the Sanctuary of the stain of human blood that still lay upon the snow outside the clamshell. Mac was long gone and Jack paced the campsite with frustration, cursing the injuries that stopped him from pursuing Swift. Time passed slowly and sounds became the events of his day: Ang Tsering groaning inside the clamshell; the hum of the power cell; a growl like a chain saw in a distant forest that disappeared with the wind, but coming back again, grew louder. Hands above his narrowing eyes, Jack stared into the sky.

It was a helicopter. But how? It was impossible that Mac could have made it down to Chomrong already. It was only a couple of hours since he had gone and Chomrong was sixteen kilometres. Jack made two metronomes of his arms and walked towards the previous landing site.

Beating the air and the snow like the white of an egg, the chopper spiralled down into the Sanctuary's bowl, hovered above the camp for a minute or two as if inspecting something, and then lunged towards the ground, whipping snow into Jack's face as he ran towards it. The markings were clear enough. It was the Royal Nepal Police.

A couple of uniformed officers, both armed, jumped out of the

321

fuselage as the rotor blades began to slow. 'Is everything all right here?' yelled one of the policemen, a sergeant.

'There's been a murder,' shouted Jack. 'And there may well be another if we don't get after the man who did it.' He pointed down the glacier, towards Machhapuchhare. 'He went that way.'

Jack tried to lead him back towards the helicopter, but the sergeant remained where he was, his eyes taking in the severed hand that still lay on the bloodstained snow.

'First we must see the body,' said the sergeant.

'You don't understand,' said Jack. 'He'll kill again unless we can stop him. There's no time to lose now.'

'Perhaps so,' said the sergeant. 'But either way we must wait to refuel before going any further. It is two hundred and forty kilometres from Khatmandu.'

Even as the police sergeant spoke the pilot was hauling jerry-cans out of the helicopter.

'This way,' said Jack. 'But please . . . *Chito garnuhos*. Please hurry.'

Boyd entered the forest in classic combat style, running to a tree, taking up a kneeling firing position, crawling on his belly towards better cover, and kneeling again. He jerked the short barrel of his carbine one way and then another, searching for a target and wishing that he'd thought to attach a forty-millimetre grenade launcher, just in case one of the yetis proved to be hard to kill with the standard nine-millimetre round.

After a couple of minutes, he felt sufficiently relaxed to lower the gun barrel and take a reading with the handheld radio wave detector. The bird's on-board computers and data transmitters utilised a local oscillator, operating around a specific signal frequency and emitting detectable electromagnetic radiation; this could be identified by the detector in Boyd's hand; and once the waveform pattern of the operating signal was found and compared with a calibrated memory within the unit, the data displayed on a small screen could be analysed by a small microchip to produce a bearing on the satellite that was accurate to within half a metre. For finding a needle in a haystack it was the nearest thing to having a giant magnet. Even so, with a working range of only fifty metres, Boyd estimated that since his arrival in the Sanctuary, a search area of some one hundred square kilometres, he had taken as many as a thousand separate readings with the little detector device, all of which had been negative. But on this occasion he found a positive reading and a bearing almost instantly. The bird lay straight ahead of him.

'Bingo,' he chuckled. 'Give that man a prize.'

He put away the detector and raised his weapon again.

'We're on our way.' He started forward between two rhododendron bushes. 'Couple of hours and you'll be out of this icebox and back at the embassy in Khat. Go find me a couple of gals in Thamel and then party.'

Another fifteen minutes of running and crawling brought Boyd to the edge of a long clearing. It looked like someone had been engaged in some serious deforestation. There were scorched bushes and broken trees.

'Something crashed here, all right,' he assured himself. Then he saw it.

The satellite looked more like the wreck of a small van than anything that had once orbited the earth. But for the stars and stripes that were painted on the dirty white fuselage he could easily have mistaken it for some kind of ambulance. And now he could understand exactly why the spy planes had missed it. The bird had crashed through fifty or sixty metres of trees and bushes upon impact, flattening them; but then it had rolled a distance, before coming to rest among some giant-sized bushes and beneath some trees. The Keyhole Eleven bird couldn't have looked better hidden from the air if he had tried to camouflage it himself.

Instinctively avoiding the clearing, Boyd started along the tree line towards his objective. Somehow he'd expected a little more opposition. After Jack's description of a whole group of yetis living in this hidden forest he'd thought he might have to squeeze off a few rounds to defend himself. But so far he hadn't even heard one of the creatures, let alone seen one. Maybe this was going to take less time than he had thought.

When he reached the bird, Boyd opened the fuselage and looked inside. Upon landing, the satellite computer should have started broadcasting a small signal enabling a remote recovery team to go into action, but this had not happened. It was easy to see why. Two lights on the warning panel, labelled MAIN BUS A UNDERVOLT and MAIN BUS B UNDERVOLT, glowed red. Something had disrupted the flow of power from both the satellite's small thermonuclear generator and the solar cell panels to all the operation and guidance systems. Bus A was easily accounted for: the solar cells had ripped off upon impact. But the thermonuclear generator feeding through Bus B should have carried on functioning. Boyd checked the voltage on the junction and found the needle indicating that it was still producing current. There was a bad connection somewhere. He searched the Bus B junction and found that one of the wires had melted, probably the result of a small fire caused inside the satellite when Bus A short circuited. Restoring power was simply a matter of flicking the Bus B switch off for a moment, reconnecting the burnt wire, and switching it back on. Bus B was now glowing green.

'Those dumb bastards,' he said, trying to imagine the reaction back in Washington when the people at the NRO realised they were on line with the Keyhole again.

'Not for long,' he chuckled and began to type out the auto-destruct code on the computer's keyboard. He had entered only half the code when the power went off again. Glancing up at the warning panel he saw the Bus B light glowing red again. There was another loose connection somewhere, but he had run out of time. He would have to use explosives to do the job after all. But at least, back in Washington, they would now know he had found the satellite. And was about to destroy it.

From his pack Boyd took out the polythene-wrapped chunk of C4 plastique. Resembling white putty, C4 was the most versatile of explosives, being easily handled, waterproof and, with the help of a little added Vaseline, able to stick to just about anything. Planting explosives had always been an important part of Boyd's job and he worked quickly, prising open the panel that protected the satellite internal machinery and shaping the C4 around the metal box that housed the radio-isotope for maximum effect. He was searching for a detonator in his pack when he heard a twig break and then a hoot series that announced the arrival of a yeti. Boyd snatched up his gun.

'Customers,' he said and fired twice in the direction of some moving bushes, with apparently no result. No scream. No collapsing body. Nothing. Boyd swore. He was losing his touch. Seven shots out of a thirty-shot magazine without a hit. He was going to have to be careful. Without a spare mag he would have to make every shot count now. And if every time he heard a yeti hoot or saw a bush move he fired a shot he would lose it.

He waited a moment, listening carefully and watching the forest for some more signs of movement. He was contemplating going back to the detonator when he heard a footfall and, whistling round, saw a clump of scorched rhododendrons swaying as if something had walked between them. Boyd raised the telescopic stock of the carbine to his shoulder and thought better of firing.

'Don't get spooked,' he reminded himself. 'Mark a hard target first.'

He took several steps back, then retired around the satellite and ran thirty or forty metres through the undergrowth in the opposite direction before turning abruptly to his right, dropping down on to his belly and crawling quickly back towards where he thought he had now placed his quarry.

Back in the States, Boyd often went hunting. In his time he had shot deer, mountain lion, coyote, seal, even a bear, but this was something new. He'd never shot a great ape. Excepting some of the men he'd killed. And hunting an animal no other man had hunted. That would be something. Boyd was beginning to enjoy himself. He crawled back round to a spot immediately behind the clump of scorched rhododendrons. Expecting to see the hairy back of some yeti he was surprised to see a mirror image of himself. It was some-one else wearing an SCE suit.

He had been followed from ABC.

Boyd cursed Ang Tsering, and then himself for not having done what should have been done. He ought to have killed them all when he had the chance. Just like he'd killed those Chinese.

Whoever it was had the automatic he had given Tsering and was crouched at the edge of the clearing, gun pointed at the satellite. Boyd was too intrigued to fire right away. He wanted to see who it was had dared to take him on before he killed them.

Swift knelt behind the cover of an enormous Himalayan silver fir, watching the satellite and wondering if Boyd was close by. She held the gun in both hands and kept it pointed in front of her in the way she had seen cops doing on TV.

A minute or so passed and then she lowered the gun. Maybe he hadn't found it yet. Or maybe he had already been there, set his charge and gone. But she felt sure that the shots had come from this direction.

She had a second or two to consider the amazing diversity of flowers around her: saxifrages, gentians, geraniums, anemones, cinquefoils and primulas. If she did manage to get herself killed she could think of worse places for her body to lie.

Gathering her courage she got to her feet only to find them kicked away from beneath her, and the gun flying out of her hand. She kicked out wildly and then felt the wind knocked out of her as something struck her hard between the shoulder blades.

It was two or three minutes before she had sucked enough breath back into her bruised body to recognise that it was Boyd who had knocked her with his rifle butt, by which time he had removed her helmet as well as his own.

He was sitting on a tree stump a short distance from her, the carbine dangling loosely from a strap between his thighs like some kind of enormous medallion.

'I might have known it'd be you,' he grinned. 'No one else with the guts, I imagine. Underneath all that ball-breaking science, you're probably quite a woman, Swifty. Of course I'm only guessing. These suits are warm, but they're hardly Issey Miyake, now are they?'

'Fuck you, Boyd.'

'Whatever you say, sweetheart.'

He wanted to have some fun before he killed her.

One of the job's perks. There hadn't been many of those. Fool around with her before he blew up the bird.

'You know, that's not a bad idea,' he said and pointed the carbine squarely at her chest. 'Why don't you take that suit off? I'd like to have a look at what you look like in your thermals.'

'Go to hell, Boyd. Just kill me and get it over with, because I'm not about to play your – '

He fired a single shot above her head, so close that she felt it touch her hair.

'I expect all you had in mind was that you should kill me,' he said. 'Any way you could get a shot in. But there are lots of ways I can kill you, Swifty. Lots of slow ways. Apache style. Or you can hang on to life a while longer. Do what you're told and stay alive. Maybe.' His tone became more menacing. 'Now get undressed or the next one will be in your kneecap.'

Swift remained motionless.

'I can tell you've never seen anyone shot in the kneecap, Swifty. It hurts. Once I've shot you in the kneecap I can do what I want with

326

you anyway. Makes no difference to me. What matters more is the difference it might make to you.'

He was right. While she was alive, she still had a ghost of a chance.

Resisting the temptation to tell him to go to hell, Swift unclipped the SCE control unit and tossed it on to the ground. Then she turned her back on him, an idea already half-forming in her mind.

'You'll have to help me,' she said. 'It's hard to get out of this thing by yourself.'

'Okay,' said Boyd. 'But no tricks now.' He placed the icy muzzle of the carbine under her ear. 'Or I can promise you won't hear my next word of reproach.'

She felt him unfasten the backpack life-support system.

'Easy now,' he said and unplugged her all-in-one underwear from its special little pipe.

Before she could do anything he stepped back.

'Now climb out of the suit. Slowly.'

Swift did as she was told and then dropped the empty suit at her feet like a sloughed skin. She began to shiver, hardly sure whether it was from fear or from cold.

'Now take the one-piece off.'

'I always knew there was something fundamentally crummy about you, Boyd. Ever since that night in Khat, when you made that crude pass at me.' She ripped open the Velcro strip covering her underwear's zip fastener.

'You should have been nice,' he said. 'Could be you'll live to regret that you weren't. But I'm not promising.'

'I think rape is precisely your style.'

She peeled off her protective underwear and stood before him wearing only her bra and panties. After the warmth of the water-heated underwear, the cold took her breath away. Only one thing was sustaining Swift. The suits had one major design limitation: virtually the only way to have a pee was to take it off or go in the suit. To rape her Boyd would surely have to remove his own suit. That might be her only opportunity.

'Come on,' he growled. 'The rest of it.'

Swift unfastened her bra and threw it on to the ground. Quickly she stepped out of her panties and, shivering endured his penetrating gaze. She was sure now: the cold definitely had the edge. But

327

there were maybe worse ways to die than cold. Surely it would be like going to sleep.

'Nice,' said Boyd. 'Very nice indeed. You and me are going to have a little party. Now get down on your hands and knees and better start praying that this cold doesn't affect me, or I'm likely to kill you out of sheer frustration.'

She did as she was told. But straight away her eyes searched the ground for the gun.

'Do you always blame the cold for your obvious inadequacies,' she said through chattering teeth.

Boyd moved around the back of her and chuckled.

'Keep talking. In just a few moments your ass is going to start paying me back for some of those smart remarks, lady. The more you say now, the more it's going to hurt. And you better understand something right now. Giving hurt is what I get off on. So talk all you like, Swifty. But just keep your eyes on the ground.'

'What's the matter? Shy or something? You're forgetting. I'm an anthropologist. I've seen an ape's dick before.'

She trembled with fear and cold as she heard something thrown on the ground. It was the control unit for his suit. Then her heart gave a leap. The gun. She could see her gun. It was lying on a clump of flowering white sandwort, no more than five or six metres from her right hand, and looking for all the world like a gift from the fairies.

Boyd was laughing.

'That's it. Keep your Bogart coming, Swifty. I'll be ready to get you warm again in a tick.'

She heard him wrestling with his backpack life support. Taking it off by yourself was like trying to take off a strait-jacket. You needed to be almost double-jointed. Virtually the only way she had found of doing it easily was to lie down on the ground and lean hard on to her elbow to force her hand back over her shoulder as far as it would go. It was a lot easier simply to have someone help you.

Boyd cursed out loud as he reached the same conclusion.

It was Swift's cue to run.

She was running before she had time to have second thoughts about her chances of surviving at low temperatures without clothing. But she had managed to grab the gun.

Instinctively she started to zigzag.

A couple of seconds later the tree beside her was pitted with small

328

explosions of wood and sap as Boyd started firing from the hip.

She felt the freezing cold breeze on her bare breasts and limbs as, her heart thumping, she hurdled a fallen tree trunk and then took off at another tangent, sprinting through the trees. While she was running it didn't feel too cold. It was when she stopped that her problems would begin. Missing her footing she slipped, somersaulted and, like an expert marksman, stood up returning fire in the direction she had come from. The gun hardly flinched as it set about its task, for it seemed to Swift that she had very little to do except point the thing, and although she was hardly aware of pulling the trigger once, she fired eight shots in less time than it would have taken her to play a piano scale.

Expecting a volley of bullets to come after her, she took off again, ducking under branches, side-stepping trees and all the time aware of the sulphurous smell of cordite, as if the air itself had been galvanised by the gunfire. The next second she was lying on her back, hearing another shot, and thinking she must have been hit until she looked above her ringing head and saw the branch of a tree sticking out like a tollgate. In her desperation to escape from Boyd she had run headfirst into the outstretched arm of the forest's own Checkpoint Charlie.

She sat up and touched her head instinctively and found a Koh-i-noor-sized bump and a small trickle of blood. But recognising the strong stink of the vegetation around her, she saw her little tunnel of rhododendrons and fallen trees again and quickly crawled inside.

Man's oldest sanctuaries were natural woods. Hidden in the tunnel and lying on a bed of ferns, Swift felt safe enough to draw an ice-cold breath and lie in wait for him coming after her. She touched the bump on her head again and winced. Sanctuary had never felt so tender, or so bitterly cold. How long could she survive with only a bed of ferns to cover her naked body? Perhaps an hour or two at the most. Unless Boyd came looking for her she was going to have to go looking for him or her clothes; or die of cold.

'Come on, you bastard,' she said holding the gun at arm's length along the ground in front of her.

Only the gun looked different now. The slide looked as if it had stuck, leaving the short barrel sticking out like a cigar's end.

It took a moment or two for the meaning of the gun's shape to pierce the shivering euphoria she felt at having escaped. The realisation that she was out of ammunition chilled her to the bone. She was waiting to ambush a man with an empty gun. She must have emptied the whole magazine when she fell and returned fire.

'Shit.'

Swift gouged the gun into the ground in sheer frustration and tried to think what to do next. Lie there and quickly freeze to death. Or surrender and hope that after he had used her he might let her live.

'Fat chance of that,' she muttered and closed her eyes. The starkness of the choice facing her was followed by the perception that it would all be ended soon.

Advancing through the forest, Boyd tried to guess how many shots she had fired.

Upon leaving ABC he had handed Ang Tsering the .38 calibre Beretta he had used to kill Miles Jameson. The automatic had a double-action magazine containing ten rounds. Swift had fired another eight shots. So the question was, how many shots had Tsering fired before giving up his weapon, if any? He had to assume that she still had two shots at the most. Enough to make the hunt interesting. He hoped he would find her in time before she froze to death. Her body would be no good to him then.

His keen and experienced eyes soon picked out her trail. The occasional footprint in the snow. And the little pile of empty brass, like the droppings of some metallic animal, where she had stopped to fire back at him. Kneeling down, he collected up the empty cases to make sure. Eight. If she had fired eight she might have fired her whole magazine out of plain fear. She was probably staring at an empty gun right now. She was probably near enough to hear him.

He stood up again, startling a pale grey and white bird with a black head that flew away with a loud flapping of wings. The noise almost cost him another bullet. It was just a snow pigeon.

'I know you're somewhere hereabouts,' he shouted. 'Why don't you come out and we can get it over with? If I have to come and find you it's going to be hard on your body. You hear me?'

He paused, ears straining for a reply, but there was only silence. Patiently, Boyd stood stock still, as if he knew that something would soon give her away. He did not have to wait long.

Another bird, only this time running across the ground from a dense clump of trees and bushes, coming towards him, racing to

330

escape someone else, and veering away from Boyd at the last moment.

Boyd frowned as he watched the bushes carefully. Scanning the dark green foliage it seemed that there was something lying on the ground beyond the leaves. Something human. He couldn't be sure. It had started to snow. Each flake brushed each leaf and made it move so that. . .

A hand. He could see her hand. Grinning he moved closer, and tightening his grip on the carbine, he raised it to shoulder level.

'I can see you,' he said teasingly. 'Hiding in there. You insult my intelligence, Swifty. I could shoot you from here, no problem. Now throw out your gun and let's see the rest of you. If I see anything other than your tits pointing at me, I'll – '

Suddenly there was an explosion of sound and vegetation as if some kind of mortar bomb had landed in front of him. Before he had time even to think or to squeeze the trigger, something huge bulldozed its way through the foliage towards him, roaring like a hurricane. Trees and bushes were literally flattened as if another out-of-control satellite was crashing to earth.

Boyd was so surprised that he turned and fled, his nerve completely gone. It was an impulse that automatically invited a chase, although not a protracted one. He hadn't gone more than two or three metres when the huge silverback yeti knocked him down, tearing at his clothing, biting his neck and back.

Boyd began to scream.

Watching the yeti attack from the comparative safety of her rhododendron tunnel, Swift had a sudden and horrific insight into the power and ferocity of the creature she had come to protect. The yeti male was enormous, much larger than she had expected. Rebecca had been a third of the size of this monster – Madonna compared to Schwarzenegger.

The yeti yanked Boyd off the ground and, still holding him by one arm, stamped him down again.

Boyd screamed again as his arm was torn from his body at the shoulder. Swift might have been glad. Instead she felt sorry for him.

Distracted by the sight of blood, the yeti sucked at the fragmented end of Boyd's arm. Mortally injured, Boyd feebly turned on to his belly and tried to crawl away. He managed only about half a metre before, with a terrible roar, the yeti fell upon him again. It picked Boyd up like an item of hand luggage, held him high above its head as if he was about to stow him somewhere and then threw him on to the ground, stamping on his torso a second time.

The yeti sat down, grunting loudly. It regarded Boyd with vague disinterest for a moment, then picked him up a third time. But instead of throwing him down again, this time the yeti brought Boyd's torn and bloody stump of a shoulder up to its huge jaws and jerked its head away, tugging at the flesh of the man's bare breast. Boyd was still alive, feebly trying to push the yeti's big head away even as he was being eaten. Watching with horror, Swift found herself gagging.

'Jesus Christ,' she said and covered her face.

When she looked up again, she saw that the yeti had cast Boyd aside and that he had stopped moving. Relief quickly gave way to terror as she realised that the yeti's big yellowish eyes were now fixed squarely on her.

Thirty-one

'Do not be amazed by the true dragon.'

Dogen Zenji

Swift remained quite still. There was no point in running. Boyd had proved that. The big silverback yeti had moved with a speed that she found astonishing for so large a creature. She estimated it to be almost two and a half metres tall and as heavy as two hundred and seventy kilogrammes. Attacking Boyd, it had moved like a gold medal Olympic sprinter, flying out of his starting-blocks. What was more it had moved bipedally, on legs as big as tree trunks, powering itself forward with arms so hugely muscled they would have made even the largest body-builder look puny. Roaring like a tiger and with hair trailing in matted red pennants, the yeti looked as formidable a hominoid as perhaps the earth had ever seen.

She didn't doubt that the slightest movement would cause the yeti to attack her. The hair on its headcrest was fully erect and the teeth fully exposed. Numb with cold as she was, Swift wondered how long she could force herself to lie there before severe chill turned to frostbite and exposure. Already her fingers and toes were without feeling and it was only the sight of the anomalously even number of fingers on Boyd's severed hand that stopped her from crying out loud with terror and discomfort.

The yeti sat down and faced her, feeding on Boyd's arm, occasionally glancing over its Rushmore-sized shoulders as if waiting for the rest of the group of which, Swift was quite certain, it must surely have been leader.

But it was not the rest of the group that came.

The yeti stood up and to Swift's surprise she heard human speech. Someone was there with her, in the hidden valley. Someone who seemed to be talking to the yeti. She knew at least the sound of Nepali well enough to recognise that this was some other language. But it did not seem to be any of the dialects spoken by the Sherpas. And she was quite sure that this was not someone from ABC who was speaking.

For a second she remembered Rebecca's imitative abilities, wondered if this might not be actual yeti speech, and almost immediately rejected this: the blood to her brain must be freezing.

The next second she saw two human feet, naked like her own. She heard a thin reedy voice and then a bearded man was kneeling down at the tunnel's entrance.

'Everything is all right,' he said quietly. 'You can come out now. It is quite safe.'

It was the sadhu. The man she and Jameson had mistakenly tracked when they had first arrived in the Sanctuary.

Swift felt her face smile with relief.

'Swami Chandare,' she panted.

'Are you training to become a sadhu?' he laughed. 'Why are you naked?'

Swift shook her head, too cold now to say anything. She felt the swami crawling into the tunnel beside her, turning her over, his hands upon her bare stomach. He wanted her too. Feebly she struck at him with her fist.

'Calm yourself. I must bring you heat. Listen to me. You must relax. Breathe calmly and listen to me. You must breathe gently and feel nothing but my hands. And hear nothing but my voice. Feel the heat in my hands. Heat coming into your body. Breathe deep and listen to my voice . . .'

For a moment, she felt quite light-headed, as if she was floating somewhere. Was he hypnotising her? If he was she felt no fear. She let herself be stroked by the honied tones of his voice. And by the healing warmth in his hands. The power in his hands seemed to come from some great underground hot spring, so potent it might have been the force of life itself. It was like the anaesthesia offered by the drugs in one of Jameson's darts, only much, much warmer than anything that might be offered at the point of a needle. She closed her eyes, feeling more relaxed now. Somehow the cold no longer mattered and for a second she felt fear, thinking that this might be death, but then there was his voice again, calming her, telling her that it was not cold, assuring her that the heat she could feel in her stomach was coming from his hands.

'. . . heat coming from my hands. There is no cold. There is only heat from my hands . . .'

There was heat. A deep, profound heat that seemed to flow out of him like a stream of hot water, warming her belly, her chest, and her arms. An inexorable tingling painless heat spreading through her limbs as if he had simply plugged her into an electric current. Feeling returning to her hands and to her feet. There was not even any pain as sluggish, half-frozen blood began to move in her bluish toes and her fingers. Just a wonderful feeling of well-being that seemed as if it would be never-ending.

'. . . listen to me. Awake.'

Swift opened her eyes and stared into the swami's bearded face. He smiled. His hands were still on her naked body, but she felt no sense of her own nakedness. She felt only warmth. Incredible warmth. The last time she had felt so warm she had been lying on a beach in Santa Monica. Her breath was there in front of her mouth, only without the accompaniment of teeth chattering together. It was freezing cold. And yet she was as warm as if she had still been wearing her SCE suit. The snow under her bare behind actually felt like the softest and warmest sand.

Sleepily she smiled back at him, and shifted comfortably.

'I must be dreaming,' she said.

'Trust your dreams,' said the swami. 'In them you will see the way to eternity. But now we must go and find your clothes.'

He helped her out of the tunnel of undergrowth took off his threadbare robe and wrapped it around her for the sake of modesty.

Swift glanced anxiously at the big silverback yeti now sitting calmly beside Boyd's broken body, and pressed herself close to the swami's back.

'My brother will not harm you while I am here.' The swami glanced sadly at Boyd's body. 'Nevertheless, your friend . . . I am very sorry.'

'He was no friend of mine.'

'A leaf does not turn brown and die without the whole tree knowing.'

The swami led her through the trees and across the clearing to where the satellite lay. The yeti followed meekly, at a short distance, like some sort of bodyguard.

'Ever since it landed here, I have been expecting someone to come,' said the swami. 'Such is the way of the world. I must confess, I have been dreading this moment.'

'That was Boyd. The dead man. Not me. He came for the satellite. I came to find out about the yeti.'

'And they led you to the same place.'

'Yes,' she said. 'But I meant no harm. I only wanted to know about the yeti.'

Swift collected her protective underwear and unhurriedly put it on, for she still felt as warm as if she had come straight out of a sauna bath.

'As an object of intellectual interest I think my brother is not much more than an abstraction to you. But to my soul, he is an object of joy. To the enlightened man he is a thing of truth and beauty, a window through which one may gaze in wonder at the universe.'

The yeti sat down at the swami's feet and allowed the holy man to stroke him with careless affection.

'You keep calling him your brother,' remarked Swift, climbing back into her SCE suit. For all the many facts about the yeti's blood chemistry that Lincoln Warner had told her, she still felt that she understood very little about this extraordinary creature. She remembered something the swami had said the first time. How he had warned her about looking for ancestors and family trees. 'Fruit may fall into your lap,' he had said. 'You may be nourished by it. But do not be surprised if the branch breaks off in your hand.' Clearly the swami knew more about the yeti than he had said. Perhaps he even knew all there was to know.

'We are like the pillars of a temple. We stand close together, but not too close together, otherwise the temple would collapse.'

'Just how close are we? The DNA says he's very close.'

'The world is not atoms,' said the swami. 'The way to understand this world and its creation cannot be achieved by studying it from the point of view of destruction. The atoms are not important. Only in the One and in the whole is there love. This is the greatest truth of all and the first seed of the soul.'

Swift handed him back his robe. He drew it about his scrawny shoulders with an apparent indifference to the cold that Swift could now understand for she had felt it herself. He helped her to fasten her backpack life-support system as if he had done it many times before.

'But what is the truth about the yeti? How did he come to be here? Why – '

'Who knows the truth?' he giggled in a way that reminded her of a newsreel she had once seen about the Maharishi. 'Who can tell how and when this world and ourselves came into being? But what is certain is that the gods are later than the beginning. So who knows where any of us comes from? Only the God in the highest heaven perhaps. Or perhaps not.'

'I don't believe in God,' said Swift.

'You cannot know God by solving puzzles.'

'Then will you tell me what you know about the yeti, not about God?'

'They are the same thing. Life itself is a temple and a religion. What I do know and what I can tell you is born of the knowledge that if one only sees the diversity of things, with all their distinctions and divisions, then one has imperfect knowledge. Great are the questions you ask of the world. But since you only know a little, I will tell you more.

'The yeti is more Man than animal, but the animal is his innocence. The innocence that Man has lost.

'According to one of my predecessors, his own grandfather's grandfather's grandfather many times over told him, whoever he was, that yetis were once abundant in these mountains. Indeed there were as many yetis as there were men. But as the men grew clever they became resentful of the yeti, for while they toiled, the yeti did nothing. What was more, the yeti were forever stealing *tsampa*, which is barley mixed with water and spices, and still the staple diet in this part of the world. Sometimes this was the only food people could get. Worse, they sometimes took meat, which is even scarcer than barley in these mountains.

'So it was that the men decided to kill all the yetis. First they left poisoned *tsampa* on the hills for them to eat. Many yetis died. And for years afterward yetis were hunted and killed. The heads, the hands and the feet of many yetis were taken to be used in religious rituals. Some ancient religions even venerate these relics as holy objects for they believe that yetis contain the souls of men. And in a way, they are not so far from the truth as I have told it to you.'

After that the swami was silent for a while and refused to answer

337

any more of Swift's questions except to confirm that a female yeti and her infant were safely returned to the hidden valley. Talk of poisoned barley had reminded Swift of why she had followed Boyd, and now she said, 'The satellite contains a radio-isotope,' she said. 'A kind of poison. Boyd planned to destroy the satellite with explosives. Which would have spread poison over the whole valley. All the yetis would have died. Not to mention you, swami.'

'What is death but lying naked in the wind?'

He smiled and threw up his hands.

'If only men thought of God as much as they think of themselves, who would not attain liberation? There is a tradition in these mountains. A great religious tradition. A puzzle if you like. There are those who call people like me the Concealed Lords and say that we worship the yeti. Some say that we are Buddhists. Some that we were here before the Lamas. The truth is sadly rather more prosaic. Merely that there have always been people like me – the religion matters not – guardians who understand the yeti and seek to protect them from the outside world. But lately this has become very hard. Every year more and more tourists come to the mountains.

'I had thought that the yetis could stay undisturbed on this holy mountain where no men are allowed to go. For many years it has been a forbidden place. The Sherpas have respected that. But things have been hard for them. There has been no money and so they have brought you here, where you wanted to go. Well, let us hope that Man will be kind to the yeti, although I can see no cause for optimism since men are so unkind to each other, as well as to other apes. The yeti himself only attacks Man because he has learned to fear Man. Really, he is quite gentle.'

The swami sat down on the ground and pulled the yeti's ear with affection.

'But you must tell me what I must do, to prevent this poison you have described.'

'I think it would be better if I were to leave this place,' said Swift. 'And take the radio-isotope with me. Without it the satellite is just scrap metal.'

The swami frowned.

'But can these things be handled safely? It is a long walk you have back to your friends. Perhaps it would be better if we were to put this source of poison in a place where it can do no harm to anyone or anything until the end of the world. There is a place. A very deep

338

crevasse. Not the one which led you here. But quite close.'

'You show me where it is,' said Swift. 'And I'll dispose of the isotope.'

Swift had spent enough time with Joanna Giardino in the UCSF Medical Center's Radiobiology Department to know that there was little chance of her being able to handle the radio-isotope safely. Not without lead sheets and lead boxes and special tongs, and a whole lot of other protective gear.

Even the isotope in the Med Center's X-ray department was treated like something from the Manhattan Project. Any radio fission product, whether biochemically inert or biochemically active, could do biological damage either outside the body or within.

Despite the SCE suit she was wearing, and her helmet, and even holding the tube containing the satellite isotope at arm's length between two ice-axes in an improvised pair of tongs, Swift was aware that radiation would pass through her body like light passing through a window. The damage it might cause on the way through would remain. Even a few minutes of exposure might easily prove fatal.

She thought of Roentgen, the discoverer of the X-ray, who had died of bone cancer, and of the two pioneers in its medical use, Madame Curie and her daughter Irene, both of whom had died of aplastic anemia, caused by radiation.

Swift had no wish to die prematurely of leukemia, or some other radiation-related disease. But she could not see how anything other than removal of the isotope from the satellite, followed by its safe disposal, could effectively ensure the yetis' continued safety in their hidden valley. There was rather more at stake than her own future to consider: there was also the future of an important new hominoid species to think of.

No contest, she told herself, and hoped she might live long enough to be able to write up her findings in a book.

Swift had the swami show her the new crevasse before she did anything. Then she told him that when she did dispose of the isotope, she was going to do it alone. There was no sense in exposing him to risk as well as herself.

Accompanied by the yeti, the swami led her to the far side of the valley and to a narrow crack in the ground that bordered the protective range of mountains. The crack was a good five minutes' walk from the satellite.

'Here,' he said, pointing into the fissure. 'This is about nine hundred metres deep, I am quite sure.'

Swift inspected it and nodded.

'That should be safe enough.'

They walked back to the open panel of the satellite next to which Boyd had left his pack. Swift took a look inside. There were several detonators, and a larger and more powerful radio than the one she had been using. At least now she could call Pokhara and organise a helicopter out of ABC.

Packed under Boyd's plastic explosive, the isotope was easy to locate. Swift peeled away the wad of C4 and then read the printed injunction against tampering with the thermoelectric generator and its Caesium 137 isotope. Caesium had a half-life of thirty years. But did that make it any less lethal in the short term than Plutonium? The fact was she had no idea.

Before opening the isotope housing she looked around for the swami. He was watching her carefully, with the yeti sitting a short distance away watching him, as if it was waiting to be told what to do.

'You'd better go now, swami,' she said quietly. 'This stuff's hazardous as soon as it's lifted out of the metal housing. No point in us both getting a dose.'

'So small,' he chuckled, peering over her shoulder curiously. 'Can it really be so very dangerous?'

'Very. Now please go.'

'You would risk your life, for us?'

Swift collected her helmet and prepared to put it on her head, hoping that it might afford her some protection against the Caesium. The swami raised his hand over her, in apparent blessing.

'The truth of love is the truth of the universe,' said the swami. 'This is the light of the soul that reveals the secrets of darkness. This light is steady in you. It burns in a shelter where no winds come. Yours is a great soul indeed and having shown your willingness to behold the spirit of death, you have opened your heart unto the very body of life.'

'Thanks,' she said grimly. 'I'll bear that in mind. Now get going before I change my mind.'

'This is an action done in God, and therefore, your soul is not bound to it.'

By this time, Swift had little idea what he was talking about and cared even less. Her mind was concentrated on the lethal job in hand. It didn't seem to matter much what he thought of her. She wasn't doing it for a garland of flowers, a basket of fruit, his good opinion, or her reward in heaven.

Swift was about to tell him more forcefully to go away when the swami turned and spoke to the yeti and now that she was nearer she knew that this was no language she had ever heard before. It was like Tibetan perhaps, but somehow more guttural – she realised that there was no other word to describe it – it was more *apelike* than she had earlier perceived.

The big silverback yeti stood up. But instead of leaving the area with the swami as she had ordered, the yeti advanced on Swift, with arms outstretched with the obvious intention of picking her up. Before she had time to do anything she found herself held gently in the creature's tree trunk arms and rising up in the air.

'Hey, what's the idea?'

'Don't worry, he won't harm you.'

'Then tell him to put me down, please.'

'He will,' said the swami. 'But only when you're away from this place.'

'Look, I can't have made myself very clear,' she said, staring uncomfortably into the yeti's big wide face. 'I have to dispose of the isotope to make the satellite safe and in order that it won't poison this whole valley.'

'Yes, you did. You were very clear. But perhaps I did not make myself clear. I am the guardian here. Not you. I have taken a holy oath to protect these brothers and sisters. Not you. I cannot let you risk your life when that is my destiny. So you see that if anyone is going to dispose of this isotope, then I am bound to do it.'

'You don't understand,' insisted Swift. She tried to wrestle herself free from the yeti's hold, but his arms were quite immovable. She might as well have been pinned by steel hawsers. 'The radioactivity will kill you if you handle the isotope.' She struggled to find a way that might help him understand. 'It would be like handling the sun,' she said.

'What could be more joyful than to melt into the sun? And you were prepared to handle it, were you not?' he said, handing her Boyd's pack.

'That's different. It's my responsibility.'

'And as I have just explained,' he giggled again. 'It is mine.'

The swami made a *namaste* with his hands.

'But the thought is appreciated. He who sees all beings in himself, and himself in all things, need have no fear. Besides, I should have thought it was obvious by now. I'm rather a tough fellow. Not so easy to kill.'

The swami spoke to the yeti once again and without hesitating the yeti began to carry Swift away from the satellite.

'He will take you back to your camp. By a different route. Oh, yes. There are many ways in and out of this place.' He smiled pleasantly. 'And you said you wanted to study him. Well, this will be your opportunity. A unique opportunity. Goodbye.'

Swift could see that there was little point in arguing with the holy man. He would only have replied with yet another enigmatic answer. But her silence didn't stop him.

'And don't be so hard on religion,' he called to her. 'God's purpose in life is like a great carpet. Seen from one side of a loom it makes no sense. It has no shape, no logic. Just hundreds of strands of wool hanging loosely here and there. But seen from the other side everything can be understood. The pattern becomes clear. There are no loose bits of wool. Just order.'

'Goodbye,' she said.

The swami was still giggling when he turned back towards the satellite and reached into the generator to remove the isotope with his thin, bare hands.

The yeti's route took them up and through the sharp pinnacles that enclosed the hidden valley like two halves of a mantrap. As they climbed higher, Swift felt her ears pop and she began to worry that the yeti would leave her on some inaccessible mountainside where she would surely die.

Dwarfed by the mountains and by the size of the creature carrying her in its arms, she felt herself an insignificant horizontal figure in an immense vertical landscape: she and her personal King Kong, two creatures that were for all the world quite different, and yet almost identical in their proteins and molecules. She was Fay Wray carried through the snow turned blue by the deeper azure of the endless sky. Gradually she began to relax and to understand perhaps a little of what he had said. What was certain except the great blue roof above her head in all its marvellous infinity? Whatever

342

happened on earth that would always be there. Perhaps she was still under the influence of the suggestions he made to her while she was in a trance. Certainly she still felt as warm, though the fact that she had yet to switch on the power for her suit. She even started to believe that in this magical place where there was no end, no finish, only vast space, the swami might never grow old, might never die. For all she knew he really was an immortal, someone to whom the ordinary laws of nature did not apply. He would go on guarding the yetis in his quiet, passive way until the end of time.

She dozed.

When she awoke they were on their way down, on a difficult-looking descent and she soon started closing her eyes when the route became too alarming. But the yeti never once lost its massive footing. Until the moment came when it was clear that even yeti feet would be inadequate for the impossibly precipitate slope that faced them. Swift guessed them to be at around six thousand metres up the side of Machhapuchhare. Below them was the Sanctuary. In front of them rose Annapurna, rising to some eight thousand metres like an ancient Egyptian pyramid. There seemed no obvious way down short of hammering a piton into the arête above them and rappelling down the one-and-a-half-kilometre-long slope.

To Swift's surprise the yeti sat down in the deep snow. She thought it might be taking a well-earned rest while considering an alternative route.

'So where to now?' she asked. 'Back the way we came, I suppose.'

Instead the yeti shifted its enormous backside forward on the ridge a little, sending a small powder avalanche down the virtually sheer gully ahead of them. Suddenly Swift guessed what the yeti was planning to do, and gasped with horror.

'Oh no,' she shouted through the hot-mike. 'You're not going to slide down this on your ass, are you? You crazy bloody baboon.' She struck the yeti several times on the chest to make her point.

The yeti grunted, before shifting forward again on the edge of the ridge.

'Oh Jesus, no. Don't do this. We'll be killed.'

Inside her helmet, she felt the sweat start on her brow. Deeper in her self-contained environment, a queasier feeling overtook her stomach as, slowly, the yeti started to slide.

'No, please.'

Swift screamed and closed her eyes as suddenly they picked up speed and began to hurtle down the steep gully in a white vacuum of snow, with the yeti roaring enthusiastically as if they had been on some fairground ride instead of the blackest-looking ski-run. As good a skier as she was, Swift would never have dared a slope like this one. She kept on screaming as they hurtled through space, buffeted one way and then the other by the falling gully. Once or twice she felt them actually take off before the yeti's great weight drew them back on to the slope. Pressing her head towards the yeti's shoulder she prayed for their precipitate journey to be over, but they kept on moving, faster and faster, until she was certain the animal holding her had lost control and they were no longer sliding, but falling inside an avalanche of their own creation that would bury them both alive.

The next second it seemed they were rising in the air and Swift braced herself for the life-extinguishing impact she felt would surely follow. But instead they kept on moving and when Swift opened half an eye she realised that the yeti had hit the ground running. They were just above the glacier at the head of the valley. She sighed with relief.

The yeti ran around an ice cliff that curled across the glacier, leaping from one rock to another like the most sure-footed of mountain goats, narrowly avoiding ice towers and crevasses. It was as at home, as agile in this high mountain landscape as a gibbon was in the tallest of trees.

Soon they reached the ice corridor and the wall with the ladder that led up to the crevasse where they had followed Rebecca and baby Esau. She would have liked to have seen them one more time, just to hear her say 'Oh-keh' again. She was almost sorry when they reached Camp One and, steaming like a carthorse on a cold day, the big silverback yeti stopped and put her down. How would she ever describe this journey in her book? And if she did, would anyone believe her? That was perhaps another thing the swami was right about. It really wasn't necessary to ask so many questions.

'Thank you,' she said.

The yeti waited. He looked almost as if he was waiting for a tip until she realised that he was looking at the equipment and tents that constituted Camp One. Gently he touched the top of a tent before pulling out a sleeping bag and sniffing it curiously.

Swift smiled. It was hard to connect this yeti with the one that had killed Boyd. But she could hardly reproach him for that. Boyd would have killed her with much more enthusiasm. Watching the yeti she felt science giving way to sentiment and realised that she wanted to give him something.

Raking through her belongings in the tent she had shared with Jutta, she thought of giving him a glove, a notebook, a woolly hat, but there was nothing that seemed appropriate. Then she remembered the yetis' predilection for shiny objects and recalled that she had carried a small makeup bag in her rucksack to Camp One. Quickly finding it, she took out a folding hand mirror and handed it to him.

The yeti looked at himself for a moment and then, grunting with pleasure, tugged at his lower lip with one enormous forefinger. She wondered if he had ever seen himself before and, if he had, whether or not he recognised himself.

Gradually the yeti's mouth split into what looked to Swift to be an enormous grin. Immediately she took off her helmet and smiled back, for she had realised that what was more important was that in this enormous hominoid she recognised something of herself. She felt a tear at the corner of her eye and blinked it away. A moment passed and then, still holding the mirror, he walked quickly away.

Swift watched him for a while, hoping he would turn and look back at her. But he never did.

It was only when he had disappeared from sight that she wondered how she was going to get back through the ice field. She had quite forgotten the serac that had collapsed across the route. If only she had remembered she might have been able to have the yeti carry her to the other side. She was about to call ABC on Boyd's radio when she saw the helicopter.

Even before the chopper landed, Jack had jumped on to the ground – his knees buckling a little as he landed – and started to run towards her. As they embraced she saw the tears in his eyes and she did not know if it was the joy of seeing her alive or the wind from the rotor blades.

Thirty-two

'Nature's stern discipline enjoins mutual help at least as often as warfare. The fittest may also be the gentlest.'

Theodosius Dobzhansky

She may not have heard any tumultuous fanfare of Nietzschean trumpets. But the ape had touched her and she had felt something change inside herself. It was not exactly an epiphany she had experienced. Rather a sense that perhaps the biggest answers were not to be had in response to questions, but only to an appreciation of the mystery of things. She had found out slightly more than she had bargained for, but with the paradoxical result that she now felt she knew slightly less. One set of questions merely posed another set of questions and the monolithic enigma of her youthful inspiration seemed just as adamantine as it had always been.

Arriving back at ABC Swift found herself curiously reticent as to exactly what had happened in the hidden valley, beyond the simple facts that Boyd was dead and the yetis were safe. It was not that she felt traumatised but that her experience already seemed too personal to share with the others. Soon she would have good reason to be glad of her caution.

Perrins took the call from Bill Reichhardt. The NRO had some good news to report. The Keyhole-Eleven satellite computer had been switched on for a couple of minutes and half the auto-destruct code entered into the on-board computer's memory before the signal disappeared again.

'I'd say the power cut out before he could finish typing out the auto-destruct sequence,' explained Reichhardt. 'The question is, did he finish the job himself? Did he blow the bird up?'

'I think we can all rest easy on that score,' opined Perrins. 'However, as we've not heard from him since, I think we have to assume that he was killed during the completion of his mission.'

'That's too bad, Bryan,' said Reichhardt. 'He must have been a good man. You must be proud of him.'

346

'Yes, Bill, I am. We're all proud of him.'

Perrins put down the phone and, picking up his American Film Institute catalogue, glanced over the early Hitchcock movies, ringing the ones he wanted to see with a red pen. *The Man Who Knew Too Much*. Perrins pursed his lips and shook his head. If only he could have said the same about himself.

Several days later, the team were back in Khatmandu, discovering that both Russia and China had urged restraint on their respective allies and, as a result, the Indians and Pakistanis had demobilised and agreed to the presence of a UN peacekeeping force in the Punjab. The crisis appeared to be over.

Jack spent a couple of days under observation in the American hospital while Swift walked around the capital city, and tried to enjoy the comforts of the Hotel Yak and Yeti, which was Khatmandu's finest. But while she was staying there, something happened that destroyed what little faith she still had in human nature.

One night she returned late from a bar in Thamel after a late-night session drinking cold San Miguel beers with Byron and Mac. The hotel night porter mistakenly gave Swift a fax intended for Lincoln Warner. By the time she was back in her room and realised it was not meant for her, she had read it. The fax was from the London *Times* regarding a paper written by Warner that was shortly to appear on the nature of the Abominable Snowman. At first Swift thought that there must have been some kind of mistake and, before accusing Warner of anything, she made a couple of telephone calls to London. These filled in what the fax had only sketchily detailed. The enthusiasm of her source, the Science Editor of the *Daily Telegraph*, and his many informed questions were sufficient confirmation of what she had feared. Warner had e-mailed a paper containing not only his own results but also a detailed account of the whole expedition to *Nature* magazine in England. While everyone else had been searching for the yeti, at no small hazard to their lives, Lincoln Warner had remained in the clamshell preparing his paper, mailing it by instalments, with the data and conclusions he had drawn sent last of all and immediately upon his arrival back in the Nepalese capital.

It was a spectacular betrayal and directly in violation of the confidentiality clause Warner had signed prior to joining the

347

expedition. Byron Cody and Jutta Henze were outraged and ceased to have anything to do with him. Meanwhile, those bravest few of the world's news media who were in India to cover the now defused crisis quickly arrived in Khat, desperate to speak to Warner about his fantastic discovery. Somehow this hardly seemed to matter to Swift and she made very little comment to Warner beyond the fact she was disappointed that he had jumped the gun.

Wondering what to do, Swift spent a whole day visiting temples in and around Khatmandu. One of these, the Hindu temple at Pashupatinath, perhaps the most famous in all of Nepal, seemed to exercise an almost hypnotic effect on her. There were other temples that were perhaps more beautiful. But with Pashupatinath there was also a sense of sanctuary. The very word now held an extra meaning for her. Located on a hilltop, away from the clamorous city streets, the temple offered a meditative spot for Swift, a place where she could get things in perspective. It was here, on the banks of the Bagamati river, that funeral biers were set alight. The sight of burning ghats exercised a mesmeric effect upon her. At first the sight of bodies cremated in the open air, like so much garden refuse, put her in morbid mind of the many millions who would surely have died in a nuclear holocaust. But life continued around these public cremations. People sold flowers, incense and firewood; outcast attendants poked the funeral fires with long poles; women washed clothes in the dirty river; and boys kicked a football. It was as if this acceptance of death added an extra dimension to existence itself.

Gradually Swift felt herself carried along on a current of life like a bundle of discarded clothes that had been removed from some blackening corpse and now floated downriver; and it was while she was at Pashupatinath that she made her most important discovery. She stumbled upon one simple and inescapable fact – not in a cave, or in the DNA of some fabulous creature, but in herself. It was a sense of responsibility for an important secret that she ought never to have given away. Publishing a paper, tenure at Berkeley, scientific laurels – none of these things now seemed to matter when set against her own conscience. It was not a Darwinian view of life she had found but her own. Perhaps it was even a life with Jack.

She knew now what had to be done, and what only she could do.

In the corner of Helen O'Connor's home that was the expedition office in Khat, Jack was preparing to return to the Sanctuary with some of the Sherpas in order to clear the campsite. At the same time he was planning to fetch Didier's body down from the crevasse on Machhapuchhare, so that he could bring it back to Canada for burial. Swift now proposed that a third task should be added to this schedule of work, and when the remaining members of the expedition – Mac, Jutta, Cody and Hurké Gurung – attended a meeting at her request, Swift outlined her plan.

The team listened to her in silence. It was Jack who spoke first.

'I'm glad you suggested it,' said Jack. 'In view of what we know, I believe we all feel we have some kind of responsibility to protect these creatures. I think we ought to take a vote on it. Anyone disagree?' Jack glanced around and saw only shaking heads. 'Okay Hurké. What do you say?'

The sirdar, whose eyes had remained on his foot, which was almost healed now, looked up with an air of surprise that he of all people should have been asked his opinion first.

'Me, sahib?' He shook his head. 'Not first. Not me.'

'This is your country. You *should* be first. So what's your decision?'

The sirdar wobbled his head, equivocating for a moment.

'Then I agree, Jack sahib. What the memsahib has said is best. Perhaps some things should be kept from other men.'

'Byron?'

'I think I'd have suggested the same course of action if Swift hadn't said it first. I vote yes.'

'I agree,' Jutta said simply and looked at Mac.

Mac sighed loudly.

'What do you say, Mac?' asked Jack. 'In a way you've got more to lose than anyone.'

'We've all got something to lose,' scowled the Scotsman. 'And I don't just mean the members of this expedition. Isn't that the point?'

'Yes, it is,' said Swift.

'I meant all those pictures.'

'Oh them.'

Mac lit a cigarette and grinned.

'Well that's an academic question.' He looked around the room with innocent surprise. 'Didn't I tell you? None of the pictures came out. Not a one. No thirty-five mill. No Hi-8. The film stock was crap. Either that or I'm a bloody lousy photographer.' He uttered a gleeful laugh. 'That bastard Warner, I wish I could be there to see his face. He'll be expecting us to publish, of course. He's going to look bloody silly when he finds that there are no photographs to support his story.'

'And when we contradict him,' smiled Byron.

'When we say none of it ever happened,' added Mac.

'We'll tell the press he was suffering from the effects of high-altitude sickness.'

'Do you think anyone *will* believe him?' asked Jack.

'Did anyone believe *you*?' said Swift.

'Good point.'

'I almost feel sorry for him,' said Jutta. 'He's going to look such a fool.'

'Don't feel sorry for him,' said Byron. 'Stealing someone else's discovery is – '

'You're forgetting something,' said Swift. 'We didn't discover anything. Just a few inconclusive bones, that's all. Which leaves only one thing still to do.'

Royal Nepal's Allouette helicopter, piloted by Bishnu as before, took Jack, Swift, Hurké and some Sherpas back up to ABC. There was no need to trek up from Pokhara this time as they were still acclimatised to living at four thousand metres, despite the week they had spent in Khat. When the helicopter landed, they found that the approach of spring and the retreat of the snows had already changed the character of their base camp. The clamshell was beginning to sag as the snow on which it was pitched started to melt; and the roof of one of the lodges was clearly visible. But none of this had any effect on their present course of action. As soon as they had burnt some incense, prayed to their gods, and drunk some *cha*, the Sherpas set about dismantling the clamshell. Meanwhile Jack and Hurké collected the Bell stretcher and one of Boyd's rucksacks from his lodge and put them on to the helicopter.

They took off again and flew up to Machhapuchhare and Camp One, on the Rognon. The pilot offered to fly them on up to Camp Two, in the ice corridor close to the crevasse. Although there was nowhere for the chopper to land at Camp Two, it would have been easy enough for them to have jumped out – a matter of less than a metre. But Jack preferred that they land at Camp One and walk back up. There were the contents of Boyd's rucksack to think about. It was not the kind of pack you just dropped on to the ground. Besides, he thought it was best that as few people knew what they were going to do as possible. The Nepalese authorities did not take kindly to people changing the physical geography of a national park.

Leaving Bishnu to smoke and enjoy the sunshine, Swift, Jack and Hurké set off down the ice corridor.

In the absence of two serviceable SCE suits, Jack and Hurké entered the crevasse wearing stormproof clothing and Petzl head-lamps. As well as the stretcher they carried the axes with which they intended to cut Didier's body free from the ice. Jack estimated that the recovery would take no more than two or three hours. While the two men were gone, Swift stayed by the tent, alone with her thoughts. Flying above the Sanctuary again, as vast as it was empty, it had seemed unlikely that such a cold and tranquil place – like a sea on the surface of the moon – could ever have yielded up any of its secrets. But now as then, she found herself looking for tracks, a figure – human, or yeti – some sign that she had not im-agined the whole thing. Above and beneath her lay nothing but pure white snow, undisturbed by anything but the wind. That any kind of large animal, let alone one so closely related to Man him-self, could have inhabited such an inhospitable environment now seemed just as improbable as it always had.

Finally Jack and Hurké returned, hauling the body out of the crevasse on two ropes. Swift had never met Didier in life and this was the first time she really looked at him. But for the missing arm, shot away by the paranoid Boyd, she could see that the body was extremely well preserved. There was only slight dehydration and although it seemed a cliché, the dead man really did look as if he was sleeping. Swift thought he had been a handsome man. Jack covered his dead friend with a groundsheet, and collecting Boyd's rucksack, started to unpack the explosive materials.

The sirdar looked at them critically, handling the plastic and the detonators with the familiarity of one who had spent many years as a Gurkha army sergeant.

Jack glanced above him at the rock face, searching for a suitable spot to place the plastic. He nudged Hurké and then pointed to a spot about fifty or sixty metres higher up the mountain, below an enormous overhang of snow and ice.

'If that lot came down, it would bury this whole area. What do you think?'

351

Hurké nodded.

'If you show me how to do it, I can set the explosives and rappel back down,' said Jack. 'No point in us both going. Besides, your foot is still bandaged. You and Swift better get going with the stretcher, and I'll see you back at the chopper, okay?'

Hurké knew better than to argue. He selected a piece of plastic about the size of a paperback novel and demonstrated how to tamp the explosive and how to insert a detonator.

'After you have placed the detonator in the plastic, sahib, be careful not to use your radio as it could accidentally set off the explosive.'

Jack nodded and shouldered a coil of rope and his knapsack, into which he carefully placed the explosive materials.

'Better to detonate from the air, memsahib,' said Hurké. 'Safer, anyway.'

'Okay.'

'Be careful, Jack,' said Swift.

'I'll be back before you know it.'

They watched him go down the ice corridor towards the rock face and only when he had disappeared from sight did the sirdar suggest that they should start back to Camp One. Swift let out a nervous sigh and went over to the front of the stretcher bearing Didier's body. Hurké stood at the rear and when Swift was ready, at his command, they picked up the stretcher and began to walk.

Neither of them said anything; and carrying the stretcher in a straight line made it almost impossible to look back. By the time they reached the helicopter, Swift's stomach was knotted with worry and she was almost certain that Hurké felt the same way.

Seeing Hurké and Swift, Bishnu jumped up and helped to slide the stretcher on to the floor of the helicopter. Then, almost as an afterthought, he glanced around and asked where Jack was.

'He'll be along in a while,' said the sirdar. He spoke with such assurance that Swift felt certain he must be right. She sat in the doorway of the helicopter, basking in the sunshine, trying to empty her mind of what concerned her most. Jack would be along in a while. Whenever he went away, he always came back again. That was how it would always be. But with each minute that passed, she became more and more certain that something must have happened to him. She stood and began to pace in front of the helicopter, her eyes straining to see along the corridor for his familiar

352

figure. When she had seen Hurké smoke his eighth cigarette and Bishnu check his watch for the third time in five minutes, she could stand it no longer, and turning to the sirdar, she reminded him that an hour had passed.

The sirdar glanced coolly at his own watch and then nodded.

'Maybe a while yet, memsahib,' he said calmly. 'Not to worry. Jack knows what he is doing.'

'Can't we radio him?'

'Radio silence is necessary with explosives,' said the sirdar. 'As is patience.'

Another half hour passed, by which time even the sirdar was worried. Having run out of his cigarettes, he had stopped smoking and began on his thumbnails, which he chewed alternately, with hands clasped, as if he hoped to add some feeling to a difficult prayer.

The sound of a dull explosion brought Swift and Hurké immediately to their feet. Bishnu glanced anxiously at the sirdar, his jaw quivering nervously.

'*Garjan?*'

The sirdar shook his head, and stared up at the face of Machhapuchhare.

'*Pairo,*' he said quietly.

For a second or two the huge mass of snow hung on the mountain before, slowly, it started to fall away like a great pile of papers toppling from a high desk.

'Avalanche,' he added, with more urgency.

Bishnu hardly needed prompting. He had already run round the far side of the helicopter to jump into the cockpit and start the engine, all the time shouting at the top of his voice. The engine added its own whine to the pilot's and slowly the rotor blades began to beat the air, drowning out his panic-stricken demands that they should get airborne as quickly as possible.

Her arm held tight in Hurké's hand, Swift found herself hustled towards the door of the aircraft.

'Please, memsahib,' he shouted. 'We have to go now.'

'What about Jack?' she shouted, twisting round to look back down the corridor. Jack was nowhere to be seen. 'We can't just leave him.'

The sound of the avalanche came closer, like an approaching thunderstorm, an icy wind the deceptive vanguard for the juggernaut of snow and rock that was on its destructive way to the Rognon. The sirdar guessed that it would be only a matter of a minute or two before the avalanche reached them and felt a surge of adrenalin through his body. If it caught them, they would all be killed. Not just Jack. He pushed Swift into the chopper and yelled at Bishnu to take off and hover about a metre above the ground, adding the threat that if he went any higher he would cut the man's hands off. Fearfully, the pilot glanced over his shoulder at Hurké. Since it was well known that it was the sirdar who had cut off Ang Tsering's hand, Bishnu did not suppose Hurké uttered the threat lightly. Uncertain if he was more afraid of the sirdar than of the avalanche now sweeping down Machhapuchhare towards them, he did as he was ordered and lifted the chopper gently off the ground.

'You can't,' screamed Swift. 'He's your friend. You can't just leave him. He'll be killed.'

'We can only wait as long as we must,' shouted the sirdar, pinning Swift's arms at her side, and nearly sitting on her to stop her from jumping out. 'But we will surely all be killed if we are still landed here when the avalanche hits.'

Swift struggled to break free of the sirdar's iron grip. She understood he was right, but after all they had come through, it seemed so unjust that Jack should be killed now. Given their decision to keep the existence of the yeti a secret, the circularity of what was happening appalled her: it was almost as if the fates had decided that Jack had always been meant die with Didier in the first avalanche all those months ago. She felt the chopper buffeted by the granular wind that was swirling round them and, uncertain whether this was caused by air blast from the avalanche, or the whacking rotor blades above her, she yelled Jack's name at the top of her voice. And then saw him, running towards them, his knees as high as the stormproof suit he was wearing allowed.

'There,' she shouted. 'There he is.'

Hurké followed the line of the arm that had broken free of his grasp to point down the ice corridor and saw that his friend would only just make it; not at all, if he was unlucky enough to fall. Now the sirdar felt real fear as, looking beyond Jack, he saw, gathering speed like an accelerating tidal wave, gaining on him all the time, a huge and angry cloud of snow that looked like the steaming hot breath of the Lord Shiva. It was as if they were being reminded that this was a holy, forbidden place, and that they should never have come here.

Jack flung himself through the open door of the helicopter, hit the floor with the upper half of his body, and felt himself hauled aboard by his waist harness.

'*Jaanu*,' shouted the sirdar. '*Jaanu, jaanu*.'

The next second the chopper lurched steeply to one side, away from the mountain and then towards the Sanctuary.

'*Hera*,' yelled Bishnu.

Machhapuchhare and the Rognon disappeared completely, as a deafening grey-white cloud enveloped the ancient helicopter like a blizzard, and the engine shuddered in its struggle to gain altitude. Swift caught Jack's eye and saw him say something, but the words were drowned in the greater volume below them. She closed her eyes as, sickeningly, the chopper seemed to turn through one hundred and eighty degrees in one direction and then the other, and for what seemed like several minutes she was sure they were going to crash. The helicopter shunted a little and then suddenly steadied itself, and they were heading smoothly back up the glacier.

Swift opened her eyes. For a second she thought that fear must have turned Jack's hair as white as some old man's until she realised that he was covered in powdered snow. They all were.

'Thank God,' she breathed.

Jack picked himself off the floor and brushed some of the snow from his head and shoulders.

'Jesus, that was close,' he said. 'I waited until I could see you before I detonated. Only I kind of underestimated the speed of it.'

'You almost got us killed.'

'Look who's talking,' he said.

But she was already leaning out of the door, surveying his handiwork. The whole of the ice corridor and the Rognon were now buried under thousands of ton of snow and ice. Certain that the route they had found to the yetis and their hidden forest habitat was gone forever, she nodded with satisfaction and took Jack's outstretched hand.

The helicopter soared over a sea of rock. The Himalayas looking like enormous waves in a petrified ocean they all hoped might still hold on to its most precious and least abominable secret.

Acknowledgements

Thanks are due to Sandy Duncan, Dr Nicholas Scott, Dr David Raeder, Dr Sara Vinicombe, Douglas Kennedy, Narendra Thapa Magar, Peter Godwin, Jonathan Burnham, Caroline Michel, Rosemary Davidson, Robert Bookman, Caradoc King, Nick Marston, Linda Shaughnessy, Paula Wagner, Marion Wood, Jerry Bruckheimer, and Michael Lynton. A very special thanks to John Walsh for helping me to formulate the story; and to my wife Jane Thynne, for her continuing patience.

I owe a debt to the work of the following scientists, explorers and writers:
Stephen Bezruckha; Peter Boardman; Chris Bonington; C. G. Bruce; W. Burrows; Jeremy Cherfas; G. A. Combe; Jared Diamond; Trevor Dupuy; Blake Edgar; Robert Foley; Dian Fossey; Murray Fowler; J. B. Fraser; John Gribbin; M. Grumley; Emily Hahn; Hooker; Ralph Izzard; Bjorn Kurten; Donald Johanson; Lenora Johanson; Richard Leakey; Roger Lewin; Peter Matthiessen; Richard Milton; W. H. Murray; J. Napier; W. W. Rockhill; Steve Roper; Carl Sagan; Eric Shipton; James Shreeve; Konrad Spindler; Joe Tasker; Ian Tattersall; O. Tchernine; Vladimir Tschernezky; L. A. Waddell and R. Windrem.